A STRANGE AND ANCIENT NAME

JOSEPHA SHERMAN

BAEN

A STRANGE AND ANCIENT NAME

A Baen Books Original.

Baen Publishing Enterprises
P.O. Box 1403
Riverdale, N.Y. 10471

ISBN: 0-671-72151-8

Cover art by Darrell K. Sweet

Printed in the United States of America

1
CEREMONIES AND CONFRONTATIONS

The hall was vast and airy, full of the clear, sunless light of Faerie and shaped by craft and illusion to seem a widely spaced forest of slender white trees that looked far too fragile to support the high, arched roof.

For all its size, the hall was also crowded. Males and females and those less easily classified thronged on either side of the wide central aisle, a sleek, sophisticated lot in finely draped gowns or tunics or wisps of mist, the colors soft as spring green, sharp as moonlight. Most there were tall and slender, their faces narrow, keen, elegantly planed, their eyes gray or smoky green, glinting with wit, magic, cruelty. Long, straight, shining hair gleamed with all the shades of gold (though here and there lurked some whose hair was green or softest blue, whose brows bore horns or backs bore wings).

None of them were human.

Ereledan, Lord of Llyrh, glanced sharply at his neighbors, his powerful form bold in a dozen fiery shades that quelled their pastels, magnificent red hair swirling like flame about his strong face as he turned from side to side. "Well?" His whisper was hardly soft. "What are we waiting for?"

Those on either side subtly shifted away, careful not to rouse his notorious temper. Ereledan was a risky person to befriend, the last link to a long-ago deposed royal line.

Across the hall from the Lord of Llyrh, Charailis

watched him and tightened her lips in distate. *Ereledan, you boor.* The lady was all tall, slender coolness in subtle blue, hair a fall of moon-touched silver, eyes those of a quiet predator. She was also, much to her satisfaction and Ereledan's discomfort, of higher status than he, bound by tenuous but true blood ties to the current royal line.

But Ereledan's impatience had infected the crowd. Throughout all that ageless, glittering company the whispers flew:

"Will he come?"

"Dare he not?"

"Dare he offer open insult to our prince?"

Their prince was wondering the same thing. Hauberin, ruler of this one land among many in the convoluted Faerie Realm, was young, even as human folk counted years, his unfashionable black hair worn defiantly long, somber against the bright silver of the intricate royal crown, his unfashionable lack of height hidden beneath the folds of the robes of state, smooth as sheets of molten silver pouring down the sides of the dais. Straight-backed, regally enthroned and seemingly composed, the prince was well aware of that one blatantly empty space amid the crowd, and he was nursing a delicate flame of anger within him.

Serein, cousin, don't presume on kinship too much!

Of Faerie though this land undeniably was, its independent-minded folk held to fewer rituals than their tradition-bound neighbors. But some ceremonies couldn't be ignored. This was the Second Triad, the sixth anniversary of Hauberin's crowning—much as Serein might hate the fact. And, much as the man might hate it, Hauberin was his liege lord. He must do the prince at least token homage this day.

And if he doesn't? asked a dry little voice at the back of Hauberin's mind. *What then?*

What, indeed?

Alliar, a sleek golden figure perched on the lower steps of the dais, twisted bonelessly about to look up at him, saying in tactfully silent mind-voice, *"You can't wait much longer."*

Hauberin glanced down at his supple, beautiful, totally genderless friend. Alliar had never been born of flesh and blood; the being was a wind spirit bound by sorcery into tangible form years back.

"I don't intend to wait." The prince looked about in feigned indifference, sensing the swirlings of emotion from his subjects: some malice, some sympathy, mostly wild curiosity and a certain subtle delight at his discomfort: He, the half-blood prince. The part-human.

The prince smiled faintly. When one grows up surrounded by sly taunts, one learns to ignore them. Or at least pretend to ignore them. He let his glance rest, as though by accident, on Ereledan and Charailis, and his smile thinned. Ambitious, those two.

How fortunate they dislike each other even more than they hate me, the prince thought wryly. *But how they would love to see me make some humiliating mistake!*

He wasn't about to gratify them—or Serein, either. The ceremonies would start now, and to the Outer Dark with his cousin.

Oh, but look: Here, with a nice sense of timing, came said cousin after all, swirlings of busy whisperings in his wake as he strode smoothly forward. As always Hauberin felt the smallest pang of envy, fiercely suppressed, at this reminder of how a proper prince of the realm should look. Serein was tall and glittering in coppery robes just a fraction less regal than those of his prince, his flowing golden hair bound back by a copper circlet just a fraction less intricate than the silver royal crown. Pride and insolence shown in every line of that elegant figure, and a sourly amused Hauberin thought that surely the man had changed very little from the haughty boy he had been.

But then Serein stepped clear of the crowd. His metallic cloak trailed out behind him, heavy and long enough to warrant a page to keep it from sweeping the floor. And that page was undeniably human.

The fact wasn't extraordinary in itself; there were

changelings enough throughout the lands of Faerie, and most of them—since even human children were cherished by a notably infertile race—were treated with more grace than they would have known in mortal lands. But this boy, obedient to Serein's every move, was so plainly terrified of his master that many of the whisperings grew sharp with disapproval.

The boy was small for his age. And slight. And dark. The whispers died one by one as he passed, and Hauberin, stunned by sudden fury, felt the weight of countless startled eyes on him. On their prince who was so lacking in height. On Hauberin of the unfashionable black hair and eyes and olive-dark skin. Hauberin, who looked most not like his regal golden father, but like his small, dark, very human mother.

No one there could miss the similarity. Or the insult. Hauberin heard Alliar's soft hiss of anger, and drew in his own breath for a shout of sheer rage—

No. Oh, no. That was surely just what Serein wanted. Hauberin clenched his teeth, struggling to keep his face impassive, remembering all the boyhood years of being the butt of Serein's sly, subtle, never quite treasonous jests, of never quite knowing how to defend himself against his older, glamorous, ambitious cousin. If he lost control now, Serein would become, as always, most innocently, most ingratiatingly humble, leaving his prince looking like a fool—worse, like a half-human ranting in totally human rage.

So Hauberin merely . . . smiled. "Welcome, cousin." For all that he ached to shrivel Serein with one well-worded spell, and the rules of law be damned, the prince kept his voice smooth and bland and level. "You come late to our court. So late that we wondered, foolish thought, if you had some reason to fear us."

He caught a flicker of unease, of anger, in the beautiful sea-green eyes. But Serein quickly broke the contact before Hauberin could read any deeper, sweeping down into an overly respectful bow.

"Fear you, dear cousin? Why, no. Never." His smile

was as fixed as Hauberin's own. "For are you not known as a most . . . merciful and . . . gentle prince?"

The faint, deliberate hesitations were an insult in themselves, implying not mercy, but weakness. Hauberin refused to be baited. "How sweetly spoken." In sudden inspiration, he added, "And how kind of you to bring me so amusing a gift."

Ha, that surprised Serein! "A . . . gift, cousin?"

"The boy, of course. The little human. He *is* a gift, is he not?"

He most certainly was not, and they both knew it. But Serein, sensing his mockery going awry, covered quickly with, "Why, what else could he be?"

"How you jest, cousin." Hauberin raised his head slightly, a prince inviting his court to join in a mild pleasantry. "And isn't it charmingly rare for one among us to be given a chance to see himself returned, as it were, to childhood?"

There was a puzzled murmuring from the court, half of them confused over their prince's motives, half more concerned with trying to remember back over the uncounted years to their own nigh-forgotten childhoods. Hauberin laughed silently. Good! Let them stay confused.

"Lady Aydris," he called.

The young woman, warmly curved and pretty, if somewhat plumper than that slender race's fashion dictated, came forward from the front edge of the crowd, giving her prince a cheerful curtsey and a smile; she and Hauberin, both young, both outside the fashionable norm, shared an amiable friendship and, on occasion, a bed. "My Prince?"

"Kindly take this boy— Ah, his name, cousin?"

Serein's eyes were smoldering. "I fear you must learn that for yourself. Cousin. I've not had the boy long enough for him to have learned our tongue."

"A pity. Lady," Hauberin said formally to Aydris, "do you take the boy under your care."

Aydris, who had been studying the boy with a motherly eye, gave him an unfeigned smile. "At once, my Prince."

Hauberin turned his attention back to the fuming Serein. "And as for you, cousin, do *you* take your proper place."

"Look you, I—"

"Take your place!"

The words were knife-sharp. They were also edged with more than a little compulsion-magic. Caught off guard, Serein was snared; for all that he fought the spell wrapping itself about his will, it had already taken hold. It would fade again in only a few moments, but for now Serein had no choice. Smiling grimly, Hauberin watched his furious cousin helplessly obey him.

The smile faded. *Ae, Serein, what game are you playing?* Hauberin wondered. *Are you really as foolish as you seem?*

In these six years since he had come to reign, Hauberin had been waiting, watching for some open attack from Serein who, being his closest kinsman, was so much more of a threat than Ereledan or Charailis. And yet, for all his cousin's blatant hate and envy, Serein had never tried anything stronger than this childish mockery.

Hauberin bit back a weary sigh, sick of the subject. Oh, yes, the man was tall and fair and golden, as he, himself would never be. But how could he envy Serein that shallow, petty mind?

Serein had reached his assigned place by now, turning sharply to face the prince again, the heavy, elegant coppery cloak whirling dramatically out behind him.

But, just for an instant, as the last of the brief compulsion-spell slid from him, Serein's self-control seemed to slip. Just for an instant, his eyes were not those of the malicious, superficial courtier, but harsh as winter ice, the will behind them cold, implacably cold. . . . Stunned by the sudden transformation, chilled to the heart, Hauberin heard without words:

"I will have your death, princeling. One way or another, I will have your death."

* * *

"On this first day of the Second Triad of your reign, I accept you, Hauberin, son of Laherin, as Prince of the Realm."

"Oh this first day of the Second Triad of my reign, I accept you as subject of the Realm."

As he repeated the ritual words of acknowledgement yet again to yet another courtier in the seemingly endless line waiting to pay their respects, Hauberin fought down an urge to squirm like an impatient child. How many times had he heard the first half of the formula so far? How many times had he replied with his half of it? At least he wasn't expected to mention everyone by name; by now, he wasn't sure he could remember anybody's name.

There had been only one small moment of suspense, right at the start, since Serein, as Hauberin's direct kinsman, was expected to swear his oath first. But, after a brief, bitter pause, Serein had yielded and sworn, though the words nearly choked him.

The prince bit back a sigh, telling himself he should be thankful neither he nor his people had a true taste for formality. He could remember all too well swearing his own oath before the High King and Queen of Faerie in their magic-glittering court soon after taking the crown. It had been an act more of politic courtesy than anything else, since his was an independent land, but even in that somewhat abridged ceremony, the oath had been couched in the high ceremonial tongue—an elaborate, archaic language in which each change of tone carried at least a dozen meanings—and had occupied a full twenty scrolls.

"On this first day of the Second Triad . . ."

Hauberin came back to himself with a jolt at this new voice. *"Don't worry,"* teased Alliar's familiar mind-voice, *"it's only me."* Amusement glinted in the being's eyes. *"And—rejoice! I'm the last one. Which means your work is done. Now it's time to play!"*

* * *

By moonrise, the festivities had spilled out from the
royal palace down to the level green valley below. Folk
whirled about in dance, gleaming, glittering in countless
shades of reds, blues, purples, of citron and jacinth and
colors known only to Faerie, muted by the light of the
full, unstained moon, brightened in flashes by the spar-
kling flames of silver, blue, and bronze from the festive,
frivolous torches set all about (frivolous, since a night-
sighted race hardly needed their light). The hems of
gowns and cloaks whispered against the long, silky grass,
a soft counterpoint to the music of harp and crystalline
flute and singers like so many silver birds. Those who
chose not to dance sipped wine fragrant as the flowers
scenting the warm night air or sharp as the sophisticated
wit being exchanged.

Hauberin sat in his chair of state and seemed at ease,
and all the while kept his attention on Serein.

But Serein did nothing more alarming than sit in
shadow, long legs outstretched, crossed at the ankle, and
drink moodily from the silver goblet in his hand. Not a
trace of hatred now, not a trace of that icy, savage will:
Serein was very much himself again, all sullen innocence.

And how can I make accusations against that?

At last the prince sighed, and signalled proud Kerlaias,
captain of his guard, fiercely blue of eye and hair, all
loyal, brave, and shining in his Faerie mail. "Keep my
cousin under your eye," Hauberin commanded softly,
and put Serein at least partially out of his mind, looking
out over the festivities with a more genuine smile.

Beyond the charmed circle of laughter and music lay
the quiet, fertile fields and, beyond them, the line of
towering mountains, snowcapped, starkly beautiful under
the Faerie moon. Hauberin felt a sudden surge of love
for them, for his whole beautiful land and the stubborn,
quicksilver-humored people on it. Ae-ye, since that stun-
ning night six years past, when he'd awakened quivering
with shock, knowing his father was dead, he had tried to
be a good, wise, just ruler. Had he succeeded? The court
sages were still wary of his youth, his human blood. But

the land was at peace and prospering, the people as content as such quarrelsome, magical folk could be.

And, damn you, Serein, neither you nor anyone else is going to take this from me!

Music caught his attention. There were at least three different groups of singers by the sound of them, to say nothing of the music from the royal musicians, all of them on separate melodies that somehow managed to blend into a harmonious whole. The dancing continued in intricate, everchanging patterns, and just beyond the adults, a group of youngsters had started up their own boisterous round, stumbling a bit on the complicated steps, half drunk on moonlight and excitement and their own youth.

Hauberin realized with a start that he wasn't all that much their senior. Ae, let him, for this night at least, be young. He had been able to shed the cumbersome silver robes of state back in the palace. Slim and lithe in wine-dark silk, the prince stepped down from the dais and slipped into one of the dances, laughing lightly with this lady and that till—by chance or design?—he found himself partnering Charailis.

For a time they moved through the steps of the dance in silence, equal in grace for all that Charailis was a good head taller than the prince, on her elegant face a smooth, secret smile.

"And what might you want of me, my lady?" Hauberin asked softly.

"My Prince?"

The last swirling chords of the dance had left them—again, by chance or design?—apart from the others, left them standing so close that Hauberin was very much aware of the subtle, not quite sweet scent Charailis wore, of the faint woman-scent beneath that. She was beautiful as ever, the clear flood of moonlight seeming by its very coldness to add warmth in contrast to her coolly perfect features, fire to her lovely eyes. Wondering, Hauberin tried to move, whether closer or away, he wasn't sure, and only then realized that strands of Charailis' long, pale hair were clinging to him.

Like spider strands. Jarred back to reality, the prince remembered who and what she was: not so far from the direct royal line she couldn't desire a crown. With a sudden prickle of distaste, he set about gently disentangling himself. "Why, lady! Are you trying to snare me?"

Her eyes glinted in the moonlight. "It pleases you to jest, my Prince."

Hauberin caught the hint of condescension in her voice, and froze. "Come, Charailis, I'm not as naive as you think me. What do you want of me?"

"The ceremonies moved me. Seeing you so proud and sure of yourself on your Second Triad— We know each other so little, for all that we are kin."

Kin. She was his grandmother's sister's child; long Faerie lives made for complicated genealogies.

"I admit," Charailis continued quietly, "I am to blame. But then, I was so much the elder, a woman when you were still only a child." With matter-of-fact Faerie honesty, "I could hardly be expected to care much for a scrawny little boy." She gave him a sly little sideways glance. "But the past is the past. And you are most certainly no longer a boy. Surely we . . . need not remain so remote."

For a moment her hand, smooth and cool, rested on his arm, as though by accident. His body responded with a slight shiver, but Hauberin thought, *Transparent, lady, transparent,* and said nothing. After a moment, Charailis continued:

"And now . . . especially now, with the moon so radiant and the night so warm . . . Look. Do you not see how folk are stealing away in secret pairs?" Again her hand brushed his arm, nails lightly grazing his skin, sending a new shiver through Hauberin despite himself. "Shall we not give each other joy tonight, my Prince?"

A flash of purely sensual wondering raced through him. *Idiot,* Hauberin snapped at himself, *you'd be safer bedding a lamia!* "No, lady. We shall not."

For an instant, the startled Charailis was at a loss.
"Why so—so cruel? Surely—"

"What's this?" cut in a sharp, hearty voice. "Cornering
our good ruler?"

Hauberin glimpsed bold red robes, a strong-featured,
cold face: "My lord Ereledan. Come to see what your
rival's about?"

"I— What?"

"I'll leave the two of you to debate it." With a cheerful
wave of his hand, Hauberin slipped out from between
them as they glared at each other, and made his way
back towards the center of music and activity.

"Well now," an amused voice said in his ear, "I was
just about to come in for a rescue."

Hauberin grinned at the sleek figure so suddenly at
his side. "Thank you, Alliar, but I rescued myself." He
gave the being a second, appreciative glance. "Nicely
shaped, Li."

His friend returned the grin with a sweeping bow.
Bound into tangibility Alliar might be, but the being
could at least control something of that enforced body's
shape. Just now, the wind spirit was tall and slender,
palest gold of skin and hair and huge, glowing eyes,
shrouded in a flowing russet cloak. But then Alliar
straightened, murmuring, "I do wish you wouldn't go
wandering off without a guard."

"What, here? Among my closest subjects? Come now,
if I dare not move freely here, I had better surrender
the crown." Hauberin glanced at Alliar. "Or were you
referring to the two I just left? No, Li. You should know
by now that for all their dark looks and thoughts, they're
no real threat to me. Not yet," the prince added thoughtfully. "Not while Serein lives to stand between them and
any hope of succession."

"Odd, having to be grateful to . . . that one."

"Speaking of my dear cousin, what has he been
doing?"

"Nothing. Save smiling, and acting disgustingly urbane
and apparently unaware of the guard watching him."

Alliar sighed. "You should thank the Powers that Ereledan and Charailis hate him as much as they hate each other."

"I do." Perhaps humans could have formed an alliance based on lies. The Faerie folk, who (save for part-human Hauberin) lacked even the concept of falsehood, could not. "Believe me— But what are all these eager looks?"

"Ach, I nearly forgot. My Prince, your presence is most humbly requested to preside over a duel— No, no, nothing serious, just two youngsters trying their strength."

Hauberin returned to his chair of state, Alliar curled comfortably at his feet, and acknowledged the cheerful salutes of the duelists: youngsters, indeed, blond and lanky, no longer quite children, not yet adult. The amused prince raised a hand for the duel to begin. It was a standard thing of shape-shifting and will against will, magic a natural thing to a folk with Power in the very air they breathed and the blood in their veins. The youngsters used little more energy than if they'd sported with swords as they slipped with reasonable ease from ferret to dog to wolf and wyvern, while their elders made lighthearted wagers.

Aha, what was this? One boy was suddenly cringing from the other, shrinking through dog, cat, mouse . . . *A trap*, the prince realized, *he's setting a trap.*

The other boy didn't see it. Fanged and furred, he pounced—

On nothing. Before he could turn, the first youngster had materialized behind him without disguise and tackled him, refusing to let him up till the boy yielded and relaxed back into his rightful form. The duelists, laughing and panting, scrambled to their feet and bowed to their prince to the accompaniment of polite applause from the dispersing audience.

"The youngsters are clever," drawled a voice. "What say you, my Prince? Shall we show them how a proper duel is fought?"

Lord Ereledan in all his flamboyant reds, eyes very bright. And what might he be about? Ignoring Alliar's alarm, Hauberin leaned down to ask sweetly, "To the death, you mean, my lord?"

"By all the Powers, no!" Ereledan's shock seemed real enough. "I meant nothing more than sport."

Alliar wasn't quite accepting that. *"Be wary,"* came the sharp mental warning, and Hauberin glanced at Serein where the man still lounged, seemingly disinterested but with a sudden tense stillness to him.

"I can't very well refuse, Li, can I? Keep your own watch on my cousin, yes?"

Hauberin stepped lightly down from the dais to face the Lord of Llyrh, and the scattered audience quickly regrouped. There would be no wagering this time; it would hardly be politic to bet against their prince. But Hauberin couldn't help wondering how many were looking to him to fail.

As challenger, Ereledan had the first move. The strong form shimmered, changed; where man had stood, a great leopard crouched, fiery orange with spots of red. "Beautiful," Hauberin acknowledged, but made no move of his own. Ereledan was under no obligation to wait. As the audience gasped, the leopard sprang—

Hauberin wasn't there. A sleek black hawk slipped easily away, spiralling up and up into the warm night, moonlight spilling from glossy wings, then plunged down again, talons outstretched, hearing the fickle audience gasp again.

But just before impact, black wings braked fiercely, talons folded. Hauberin rapped Ereledan sharply on the head with a fisted claw, then swooped up again, enjoying the crowd's ripple of laughter.

Ereledan wasn't amused. With a snarl, the leopard reared up into the form of a blood-red griffin. With a thunder of wings, he was airborne. An astonished Hauberin saw the wild rage blazing in the griffin's eyes and thought, *What's this? Did you forget this is only sport? Did you* mean *to forget?*

Ae! That fiercely curved beak had nearly caught him! Whatever game Ereledan was playing, it had suddenly gone far beyond sport. The griffin lunged, and Hauberin hastily sideslipped, not quite in time. A powerful red shoulder crashed into him, sending him tumbling. The prince abandoned hawk-form, somersaulting in mid-air, landing on his feet with a jolt, unhurt, breathless and furious, craning his head back to find Ereledan. Ah, the fool was diving at him!

The crowd going mad about him, pleading with their prince to move, defend himself, do *something*, Hauberin stood still, timing the griffin's plummet. The prince scooped up a handful of dust, murmuring quiet Words, feeling the responsive magic tingling in soil and self, waiting . . . Now!

Hauberin hurled the dust right at Ereledan, then threw himself aside, gasping out the final Word to bring the spell to life. Ereledan went crashing to the ground, sprawled in an ignominious tangle of dust-become-web, helpless as a bird in a fowler's net.

Ereledan's furious struggle stopped abruptly as Hauberin approached. Under the crowd's roars of laughter, the prince asked quietly, "What were you trying to do, my lord? Were you trying to kill me?"

Eyes wild with confusion, Ereledan let the griffin-shape fade. "No! I . . ." The man lay in self-contemptuous submission as the web faded back into dust about him, then propped himself up on one elbow. "My Prince, I don't know what happened. Somehow I . . . lost control." The admission came bitterly from that proud lord. "Believe me," he added in a voice savage with repressed rage, "if I had meant to kill you, I'd not have been so clumsy about it."

"Rise," Hauberin said shortly. Politic to let the man regain some self-esteem in privacy. "You may leave us."

Dourly he acknowledged Ereledan's bow, wondering, *Lost control? Experienced Ereledan?*

And yet, of course, Ereledan couldn't lie. Besides, it really had been a clumsy attack, almost as though someone else had tried to control— Nonsense. The Faerie folk just weren't susceptible to possession.

He was starting to tremble a bit with delayed reaction. Someone was putting a cloak about his shoulders—Alliar, who was handing him a wine-filled crystal goblet. Hauberin sipped gratefully, letting the cool, mellow, golden wine trickle down his stress-parched throat.

But then the prince found himself glancing over the goblet's rim at Serein. His cousin met his gaze without flinching, smiling. Hardly knowing why he did it, Hauberin strolled over to the man and murmured:

"What of you, cousin? Were *you* trying to kill me?"

For the faintest fraction of time, Hauberin was certain Serein was going to admit it. But all the man said was, "Why cousin, what a question!"

"Answer it."

"The answer, dear Hauberin, is that while I might not mourn your death for very long, no, my overwrought little cousin, I was *not* trying to kill you."

With that, reluctantly, Hauberin had to be content.

11
BROODINGS

Alone, Alliar stood upon a narrow balcony of the royal palace, wrapped in night and silence. The hour, the being guessed (though time meant little to a spirit) was very late, closer to morning than night, and very dark. The moon had long since set, the last of the festive torches had been extinguished with the prince's retiring, and save for a few reluctant stragglers whispering or cuddling together, the darkness no barrier to night-keen Faerie senses, the exhausted royal court slept.

Alliar never slept, not as the flesh-and-blood folk understood such things. And though normally the being hardly felt the lack, this once a spate of peaceful mindlessness would have been very welcome. Despairing, Alliar looked out at the cool, black velvet sky, unaware of the chill, tormented by the touch of the first sweet breezes of morning.

Was I ever part of that? Was I ever . . . What? There were no words for what had been; the winds needed no words. After a moment, Alliar continued the thought awkwardly, *Was I ever not-self? Not this narrow thing, this "body," this stupid, solid "I"? Was I ever . . . free?*

The courtiers would have stared to see this. They all considered the wind spirit little more than a pet, a clever oddity that came and went as it would, all too conscious of the thoughts they never quite voiced aloud: How pretty it is, how intelligent it seems, what a shame it can never be our equal.

Your equal. Alliar remembered storms as mighty as the birth of rage, as primal as Beginning, remembered skies bright and sharp with fire, remembered sweeping down the length of freedom, part of it as no finite little flesh-and-bloodling could ever be, one with the fury, one with the glory— *As though I would ever want to shrink to being merely your equal.*

Finite. Alliar glanced down at the solid, undeniably tangible body, the possibly forever-binding shape that imprisoned spirit, and shuddered.

(That one devastating moment when the trap had first closed fast . . .)

The being groaned, trying in vain to block the surge of memory.

(The sorcerer had dragged his captive down from infinity, forcing shape and a single, lonely identity on it, heedless of that captive's fierce, bewildered terror. Ae, ae, the storm of sensation: sight and sound distorted, shrunken, wrong, the alien new senses of scent and touch, the unbearable horror of being so suddenly bereft and alone, alone . . .)

Had Alliar a fragile mortal mind, the spirit would surely have gone hopelessly insane then and there. But the sorcerer, the one who named himself Ysilar, had wrought his spell far too well. The new slave had survived. Endured. Served. Learned new lessons in fear and pain and shame—

No! I will not remember!

But Hauberin was also a part of that past. Alliar smiled faintly. At least this one memory could be cherished: the young prince, then little more than a boy, so small, so defiant and brave at their first meeting. . . .

Ysilar, raging, had dragged his magic-stunned slave down here to the deepest cellar in the castle. Even as Alliar groggily roused, it was to the feeling of the sorcerer fastening a chain around one slim golden ankle.

"What— No, master, please! You can't leave me down here!"

But Ysilar was already gone, and Alliar was alone, shut away from the sky amid dark, dead stone. . . .

There was a time of screaming. There was a time of sheer, mindless, claustrophobic terror. But at last, through sheer exhaustion, the being lost the first sharp edge of fear. If one huddled as tightly together as one could, and kept one's absurdly limited eyes shut, this terrible dark confinement was almost bearable.

Almost. Though Alliar knew with the last shreds of sanity that there was open space, that the cellar wasn't that narrow, the terrible cold weight of the castle still seemed to press down and in till it seemed this frail body would be crushed.

What if it is? Flesh-and-blood folk do something called dying when their bodies are destroyed. Maybe since I am tangible now, I would die, too, and be free.

Free? Down here? Trapped forever in close, cruel darkness? The being huddled in a tighter ball and rocked miserably back and forth.

There was a rustle, a scratching. There was a muffled yelp, and something warm and heavy fell over the being. Alliar quickly uncurled, staring, unhindered by darkness, at the dirty, disheveled form of . . . a man? No, not quite a man; he *felt* too much of flesh-and-blood youth. A boy, then. One of the Faerie kind, like the sorcerer? He seemed small for that, too dark of hair and eyes and filthy, mud-stained face, though the proper *feel* of Power hung about him.

The boy scrambled to his feet, straightening clothing and the knife at his belt, staring right back. "Who are you?" he asked in a fierce whisper. "His enemy?"

The jerk of the boy's head indicated the upper chambers and the sorcerer. The being gave the ghost of a laugh. "His slave."

To Alliar's surprise, the boy frowned and crouched down again, a small hand gentle on the being's naked shoulder. "No. . . . Not just a slave." The earnest dark eyes stared anew, full of true Faerie sight. Suddenly the boy sat back on his heels in surprise. "A spirit, a wind spirit! And he d-dares do *this* to you?"

"The body, you mean? Or this?" Alliar's sweep of arm took in the cellar. "He dared. I . . . bit him."

The boy fought down a frantic giggle. "You did *what*?"

Alliar was astonished to feel a grin forming in response. "I was scared. And angry. There wasn't anything else I could do; the spell on me keeps me from truly harming him. It was almost worth . . . this to see the look on his face."

The boy hastily buried his face in his hands to muffle laughter. "I—I suppose it was!" He took a deep, steadying breath. "Look you, there's only the one shackle holding you. There's a hole in the cellar floor, back there in the corner, where the mortar wore out and some stones fell away; that's how I got in. I think I can get you loose. If I do, can you dissolve and escape through—"

"No. I cannot lose this solid shape." Alliar gave it a savage slap. "Nor can I leave this castle while my . . . master lives."

"Oh. Well. That sh-should work out all right. Because I've come here to kill him."

"But—you can't— He'll—" Alliar took a deep breath, amazed at this sudden urge to protect a flesh-and-bloodling. But . . . what the boy had shown was called *kindness,* the being knew that from the pleading of the sorcerer's poor victims. Kindness. "Boy, whoever, whatever you are, you're safe enough down here for the moment. There's no one else in the castle, only you and I and . . . him—"

"I know. He doesn't trust anybody."

"—so get out of here now, before he comes down to investigate."

"No." The boy straightened proudly, suddenly looking far older than his slight years. "I am Hauberin, son of the ruler of this land, and your—your master, Ysilar, is his foe. Ysilar is a cruel, callous man, and I . . . don't guess he's really sane any more, He's guilty of murder and—worse things, several times over." The young prince stopped, flustered. "But you would already know all about that, wouldn't you?"

Alliar winced. "Yes."

"My father has placed him under sentence of death for his crimes but, so far, he hasn't been able to carry out the sentence."

"Why not?"

Hauberin sighed. "Though Ysilar doesn't dare leave his castle, it's so well Shielded that up till now no one has been able to get past the Wards. And any magics strong enough to break the Shielding from afar would destroy the land around as well. But I . . ." The boy hesitated, then continued defiantly, "I am half-human. Do you know what 'human' means?"

"Yes." Ysilar had used one or two of the poor, lost, magickless creatures in his studies. "Ahh, of course. The Wards were set strictly against Faerie blood. They wouldn't have sensed someone partly human."

The prince nodded. "I got past them without any trouble." He added in a bitter undertone, "First time I've ever been glad of human blood."

"You are unhappy with your shaping, too?" the confused being asked.

"No. I mean, yes. I mean— Look you, we can't stay down here talking like this. Ysilar is sure to find us. But if we can find him first . . . If I free you, wind spirit—"

"Alliar. The sorcerer tried to put a name of his own devising on me soon after Binding me. But I secretly chose my own."

The young prince dipped his head politely. "Alliar, then. If I free you, will you guide me to him?"

"I . . . no . . ."

"I'm not asking you to raise a hand against him. Just guide me. Come, hurry, decide! If you don't want to help me, I promise I'll free you anyhow. Then I'll go find Ysilar on my own."

And almost certainly get himself slain in one of the sorcerer's traps, and put an end to kindness. *If I go with him,* Alliar mused, *maybe I can save this bright, brave young thing. Somehow.* "Yes," the spirit said reluctantly. "Remove this shackle and I will guide you."

It took some time for Hauberin to unlock the chain, murmuring wary Words, their Power muted so he wouldn't alert Ysilar. But at last the shackle yielded and Alliar scrambled up, headed for the stairway down which Ysilar had dragged his slave.

They met the sorcerer halfway up.

Ysilar, tall and lean, long hair silvery-fair, ice-gray eyes wide and flat and mad, had presumably been descending the winding stair to see if his slave had learned proper submission. All three stood frozen for what seemed an endless time. Then the sorcerer smiled.

"You. Slave. Come here."

Sick with fear, Alliar looked into Ysilar's terrible eyes and trembled, remembering all the length of captivity, all the cruelty witnessed and, perforce, performed. And all at once it was quite beyond bearing. "No," the being said in desperate defiance. "No. This time I will not."

But the spirit *felt* the sorcerer draw in magic and knew the target—

The boy! He'll kill the boy!

With all the speed the imposed body knew, Alliar threw Hauberin aside onto a landing, then hurtled up at Ysilar, bowling the astonished sorcerer off his feet. But then Alliar hesitated, ready to howl in frustration, helpless to do anything to harm him. The furious Ysilar backhanded his slave across the face, sending Alliar tumbling. Sorcery struck, white-hot, merciless as the rest of Ysilar's punishments, and the being screamed and screamed again, struggling futilely to escape.

"Stop it." That was Hauberin's voice, and even through the pain, Alliar had to wonder at how regal it sounded.

And, miraculously, the pain did stop. Shaking with relief, the being tried to rush to the boy's side, but a magic-stunned body refused to move.

"Who are you, boy?" Ysilar was amused. "You have the feel of magic to you, but the look of a mongrel."

That must have stung, but the boy answered proudly, "You should know me, traitor. I am Hauberin, son of Prince Laherin, your rightful liege lord."

Alliar managed to work the weary body up onto one elbow, in time to see the humor fade from Ysilar's face. Not even a Faerie child could have sensed the subtle tremor of air that meant the gathering of death-magic by a master. But the wind spirit knew, the wind spirit shouted out a frantic "Look out!" to Hauberin.

Ysilar was prepared for spells—not a quickly thrown knife. Silver flashing, Hauberin's blade took the sorcerer full in the throat.

Choking, wild-eyed, already dead, Ysilar clawed frantically at the hilt of the knife (a distracted part of Alliar's mind noted that Faerie blood, like that within the imposed body, was quite red), then crumpled. The being twisted aside in a spasm of disgust to let the body tumble past, then scrambled up to stand beside Hauberin, staring back at the corpse in disbelief.

"Come on." the boy pulled at Alliar's arm. "It's all right, he—he's dead. Alliar, come on!"

Only then did the being realize that the castle was shaking violently around them. "His spells are falling apart!"

"Can you walk?"

Alliar ached in every muscle, and longed for nothing so much as to let this ridiculous trap of a body rest. But if rest meant being buried alive— "Walk?" the being retorted with a flash of humor. "I can run!"

Alliar, out on the palace balcony in the present, smiled. Run they had, narrowly escaping as the last of the castle settled with spectacular noise into so much broken stone behind them. Only then, once he was sure they were safe and it was really over, had the young prince, white-faced with shock and the realization of what he had done, stopped to be thoroughly sick.

"Ah, Hauberin." It was a whisper of pure affection.

Of course Alliar had returned to the royal palace with Hauberin—where else was there to go?—and heard the young prince punished and praised for his rash, heroic actions. The being had defended Hauberin hotly, and earned the amused approval of the boy's tall, golden father, Prince Laherin.

But then had come bitter, bitter disappointment. The court sages all studied Alliar and came to the same regretful conclusion: insane Ysilar had worked a binding spell on the spirit so foreign it could not be broken. For a dark while after that, Alliar had wanted only death, not caring that suicide for a bound spirit would probably mean extinction.

But Hauberin had pierced the darkness. "Look you, I know I can't even begin to understand what you've lost. And the Powers know you've been given no reason so far to live. But . . . oh, Alliar, there are such wonderful things to flesh-and-blood life, and you don't know any of them."

"I don't care to—"

"Don't interrupt! I saved your life, I'm responsible for it, and—d-dammit, I'm not going to let you go till you've learned to enjoy it!"

And the boy had won. There had been small time for despair amid the shining new wonders of *taste* and *touch* and *smell*. Alliar smiled, remembering lying in sweet-scented grass, listening to birdsong, feeling the living earth beneath. And swimming—ha, what a lovely, alien pleasure that had been, moving easily through water cool and clear as air. There had been the bliss of music, too, and song, and oh, the joy of realizing all magic didn't have to have a tang of pain to it. Most wondrous of all, there had been laughter.

Hauberin, Hauberin, I owe you a debt I can never repay.

No. "Debt" was a cold, hard word. It wasn't obligation keeping Alliar here, but love. Not, of course, anything like that pleasure gendered folk seemed to take in each other's flesh; there were some things even a tangible spirit could never understand, physically or emotionally. But this love of friend and friend Alliar *did* know, and it was a wonderful thing, refreshing as . . . swooping down summer skies, comforting as . . . as . . . Ae, useless. There were no wind spirit equivalents for it. Except—joy.

The being stared out into the directionless brightening that meant the coming of dawn in sunless Faerie, and smiled.

Charailis stretched languorously, a sleek figure in soft, silky blue, unbound hair rippling down her back in a fall of pale silver. The hour was very late, and she was truly weary after the festivities at the royal palace and the journey in her carriage drawn by matched winged steeds back to her own estate. But Charailis stood at the window of her elegant white bedchamber, too lost in thought for sleep.

What an odd night this had been. Particularly in regard to Hauberin. Charailis, bored with courtly matters, had involved herself for some time with personal magics, personal affairs. But she really had been away from court too long if that unprepossessing boy had had time enough to grow into manhood.

Charailis laughed softly. Who would ever have expected the little mixed-blood creature to become anything of worth, let alone a ruler who had actually held the throne safe for six years? She had underestimated the young one, no doubt of that. So blatant an attempt at seduction would only have amused a subtle Faerie man. But she had been so sure the prince's human blood would overwhelm him!

Fool, the woman told herself without heat. *Were he that weak, he wouldn't have held the throne for a day.*

Charailis smiled sleepily. More experiments were definitely in order, not merely because on a purely sensual level she was wondering if Hauberin's so exotic coloring meant an exotic taste in lovemaking as well. Sexual magic was a powerful force when properly controlled; bind Hauberin to her, mind and body, and who knew where it might lead? Of course, Serein would still need to be removed, and Ereledan (that hulking boor who couldn't even control his own will). But they were both fools; they shouldn't pose any real problems. Particularly once Hauberin was hers.

Charailis raised a graceful hand to her head, indulging herself in a moment's fantasy, imagining a crown there. Naturally, once fantasy became fact, she wouldn't need Hauberin any more. But with one of the true Faerie blood on the throne, who would miss one little half-human?

Looking out into the coming dawn, Charailis smiled again.

Ereledan hadn't any intention of rushing off to his home this night. If Hauberin was urbane or foolish enough to offer hospitality to those guests who wanted it, so be it. For one thing, unlike that icy, so-proper Charailis, Ereledan had no pretty little team of winged steeds to whisk him away. For another, after that near disastrous duel (he didn't want to think of that too closely), leaving now would have looked like panicky or, worse, guilty flight.

Besides, what better chance, when the nobility was gathered here from all over the land, to do some delicate prying? To see how many folk were discontent and just how many might consider a chance of leadership?

But there'd been nothing but frustration! Even before the duel had spoiled everything, Ereledan still had uncovered no secret plots, no festering hate, nothing on which to build. Though, admittedly, there was a certain simpleminded thrill in meeting here, illicitly, within the walls of the palace, with these his fellow conspirators.

They were his distant kinsmen, actually, related to him in such convoluted Faerie ways that even Ereledan wasn't sure exactly how. At least, he thought with a touch of wry humor, if he was surprised by Hauberin's guards despite the faint Warding he'd put on the room, he could always claim this was nothing more than a small family reunion.

The Powers knew these . . . conspirators weren't good for much else. Ereledan glared at the six of them and thought, *What a lifeless lot!* None had inherited the main stock's flaming red hair or solid build. They were downright trite, alike in slender height and golden hair and that carefully developed air of world-weariness. As Ereledan paced, they sprawled at their languid ease, watching him from half-lidded, amused eyes.

As though they expect me to entertain them, damn them!

Of course. They were almost surely here out of boredom, not any true hatred for the prince; long Faerie lives led to mischief in those without any depth of mind. However, Ereledan told himself, one worked with the tools at hand.

"You know why we're here," he began, and languid Astyal murmured:

"Because you have dreams of glory."

"Because we've been ruled by a mongrel too long!" Ereledan snapped. "Because it's time to put someone of the true blood on the throne."

"Your blood?" mused slender Sharial. "It seems to me I remember your grandsire's deposing some time back. Mm, yes, and the elimination of most of your branch of the family." A cold light flickered in his eyes. "It wasn't a comfortable time for the rest of us."

"What of it? The past is dead, and we—"

"Must live in the present," Astyal finished with a yawn. "Yes, yes, we've heard all the platitudes before. We know what you want, Ereledan. Tell us why we should support you."

Ereledan opened his mouth, shut it, realizing to his horror that suddenly he couldn't think. Without warning all his carefully planned reasons had vanished, and what thoughts he had were fluttering frantically about in his mind. Ae, Powers, he must say something, anything:

"Hauberin has seemed to rule well so far."

"Well, indeed. The land prospers."

"Yes, but . . ." But *what?* Desperate, Ereledan forced out, "But that won't last, it can't. We all know what humans are like: flighty, animal, easy to control—"

"Like you?" Sharial murmured maliciously.

"No! How dare you—"

"We saw that duel, that ridiculous outright attack. What happened, kinsman? Were *you* controlled?"

"No! That's impossible, I—"

"Then you simply lost control. While the prince, that 'flighty animal,' did not."

"It was a fluke, an accident."

"An accident that just might happen again."

"It won't—I won't— Wait!"

But his kinsmen were getting smoothly to their feet. Astyal gave him a flat, polite smile. "We, too, would prefer one of true Faerie blood on the throne. But so far, save for his . . . unfortunate taint, we have no reason to quarrel with the prince. Perhaps he will, indeed, reveal a weaker nature someday. Till then: Your branch of the family once nearly destroyed us all. Why should we endanger ourselves for you now?"

By the time Ereledan could find an answer, he was alone. And, for the first time in he knew not how long, afraid.

What was happening? In all his long life, he'd never been so confused! Arranging for this ridiculous meeting, then forgetting what he'd wanted to say— Powers! It had almost felt as though someone else had rummaged through his mind, then discarded him.

But that's impossible! No one has such magic!

Despairing, Ereledan sank to a chair, head in hands.

The slave had fallen asleep long ago (or was feigning sleep), her long green hair fanned out across the pillows. But Serein remained awake, staring blankly up at the smooth golden ceiling of his bedchamber, fear a cold weight within him.

Ae, ae, what was wrong with him? When Hauberin had accused him of attempted assassination, he had smiled and denied everything, and prayed he had sounded convincing—because he couldn't remember a thing!

It hadn't been the first time. These frightening moments of blankness, these empty gray patches in his memory— Could it be Hauberin's plot? Was that little animal working some bizarre revenge? No. Cousin Hauberin was far too moral, too human, for that, damn him. *I'll have his throne, and him as my pet.* But the familiar litany failed to soothe. He had made this vow often enough, yet somehow had never seemed to do anything about it. *This time it will be different. When my plan begins to work . . .*

If the emptiness allowed it.

All at once Serein found himself remembering Ysilar, the long-dead sorcerer brooding over his envy and empty plots till at last his sanity fled. Maybe he, too, had begun by losing memory—

No! I'm not like him!

The room was freezing. Shivering, Serein glanced at the slave, aching for her to wake, to hold him in her arms and let him be a child again (but childhood had been a cold, sharp time, no weaknesses permitted), to let down his guard and for once be sheltered, safe. . . .

But the slave continued to sleep, face turned from him. Suddenly furious that she was so peaceful while he suffered alone, Serein shouted at her:

"Wake up!"

She started, blinking in confusion. "Wh-What . . . ?"

"Wake up, you lazy bitch!"

The slave stifled a scream as he slapped her, and tried to squirm away. Serein caught one slender arm and pulled her roughly back.

"Go ahead," he gasped, "fight me. Fight me!"

His last bedmate had fought splendidly, savagely. Serein's lips peeled back in a fierce smile as he remembered. How the creature had hated him, right up to the night when she had actually tried to kill him! Of course he had destroyed her, but with sincere regret. But this timid little thing—

"Fight me!" he ordered, slapping her again. "Come on, fight!"

But the slave went limply submissive instead, whimpering, mossy-green eyes dark with pleading. Her meekness enraged him, aroused him, and suddenly he threw himself on her, forcing her thin legs apart, taking her savagely, frantic with the need to prove himself alive and real and in control.

At last, exhausted, he rolled aside, drenched with perspiration. The slave's muffled sobbing annoyed him, and Serein snapped, not looking at her, "Go on, get out of here." He reached out blindly to give her a rough shove. "Go on! Get out!"

Still sobbing, she scrambled up and out.

Serein hardly noticed. Terror as sharp within him as ever, he lay amid the crumpled bedclothes and stared bleakly into space.

III

THE MIND OF A CHILD

It was not yet halfway into the next moon-cycle after the celebration of Hauberin's Second Triad, and gifts and polite congratulations were still pouring in from neighboring lands, but the royal court was in session once again; festivals or no, life must go on.

Hauberin, by this point totally weary of ceremony, had refused any elaborate court robes. His silky gray tunic and cloak, simple of design but soft and comfortable, were close enough to royal silver to pass, and the beautifully curved silver circle of the everyday coronet was a relatively lightweight burden on his brow. But he couldn't avoid the chair of state on its slightly raised dais; his people insisted on some splendor.

Splendid the chair undoubtedly was, silver wrought in elegant little ripples like the waves of the sea. Unfortunately, though, it had been all too evidently designed more for style than comfort.

His discomfort wasn't eased by the half-finished Word of Power, lacking only the final syllable, that he was holding in his mind. It was a traditional means of royal self-protection, the theory being that a ruler could complete and shout out the Word faster than any would-be assassin could move. But it was also a prickly thing to hold, prodding at his thoughts for completion, uneasy as a mental itch.

So Hauberin sat within the spacious council hall with its shining walls of amber and nacre, struggling not to fidget, surrounded by sages and courtiers and the merely curious, and tried his best to keep his patience.

Before him stood the co-complainants (*combatants, is more like it,* thought the prince): Lietlal, Lord of Cyrran, and Ethenial, Lord of Akalait, grand titles for two whose bordering lands could be walked from end to end in a day. Old rivals, Lietlal and Ethenial, though they could just as soon have been brothers to look at them, nearly alike in youthful-seeming hawk-fine features and silvery hair. Only their slanted Faerie eyes betrayed their age, dry with too much life, too much boredom.

And so, out of boredom, they fought. In fact, they had been fighting over land, over horses, over whatever excuse came to mind, for longer than Hauberin had been alive. But this time the quarrel had turned bitter. Hauberin leaned forward in his elegant, uncomfortable chair and asked Ethenial bluntly, cutting into the man's flowery, empty speech:

"Did you kill the man?"

Ethenial blinked, offended. "My Prince, the land is mine. Any who enter onto it without my permission trespass and—"

"Yours!" Lietlal interrupted. "That land has been mine since before the days of—"

"Yes, yes!" shouted Hauberin before they could start their argument all over again. "But did you kill the man?"

"I am not a murderer, my prince."

The prince took a calming breath. "Lord Lietlal has brought complaint before me that you slew his servant."

"A slave. Only a foolish old hu—" Ethenial broke off sharply, fair skin blanching, and Hauberin guessed that the unfinished word would have been "human." "Only a slave," Ethenial finished lamely.

"A life." Hauberin's voice was cold. "Which neither you nor Lord Lietlal can restore. Now, one last time, my lord: Did you or did you not kill the man?"

Ethenial hesitated, as though hunting for an excuse. Then his proud head drooped ever so slightly. "It was an accident," he murmured. "I meant only to frighten him away. No one dreamed he would prove so fragile."

"Ah." Hauberin sat back again, thanking the Powers

for innate Faerie truthfulness; without it, this case might have dragged on for days. "Then I order you to pay a blood-fine of—"

Neither lord was listening to him. "What are you laughing at?" Ethenial hissed at his rival.

"You, you land-thief."

"Land-thief! That land is mine!"

"Impossible! My father drew the lines himself!"

"Your father couldn't have drawn a true line if his magic hung on it!"

"At least he wasn't a treacherous land-thief!"

As they argued back and forth, voices growing shriller and fiercer by the moment, Hauberin slumped in his chair, fingers steepled, glaring darkly down at both of them. There were so many other matters demanding his attention—not the least of them Serein—but he couldn't do anything about anything while he was trapped here. Yet if he dared complain, the prince knew he would get nothing but mild contempt from those around him, not, this time, because of his human blood but because of his "youthful agitation."

Youth. Though of course they showed few overt signs of age, none of the men or women about him had been young for . . . Powers, who knew how long? Most of them had served his father, some his grandfather, some of them might even have served—

Hauberin tensed in sudden alarm. Magic— The two idiots were arming spells against each other! The prince sprang to his feet on the narrow dais, completing and shouting out the Word of Power he had been holding in his mind, just barely tempering it in time to keep it from killing force. Even so, the Power was enough to slash through the half-formed magics, dispelling them, and send Lietlal and Ethenial staggering back as though he'd slapped them with all his might, stunned into silence. Hauberin blazed out at them:

"How dare you bring battle-magic into my court! You've already killed one man over that barren strip of land. How many more were you planning to add?" Their

guilty glances only fed his fury: They hadn't even stopped
to consider the risks of war-spells in that crowded hall!
"By the Powers, I should seize that land as Crown
property!"

The prince looked sharply about, hunting a scribe to
take down his decree.

No . . . wait. He had a better idea.

Hauberin whirled to face the two lords again, smiling
fiercely. "You are so eager to fight for that land? So be
it! You *shall* fight, one moon-cycle hence, at a site of
my choosing: one to one, alone, with no one to aid or
interfere."

They stared. "Do you mean . . . death-spells, my
Prince?" Ethenial asked nervously.

"Whatever it takes. One way or another, my lords, the
matter shall be settled!" With a deliberately dramatic
swirl of cloak, Hauberin settled back in his chair. "You
have my permission to leave."

As the chastened lords slunk away, a wary voice asked,
"But is this wise, my Prince?"

Hauberin turned his head to see Sharailan at his
side: Sharailan, oldest of the royal sages, so old no one
could remember him as other than he was now: his
fair skin still smoothed and unmarked, his back
straight, but seeming somehow so brittle he would
shatter at a touch. Even the once-bright hair and eyes
had changed, their color faded under the weight of
untold ages. A truly wise man, Sharailan. Also, unfortunately, literally a royal nuisance, devoid of wit and
spontaneity. "Why, yes, Sage," Hauberin replied. "I
think it is. Do you really believe those two want to
give up their cherished bickering? No. They'll ponder
awhile, come up with some excuse not to duel, and go
right back to their quarrels. Only this time they will be
more careful of what they do."

"But, my Prince," Sharailan insisted, "are you sure?"

"I am."

"Yes, but—"

"I said, I am!" All at once at the edge of his patience

with Sharailan and the whole tedious day, the prince sprang to his feet once more. But he couldn't just go storming out of there, not without leaving condescending whispers in his wake. In a pretense of proper princely duty, Hauberin snatched at random one of the scrolls the startled sage had been holding for his signature. But then the prince glanced down at what he held, and stifled a groan. He wasn't going to escape with anything so simple as a signature with *this* thing. Still, he could hardly stuff it back into Sharailan's hands!

"I did promise to work on this spell," Hauberin admitted. "And so I shall. Now. Outside. Alone!"

Hauberin, his crown sent back to the royal treasury, his cloak abandoned in this soft weather, sat out on a palace terrace in the warm afternoon light, inhaling air sweet with hay and flowers, and tried to concentrate only on the spell-scroll spread out on the small stone table before him.

It wasn't easy.

Powers . . . what if he had been wrong about Lietlal and Ethenial? What if they did fight, and killed each other? Maybe Sharailan was right. Maybe he shouldn't have acted so rashly. Maybe—

Hauberin exhaled sharply, angry at himself. Alarming though the fact sometimes seemed, even after these six years of rule, he *was* the prince. While he might listen to his advisors as much as he pleased, he must not let anyone else make his decisions for him.

Besides, I was right, Hauberin told himself. *They will not duel.*

He hoped.

Ah well, to the scroll. Hauberin studied it for a long while, frowning. And gradually he became engrossed in the problem despite himself, plotting out the steps he would need to take. . . . Decided, the prince set to work.

Some sage in ages past had inscribed a basic wheat-fertility charm on the parchment, the Powerful symbols twisting elegantly about each other. Hauberin, delicately untangling and widening the twists, was attempting to widen the charm's narrow application by including his own magical additions.

A few days back, he had argued that surely an older, more seasoned scholar would be a better choice for this. But the sages had all insisted the spell would have increased potency if the prince himself worked on it, citing the magical correlation between ruler and land. Hauberin wasn't so sure about that. He was the rightful prince, no argument there, and as far as he knew, his half-human status had no effect one way or the other on his fertility. But it wasn't as though he had actually sired a child, after all.

Still, Hauberin had to admit that testing his abilities like this (assuming the spell worked and all this wasn't for nothing) was fun. Besides, there was a limit to the strength of the little field-magics most farmers used, and anything that coaxed the land into greater abundance . . .

The prince gave a dry little laugh. Whenever he turned his talents to some such less . . . fashionable subject, he bewildered his nobles. Why, they wondered, worry about something as plebeian as crops and harvests?

Let those harvests fail, and we'll see how quickly they learn the answer to that! There's a limit to what magic alone can do. Without the farmers they hold in such contempt, none of us would eat or—
"Oh, damn!"

The moment he'd released his will from them, the stubborn spell-syllables had curled themselves back up on the page into their original form. Yet again.

Hauberin leaned back in his chair, rubbing his eyes. There was such a thing as being too conscientious. Maybe Alliar was right. Now that he had the fundamentals of the new spell set, he should just turn the whole thing back over to the sages.

The prince straightened, resting his gaze on his lands. The view from here was glorious: a sweep of fertile fields and meadows rich with flowers—solid

patches of red, blue and yellow from here—merging
into a dark green tapestry of forest folding itself up
against the wild mountains beyond, and over all the
clear, sunless, achingly blue sky of Faerie and the luminous Faerie light.

Hauberin got to his feet, soft gray tunic whispering
silkily at the motion, and moved forward to lean on the
terrace's smooth white balustrade, enjoying the moment's
idleness.

But then his gaze sharpened. There amid the peaceful
fields lay Serein's estate.

Serein. So far there had been nothing but sweet innocence in all the man's actions. By now, Hauberin could
almost convince himself he had imagined the threat in
Serein's eyes the day of the celebration— No. It had
been real enough.

And why hasn't he acted on it?

The law, of course, was in Serein's favor. Hauberin
couldn't exile his cousin, or slay him, or even hold him
as a royal "guest" without some very real proof of treason; his magical folk, being by nature so near to chaos,
clung to their laws as the only true stabilizing factor,
and not even a prince dared go against them. Hauberin slammed his fist down on the balustrade in
frustration.

"Damn you, cousin," he muttered, "what game are you
playing now?"

A mind brushed his, briefly, questioningly, and the
prince sighed and answered silently, *"Yes. Come."*

He didn't actually hear Alliar approach. But then, no
one ever did. A flash of motion, and the wind spirit
was at his side, at the moment no taller than Hauberin
and vaguely elfin in shape, fairly glowing in the clear
light, deeply golden of hair and skin and luminous eyes.

Worried eyes. "My Prince." The being swept down in
a bonelessly graceful bow, and Hauberin frowned.

"So formal, Li? What is it?"

"Am I your friend? Do you trust me?"

"Yes, and yes. Look you, I'm in no mood for word games."

"Serein again?"

Sometimes his friend could read him too clearly. "Serein," Hauberin agreed.

The being shivered. "You're going to have to kill him someday."

"Alliar!"

"It's true. For the sake of the realm as well as your own."

"Ach, Alliar." Very gently, Hauberin said, "He . . . isn't Ysilar. You don't have to fear him, I promise you."

Anger flickered in the golden eyes. "I don't fear him. But maybe you should! Wait, let me finish. Serein may be next in the line of succession, curse him—but can you picture him in your place?" Slim hands flew in a quick, fierce protective gesture. "Winds prevent! A fine prince he'd make, for all his fine looks, he, who dares hunger for your lands when he can barely manage his own!"

True enough. "But he *is* next in line. And aside from the fact that I don't intend to make things easier for Charailis or Ereledan by removing him, I'm not about to murder my own kinsman. Particularly when I haven't been able to coax out the slightest hint of whatever plots are hiding behind that pretty face of his."

"You . . . could use force."

Hauberin snorted. "How long do you think my people would support a half-blood prince who bent the law for his own use?"

"Ah. There is that. Ay-yi, at least the boy is free of him!" It was said with an ex-slave's fervor.

"The boy."

"Had you forgotten? The human! Serein's little captive." The being paused. "He . . . *is* free now?"

"Oh, Alliar, of course." Hauberin *had* forgotten; he'd had more things on his mind than one small human. A touch abashed, he asked, "How is the boy?"

Alliar shivered. "Not overly well."

"He's ill?" It was sharply said; a half-human might not be immune to human disease.

"Not ill," the being hedged, "not exactly . . . My Prince, Serein is your kinsman . . ."

"I thought we had already established that. Come, speak."

"At your will be it," Alliar said formally. "The boy has been hurt. Deliberately, repeatedly, willfully hurt."

Hauberin stared at his friend in horror. Who could ever have been dark-souled enough to torture a child? "It . . . must have been some human, back in the boy's Realm."

"I'm sorry. No."

"One of *us*? No, that's impossible. None of us would ever—"

"One man would. And did. Your cousin."

"But—Alliar, that's obscene! Not even Serein would— Look you, I know you don't like him—"

"Ha!"

"—but he would never do anything so foul—"

"The proof," Alliar said sadly, "is there."

"It *can't* be! You've been among us long enough, you know that none of us, not even the—the lowest, would ever hurt a child: a rare, precious child!" But Alliar was watching him steadily, never flinching, and Hauberin hurried on, "Granted, the boy was terrified of him. But what else would you expect from a magickless little creature snatched from his Realm and dropped into ours? That doesn't mean Serein. . . . He . . ."

Hauberin stumbled to a halt beneath the weight of that quiet, unblinking gaze. "Ahh, Li . . ." Sickened, the prince asked softly, "What proof?"

"I'm . . . not sure exactly what torment was worked on him." A new shudder shook the sleek golden form. "Not very much physical torment; at least I don't think so; there aren't any lasting scars. But mental harm, magical harm . . ." Alliar waved a helpless hand. "Who can say? The torture was real enough. The boy will not speak, or laugh, or even smile. And whenever anyone approaches, he shrinks away in terror, even from the Lady Aydris."

"Aydris! Who could possibly be afraid of Aydris?"

"It's the slant of eye, I think," Alliar said delicately, "and the color of hair and set of features. They must remind him of your cousin. And so the poor little wretch cringes like some beaten animal expecting further blows. Of course," the being added, "some of us have cringed from him as well."

"What does that mean?"

"The boy has a human's knife: Iron."

Hauberin felt his heart miss a beat. That deadly metal . . . Iron was found only in certain human Realms. Tied totally to the human Earth, with no tempering ties to other forces—not Moon-magic like silver, Fire-magic like copper—its power was so alien to Faerie and magic that the merest touch charred Faerie flesh. A cut, even a scratch, from an iron blade meant certain, agonizing death. "And you let him keep it? By all the Powers, Li, where's your sense? You're the only one here who can touch it. Get the thing away from him before he kills someone!"

"The Lady Aydris wouldn't let me. She says that the boy sees it as the last link with his homeland."

"The Lady Aydris is overruled. Sooner or later, the boy must learn to live here. Oh, and don't give me that wounded wood-sprite look! I'm not being heartless! Alliar, think. Even if we knew which of all the many Realms in space and time was his, human years fly too swiftly. The boy would stand a good chance of—of crumbling to ancient dust the moment he touched mortal soil. Now go, get that dagger away from him."

As far as Hauberin was concerned, the subject was now closed; pity wasn't a Faerie emotion, and the half-human didn't care to be caught in the middle of it, even by a friend. But Alliar continued to watch him so hopefully the prince added shortly, "All right, what else? Will the boy at least speak to— No, that's right, he doesn't speak our language."

"I don't suppose that you . . . ?"

"No. You know the only human tongue I speak is of my mother's folk. I doubt the boy is even from her Realm, let alone her land. And stop staring at me!"

"I only meant—"

"I know what you meant. And I know what you want of me." Hauberin threw up his hands in defeat. "Since the boy is, after all, under my protection, I suppose I can find the time to pay him a visit."

Hauberin eyed the small human dubiously. What a scrawny little thing it was! All unlikely lengths of arms and legs—too thin, surely?—with those enormous dark eyes peering out from beneath that wild mass of black hair.

Did I ever look like that? I hope not!

But the boy seemed to see a resemblance, in coloring if in nothing else. He left the bed on which he'd been huddling and approached the prince with a wild animal wariness that struck an unexpected note of purely human sympathy in Hauberin and left him standing stock still and ill at ease.

And what was he supposed to say to the child. "It doesn't matter, does it, boy? You can't possibly understand a word I say."

The human stopped, blinking, uncertain. After a moment he spoke, a rusty, hesitant string of sounds. Hauberin listened dutifully, then sighed. "No, boy. I don't understand you." He tried an experimental shift of languages. "And I don't suppose you know my mother's tongue, either? No. I thought not."

So. Surely this satisfied Alliar and the maternally beaming Aydris? The prince turned to them—but in a little flurry of those gawky limbs, the boy caught him, clinging to him desperately. The startled Hauberin froze, confused and embarrassed, thinking with a moment's wild gratitude, *At least they managed to bathe him,* not quite certain how to free himself.

"Hey now, boy, let go. I'm not your kinsman after all."

No reaction.

"Let go, child."

Ridiculous. If some presumptuous adult had dared seize him, Hauberin would have loosed his magic. But of course he couldn't use magic now, not against a child!

"Come now, enough."

If Aydris was so maternal-minded about the boy, let him go cling to her! Or Alliar, who was fairly choking with laughter. Hauberin glanced down at his small, determined captor, wondering if he could peel the boy off bit by bit. Like a limpet.

But all at once Hauberin glimpsed the boy's eyes, and suddenly it wasn't funny any more, because where they should have been dark, they glittered a cold, familiar sea-green—

Serein!

No wonder he'd surrendered his slave so meekly. No wonder he had made no outward attack during all this past moon-cycle. He'd needed none. This child was his weapon!

The child who was armed with iron. Hauberin twisted desperately as he saw metal flash, but he couldn't pull free from the tangle of limbs in the instant of time before—

With a wild, unfocused blaze of will, Hauberin hurled the boy from him, not quite in time. Something white-hot seared his side and he cried out in anguish, hearing Aydris' terrified scream like an acho. Then a frantic Alliar was at his side.

"Let me see! Oh Winds, did the blade cut you?"

If it had, he was already dead. "Let me be." The boy still had the knife and was about to strike again— "Alliar, let me be!"

This time the surge of will was controlled, a lance of light flashing from Hauberin's outflung hand. The boy screamed, falling back against a wall, knife dropping from numbed fingers, and the prince lunged at him, catching the thin shoulders in a fierce grip.

"Link with me, Li."

"My Prince—"

"Link with me!"

He felt Alliar's consciousness, cool and clear as wind, obediently touch his, then reached out to catch the boy's mind with his own, brushing aside the unskilled, frightened attempts at defense, searching— There! As elusive as shadow, there was Serein's presence, the merest trace, barely enough to say, *I am,* slipping, sliding away from him. . . .

In the next instant, it was gone. Only the boy was left, trembling so violently only Hauberin's grip on his shoulders held him upright. Sick with guilt, the prince gently touched his mind again in an attempt to soothe him, only to recoil in disbelief. There was nothing of the child-essence to be read, nothing save shadow.

That's impossible, Hauberin told himself hurriedly, *it's only that he's exhausted, he'll recover,* and prayed he was correct.

But he had to do *something.* If he couldn't touch the boy's mind, maybe he could at least reach him with words. "Poor child. Between us, my cousin and I have used you cruelly. But you're safe now, little one. And the Lady Aydris will see that you remember nothing of this."

His voice faltered. The woman quickly took the boy from him, and the small human fell helplessly against her, still shaking convulsively. Hauberin, feeling the onset of shock, fought his own shivers, straightening slowly, biting his lip at the movement.

"Now you *will* let me see the wound," Alliar ordered grimly, parting the slash in the gray tunic with gentle hands. Hauberin glanced down in time to see the iron-scorched fabric crumbling away into little black flakes, and hastily looked away, stomach protesting. "Winds be praised," he heard the being murmur after a time. "Not the slightest break in the skin."

"I knew it." *When I didn't start to die,* Hauberin added silently in dark humor. "An iron-burn, no more."

It was enough. It was beginning to hurt sickeningly, as

though someone had pressed a fiery brand against his skin, and the pain was making him dizzy. But he waved off his solicitous friend, mind racing.

"He's finally done it. Finally declared himself."

"Serein?"

"Of course." Hauberin closed his eyes for a moment, struggling to will his shaken body under control. "Oh, monstrous, to use a child as assassin!"

"And I am witness," Alliar said sharply. "That's why you had us link minds."

"Exactly! Serein, Serein, I have you at—"

But Aydris' scream of sheer horror slashed across his words. As Hauberin and Alliar turned to stare, the woman, white-faced, backed away, arms falling to her sides. The boy's body sagged briefly against her, then slid slowly, bonelessly, to the floor.

"Winds protect," Alliar gasped. "What . . . ?"

Hauberin reached out with his will, searching frantically for any sign of life. *There has to be something, anything, he can't be . . .*

But then he knew the truth. The prince staggered back, this time glad of Alliar's supporting arms.

"Nothing," he murmured to the being, shuddering helplessly. "Alliar, there was nothing, not even a fading essence, nothing but that . . . shell." The prince wanted to do something, cover the body, comfort poor, weeping Aydris, but his legs refused to obey him. Limp within Alliar's support, Hauberin heard himself chattering feverishly, "I should have guessed. There was shadow in the boy's mind before, I mean, when I touched him, shadow where there should have been—should have been life, but I never suspected, I—"

He broke off abruptly, struggling for self-control. "Oh, Li," the prince said softly. "Serein's magics ruined the child's mind, tore it apart. When my cousin fled me, he destroyed what little essence-spark remained. There was nothing left, nothing that could cling to life for more than the few short moments we saw.

"My cousin is a murderer. Serein has murdered a child."

IV

"WHO WAS YOUR MOTHER'S FATHER?"

Hauberin, clad in light, supple Faerie mail, astride a sleek white Faerie stallion, glanced back over his shoulder at the grim-faced royal war troop following him. As was to be expected from his independent people, none of them wore anything that could have been interpreted as livery—their armor was covered by cloaks and tunics in a wild range of color, from subtle pastels to flaming yellows and reds—but they had answered his summons quickly enough. The prince wasn't vain enough to think it had all been for love of him or concern about treason against him; no, they had been as shocked as he by that most horrifying murder.

The troop rode in silence, the only sounds the thrumming of hoofs against the ground, the flapping of a cloak or clink of a sword hilt against mail, or a snort or whicker from a nervously prancing horse. Hauberin ran over in his mind yet again the complex spells of attack and defense he would surely need (so much more difficult than any everyday magic, so much more dangerous to the magician), and tried to shut out his uneasiness.

Uneasiness, ha! Hauberin thought. *Downright fear is more like it.*

Not fear of Serein, never that. But . . . he had never ridden to battle before. What if something went wrong? What if he misspoke a battle-spell? He had never actually used one, after all. Powers, what if he did misspeak one, and the backlash killed him? He had no heir (save Serein, of course, and no one was going to follow Serein now). There would be civil war, chaos—

Enough of this! As fiercely as any magician mastering a spell, Hauberin forced doubt from his mind.

Just in time. The high white walls of Serein's estate stood before them. Hauberin raised a hand, bringing his company to a halt, studying the estate. Those smooth white walls were pretty, but even his less than battle-trained eyes could tell they would never hold off a determined attack. Yet he didn't feel the peculiar psychic tingling that meant Serein was placing magical reinforcements on them, either.

Wary, the prince waited, alert to the slightest change in air currents that might signal magic, There was silence, such total silence that when one of the horses shook its head, the chinking of the bridle rang out startlingly loud.

"What is this?" one of the warriors muttered. "Not even a token assault from them? Not even a little spell, or an arrow? *Someone's* in there, I can sense them."

So could Hauberin. And they could hardly not have seen his troop approach. Serein had already declared himself a traitor by his acts; he could hardly have developed scruples now.

For an instant more Hauberin hesitated, nerves tight, then signalled to his herald, who rode boldly forward, her gaudy herald's robes—deliberately bright to mark her as a noncombatant—fluttering in the wind. Standing in the stirrups, she called out in a voice like a silver trumpet:

"Open, in the name of the prince! Open for Prince Hauberin!"

There was a moment more of silence, during which Hauberin could feel unseen eyes watching him. And then, almost in anticlimax, the gates swung smoothly open. Figures lurked in the shadow of the doorway, lowly servants, most of them the unlikely mixes found in magical lands: human-sprite-woods creature hybrids and the like to judge from their greenish hair and rough brownish skin. Hauberin had always known Serein liked to surround himself with ugliness (save in the women he took to bed, of course), to make his golden elegance shine the brighter by contrast, but the sudden impact of so many warped beings couldn't be anything but startling.

Particularly when he sensed that much of that warping was relatively recent, and quite deliberately wrought.

Ach, Serein, Hauberin thought, remembering mad, cruel Ysilar.

One of the servants, a thin, wiry creature as much animal as man, moved shyly forward, peering up at Hauberin. "It *is* you!" the being gasped.

With that, as though a wind had stirred them, the servants all sank to their knees. "Spare us, merciful prince," they moaned. "We are innocent. We had nothing to do with it."

"Never mind that," the prince said shortly. "Where is your master?"

They looked blankly up at him.

"Serein!" Hauberin snapped. "Where is he?"

To his amazement, the creatures all, slowly, began to smile. "Why, fled," one said in rich pleasure. "Our once and no longer master has fled for his very life."

"He wanted us to help him in his flight," a thin, ragged creature continued, its face hidden by a wild, tangled mane of mossy hair. With a sudden frantic motion, it tossed back that hair, and Hauberin realized with a shock that the face revealed was a young woman's, haggard traces of beauty still lingering. "He said we must help. He reminded us that we are nothing, only slaves. His to do with as it pleased him. So it was in the past," she added bitterly.

"No longer!" cut in the animal-man. "He raved at us, but we—oh, we wouldn't help him, not that child-tormentor, not that killer of the wee little one." The creature grinned, revealing sharp white teeth. "He could not torment all of us at once, not when he was in such haste. Follow the trail to the mountains, merciful prince, and you shall find him."

Stunned by the raw hatred radiating all about him, Hauberin heard his voice come out more harshly than he'd intended. "How? Is he winged? On horseback? Why are you all smiling?"

"He thought us powerless," they murmured. "And, one and one, we are. But the forest blood is in our veins, however weak. Together, in our deepest need and rage, together we called on it. And this once we were answered. We could not kill him, oh no, he was too clever for that. But when he would escape, we blocked his spells with forest magic, we would not let him take the air. His horse is swift, but horses tire. Follow, merciful prince, follow. Then—kill him, merciful prince!"

The savage despair in that cry made Hauberin wince. "I . . . will do what I must."

That wasn't enough for the haggard-faced woman. "Kill him," she hissed. "Kill him for the sake of that wee little one. Kill him for those of us he raped, those of us he maimed and slew. Kill him."

And, "Kill him," the others chanted, all the while Hauberin, not quite trusting these not quite sane wild things, had his warriors search the entire estate. "Kill him," they chanted when, not having found the slightest hint of Serein-in-hiding, the prince and his troop turned their horses towards the mountains. As he urged his mount on, Hauberin, chilled, could still hear that joyous, savage litany, and thanked all the Powers the hate behind it wasn't aimed at him:

"Kill him. Kill him. Kill him."

Whatever primal Power Serein's slaves had roused, it had done its work well. Serein had tried to erase his trail, but his magic was plainly working only sporadically; Hauberin, extending his senses to their utmost, could track his cousin as surely as hound tracked prey.

The forest thinned with Faerie abruptness, the land all at once becoming rocky and rough. Then suddenly

Hauberin and his troop were out of the trees altogether, seeing a great wall of mountain looming up before them.

They found Serein's horse wandering loose at the mountain's base, still sweating, its flanks still heaving. Faerie horses had their own strong animal intelligence, and this one, pushed to the point of exhaustion, must have simply refused to move.

"That means the traitor can't be too far away," an archer said, fingering his bow uneasily.

Hauberin nodded, craning his head back to look up and up the mountainside. "He didn't reenter the forest; I would have felt it. He could only have gone up."

Yes. There amid the crags was a metallic glint— Serein's armor, or his golden hair.

"Within range," the archer muttered, fitting arrow to bow.

"No!" Hauberin hastily struck down the man's arm, then had to wonder at himself. A well-placed arrow would have been such an easy, logical solution. Now it was too late; Serein had heard or sensed them, and was scrambling out of range. As his warriors stared at the prince in bewilderment, all Hauberin could answer was a simple, "He is mine."

Halfway up the mountainside, Hauberin realized what a fool he was. All Serein had to do was drop a rock on him, and his people would be searching for a new ruler.

But Serein didn't do anything at all, possibly out of the same misguided idea that they should meet (and maybe kill each other) with honor. Or at least suitable drama.

Or maybe he just can't find a big enough rock.

It was a rough climb, and not getting any easier. Maybe he should have shape-shifted— No. Flight would take just as much effort. More, probably, since he'd have the added weight of mail and sword. Besides, he was gaining. He could hear Serein somewhere just ahead of him, scattering tiny avalanches of pebbles as he hunted for a better place to make a stand. Suddenly inspired,

Hauberin left the rugged trail he had been climbing, scrabbling up the bare mountainside instead by fingers, toes, and sheer will, struggling to get ahead of Serein, somewhere off to his right, succeeding by being smaller and lighter than his cousin. Spread-eagled against the mountainside, struggling to catch his breath, the prince glanced back down over his right shoulder, and saw Serein reach a relatively flat, relatively wide ledge.

There isn't likely to be a better place.

Resisting the urge to yell a melodramatic war-cry, Hauberin pushed off from the mountainside and sprang down to confront him.

The impact left him winded. Fortunately, Serein was just as breathless from his climb. And so it came down to this: not elegant prince and noble, not kinsmen making claims on memory, only two tired warriors on a mountain ledge, clad in dust-stained mail.

For a long time they faced each other in tense, weary silence. Then Hauberin said softly, "It's over."

"Not quite."

"Face facts! You failed. Now you're cornered and alone."

The sea-green eyes were bitterly amused. "For which you're so pleased to take credit."

"It wasn't difficult!" Hauberin snapped. "I knew there wasn't any well-planned revolution behind you." Remembering those desperately hate-filled slaves urging him to the kill, he added with a shudder, "Powers above, you couldn't have expected even those maltreated servants of yours to cleave to you!"

A shrug of elegant shoulders. "I confess, I never thought it would come down to my needing an army. After all, there was the boy." Serein's smile was a slow, chill thing. "Ah, the boy. These six long years struggling to find a weakness in your shields, and then to chance upon him— My little human truly had you off your guard, didn't he? Granted, I never expected you to steal him from me. But that only made my task easier!"

"You failed."

"But it was such a narrow thing, wasn't it?"

Serein's abstract calm was beginning to grate. "How could you do it?" Hauberin asked.

"What, try to kill you?"

"No, curse you! Do you think I'm so human I'm surprised at that? The child! How could you torment a child?"

"Why, the whelp had to be in the properly receptive frame of mind. Even you must know how such spells work."

"No, thank the Powers! No matter how much you ached for my crown, how could you ever have stooped to such foulness? You, who always taunted me with how truly of Faerie you are?"

"Oh, cousin, really. It wasn't a Faerie child, after all."

"He was still a child! To use him, torture him, not caring if you broke his mind, if you killed him—"

Hauberin broke off sharply, sickened by the unreachable serenity of the sea-green eyes. His cousin smiled.

"Oh, Hauberin, what a sentimental little half-blood you are! A child? How should that ugly, dirty vicious creature be anything but a tool?"

Hauberin bit back the hot, useless words he'd been about to shout. "Were it not impossible for our folk," he said in a rigidly controlled voice, "I would call you possessed. But I'm not going to waste any more time arguing morality. Come, yield."

"And you'll let me live? What, have you a pretty picture of me humbled in silver chains? Oh no, cousin, I'll not surrender for that!" Serein's smile was thin and sharp. "In fact, I don't yet see the need to surrender at all. Tell me, what moved you to come after me yourself? Surely you could have sent your faithful warriors to find me." (*I could have let that archer shoot you*, Hauberin thought.) "Why come after me alone? Honor? Powers above, *pity*?" He made that human emotion sound like an obscenity.

"Just this," Hauberin said slowly. "Traitor though you are, murderer though you are, you are still my kinsman, reluctant though I am to admit it. I . . . couldn't see you hunted down like a stag."

"Such scruples." Serein's eyes glittered. "But here we are, alone. Tell me, cousin, what's to stop my escape after I kill you?" There was the faintest, subtlest trembling of the air. "I'm of the blood royal, more so than you. And you have no heir—save me." The trembling heightened ever so slightly, became a barely perceptible glowing. "With you slain, how long do you think it would take our oh so practical people to forget the past and welcome me to the throne? With you dead, how long before they come to prefer my rule to that of a mongrel? With you dead!" The glowing was a surge of raw Power that came crashing fiercely down—

Against a suddenly upthrust wall of force. Power broke apart like a wave against rock, and flowed harmlessly aside.

"Oh, well done, cousin!" Serein gasped, unable to hide the drain from that wild waste of strength. "But the force-wall must have cost you dearly."

It had, but Hauberin was hardly about to admit it. "You never would admit the truth." He managed to say that in an almost steady voice. "There's no lack of magic in my blood." (*True enough; I never would have ruled if I hadn't inherited it from both sides of the family. Though what Power was doing flowing through a human woman's veins . . .*) "And— Swords, now, is it? So be it!"

That first savage clash of blades almost threw Hauberin off his feet. He stumbled back, nearly falling, wishing he hadn't been so hasty to agree to this, painfully aware that he was at a disadvantage of height, of weight, of reach. A flash of memory raced through his mind, of himself as a boy, and the royal master of arms saying bluntly to his disheartened charge:

"You'll never have your sire's height. Accept it. You're likely to be smaller than most of the swordsmen you may have to meet. Accept that, too. But you're quicker than most, light on your feet. There's your edge—use it!"

Use it, indeed. With a hiss, Serein attacked. But his

sword only shrieked against rock. Hauberin had twisted out of the way, gaining firmer footing with a sideways leap—daring, on so perilous a ledge—trying to find enough room to make use of his supple speed, cutting and cutting at Serein dazzlingly, both of them knowing he must end the fight quickly or burn himself out.

And so Serein braced himself, feet planted firmly, forcing Hauberin to bring the fight to him, waiting with inhuman patience.

Stalemate! Hauberin could still move too quickly to be cut down, but he just could never pierce his cousin's guard. His side was beginning to ache now, too; he really had been straining that only half-healed iron-burn. The royal physician would be furious with him. If he lived that long.

As though he'd overheard the prince's thoughts, Serein slashed out at him, connecting with Hauberin's injured side. The good dwarven mail absorbed most of the blow, but even so, the sudden blaze of pain forced a gasp from Hauberin and sent him stumbling helplessly back. Serein gave a soft, delighted laugh.

"You're tiring, little cousin. Oh yes, there's no doubt of it."

Without warning, Serein slashed out again with all his strength behind the blow, fierce enough to cut through helm and head alike, but Hauberin desperately brought his blade up, two-handed, to parry. The sword held true, but the shock of impact upset his already shaken balance. He went sprawling.

Ae, and here came the death blow!

Frantic, Hauberin rolled, slipped, fell right off the ledge, twisting about blindly in mid-air, sure he was about to die—

And landed with jarring force on his feet, on a ledge a man-length below. Struggling to catch his breath, he saw Serein spring down to the far end of the ledge with a light chiming of mail, ready, wary, deadly. And in that moment, Hauberin accepted with true Faerie fatality what he hadn't really believed till then: Death could be the only end to this.

Both saw their chance at the same time. Both struck from where they stood, heads thrown back, swords outthrust, extensions of their arms. Lightning flashed in a clear sky, twin magics cut the suddenly acrid air, gleaming, blinding—

Both men fell.

Only one regained his feet.

Hauberin stood gasping, at that moment helpless to the slightest attack, mail scorched and torn, mind dazed, able to think only, *Serein . . . Is he . . . ? Did I . . . ?*

Oh, Powers, no! The prince had meant to kill cleanly, since kill he must, but though his cousin's body was too broken to survive, somehow, horribly, Serein still breathed. . . .

I . . . can't. . . .

There wasn't any pain in the dying man's eyes, not even the hatred Hauberin expected. Nothing but mockery burned there, sharp and cruel. As his exhausted cousin stood over him, sick at heart, sword still in shaking hand, Serein laughed faintly.

"Do you think yourself rid of me, kinsman?" It was a whisper. "Oh no. You've only slain this shell, that's all."

"Serein . . ."

"You're not rid of me." The soft, mocking voice dragged to a stop. For an instant, Serein's will faltered, for an instant sheer terror of his approaching death flickered in the sea-green eyes. His eyelids drooped. Hauberin leaned forward warily, sure it was over. Not a breath stirred his cousin's chest. . . .

But all at once Serein was staring up at him again, eyes once more wild with mockery. "Tell me this, dear Hauberin," he cried out in a voice sharp as iron. "Who was your mother's father?"

"What—"

"Are my words not plain enough? Where did her magic come from? Who was your mother's father? Can you name him? No?" Serein's smile was triumphant.

"Then, poor little half-blood, my curse on you! My curse that you know not peace, not sleep, till you learn your mother's father's name! My curse on you in the Binding Names of—"

But what terrible forces he might have invoked were silenced by the fall of the sword.

Hauberin straightened slowly, wondering at his numbness: no grief, no joy, nothing. . . . He took one determined step away. But then legs still trembling with strain buckled under him, and he fell.

The prince hadn't actually lost consciousness, and the rough, hard stone on which he lay wasn't particularly comfortable, but for the moment it was enough not to have to move or think, to just let his body regain its strength. But of course after a time Hauberin heard his warriors come climbing up, looking for their prince, and he sighed silently at the thought of having to move.

"Ae, terrible!" he heard them cry from the ledge just over his head. "The two of them fallen!"

"And are they both dead? The last of the royal line— Are we left without any prince at all?"

"Not quite," Hauberin muttered drily, raising himself on one elbow, watching them start. "Your concern for my well-being touches me."

They jumped lightly down beside him. "Are you hurt, my Prince? Are you badly hurt?"

"No." Weary, yes, weary nigh to death, and with a side that burned like living coals. . . . But he wasn't going to admit it to them. "Only bruised a bit."

Somehow he struggled to his feet unaided, standing as proudly as he was able, one slender, bedraggled, dark young man amid their sleek golden height. "Come," the prince said shortly. "There is still work to be done."

Yes he hesitated for a confused moment.

Serein. He would have to do something about Serein, see to his proper burial. Till then, someone had better cast a Shield around the body. One of the men would have to manage it; right now he didn't have the strength to spare. Not that he was going to confess that, either. Let them think him ruthless enough not to care what happened to a traitor's body. Good for the royal image.

It hardly seemed possible, but it was over. Serein was dead, his curse weightless. It was surely over.

Wasn't it?

V

NIGHTWALKER

A sleek Faerie woman curled up on either side of him, Ereledan, smoothly golden in candlelight, hair a bright, tangled flame, lay awake and brooding.

He had waited so long, more patiently than anyone who thought they knew him would ever have believed. He had let the tedious years go by without a hint of regal ambition, hiding behind the mask of a shallow, sensation-hungry fool, waiting only for the passing of time to safely dull the memory of late, deposed Grandfather. Perilous Grandfather.

But he had waited long enough! Serein had been dead for nearly a full moon-cycle, and yet here Ereledan lay, no closer to his goal since before the night of that disastrous duel with the half-blood prince and the equally disastrous meeting with his kin, when he had rambled and stammered like a mindless fool. . . . What if something like that incredible loss of control happened again? It could destroy him. . . .

"Nonsense," Ereledan muttered. The first had been . . . too much wine. The second, too much tension. He was thoroughly himself again, as both these lovely creatures could attest. And his difficulties these days had nothing to do with wine or mental quirks. No one would meet with him, no one listen to him— Dammit, he wasn't even sure anyone was receiving his messages. Ever since that message-bird had returned to him with great, bleeding gaps in its side, as though some larger, more deadly creature had deliberately driven it back, Ereledan had suspected the truth:

"Charailis."

She was next in line for the crown, the cold-blooded creature. And so, while she plotted whatever lurked in that devious mind of hers, she was making sure he stayed neatly in his place, no threat to her, nicely submissive—

"Ha!"

It was nearly a roar. The women stirred sleepily. One of them giggled and reached out a caressing hand. At first, Ereledan almost knocked it away, angry at her singlemindedness. But wasn't that total devotion to her art exactly why he'd taken her and her sister to his bed? What he wanted in all his women? (And yet, once there had been another . . . a woman unlike any he had ever known, sweet and lovely though fully human. Blanche, gentle, lonely Blanche. . . . She had loved him. But, unlike Prince Laherin and his own human love, he hadn't appreciated the gift offered him. Oh no, he'd been a fool, he'd lightly used and abandoned her. And only then, far too late, realized he'd forever lost that one true love.)

No. He wouldn't think of the past. Ereledan forced himself to relax, letting the woman's soft hand rove where it would, toying just for a moment with the fantasy of it being Charailis in his bed instead, her long, elegant body cool against his own, her hand, with its silvery nails, exploring his body. Powers, no! She'd probably gut him like a fish with those claws!

He shivered as the hand ran ticklingly down his chest, down his stomach, down. . . . And after a bit Ereledan grinned, mentally murmuring the words of a restorative spell, and pulled the giggling woman to him. But just before he let his mind surrender with his body, the Lord of Llyrh told Charailis silently:

Try to block my plans, will you? We'll see how you like it!

In her white and silver bedroom, lovely Charailis lay alone, fuming. Serein dead for a moon-cycle now, and she no closer to Hauberin than she had been on that night of his Second Triad celebration.

"Ereledan."

When none of her little messenger-sprites had reached the palace, returning instead with their small forms trembling with fatigue, whispering words of blinding fogs and swift, perilous winds, she had suspected. When her prized matched team of white, winged steeds had literally grounded themselves, suffering broken flight feathers in a fight—they, who never fought—she knew who must have goaded them on.

"Ereledan," she repeated softly.

Who else could it be? Who else was her chief rival for the throne? Though if that fool thought anyone would support him in a power-drive—he who came from traitor stock—if he thought anyone would stand by him if by some wild mischance he came to rule, or prefer his bluster to her subtlety . . .

Charailis smiled coldly. But then, slowly, the smile faded, leaving her face bleak as she considered the years, the long, weary years behind her, before her. . . . Boredom was the cruelest threat to one untouched by time. Oh, there were some, she knew, who claimed to savor every moment of life, like elderly Sharailan, who never seemed to weary of the intricacies of law and politics, or those others who jumped delightedly from interest to interest, announcing to one and all that even with their lengthy Faerie spans there could never be enough time to learn all there was to be learned, do all there was to be done.

"Fools," Charailis whispered bitterly. "Self-deluding fools."

She had done so many things in her life already, though she was hardly old by Faerie terms, played so many roles. But it was all in vain. No matter what she did, there was still the emptiness, the hopelessness, waiting for the moment when the thrill of *new*, of *unexpected*, was gone.

Charailis bit her lip. If it was only now, belatedly, that

the idea had struck her to vie for a crown, for the heady
new challenge of royal power that just might stave off
the emptiness for a time, that didn't mean she wasn't
totally determined. To escape that emptiness, she would
do whatever she must. Including destroying anyone who
blocked her path.

Especially you, she warned Ereledan silently.

Strangling, smothering, Hauberin clawed his frantic
way up from darkness and—

Awoke. He twisted free of the cocoon of blankets, sitting up in his perspiration-soaked bed, alone, shaking.
Gradually the bedchamber took on reality about him,
chairs, tables, lovely silken tapestries, comforting him
that, yes, it had been only a dream.

Only another dream.

Only another time of broken sleep and little rest—
Powers, oh, Powers.

Hauberin sat for a time, head in hands, trying to steady
his breathing. How many foul nights did this make? So
far, he had covered this . . . weakness well. No one at
court suspected the truth. He had managed to keep
Ereledan and Charailis neatly at each other's throats and
away from his own, with each blaming the other for whatever went wrong. He had even had the satisfaction of
seeing a prediction he'd made come true: quarrelers
Lietlal and Ethenial, the date come round for their duel,
had begged off, both pleading, a bit too coincidentally,
incapacitating illness.

Hauberin smiled faintly. *That* had made Sharailan
regard his prince with new respect! And as for his ever
more darkly circled eyes and gradually increasing slips
of logic, why, the nobles all believed them the signs of
a man deeply engrossed in magical research. (Commendable, they murmured, citing that expanded
wheat-fertility spell as evidence, shows that despite his
unfortunately mixed blood, he takes his Faerie heritage
seriously.) The prince hadn't said anything to dissuade
them.

Powers, if they learn I can't even deal with dreams . . .

Hauberin rubbed his burning eyes with the heels of his hands. He didn't dare return to sleep (*to the darkness, to the dream . . .*), but his body was crying out for rest. At last, reluctantly, he murmured the words of a fatigue-banishing spell and waited tensely for it to take effect. But too many uses of the spell in too short a time had weakened its effect on him; instead of a rush of new energy, all Hauberin felt was the slightest lifting of his fatigue. It would have to be enough.

And what was he going to do when the spell stopped having any effect at all?

No. He wouldn't think of that.

The prince slipped from his bed, flinging on the first clothes that came to hand, and set out to wander the palace halls yet again. Black of hair, clothes, cloak, he was very nearly invisible in the dark corridors that night of Moon Dark. His silent approach startled two guards, who whirled, silver-headed spears at the ready, only at the last moment recognizing:

"Ae, my Prince, forgive us! We didn't realize—"

"No matter. No. Don't follow. I would be alone."

Hauberin kept himself most regally proud of carriage till he was out of their sight, then slowly let his shoulders sag. Those guards were supposed to have been actively patrolling. He should have said something. But he just hadn't been able to find the energy.

And was this what Serein had meant by his strange curse? That every time Hauberin slept, he would start to—

Phaugh! I will not carry his words around like some idiotic little spell-slave!

No? Then what was he doing wandering the palace corridors like some sleepless wraith? Hauberin gave a dry little laugh, stopping to lean against a wall, welcoming its support, enjoying its smooth coolness, his head thrown back.

If anyone should ask, I can always blame my father's blood.

Prince Laherin had truly been a born traveler, wandering even into other Realms whenever time and royal duties permitted. Hauberin saw himself in his mind's eye, a small, dark child staring wide-eyed up at the tall, golden-haired being who always seemed far too splendid to be merely Father, shyly asking the man to travel with him. Laherin had laughed, ruffling his son's hair, promising lightly that yes, he would take the child-Hauberin with him some day.

Some day. After the death of Hauberin's mother, that promise had been forgotten. Prince Laherin had thrown himself into a frenzy of grief from which, in time, he had emerged apparently unchanged. Only Hauberin knew that some small corner of Laherin's soul had died as well. There had been wilder and ever more perilous journeyings over the years, stolen in secret stretches of other-time, with none suspecting but his desperate son, helpless to stop him.

And at last Laherin had found what, perhaps, he had been seeking all along: his death.

Jaws clenched, Hauberin blinked fiercely, telling himself it was merely weariness lowering his defenses. After all, he and his father had never been truly close. And yet, and yet . . .

Damn!

The prince wiped angrily at his eyes and strode determinedly forward. Even after these six years, he hadn't forgotten the anguish of suddenly waking knowing with a dreadful psychic certainty that his father was dead, slain by mischance or some yet-unknown hand—

No. He wouldn't dwell on unhappiness. If the past insisted on being recalled, he would think only of the bright days, of his father as happy explorer. As romantic, too, though none would have guessed it from that cool royal facade.

Hauberin smiled. The man had definitely been a romantic. Who else would have fallen so deeply in love with a human woman, slight, dark little Melusine? Who else but a romantic would have ignored all the warnings and shocked murmurings from his court to make her his wife and royal consort?

And what of Melusine? Hauberin could understand a human woman falling in love with a tall, golden Faerie prince. But what courage she must have had, even with love's support, to come here to an unknown land and people, forever leaving behind all she knew.

But she had succeeded in making herself a new life here.

Hauberin's smile softened tenderly. *Ah, Mother. I do miss you, too.*

Of course he hadn't realized her courage back then when he'd been a boy. She had been merely Mother, warm and loving, but with a wry wit to her that hadn't allowed her son self-pity or shame. But his memories of her were a child's memories; she had died so unexpectedly young, when he had been barely eight. Had things been different . . .

Ah, but who could avoid Destiny? At least, Hauberin told himself, she had had the chance to love and know herself loved in return.

And so I come to be small, like her, and dark. And half-human.

Less than half-human.

Hauberin shivered, and caught his cloak more tightly about himself. Serein's odd, odd curse . . . What rumors had he heard? What secret whispers that the witchly consort's father had been other than human?

The prince shivered again, all at once feeling very young and very, very alone, aching for someone in whom he could confide, someone who wouldn't use whatever he might confess as fuel against him.

Alliar. If ever there was a friend who could be trusted . . .

But Alliar had vanished for a time, in the manner of that restless wind spirit. Hauberin didn't begrudge his friend the need for privacy, and of course the being would be back eventually. But until then he must be alone, and live with loneliness and—

"Oh, enough!"

The prince turned sharply in the direction of that terrace with the mountainous view. All this maundering self-pity was surely the result of too little sleep. The cold air should clear his mind.

Hauberin stopped short, feeling a twinge of annoyance because someone was already out there on the terrace.

Eh, but that someone was slim as a statue, sleekly golden against the darkness: Alliar!

The being was perched casually on the very corner of the balustrade, staring dreamily out into the night, sharp, beautiful, sexless profile softened by a faint smile. One leg was curled bonelessly under, the other bent at the knee, arms wrapped around it, chin resting on it, Alliar apparently quite comfortable and at ease in that precarious pose.

Hauberin hesitated, afraid to startle his friend while the being was so delicately poised on the edge of a sizeable drop. But a moon-moth large as his hand brushed his arm, wings flickering softly silver as it fluttered off, and he started involuntarily, not quite stifling a yelp. The faint sound was enough to alert keen-eared Alliar, who uncoiled back onto the terrace and around to face him in one lithe, wild-eyed leap.

"Hauberin!" The being laughed softly in relief. "For a moment I thought you were a Night Gaunt."

"Oh, thank you!"

Alliar grinned. "I didn't mean it the way it sounded. But . . ." Wide golden eyes studied the prince, and the grin faded. "What's wrong? No, don't try to deny it. I've only been away for a short time, but there's been such a change in you. . . . And your eyes are so very weary."

"I . . . simply haven't been able to sleep."

"Tchaugh! I can see that. But I think that's a symptom, as the healers would say, not the disease." The being slipped silently to Hauberin's side. "I'm not Ereledan, you know, or Charailis, or—"

"Oh, Li. You know I trust you."

"Well?"

Hauberin shook his head. "You were never meant to bear the weight of—of flesh-and-blood emotions."

"Don't patronize me. Do you think wind-children have no emotions?"

"Not normal wind— Ae, I'm sorry, I didn't mean that."

He could have struck himself at the shadow that passed over his friend's face. "It's true," the being said levelly. "It wasn't till I . . . became flesh-and-blood myself that I could fully understand certain things. Fear. And hate."

"Li, I—"

"And love, and friendship. Those two you taught me. Come now, what troubles you?"

Hauberin stared into the earnest golden gaze, then glanced quickly away. "Serein," he admitted.

"Serein! But it's been nearly . . . Surely you don't still regret his death?"

"Yes. No. Ach, wait. Li, the man *was* part of my life. Even if I did hate him for most of it. I can't that easily forget him, or that he's dead, or that mine was the hand that . . ." But Hauberin couldn't finish that. "No, Li. I'm not a hypocrite. If I hadn't . . . if he hadn't died, he would have killed me."

"Then why let a dead traitor— Oh, don't look at me like that, that's exactly what he was. Why let a traitor haunt your thoughts?" The glowing eyes narrowed warily. "Unless he really is haunting you . . . ?"

Serein's mockery, his certainty: "You're not rid of me." Hauberin forced a laugh. "Credit me with enough skill to banish a ghost." He took a deep breath. "Serein cursed me."

"*What!* And you just stand here? By what Powers did he— Ae, what Names did he—"

"None. I had more sense than to let him finish."

Alliar blinked. "Why, then, whatever curse he began can have no hold on you!"

"So the rules of such things would have it."

"But?"

Hauberin sighed. "But, as I told you, I've been sleeping poorly of late."

"I don't understand. Surely there are aids for those who can't sleep? Potions? Or ... some willing lady, Aydris or—or Charailis?"

The prince snorted. "You saw her trying to seduce me during the Second Triad celebration, didn't you?"

"I ... uh ... assumed that's what she was trying to do," the sexless being said uncertainly. "But you didn't seem to want to—"

"And you don't know why. Oh my dear Li, the woman despises me. The only reason she wanted to bed me was to snare my will."

Alliar's eyes widened. "You mean, flesh-pleasures are that dangerous?"

Hauberin bit back a laugh. "Not usually. In her case, however ... With Serein dead, she's virtually next in line for the crown—unless, of course, Ereledan murders her. If she could control me and take the throne, why, how long do you think she would leave me alive?"

Alliar shuddered. "But I wasn't thinking of politics," the being said plaintively. "All I meant ... I thought gendered folk found relaxation in that odd act of—"

"Oh, we do." He grinned. "But it would hardly be polite to use someone as a living sleeping-potion, would it?"

The being let out a long sigh of frustration. "*Will* you stop playing games? If the difficulty isn't simple lack of sleep, what in the name of all the Winds is it?"

Hauberin winced. Unable to meet his friend's fierce stare, he turned away, leaning on the balustrade, looking blankly out into space. "Dreams," he said softly. "But then, you don't dream, do you?"

"Not as you do."

"You can't possibly know the power our unconscious minds can hold over us." He glanced at Alliar. "Do you want to hear the exact words of Serein's curse? That I 'know not peace, not sleep,' till I learn my mother's father's name."

"Now, that's an odd thing!"

"Isn't it? I didn't take it seriously, of course, not at first, particularly since I knew no Binding Names had been invoked. But since then . . ." Hauberin paused. "It began so slowly, with the slightest troubling of my dreams." He glanced at Alliar again. "All dreaming beings have such things from time to time. And I . . . was more disturbed by Serein's death than I admitted even to you; I told myself it was natural for my sleep to be uneasy for a time after . . . that."

The prince felt himself starting to shiver, and snatched at his cloak, wrapping it tightly about himself, struggling for composure. "But with each night of the moon's waning, I've been falling deeper and deeper into nightmare. Now, at Moon Dark, I—I can't sleep, I dare not sleep— oh, Alliar, how do I rid myself of a curse that all the rules flatly state can't exist?"

"You *have* tried magic?"

"Everything from the slightest little charm for sweet sleep all the way up to the Spell of Ryellan Banishment."

Alliar raised a startled brow. "And even *that* didn't work?"

"Other than alarming half the court sages, who were wondering just what their prince was trying to do, no. And if such a powerful spell failed, it . . . seems to imply something very unhappy."

"Eh?"

The prince hesitated a long while. Alliar, with all the alien patience of a spirit, did not push him. And at last Hauberin said painfully, "I am a half-blood, after all. Not fully of my father's kind, nor of my mother's. Not quite looking or acting like either."

Even as he said that, Hauberin wished he could have taken it back; Alliar, after all, resembled no one in all the Realms. But the being only shrugged. "So? That just makes you—ah, what did I hear a lady call you?— 'intriguingly exotic.'"

"You're missing my point, Li. Powers, not only don't I know my mother's father's name, I don't even know *what* he was! What if the mixture of races brought out some . . . instability, some slowly surfacing . . . weakness of mind—"

"How dare you!" Alliar's form blurred and shifted with the force of the being's sudden indignation. "How dare you belittle yourself!"

"Ai-yi, hold to one form! You're making me dizzy."

The being grudgingly solidified, golden hair a wild aureole about the fine-boned head, eyes still fierce. "I just will not hear you talk about yourself that way. The boy who slew my . . . master, who freed me from horror: that boy had no 'weakness of mind,' and neither, by all the Winds, does the man he's become!"

Even Alliar had to stop for breath by that point, and Hauberin, half astonished, half touched by his friend's vehemence, began warily, "But the curse—"

"Damn the curse!" Alliar stopped again, panting, wild golden mane gradually settling sleekly back into place. "So. Enough. It's the lack of sleep talking, not you."

"Probably."

"Certainly. Come, let me hear the plot of your dream."

The prince gave the ghost of a chuckle. "Yes, Mother."

"What?"

"Nothing." He was deliberately keeping his voice light. "You do understand that such things can't possibly sound so terrifying in the telling as they are in the dreaming. But, if you must have it:

"I'm walking down a smooth-walled, featureless corridor, dark, but not so dark I can't see where I'm going. What I can't see is the corridor's far end, but the air is so close and chill that I very much want to turn and run. But I can't run. Some terrible compulsion drives me on and on, even though I'm becoming almost sick with horror, even though I know there's something waiting, even though I know that when I see the truth, I will—die."

Hauberin broke off with a gasp, shaking. "It's all right," Alliar murmured, putting a gentle hand on his arm. "You're not alone now."

"No. Of course not." After a moment, the prince

continued softly, "Each time I sleep, I find myself further down that dark corridor. And lately I've been hearing a voice in the dream. All it says is a toneless, "Grandson, welcome." But there's something behind the words that's so very unbearable that I find myself screaming like a child, 'I will not look! I will not look!' And with that, of course," Hauberin finished wearily, "I wake myself up." He glanced at Alliar. "It sounds foolish now, doesn't it?"

"No," the being murmured. "If, as I've heard, dreams seem quite real to the dreamer, then it doesn't sound foolish at all. But why have you been trying to solve this all by yourself? Did you never think of finding help?"

"Li, please. That's the last thing I want to do."

"But—"

"I did consult with Sharailan privately, pretending I spoke of some hypothetical case I'd come across in my studies. I think he believed me; our Sharailan has outlived any deviousness he might once have had. And he seemed genuinely intrigued by the problem. But for all his musings over past magics, he couldn't come up with a solution. I didn't dare press him, or go to anyone else. By that point, I couldn't keep up the pretense long enough or convincingly enough for that. And if anyone should begin to suspect the truth . . . No, Li," he added before the being could interrupt, "I'm not being overly cautious. Remember that time three years back, when I fell so feverishly ill from drinking *seralis*, because no one had remembered that the wine was poisonous to humans and might harm me, too?"

Alliar shuddered. "Of course."

"Remember the whispers? 'Sickly half-blood,' 'unfit to rule'—I wasn't so ill I didn't overhear them. Remember how many loyal vassals were ready to forget their loyalty? How many would-be rebels I had to put down—all the time worrying that I was bringing the land into civil war—to prove that human blood or no, I was still their prince? Li, I don't want to go through that again."

"Oh, but surely things are different now. Your people love you."

Hauberin grinned fiercely. "Don't be naive. Some do, some don't. Most are merely . . . politic. As long as their prince keeps the land peaceful and prosperous and lets them live their own lives, they don't really care who sits the throne—as long as he can wield sufficient strength. I've worn the crown for only six years, a mere eyeblink of Faerie time, nowhere near long enough for everyone to be totally trusting of me."

"Ah."

"The slightest sign of human failings from me, and off they'd go again. With Charailis and Ereledan, doubtless, in the lead."

Alliar sighed. "What complicated lives you solid folk lead! But I agree: You really can't go to anyone for help. Except to me, of course." The being paused, head cocked to one side, considering. "Now, here's a thought . . . Thanks to your mother, you know some spells foreign to this Realm. Suppose Serein had learned some, too."

"I doubt it. Can you see him ever sullying his hands with human magic?"

"Ah well, we can hardly prove it now. It would have made such a lovely answer, though: none of your Faerie magic working against his curse because that curse wasn't formed of Faerie Power."

Hauberin stared at the being. If the curse was real, if Alliar was right, and it was formed of alien Power . . . Without the Name and shape of that magic, he would never, ever, be able to lift the curse. . . .

The being could hardly have missed the sudden bleakness in his eyes. "There's still one very simple solution, my friend," Alliar said, "and I suppose only weariness has kept you from seeing it. Since you need your grandsire's name, send someone into your mother's Realm to learn it! Then whether Serein's curse really is fueled by some outside Power, or whether you've—forgive me—

fallen victim to the simpler power of suggestion, we've drawn the fangs of his malice."

Plain enough. Sensible enough. And Hauberin *had* already thought of it, and flinched from the idea. Now he turned away, biting his lip, feeling Alliar's gaze piercing him like two golden darts. "Li, I . . ."

"What is it?" The being moved to face him, but Hauberin angrily turned away again. "Why, you're afraid!"

"That's ridiculous."

"Oh, really? Then why won't you look at me? You're terrified of the very thought of learning that name."

He wanted to shout, *No! How should I be afraid?* But not even a half-human Faerie prince could lie. At bay, furious at his weakness, and at his friend for exposing it, Hauberin whirled with a savage, "You go too far!"

A responding flash of anger crossed Alliar's face. "Pray forgive me." The formal words were laced with mockery. The sleek form shifted, quick as thought. A lithe elf-girl, golden-maned, knelt in supplication at Hauberin's feet. After a moment, the prince murmured, "Prettily done, Li. Come, get up. I apologize. Ach, Li, please," the prince added wearily when the being didn't move, "I'm not up to feuding right now."

A bright golden eye glanced up at him. "No. I can see that."

Alliar straightened, blurring. Hauberin waited till the malleable being had shifted back to sexlessness before confessing quietly, "I shouldn't have shouted at you. And . . . you're right. I *am* afraid."

"Of what?" Alliar had apparently let anger flow away with the change of shape. "Of whom your grandsire might have been?"

"Of *what* he might have been. All I know for certain is that he wasn't—isn't?—human."

"What of it? *I'm* not human. Your *father* wasn't human."

"Don't be clever. You know that's not what I meant. Of course there's other than human, better than human. There's also . . . worse. I . . . never told anyone this, but

I used to have nightmares about that. I used to lie awake,
ashamed to call my mother, afraid to call my father, wondering: what if my grandfather turned out to be something—something— Damn! I thought I had conquered
that fear long ago." Hauberin took a deep breath. "Look
you, I really don't want to learn the truth. But I don't
want to die from lack of sleep, either."

"Why are you so sure the answer is something terrible?" Alliar asked gently. "I never met your mother, but
from all I've heard she was too good of soul—as is her
son, I might add—for her father to ever have been anything Evil."

Touched, Hauberin murmured, "Thank you, Li."

The being shrugged, embarrassed. "So, now. I suppose the next question is who you're going to send into
your mother's Realm. The answer is obvious enough:
me."

"No!" Hauberin had a sudden sharp image of Alliar in
human lands, making some fatal blunder in all innocence,
of human fear and hatred, of the stake and the
flames. . . . "Thank you, but you don't know enough
about being human to pass as one."

"But who else could you possibly—"

"No one." Hauberin paused. "Except myself."

"You! But— You— That's too dangerous! Leaving
the throne at a time when Ereledan—Charailis— By
the Winds, think! As soon as they knew you were gone,
they would declare you dead, and you would return
to find your throne usurped and some quiet assassin
waiting—"

"Hush, now. I'm not a complete fool, Li, truly I'm
not."

"But—"

"My father used to go off into other Realms whenever
the whim took him, without needing to worry about
throne or life. I've studied his scrolls. And now I know
how he did it: Time."

"I don't understand."

"You know that time flows at different speeds in different

Realms. My father found the magics to play all manner of
tricks with those speeds. He could spend long moon-
cycles of mortal time in mortal lands, and have them
translate into only a day or even less of Faerie time."

"But can you do that? Have you ever even tried?"

"No," Hauberin admitted. "But I have a firm grip on
how his magics work."

"You hope."

"I know. Li, Li, have I a choice? Can you think of a
better idea?"

"What I think, my friend," Alliar said bluntly, "is that
you've gone giddy from lack of sleep."

Hauberin stifled a yawn, wondering if he dared try
that fatigue-banishing spell yet again. No, he decided
reluctantly. Casting it again so soon would either have
no effect at all, or hit his mind with enough psychic
backlash to leave him in coma. "Probably," he admitted
belatedly. "But that doesn't change the facts."

"Yes, but I— You told me I didn't know enough about
being human to pass. Well and good, but do you? My
Prince, you've lived in Faerie all your life. Just because
your mother happened to be human doesn't make you
an authority on the race!"

"Granted. But I do remember almost everything my
mother told me about her people and their customs. Yes,
I know, that hardly makes me an adept. But I do know
human ways better than anyone else at court, give me
that much." Seeing the being's blatant skepticism, the
prince added defensively, "And I do speak the human
language well enough. You know that; I've practiced it
on you often enough."

"True," Alliar conceded with a quick laugh. "You've
made *me* fluent in it! Ae, but that doesn't wipe away
the danger. To go into a human Realm . . . You once
told me that humans hold even their own witches in
low regard."

"Low regard! They think them spawns of Evil."

"Oh, that truly puts my mind at ease! If you make a
mistake, reveal your talents—"

"I won't."

"Mm. And for all your 'exotic' coloring, my Prince, you just don't look particularly human."

"My own mother had slanted eyes, Li, and these high cheekbones."

"And how do you plan to explain those? Or do human ears vary wildly in shape, too?"

Hauberin touched one elegantly pointed ear with a light fingertip. "They're not all *that* different."

"Huh!"

"Besides, my hair is long enough and thick enough to hide them. And no one would believe what he or she might chance to glimpse." He grinned. "After all, what human would ever believe a creature of Faerie would be brash enough to walk among them? In broad daylight, to boot."

"That's another point. Sunlight doesn't bother me. What about you?"

"I can bear it. Inherited protection from my mother. All I need worry about is avoiding iron."

"Lightly said, considering your mother's culture is based on it!" The being sighed. "At least iron can't hurt me."

"You! Li, I told you—"

"Not to go alone. I have no intention of letting you go alone, either. Come now, you hardly thought I'd let a friend go wandering off into who-knows-what all by himself!"

Hauberin forced a smile. "I don't suppose there's any way to stop you."

"Short of outright imprisonment, no."

"And that, I would never do." This time the yawn escaped before Hauberin could stop it. All at once he realized that his legs wouldn't support him. He sank to a bench just in time, Alliar at his side. Feeling as though his words were coming from a vast distance, the prince forced out, "Then . . . thank you, my friend. I . . . will be . . . glad of your . . . company. . . ."

The last shred of the fatigue-banishing spell dissolved. As suddenly as a child, the exhausted Hauberin fell into a warm black ocean of sleep. And this time there was no room for dreams.

VI

ALARMS AND EXCURSIONS

Alliar leaned nervously over Hauberin's shoulder, shifting softly from foot to foot as the prince tried to concentrate, breathing down his neck until Hauberin turned with an impatient hiss and seized the being by the shoulders, moving Alliar firmly to one side. Undeterred, the being asked, yet again, "Are you sure this is going to work, my prince?"

"Yes, Alliar. I am."

"But if the spell isn't precise, we could wind up lost, or—or in a place not even tangible enough to be lost *in—*"

"The spell is precise."

"Yes, but what about you? Can you control it? I mean, you didn't get all that much sleep out there on the terrace—"

"More than I'm likely to get indoors, things being the way they are. And conditions aren't likely to get much better if we simply stay here. Alliar, please." The last thing Hauberin would have expected from a wind spirit was nerves. *As if I wasn't nervous enough for the two of us.* But he dare not give in to nerves, or to any other strong emotion, not if he meant to control the magic he was about to release. "If you would rather not come with me . . ."

"I never said that."

"Then, hush. Let me concentrate."

The spell-words were remarkably simple. As Hauberin

spoke them, he felt a shiver of amazement at how swiftly
Power was building about him, surging almost before he
was ready for it. He couldn't hold it in place much
longer; something . . . must . . . happen. . . .

Yes! All at once the air before his eyes had turned
translucent, shimmering eerily. A doorway between
Realms had opened, and so easily the prince knew a
moment's sheer wonder at his father's skill in spell
design.

But then the doorway was drawing him in, whether he
willed it or not, and Alliar with him, submerging them
in a whirlpool of not-color, not-sound, not-shape. For a
brief, terrified moment, Hauberin wanted to pull back,
to cancel the Power, to cry out, childishly, *No, I'm not
going, I changed my mind.*

But of course it was already too late for that, and . . .

. . . in the next moment, they were stepping out upon
solid ground once more, ground carpeted with moss and
a litter of dead leaves.

Hauberin's first clear thought was a bemused, *Well,
what do you know? It worked.* There was air for his
lungs to breathe, a forest all about him, as the arcane
doorway closed behind him.

"Ah . . . my Prince?" Alliar, sleek and sexless, stood
uneasy at his side, clinging to both their packs. "Where
are we?"

"I'm . . . not quite sure yet," Hauberin admitted honestly. "Somewhere in my mother's Realm." *I . . . hope.*
"I was merely following my father's spell-coordinates."

Alliar glanced thoughtfully up at one stout tree. "That
looks tall enough. Shall I see if I can find out where we
are?" At Hauberin's nod, the being swarmed up the tree
as swiftly as any squirrel, disappearing from sight amid
the thick roof of leaves. The prince waited below, thanking the Powers they had landed anywhere tangible at all.
It had been a damnably foolish thing to do, risking a
new spell like that—and one so Powerful and potentially

dangerous—without any prior experimentation; he really *must* have been mind-fogged to try it.

But it had worked, no doubt about it. More important, he could feel the knowledge of how to get home again staying, safe, there at the back of his mind, ready to be retrieved whenever he needed it. At least, mused Hauberin, he had been awake enough back in his palace to teach the spell to Alliar as well, just in case.

He wasn't sleepy now. Someone really should have listed Realm-changing as a means of banishing fatigue. As he stood breathing in mortal air for the first time in his life, the prince felt as rested and whole as though he'd slept the day around.

Whole in body, at any rate. Now that his mind had recovered from the transfer of Realms, he was growing increasingly aware that there was a peculiar sense of *lack* hanging heavily about him, weighing on his spirit. It was almost, he thought in a surge of panic, as though he'd lost one of his senses, not anything as simple as sight or hearing . . .

Then Hauberin realized the lack wasn't in himself, but in the Realm. In Faerie, magic shimmered in the very air. He didn't doubt this Realm held magic, too; every living world must, to some degree. But here, whatever Power there might be was far more subtle than any he knew, more difficult to touch.

Hopefully he wouldn't need to touch it.

Not that there seemed to be anything menacing about this forest. Hauberin guessed he and Alliar had arrived in mid-afternoon, though he couldn't be sure; the light here was strange, somehow flat and lifeless. The colors about him, brown of tree, green of leaf and mossy ground, were . . . darker, less alive, though not without a beauty of their own, like the colors of an ancient painting gone deep-hued and mysterious with age.

If the air wasn't the crystal-bright wine of Faerie, at least it was clean and green-scented, cool beneath the rippling ceiling of leaves. Hauberin spent a moment bemused at the novelty of shadow by daylight; there were no shadows in sunless Faerie, with its directionless light, save for those cast at night by the moon or those cast by flames. Then he pushed back the folds of his cloak (good, thick stuff, as close to mortal weave as he could find, as were his plain brown tunic, leggings, and boots) to rest a hand on the trunk of the tree up which Alliar had scrambled, staring up and up its height to the point where bark greenish-gray in shadow became most intriguingly dappled with a gold that must surely be mortal sunlight.

"Alliar?"

"Here, my Prince." The being came speeding lightly down, barely touching foot to branch, landing soundlessly at Hauberin's side. "Ah, but it's beautiful up there: forest and forest in a carpet of a hundred greens, and the sky lovely blue for all the garish sunlight."

"Nothing but forest?" Ae, that couldn't be right!

"Far to the—north? This sun goes from east to west? To the north, then, there's a great hill, and someone's fortress brooding on the crest."

"Ah! Describe it."

"The fortress or the hill?"

"Both." In sudden impatience, Hauberin glanced up the tree, wondering if he could make the climb and see for himself.

"Ae, no, my Prince! The upper branches are too thin to hold even your weight. Come, here's the fortress."

They touched minds, sharing the image, saw the hill, its grim spurs of weathered rock thrusting up from grassy roundness. *Yes,* thought Hauberin, *a rounded hill, yes, it could be . . . And the fortress?*

But even with Alliar's sharp wind spirit sight, it had seemed only a confused jumble of gray stone walls and crenellated towers. "There was some sort of banner on the tallest tower," the being added.

"Couldn't you make out the insignia?"

"Without a breeze to unfold the crumpled thing?" Alliar's tone was reproachful. "There *are* limits."

"Of course." Hauberin sighed. "It *might* be the castle

my father described. I don't remember him mentioning
it being quite so elaborate, but the humans would have
had . . . who knows how many years of their time to
rebuild."

Alliar glanced at him in alarm. "I trust we're not too
far into their future?"

"No, no, my mother's kin should still be very much
alive. I didn't dare focus the mortal-time aspects of the
spell much more tightly; I don't *think* we would have
run into any time paradoxes, but . . ."

"Paradoxes like meeting your mother before she'd met
your father?"

Hauberin nodded. "And just possibly negating myself
in the process. If only he'd been more specific about
where he met her!"

"He could hardly have expected you to make a—a
pilgrimage to the spot."

"Granted. Were there any other signs of human life?"

"A few traces of smoke along the way, from chimneys,
I suppose. And there was a regular break in the trees
that hints at a road." Alliar grinned. "A most conveniently
northbound road."

Hauberin grinned back. "Sorry, I can't take credit for
it; it's just a fortunate coincidence. Come, my friend,
north we go." The prince lightly shouldered his pack,
more carefully shouldered his elegant little harp: no one
of Faerie travelled without music. "Ah—aren't you forgetting something, Li?"

"Eh?" The being glanced down at smooth, patently
sexless flesh, then up again, with a rueful grin. "Oh. Of
course. They'd think me a demon like this, wouldn't
they?"

The sleek golden form lengthened, broadened,
blurred. Hauberin blinked, dazzled, then nodded, calling out corrections: "A little taller. . . . Yes. Less mus-
cling to those arms . . . Ah. Good."

He smiled at the final result: a very likely imitation of
a human male, convincingly strong of build and half a
head taller than the prince, dusky gold of hair, beard,

and apparently well-tanned skin. Face and form were pleasant but unmemorable; Alliar had no intention of attracting too much attention. "Nicely done, Li."

"Of course," Alliar agreed smugly. The being settled into a blank-eyed trance for a moment, then came out of it with a shiver like a dog shaking water from its fur. "There. I've set the shape in my memory. No chance of absentmindedly losing it now."

The being quickly settled into the unfamiliar human-styled clothing Hauberin handed over from Alliar's pack, then took the pack itself, adjusting easily to its weight in this strong new shape. The prince, with mock solemnity, proffered sword and swordbelt over his arm. "Your weapon, milord."

Alliar made him an elegantly formal bow, then spoiled the effect by adding plaintively, "If you wanted to go castle-viewing, did we really have to land so far away?"

"I cut it as closely as I dared." Hauberin raised a wry eyebrow. "Would you rather we'd materialized inside a wall?"

"Ugh. No. But if we're to wander in the wilderness, we should at least have brought horses."

"And expose Faerie beasts to sunlight? Come, watch, lazy one. I'll provide for us."

The prince gathered a double handful of twigs from the forest floor, grinning at Alliar's confusion. "Now I bind them together, so . . . These reeds should do the trick."

"What *are* you doing? That looks like the framework for two little house-models: four rafters, two ridgepoles . . ."

"Hush, Li." Hauberin was busy adding new twigs to his constructions. "They're not *house* models, they're *horse* models, and this is a spell my far-distant kin the wood elves are supposed to use whenever they need transport. Now, then . . ."

It wasn't a very Powerful spell, and shouldn't be affected by the lack of magic in this Realm. The words of it didn't mean too much to him; he wasn't well acquainted with the odd, antique dialect. But that didn't matter; the words were just a focus for the will, and the Power was gathering nicely. When it reached its peak, he cast it forth into the shaping—

And where two twig models had stood were now two full-sized horses, shadowy and vague at first, then tangible as any born of mare. If their eyes were dull, if their manes and tails looked more like tufts of wilted grass than hair, what matter? They were illusion made solid, and with a little laugh of triumph, Hauberin vaulted up onto the back of one—

And fell ignominiously right through the suddenly dissolving thing, landing on the ground with a thud. The astonished prince scrambled to his feet, too proud to rub his sore rump, staring at two crumpled bundles of twigs as Alliar burst into laughter.

"That's right. Laugh at your prince."

"Of—of course!" the being gurgled. "You sh-should have seen yourself! Lying there with—with a bunch of twigs clutched in your hand, staring like an—an owl in daylight—"

"Daylight! Of course!" Hauberin wasn't about to give Alliar the satisfaction of hearing him admit how foolish he felt. "None of the elf-folk can stand the touch of daylight, and neither can their enchantments. Eh well, I suppose we'll be able to purchase earthly horses when we reach a human settlement."

The being raised both eyebrows. "Purchase?"

"Purchase. With silver. Not magicked leaves. Until I learn what I'm here to learn, I don't want to cause any alarm."

"Ay me, so be it."

"And till we get those horses, it won't hurt either of us to hike a bit."

Humor glinted in Alliar's eyes. "No more harm than throwing ourselves on the ground, eh?"

Hauberin couldn't hold back a grin. "Enough, enough. Let's find that northbound road."

They were both skilled enough in forest ways to move smoothly and swiftly through underbrush that would have checked mere human woodmen, and were soon stepping out onto the bare earthen road with no more sound than two deer would have made.

Hauberin froze. The interlaced ceiling of leaves was broken here and there over the road, and he felt a surge of intense Faerie curiosity. "Sunlight, Li! Sunlight, with nothing between earth and sky."

"Yes, but don't look—"

Hauberiun had already glanced skyward, and stumbled back with a stifled yell of pain. Alliar's hand shot out to steady him as the being finished lamely, "—directly at the sun. Are you all right?"

It was a moment before the prince could gasp out, "Yes." He had flung both arms up instinctively for protection, and had to force himself to lower them again, blinking, seeing nothing but garish afterimages, eyes watering and aching. "So bright— How do they manage to live with something like *that* blazing down on them?"

"Not by trying to stare it in the eye," Alliar said reproachfully. "Particularly not when your vision's adjusted to dim forest light. I thought you'd done enough experiments to know better than that."

"Obviously not." Hauberin's head still felt as though two darts had pierced it front to back, but he managed a rueful little laugh. "At least I wasn't struck to dust like some night-thing. Ah no, Li, don't worry. Just give me a bit for my sight to clear." It . . . would clear, wouldn't it?

The prince tensed, even as Alliar went suddenly alert at his side. "Now, have I damaged my hearing as well," he murmured, "or do I hear hoofbeats?"

"You do," the being replied softly. "I have for some time. Horses don't tend to run loose in this Realm, do they?"

"I doubt it. I suspect we're about to meet our first humans."

"Should we hide?"

Not till my vision clears enough for me to see what I'm doing. "Why? We're two honest travellers."

"Yes," said an uneasy Alliar as the riders came into sight, "but they're fifteen ... twenty, and—ae, be wary!—covered with cold iron!"

"Cold steel," Hauberin corrected absently. "Mail shirts under those bright tunics."

But what was this? The riders couldn't help but see them, but weren't making the slightest attempt to avoid them.

Foul manners, to choke us in their dust.

Manners, nothing! The riders were going to run right over them! "Alliar, look out!"

One moment Hauberin was surrounded by a confused blur of hooves and cloaks and deadly swords, the next, reacting with Faerie speed, he was aside in one feline leap, choking on dust and blazing with regal rage, instinctively calling Power to him—

But no Power came. This was a mortal realm, not Faerie.

And if I'm to stay in it, Hauberin told himself, *I must fight only in human terms, sword to sword. And the fools are already too far down the road for a challenge.*

But their leader ... Hauberin's sun-dazzled vision had cleared enough for him to see that young man's face, outlined for a moment as cleanly as a cameo: grim, fierce-eyed, rimmed by a thin, dark gold beard. "I'll remember you," the prince murmured after him. "Oh, I will remember you."

He whirled to Alliar. "Are you hurt?"

"Shaken, no more. And you?"

"The same." Hauberin brushed dust from his clothing and said with determined calmness, "Come. The road's not getting shorter for the waiting."

They had been travelling for some time, long enough for Hauberin to have quite lost his fascination with foot-travel and sunlight. The brightness hurt his eyes and head, and the prince gave a little sigh of relief when that dazzling ball of light sank below the level of the trees. Almost at once, the forest around him seemed to fade from muted green to the mysterious, shadowy blue of coming night, though the sky overhead remained quite bright.

Odd phenomenon, he thought, wondering if this was what his mother had called "twilight." The foreignness of it took his mind somewhat off this unaccustomed trudging, if not off the fact that every time he looked down, he saw earth printed by hoofs, reminding him of that golden-bearded young human. The folk of Faerie didn't easily forget an injury.

"My Prince!"

The urgent whisper brought Hauberin instantly alert. "Yes, Li," he whispered back. "I hear them, too. Come, off the road."

They melted silently into cover just as their bewildered, would-be ambushers crashed out through the bushes on the other side of the road.

"Humans," Alliar murmured doubtfully in Hauberin's ear.

Hauberin eyed the men in distaste, reluctant to claim any manner of kinship with them. "Some form of humans, at any rate." Filthy things, all rags and roughness— Phaugh, and stench! Not a sword among the eight of them, but common clubs enough, and a few glinting daggers.

Iron daggers. For safety's sake, Hauberin switched to mind-speech. *"The ruler of these lands is lax. I would never allow such vermin in my forest."*

"The ruler of these lands doesn't have magic," Alliar reminded him wryly, then paused. *"What in the name of the Winds are they speaking?"*

Hauberin listened intently, struggling to understand them. It seemed to be some manner of human dialect. But full of words his mother had never included in her lessons:

"Thot I saw 'em."

"Trick a the **** light. So **** dark, can't see a **** thing."

"Was 'er a trick? That all? Shouldn't be 'ere, not now. Maybe they's about."

"Don't be a **** fool!"

"*I think,*" Hauberin summarized uncertainly, "*they've decided we're a mirage. They're also afraid of the night and what might be abroad in it.*" He paused to listen again. "*Which isn't stopping them from complaining because they didn't have enough men to catch their original prey.*"

"*The mail-clad riders?*" Alliar tensed. "*Eh, but I hear hoofbeats!*"

"*Yes. One horse, coming from the south . . . and at a gallop.*"

Tsk, bad timing. These creatures couldn't help but hear.

And hear they did. They hastily rustled and crashed their way back into hiding, while Hauberin and Alliar watched with detached Faerie curiosity.

Here came the horseman now, one small figure bent low over his mount's neck, dark blue cloak flapping out behind him.

He rode right into ambush. Two of the would-be robbers sprang out in front of the horse with wild shouts, waving their arms, and the startled animal shied to a stop. The rider barely kept his seat, trying frantically to spur the frightened horse forward, fumbling with the hilt of his sword at the same time. There! He had the blade free.

But the rest of the robbers rushed him, grabbing at the bridle, dodging the rider's desperate slashes. They snared him by arm and leg, dragging him from the saddle and hurling him to the ground. The rider struggled to his feet, but one leg gave way beneath him and he fell again, still trying to slash at his attackers with his sword. Someone cursed and kicked his sword arm viciously, sending the weapon flying. Hauberin heard the rider's choked cry, saw a club raised over his head where he huddled, helpless with the shock of sudden pain, caught a glimpse of a wild, desperate face— A young face, a child's face!

And suddenly Hauberin remembered another child, small and dark and so piteously afraid. A child he'd failed to save.

No! Not again!

Hauberin sprang from hiding and said aloud, "Now, I do think that's enough."

As startled heads turned to him, the prince hurled forth a spark of will, no mighty thing of Power, just the easy little spell anyone of Faerie would have used to light a campfire. It worked, even in this magic-poor Realm. There was a concerted yell of horror from the robbers as a club blazed up into flame. The man holding it threw it from him, eyes wild with terror, and the other robbers backed away.

Hauberin smiled a sharp, feline smile in the growing darkness, eyes glinting. "Good evening."

"Who in 'ell be ye?"

"Do you really want my name?" the prince purred, enjoying himself. Beside him, Alliar had risen—and kept right on rising, smoothly shifting shape till a sleek golden form towered over the robbers. "You were right," Hauberin said gently. "They *are* abroad this night."

"My, my," murmured Alliar, returned to human form. "Look at them run. Aren't you going to slay them, my Prince?"

"Waste my strength on vermin?" Hauberin glanced down at the fallen rider, who was staring up at him, white-faced with shock and pain, defiant with fear. "Don't look at me like that, boy," the prince said in the human tongue, hoping the child could understand him. "We won't harm you."

"You— I saw— In God's name, what are you?"

The boy made one wild effort to rise, which was a mistake. His injured leg gave way again and he fell, striking his injured arm against the ground and going limp.

"Is he dead?" Alliar asked uneasily.

"Only fainted." Hauberin knelt by the boy's side. "That arm is definitely broken. The leg . . . mm. It seems to still be whole, though he clearly can't put weight on it." He glanced up at Alliar. "Now what, by all the Powers, are we to do with him?"

"Heal him, I should think."

"I was hardly planning to leave him for the scavengers." Hauberin sighed. Night being no barrier to either Alliar or himself, he had planned to go on at least a bit further. But . . . he couldn't abandon a child. "So." He looked thoughtfully down at the pale young human face. "We'll get no further tonight. Let's do our best to patch the boy up, and maybe we'll be able to send him on his way and be free of him tomorrow."

While Alliar retrieved the boy's horse (the animal seemed bewildered by the wind spirit's lack of a scent), convincing it with gently bespelled words to stay by them in the sheltered little grove they'd found, Hauberin quickly charmed a campfire into being. He hardly needed the light, but the night was growing chill. Besides, he had managed to dispatch two rabbits, as neatly and swiftly as any four-legged predator; they would soon be cooking for dinner.

A groan from the awakening child alerted him.

"No, boy, don't try to move."

Pain glittered in the light brown eyes. "My arm . . . is my arm . . . ?"

"Broken. Nothing worse. I was just preparing to tend it."

The boy blinked up at him, still dazed. "Are you a physician?"

"No. Come, I told you, don't move."

"Milord, I—I must apologize. You saved me from those scum, and yet I acted like a frightened child. You see, I thought I saw—"

"Hush. You were stunned and in pain, and not responsible for anything you . . . might have believed you saw."

"I . . . fainted?"

"From pain. No shame in that," Hauberin added with the faintest of chuckles, remembering his own desperate pride when he'd been a boy. "Now, enough. Lie still."

It was a royal command. And it was obeyed. The prince reached out a hand, holding it outstretched above the boy's eyes. His own eyes shut, Hauberin searched inward . . . inward . . . till he had found a well of quietness within himself and tapped it, *feeling* the rising psychic energy spreading out from him like a soft gray fog, *feeling* the boy's senses slipping away beneath it into heavy sleep.

"So-o." Hauberin took a deep breath. "That was easy enough."

"Not as easy as it might have been," Alliar warned softly. "Remember you're not used to working with a purely human essence. You might not be able to control it. Maybe I should link with you?"

Hauberin shook his head. The intrusion of another personality would only confuse the spell. "Just keep watch. Warn me if I'm going too deep." He lowered his hand from the boy's head to the fractured arm, tracing gently down, not quite touching the skin, till he had found the point of the break. *Points, rather. The bone is broke twice. Ah well, now . . .*

He had healed fractures before; Sharailan and the other court sages had been right about one thing at least: there did seem to be a healing virtue to the rightful ruler's touch.

(*In your rightful land,* his mind whispered, *only in your rightful land.*)

Hauberin ignored the whisper. This healing should be no different; Faerie or human, the basic skeletal structure was almost identical.

(*Yes,* his stubborn mind insisted, *but this isn't Faerie now. This Realm may fight you. . . .*)

Oh, thank you, Li, for planting that *idea!* A fracture was a fracture, no matter what its surroundings. And magic depended on the certainty of the magician. If he started doubting his abilities now, he'd never get anything done.

The prince closed his eyes again, softly, carefully emptying his mind of extraneous thought, leaving the outer, conscious layer behind. Delicately he attuned himself to the boy on a primal level of color and form, seeing healthy bone surrounded by a clean white aura, the jagged ends of the fracture burning a sullen, angry red. . . . He slid deeper, *feeling* the very pattern of cell to cell, *feeling* where the fabric of being had been torn. Warily, he began to reweave the strands, pulling bone to bone, muscle to muscle. . . .

But all at once it was going terribly wrong! It was hurting him, burning him, pulling him from himself—

Alliar's thought slashed down like a wall of dazzling blue: *"Enough! Withdraw!"*

And Hauberin fell back abruptly into his physical self, back into the physical world, crumpling to the ground, panting.

"My Prince?"

"Head," he gasped, and Alliar understood. Hauberin felt his friend's mind-touch like the coolness of a welcome breeze, and the wild pain dissolved. He sat up warily, trying to catch his breath. Ach, he hadn't felt this sick after a spell since . . .

Since he had been a very little boy experimenting with magics too strong for him. Thanks to cousin Serein, who had taunted him into it (though of course he couldn't blame Serein altogether; he never should have believed human blood might keep him from the higher magics).

"Ah well, it was an interesting experiment."

"My Prince?" Alliar repeated warily.

Hauberin threw his head back, then quickly changed his mind and put it down instead lest he really be sick. He waited till his body had quieted enough for him to straighten and continue, glancing at the being, "That charm should have worked, even on a magickless human. I just couldn't pull enough energy from this Realm to hold the focus." He smiled wryly. "And thank you for not saying, 'I told you so.'"

The being grinned and gave an expressive shrug.

Hauberin brushed disheveled black hair back out of his eyes. "At least I aligned the breaks correctly and started the arm to healing."

"Then I'll splint it."

The prince watched the deft fingers at work. But those fingers lengthened or shortened at need and, dizzy, he turned away.

"Done," Alliar said in satisfaction.

"And well done, too. You've bound the ankle, too? It's only wrenched; time should heal it and— What's burning?"

"Ae, the rabbits!"

Alliar dove for the fire, retrieving two spitted forms from the flames. Hauberin accepted one gratefully, though he couldn't resist a sly, "Quite the efficient camper, aren't we?"

Alliar bowed from the waist in mock solemnity. "One does what one can, oh gracious Prince."

"Mm." Hauberin's energy-depleted body wouldn't let him wait a moment longer. Granted, the meat was charred without, nearly raw within—and, ugh! Alliar, in ignorance, hadn't even gutted the creatures!—but who expected a wind spirit to know anything about cookery? The prince devoured his rabbit with blissful disregard for regal manners, feeling a lovely surge of renewed strength flowing through him. "Eh, Li, aren't you going to eat?"

"Not yet." Alliar glanced down at the pseudo-human form thoughtfully. "I don't think I'll need food in this shape for perhaps another day or so." The being looked sharply up again. "My Prince, I almost hate to mention this, but what about the robbers? What if they or others of their ilk decide to pay us a visit?"

"They die," Hauberin said shortly.

"Of course. But shouldn't I stand guard?"

Hauberin got reluctantly to his feet. "No. You may not

need food or sleep, but even you need rest. I'll set the Wards about us." He gave his friend a weary grin. "At least I should be able to manage *that* without endangering mind and body."

The boy's horse was watching him with amiable equine curiosity. Hauberin gave it a friendly scratch under the jaw. "Now you," he told it as the horse pushed against him, "like all your race, will be spending half the night awake and grazing, and wandering about no matter what binding Words I might put on you. That means the Wards can't include you. But you'll warn us with your whinnies if you're in any danger."

The horse snorted, for all the world as though in agreement, and Hauberin chuckled.

But now to the work at hand. The prince pushed the friendly equine head away and stood motionless, eyes closed, arms held slightly out from his sides, hands palm down. Once more he let himself slip below the conscious level, *feeling* first the busy little animal and insect lives about him, then the deeper, slower pulsings of the green, vegetable lives. Warily, he slid deeper yet, trying to attune himself to the earth itself, sensing the pull of it at last through his flattened hands, so strong a pull, so alien. . . .

The prince came back to himself with a start. So alien, indeed! He should be feeling refreshed, not as though he had been trying to move a crushing weight.

So now. Let me try again.

The earth . . . the heavy, heavy earth . . . What if he didn't fight? If he let it pull him this way and that . . . ? Yes . . . he could see color now through his closed lids: red, blue, green, brown, the colors symbolic of the cardinal points.

Oriented, Hauberin opened his eyes, staring at true north. "Earth," he said firmly, and summoned an image of a little circle of bare earth, rich, deep brown-black, fertile earth, the element of the north. For a moment he held it firm in his mind.

But all at once the image was wavering, fading—

Hauberin caught it, set it firmly, ignoring the nagging little doubts as to why he should be having trouble with this, the most basic of protective spells.

The prince turned sharply to the east. "Air." It was an image of the luminous air of Faerie, and it, too, fought his will, shimmering and darkening until Hauberin needed all his strength to fix it in place.

(Ae, ae, what was wrong? He'd never had such trouble before, never! But he couldn't stop now, not with the Wards only halfway built and the Power still unbound.)

Hauberin turned towards the south, standing silent till he had blocked knowledge of his body's weariness from his mind. "Fire." A tiny flame sprang up, thin and pale and wavering, forcing him to feed it with his own energy to keep it burning. There, now! It was blossoming at last into healthy red and gold, and he dared turn away to face the west.

"Water." The last of the Elements, the Powers be praised: a bright little pool, clear and still and perfect as he poured more and more will into its being, extravagant of his strength now in the desperation to be finished.

One thing more, only one thing more to complete the Warding. Hauberin caught his breath, then willed an arc of clear blue flame from earth to air, from air to fire, from fire to water, from water to earth. None save someone skilled in Power could have seen it, but it was there. The Warding was complete, and he, Alliar, and the human boy were safe within it.

And Hauberin, spent, toppled sideways, only Alliar's quick move keeping him from striking his head as he fell, asleep, quite literally, before he hit the ground.

VII
AIMERY

Hauberin awoke completely disoriented. A forest . . . ?
Had they been hunting . . . ? He looked lazily up at trees
towering over him, their leaves so intriguingly dappled—
Dappled by sunlight!

Oh. This was the human Realm. And he was lying on
the ground more or less where he had collapsed,
wrapped warmly in both his and Alliar's cloaks. (That
had been kind of Li. . . . But then, the wind spirit hardly
needed a cloak, not feeling the cold.)

Mm. A night spent on the hard, bare ground, and yet
he had slept so well. . . .

Hauberin's eyes shot open again. Slept well, indeed,
without the faintest hint of nightmare— Ha, just as he
had that night back on the terrace.

*Wonderful. All I have to do to escape Serein's curse is
work myself into total exhaustion every day— No, thank
you. I would rather continue this ridiculous name-quest.*

He had better see about lowering the Wards before
the boy began asking uncomfortable questions. It was
almost a shame to destroy the things after all the struggle
of setting them. Remembering that battle, the prince felt
a sudden cold horror.

*Powers, Powers, I could have burned out my mind,
destroyed myself with the backlash.*

Hauberin stared bleakly up at the leaves far overhead.
Granted, the healing charm might have been too much
of Faerie to work efficiently here. But setting the Wards
was one of the simplest defensive spells known! Even away
from Faerie, it shouldn't have given him any trouble,

even though he'd been forced to impose foreign imagery on a mortal Realm—

Unless the Realm itself was hostile to Faerie.

Hauberin shuddered. A would-be magician must have the innate talent for Power if he or she was to work any spells at all. But that magician must also have deep inner resources, for Power fed directly off whatever energy was at hand. In Faerie, no one worried much about it, since Faerie *was* magic; anyone with talent and training could call upon fresh energy from land or even air almost without thought. But here, where the land was jealous of its strength, refusing to yield its energies to one not of its own . . . To all extents and purposes, he was Powerless.

No. Not quite. Hauberin realized he had already proved that lightweight magics fueled from his own will still were possible, such things as the sparking of a fire into life or the using of mind-speech. He could almost certainly still manage even a persuasion spell, or any other magic worked directly mind to mind.

But anything stronger, anything requiring more strength than one mind and body could surrender, would be suicidal.

Ay me, Hauberin decided after a moment, *if my father could endure this loss* (which would, after all, last only till he returned to Faerie), *so can I.*

No doubt about it, though: Prince Laherin had truly had a bizarre taste in Realms.

Hauberin stretched, pulling his arms free from the double wrapping of cloaks. As he began to wriggle out of the cocoon, a cheerful voice chirped:

"Now, God give you good morning, my lord."

It was the human boy, arm in sling, foot neatly bound up, back resting comfortably against a tree. All in all, he looked vastly improved from the pale-faced child of last night.

Hauberin raised a surprised eyebrow. Child? Not quite. Without the fog of pain and terror shrouding him, he was clearly older than the prince had first believed,

perhaps close to the age Hauberin had been when he'd
rescued Alliar. And killed Ysilar. Hardly a child, indeed.

Would I have still saved him if I'd known?

It was a little late to worry about it now. The prince
cocked his head to one side, studying his catch. A stocky
form that promised strength to come, short, thick, sandy
hair topping a broad, engagingly homely face ruddier and
rougher than the clear, pale Faerie skin, and sprinkled
with odd little brownish spots (natural? an affliction of
some sort?). The boy's accent was a touch strange to his
ear—or else, more likely, Hauberin's own accent, learned
from his mother, was a bit out of date, and flavored with
the music of Faerie as well—but at least the language
still was the one he knew.

"What part of the morning is it?" Hauberin asked
belatedly.

The boy glanced up as though hoping to see the sun
through the screen of leaves. "Somewhere near the noon
hour, I would think."

"What!" Hauberin sat bolt upright, and heard Alliar's
amused chuckle.

"It's quite true," the being said in the human tongue.
"You slept like Azerion the Entranced. And how do you
feel?"

"Quite recovered." *And here I'd hoped to make an
early start.* He glanced at the being again, and added,
mind to mind, *"Why, Li, how elegant, all in deep blue."*

*"I humble myself before my gracious liege for his cour-
tesy. Besides, the boy seemed to expect a brave show:
What, are we not of noble birth?"*

"Are we not, indeed."

The silent exchange was, of course, literally as swift as
thought, and Hauberin turned to the boy as though
merely continuing his spoken conversation. "And you,
lad— First, what do you call yourself?"

"Aimery, my lord. Aimery de Valen."

"So. How do you feel this day?"

"Oh, much better than I ever thought I'd be feeling
after last night. There isn't even any pain! Or not much,

anyhow." The boy gave him a quick, grateful grin. "Your hands have a most wonderfully healing touch, my lord." He bowed from the waist. "Pray forgive me for not doing this properly."

"Ae, no," cut in Alliar. "Stay off that ankle."

The boy glanced from Alliar to Hauberin. "Ah, did I thank you last night for saving my life? I'm afraid I—I don't remember."

"You did." Hauberin was on his feet, stretching stiffness from protesting muscles. He disentangled the two cloaks, shaking twigs and leaves from them, and tossed one to Alliar with a nod of thanks. "I'm surprised you remember anything at all. You were in a sorry state."

"Oh, and don't I know it. I . . . did get a chance to use my sword on them," the boy added wistfully, "didn't I?"

"The robbers? Yes."

"So." Aimery was clearly pleased with himself, though he added with determined modesty, "Of course I'm nowhere near being a knight. As I admitted to Sir Alliar, I'm still very much in training."

" 'Sir' Alliar?"

A mental shrug. *The boy expected a title. He has a very feudal mind.*

Hauberin eyed Aimery skeptically. "Is that a uniform you wear?" The tunic was sadly stained and torn, but its pattern of red and blue was still plain.

"It's livery, my lord! I'm a squire," he added with considerable pride, "to my good Baron Gilbert."

Who obviously has more submissive underlings than I if he can get them into livery. "And would said baron be the owner of that castle to the north?"

The boy's look of astonishment said plainly, how could anyone not know that? "Of course, my lord."

"Pray forgive my ignorance," Hauberin drawled. "I'm a stranger here."

"Oh, I could see that." Aimery stopped, reddening. "I'm sorry. It's not my place to—"

"You'd be singularly unobservant if you hadn't noticed

my . . . shall we say foreignness." Hauberin paused, considering. "Now, I do think you'll be able to repay us for the rescue."

Aimery stiffened. "Ask of me anything, my lord. Anything that might be honorable for a squire."

Hauberin and Alliar exchanged wry glances. "I wasn't planning to compromise your honor," the prince said. "All I want is a guide to your baron's castle."

"Ah! You've business with—" He broke off in dismay. "Forgive me, my lord. I don't mean to pry, truly I don't, but sometimes a devil seems to get into me—"

"The creature's name is Curiosity, Aimery. And in my land he's not considered a devil at all." Hauberin turned to Alliar. "So, 'Sir' Alliar, do I or do I not scent water?"

"You do, my—ah—lord. A neat little pool some hundred paces to your right."

"Good." Hauberin scooped up his pack. But then he froze, staring. *"Li! Where are the Wards?"*

"Down."

"But—"

"The sunlight touched them," the being said laconically. *"They dissolved."*

"I'll never get used to this Realm, never!"

With that, Hauberin went in search of the pool.

There it was, clean and clear and so deep the water looked almost black, ringed by thick carpets of moss and screened by trees. The prince stripped and dove silently in, only to surface a moment later, gasping. Ae, cold! But refreshing. He took a few supple strokes; Hauberin could swim like one of the seal-folk. He turned easily onto his back, looking up at the interlaced branches shielding him from the sun, and was suddenly sober, wondering about his people, wondering just how much time was passing in Faerie. If he'd worked his father's spell correctly, the answer to that should be: virtually none. But what if something had gone wrong? What if— No. He wasn't going to start worrying over "what ifs." Or ponder the restrictions on his magic, either.

*But I'm forgetting how swiftly mortal time passes.
Enough of this.*

He returned clad in soft russets and browns, black hair
neatly combed. *"So-o,"* Alliar said slyly, *"I'm not the only
one to impress the boy, am I?"*

"One must keep up appearances," Hauberin retorted
with mock dignity. He was nibbling a last mouthful of
cold rabbit, trying not to taste what he was swallowing.
"Aimery, lad, if we get you into the saddle, do you think
you're strong enough to ride?"

"Of course, my lord."

"So be it," said the ever-practical Alliar, who calmly
picked the startled boy up and put him on his horse.

"Uh . . . thank you, Sir Alliar. I . . . think I can manage
from here. But what about you, my lords? Where are
your horses?"

Alliar shot a wry glance at Hauberin. "We have none."

The boy stared, opened his mouth, then shut it again,
plainly struggling not to ask the questions they could
practically hear shouting in his mind. "B-but it's not
proper for me to ride while you walk."

"Aimery," Hauberin said, "you can't even stand. How
could you walk?" He returned Alliar's wry glance. "As I
believed I mentioned some time before, 'Sir' Alliar, it
will do neither of us any harm to hike a bit."

"Aimery."

"My lord?" The boy seemed to be holding up well
enough at that easy pace, but he looked glad at the
chance to take his mind off what must have been considerable discomfort.

"You are a squire. Blame this on my foreignness, but
what, exactly is a squire?"

"A station below knight, my lord, and one above page."

"Of course," flatly.

Aimery gave him a rueful smile. "That didn't tell you
very much, did it?" He pondered a moment. "Well now,
I'm in training at arms, of course, with sword and lance
now that I'm no longer just a page. The sergeant-at-arms

thinks I'll have the shoulders to handle a war axe, but I don't know about that." The boy glanced down at Hauberin's supple slimness. "You're a swordsman, my lord?"

"Among other things," Hauberin replied, and heard Alliar stifle a laugh. "Go on."

"Ah . . . of course I have my duties within my lord baron's castle, serving at table and the like. There are the three of us, Bertran, Denis, and myself, to take turns as my lord baron's personal squire. And of course if he rode to battle or tourney, one of us would go with him to assist or—saints defend him!—rescue or protect him should the need arise." He was plainly reciting something learned by rote. But then Aimery added with an embarrassed little smile, "I'd be perfectly safe. No knight, of honor, would ever stoop to attacking a squire."

Common men-at-arms wouldn't have such scruples, but Hauberin wasn't about to dishearten the boy by reminding him of that. "Now, what was a young squire— for all his undoubted abilities—doing riding alone through a dangerous forest at night?"

The boy reddened. "Oh. Well. Through my own foolishness. You see, my lord baron had given me leave to ride with Sir Raimond and his party—"

"Sir Raimond."

"The baron's younger brother, my lord."

"So. Continue."

"We were all going to— Well, I don't suppose you want the name. It's a village belonging to my lord baron, on land he holds from— Ah. Yes. I'll just tell the story. Sir Raimond was going there in his brother's name—and not liking it overmuch, either. We were all in a hurry to return. But my horse picked up a stone in his hoof and went lame. I was supposed to wait in the village overnight and return the next morning. But . . . well, I didn't want to stay there. I don't mind serfs, someone has to tend the fields and all that, but . . ." He sighed. "At any rate, my horse stopped limping almost as soon as I'd pried the stone loose. I thought that if I set out at a good speed,

I would be able to catch up with Sir Raimond." He sighed again. "As you know, my lord, I didn't make it."

"This Raimond," Hauberin mused. "Is he young? Dark gold of hair and beard? Yes? I do believe we've seen the man, eh, Alliar?"

"One could say his party passed us on the road," the being drawled. "He was in something of a hurry."

"Sir Raimond does have a quick temper." The boy's voice was apologetic, as though he'd guessed what had happened. "And he was angry at having been sent out by his brother to play messenger. Particularly since he didn't have a choice."

"Ah?" Hauberin purred, a slightly malicious curiosity aroused. He put just a touch of magical persuasion into his next words. "And why didn't he have a choice?"

"He's in his brother's custody, as it were. You see, being the younger son, he had originally been destined for the Church."

Alliar blinked. "I don't see the connection."

"I think I do," Hauberin said. "Humans are so much more fertile than— Ah, what I mean is that with only the eldest child inheriting, the family lands don't have to be divided." At Aimery's doubtful nod, the prince continued, gently increasing the force of his persuasion-spell, "But Sir Raimond wasn't fit for this Church, I take it?"

"Uh . . . no. And so he was given a portion of land to rule after all, against custom. But he . . . became involved with . . . He wasn't a traitor, it was just that he—he met up with certain comrades who plotted against the duke our baron's liege lord."

"And the duke was merciful, I take it, and put Raimond back in his brother's safekeeping." *"Ensuring at one time the baron's continued fidelity and the hotheaded younster's restraint. Practical man, eh, Li?"*

"And how said hothead must hate his brother," the being added.

"Almost as much as Serein hated me, I should think."

Just as gently as he'd placed it, Hauberin released his persuasion-spell. Aimery, confused, said quickly, "Forgive me, my lords. I—I don't know what devil started me gossiping like an old woman."

He fell determinedly silent, while Hauberin and Alliar and the bored, sagging-eared horse walked on. But Hauberin was beginning to feel a tormenting uneasiness. This chattering, cheerful boy seemed to know all the doings of the area. What if he also knew . . . ?

"Aimery. No, don't look so alarmed. I'm not going to ask you to gossip about your betters." The prince hesitated, angry at himself for his suddenly pounding heart. "But I have an interest in the—the tales of the region."

Aimery gave him a puzzled look. "I don't know if I can help you with anything like that, my lord. You see, I've only been in my lord baron's service for two years. Ever since my first lord was slain at Touranne. But if I can be of any assistance . . . ?"

"Do you know any tales of a woman, a—witch-woman, called Melusine?"

The boy frowned. "Well, of course there's always the story of that female devil."

"Ae!"

Aimery gave him a startled glance. "Oh, d'you know that one, then? Half-serpent, half— No, wait. You wanted a local tale, and that's not a local one at all. Mm . . . a story about a woman named Melusine . . ." He shook his head. "Sorry, my lord. I don't know anything like that. But then, as I say, I've only been in service with my lord baron a short time."

Hauberin, sorry and relieved in one, forced a smile.

Hauberin had long since grown disenchanted with walking. His feet hurt, his legs hurt, and his head was beginning to ache most thoroughly from the unaccustomed rays of sunlight piercing through the leaves like so many fiery little daggers. "Does this forest never end?"

"It does, my lord." Aimery's voice was encouraging. "Just a little further and we'll reach the crest of this hill and be out of it, and you'll be able to see my lord baron's demesne."

"Demesne?" Alliar queried.

"The baron's personal lands, Li. And— Ah, what a splendid sight *that* is!"

Prince and wind spirit stood frozen, staring out from the hilltop at the alien view. Light green fields and deep green hedges, low stone walls and here and there clusters of huts roofed with thatch turned black with age, the castle in its heavy-walled might upon its rugged hill, and beyond, the dark folds of forest beginning anew, and all beneath a sky glorious with racing clouds tinted pink and red and orange by a late afternoon sun. . . .

"Splendid," Alliar echoed softly.

Hauberin thought he caught the faintest hint of pain in his friend's voice, and winced in pity. How the being must ache to soar freely out over that expanse! To know one's self hopelessly trapped instead within a solid, earthbound form— Ah, poor Li!

But Alliar rarely wasted time in self-pity. "Splendid, I repeat. But night comes after sunset, and if I'm not mistaken, the sun isn't far from setting." The being cast an appraising eye over the prince, who guessed his weariness must be easy enough to read. "Shall we camp out again?" Alliar asked. "Or continue on to the castle?"

"I think that castle is further away than it looks. Distances in mortal—ah, in these Realms can be deceptive. We would never reach it before full night, and I highly doubt they would let anyone in after nightfall. Eh, Aimery?"

"No, my lord."

The boy's voice sounded so weak that Hauberin stared at him. "You look terrible. Why didn't you tell us you were in pain?"

"I—I didn't want to delay you. Besides," Aimery insisted, gray with fatigue, "I'm only a b-bit faint."

"And faint is exactly what you'll do if we travel on much further."

"We may have another problem." Alliar, head back, was scenting the wind. "See how rapidly the clouds are thickening. I smell rain moving in very quickly."

"So do I. That settles it. We can't possibly reach the castle in time. And you, boy, are in no condition to go much further—and don't argue with me. I'm assuming that since this seems to be a well-travelled road, free from vegetation, there must be an inn of sorts somewhere along the way. Am I right?"

Aimery had plainly gone past the point of caring, but he murmured, "Down there. That building at the end of the village. They take in travellers sometimes."

It wasn't much of an inn, more a small farm—and, to judge from the reek, brewery as well—but by the time they had reached it, Aimery was sagging in the saddle and both Hauberin and the seemingly tireless Alliar were footsore enough to be glad of any chance to rest.

"Can you help the boy down, Li? I'll just hitch his horse here in the shed. Ae, and here comes the rain! Let's get inside."

"*Wait. Look.*"

There over the lintel an iron dagger had been most conspicuously stabbed. Hauberin frowned at it. "*Now what do you suppose that means?*"

"*I think, my Prince, that's to ward off such as you and I.*"

"*Charitable.*" The rain was beginning to fall in curtains, and Hauberin mentally consigned warding daggers to the Beyond, and reached for the door.

"*No!*" Alliar mind-shouted. "*Iron again, in the latch.*" Aloud, the being said chivalrously, "Allow me," and cast open the door with one arm, supporting Aimery with the other. Hauberin hurried inside, then stopped warily, glancing about.

This was hardly an elegant place: one large room with a floor of hard-packed, dully glossy earth, a step lower than the land outside, and a wooden ladder leading up to a loft. An enormous square-sided bed occupied one side of the room, which was otherwise sparsely furnished with a table and a few benches of plain, solid wood darkened with age and, Hauberin guessed, almost as impervious to wear as the house's stone walls. The chimney of the deep fireplace did seem to be drawing well, though the prince had his doubts about how long that would last now that the rain was already splatting down on the flames. He eyed that fire uneasily, sensing the cold, cruel burning of iron fire-dogs, iron pokers, an iron cauldron. . . .

A human was hurrying forward to meet them, a solid, leathery-skinned man in the plainest of brown woolen tunics and trousers. Hauberin forgot his iron-uneasiness, staring in sickened fascination. As with Aimery, this man was far ruddier than anyone out of Faerie, and his skin was . . . ugly, worn and wrinkled, rough as a file. Worse, not only was the human's hair losing its color, in places the scalp was actually visible. . . .

"What ails the man?" Alliar asked warily.

"I . . . think it's nothing more than mortal age. A . . . disease common to all full-blooded humans." Oh, Powers, let it be one common only to full-blooded humans, not to a half-blood as well. . . .

Alliar's distaste was sour in his mind. *"Be thankful for Faerie blood, then."*

I am, Alliar, I truly am. . . .

But then Hauberin realized that the human—the inn-keeper?—was watching him as though he were a wild thing that might pounce. "Come, man, stand aside and let us enter," the prince said regally. "Is this not an inn?"

"I . . . take in travellers now'n then."

"What *are* you staring at? Do I look like a monster to you?"

The man flushed. "Oh no, m'lord, of course not. It's just . . ." Wary brown eyes flicked from the quality of Hauberin's clothing—obvious even under the layer of road dust—to the hilt of his sword, to the proud, sharp lines of his face. "M'lord, to be honest, we don't have lodging fit fer gentry, only for farmers 'n the like."

"No matter. We're here. And the boy is hurt and in need of rest."

The innkeeper's eyes widened as he saw Aimery sagging in Alliar's grasp. "That's the baron's livery."

"The boy is a squire in his service. Now stand aside and let us enter!"

In a quick, efficient flurry of motion, a woman the innkeeper's match for solid human middle age and ruddy skin (though, noted the bemused Hauberin, she seemed to be retaining her hair) came forward to take charge of Aimery.

"Bed's the best place for him," she said over her shoulder in a no-nonsense voice. "Beggin' yer pardons, m'lord."

"My Meg'll take good care of the lad," the innkeeper assured Hauberin. "And my son'll see to your horses."

"Horse," the prince corrected to the gawky adolescent shape that had materialized out of the shadows. "Only one." He turned smoothly back to the bewildered innkeeper with a charming smile. "So now. You *do* have beds, I take it? And food and drink?"

The human's eyes brightened a bit. "Yes, m'lord. Best beer in the barony, saints forgive me fer boastin', good as what they brew up in the castle." He beamed. "Brew our own, y'know."

"We noticed," Alliar murmured.

"Ah well, yes. Guess it is a bit strong to the nose, what with the wet outside 'n all." But then the brightness faded. "Food's goin' to be plain, m'lords, I'm warnin' you now so you won't be blamin' m'wife or me."

Alliar raised mental eyebrows. *"Does he expect us to take our swords to him if we're displeased?"*

"Possibly." "Is the food hot? And filling? Good enough, then. Wait, now . . ." Hauberin rummaged in his belt purse; his people had no need of coins, but he imagined that links from a pure silver chain would suffice. "There, man. I assume that's enough."

Too late he remembered that humans didn't necessarily tell the truth. The innkeeper stared down at the shining metal in his hand, obviously fighting a battle between greed and honesty. "More 'n enough," he admitted with obvious reluctance.

Lessons in the fine art of bargaining for food certainly

weren't part of a princely education. "Never mind," Hauberin said helplessly. "Keep it."

He sat without ceremony, close enough to the fire to be warmed, far enough from the iron tools to be at ease. Alliar sprawled beside him, the very image of a road-weary human. "Aimery looks comfortable enough over there."

"He does. I think that's a feather bed." Hauberin winced inwardly at the thought of the fleas probably inhabiting it.

"And where are we to sleep, my Prince?"

"Up in the loft, I would think."

"Among the rafters? I trust the roof doesn't leak." "Heigh-ho for a life of luxury," the being added aloud, and smiled innocently at the now cauldron-tending Meg when that harried woman looked up in surprise. *"Not exactly the image of the buxom tavern wench."*

It was Hauberin's turn to stare. "Now, where in the name of all the Powers did you learn about tavern wenches?" he said, absently aloud, and received a second startled glance. *"For the poor woman's sake—and she's an honest farm wife, Li, not a wench—let's be more careful with our mind-speech."*

"Mm. Our hosts are eyeing us oddly enough as it is." "Ah, here comes dinner."

It might have been plain, but neither Hauberin (after that half-raw rabbit) nor Alliar, whose pseudo-human form at last needed food, could find fault in the good hunks of bread and cheese and the bowls of soup thick enough to be called stew. Hauberin took a wary sip of the home-brewed beer, then, pleased, a second, savoring the unfamiliar tang on his tongue. He called out to the innkeeper, "My compliments. Your boasts were justified."

The human, too proud to grovel, too pleased not to react, gave him a quick, surprisingly charming smile, and Hauberin thought, *He's no fool. And what tales might he know about the region?* "Come, host, and join us." Now, how could he win the human's confidence? "I really can't recall ever tasting finer beer." True enough; he'd never tasted *any* human drink before. "No, man, I mean it. It reminds me almost of heather ale."

To his surprise, the human let out a shout of genuine laughter. "Caught me there, m'lord. Heather ale, indeed. You'll be knowin' some of our local tales, I see."

For an instant, Hauberin was puzzled. Ah, wait . . . heather ale might be brewed in Faerie, with magic's aid, but here it was probably only a drinker's myth. "And why shouldn't I know your tales?"

The human's smile faded. "Pardon, m'lord, but . . . Well, it's plain you're a stranger here."

Hauberin grinned. "Stranger, indeed. Come, your eyes are fairly burning holes in me. Ask your question."

"No, wouldn't be proper . . ."

"Ask!"

"Be you a . . ." his voice sank almost to a whisper, "a Saracen?"

Hauberin and Alliar exchanged a blank glance. "A . . . what?"

"Why, a Saracen, m'lord! A—a paynim from the East, a worshipper of Mahound." At that name, the farm wife, en route to Aimery, stopped to piously cross herself. Hauberin raised a brow, more bewildered than before.

"No, man. Whatever else I may be, I am most certainly not a worshipper of this . . . Mahound."

"Didn't mean no harm by it, m'lord. But you did ask me t' ask, and . . . It's just you lookin' so dark 'n foreign 'n all. . . ." His voice trailed into silence, and the prince was uncomfortably aware of a building tension. Alliar could hardly miss it.

"By the Winds, he's afraid of us! Why? He doesn't even know who we are."

"He knows we're nobility and he's a commoner. Didn't you hear the contempt in Aimery's voice when he mentioned serfs? Human nobles are allowed cruel license over human commons."

"Our good host looks quite capable of defending himself."

And a man frightened for himself and his family, a man wielding cold iron. . . . Hauberin smiled reassuringly. "Come now, don't look so grim. I'm not offended. Eh, enough of this! Since I am, indeed, a stranger, perhaps you can tell me something about the region. As innkeeper and brewer, you must know a great deal."

The flattery struck home. "Ah. Well. Somewhat."

"The land seems peaceful enough," Alliar prodded. *"Barring the occasional bandits, of course,"* the being added silently to Hauberin.

"It *is* peaceful," the innkeeper said, "saints be praised. Fer now, anyhow. Hasn't been real trouble—the kind a' thing where we all pick up and huddle up in the castle hopin' there'll be somewhat left unburned to get back to—hasn't been anythin' like that since Lammas two summers past."

"Touranne?" Hauberin hazarded, recalling Aimery's words.

"That's it, m'lord. We were lucky then. Fightin' didn't really reach us here. Left a lot a' hard feelin's, though, some on the good duke's side, some on t'other. . . . You've not come through Baron Thibault's lands, or you'd be knowin' all about that."

"Feuds?" Alliar asked uncertainly.

"Oh, aye, feuds." The human broke off abruptly at a glare from his wife. "But ain't my business, talkin' a' such."

Hauberin gave a mental shrug. Let the humans have their feuds; they meant nothing to him. "We were mentioning local tales just now. Are you well acquainted with them?"

The innkeeper grinned. "The old tales, you mean? We all know 'em; they're good for tellin' during those long winter nights. Tales o' magic creatures. Like the *galipote,* who can make himself look like your favorite hound, just waitin' for you to turn your back. Or the Evil Herb— that's a nasty thing, looks just like grass, but it *thinks,* it *hates.* If you step on it, it tricks your mind so you walk right into a bog or off a cliff. . . ." After a moment, his grin returned. "O'course we don't believe in such things any more; we're all good Christians here, God save us."

But Hauberin saw a flicker of superstitious fear in the man's eyes, and fought down a smile. *No. Of course you don't believe.* "There's one tale in particular I'd like to know. Perhaps you can help me. Have you ever heard folk tell of a—witch, Melusine?"

The man and woman hastily crossed themselves. "There's many a tale told a' witches, m'lord. Some of 'em more than just tales, if you take my meanin'. But can't say I've heard of a Melusine. You, Meg?"

"Hush, now. The poor young lord's just fallen asleep." The woman turned a red, earnest face to Hauberin. "Never heard of a Melusine, m'lord. They might know at the castle, if it's important to you."

"Perhaps." The prince refused to discuss his affairs with humans. "But the hour grows late, and we are both nearly as weary as the boy."

Did relief flicker in the humans' eyes? "Of course, m'lord," said the man. "This way."

"Your bed? Oh no, man. I'll not dispossess you and your wife." It was said out of Faerie fastidiousness, not charity—Aimery might not mind sleeping there, but there *were* limits—but the human only nodded, accepting without question this one more sign of eccentricity on the part of his strange guests.

"You must be understandin', we've only got straw pallets up there on the loft."

"Fresh straw?"

"My son'll just be fixin' it." The long-legged adolescent scrambled down the ladder, bowing nervously, and disappeared back into the shadows.

"Fair enough," Hauberin said lightly. "Lead on."

But the human paused at the foot of the ladder, plainly fighting an inner battle. At last he said, "Was it bandits, m'lords?"

"Eh?"

"That wounded the youngster. And stole your horses.

It was bandits, wasn't it? The baron's men do patrol, but the forest's big."

"Bandits did hurt the boy," the prince said evasively. "As for us . . ." Hauberin smiled and neatly skirted falsehood. "Let us merely say that when we tried to ride through the forest, things just—fell apart." Ignoring Alliar's frantically stifled gasp of laughter, he nodded regally. "Good night, good host."

VIII
STORM WINDS

Hauberin woke suddenly to a screaming that seemed to shake the very walls, woke trying desperately to pull Power to him, Power that just wouldn't come—

But after that first shocked moment, he sank back down again. This was the humans' inn, somewhere in the small hours of the mortal night, with the storm outside turning from rain to fierce wind.

The prince lay for a time staring up through darkness at oaken beams and gray-black masses of thatching, aching with the lack of magic, all at once overwhelmed by so strong a sense of the sheer alien strangeness all around him that he shivered, thinking suddenly of home, of Ereledan and Charailis, wondering once again if, indeed, he had judged the difference between Faerie and human time accurately, worrying as to what he would return.

When he returned.

If.

No self-pity, Hauberin told himself.

But how he wished he had been able to cut across Realms closer to the castle! So much mortal time already wasted. . . .

The prince sighed and stretched, trying to straighten out the clothing in which he, perforce, had been sleeping, and heard the straw mattress crackle under him. At least he had slept well so far, Serein not withstanding: exhaustion did seem to hold the curse at bay. And straw made a reasonable bed, if one was tired enough. Providing it wasn't already . . . inhabited, of course. There were piles of alder leaves in all the loft's crevices, guaranteed, according to the innkeeper, to chase away fleas. At least whatever creatures might still be up here didn't seem to care for the taste of Faerie blood.

Chuckling, the prince closed his eyes. But sleep was impossible now, what with all the shriekings and whinings and house-shaking buffets. "Eh, Alliar, are you—"

Alliar was gone.

"*Li?*" No cause for alarm. The being must be downstairs, discovering that the so skillfully detailed pseudo-human form, after eating and drinking so well, had certain needs for relief as well.

Still ... could Alliar counterfeit humanity *that* completely?

"*Li? Everything all right?*"

No answer.

"*Li!*"

Not the faintest of mental touches. Hauberin sprang to his feet, now genuinely alarmed. "*Alliar!*" It was a mental shout. "*Alliar!*"

Was there...? Yes! No coherent thought, only the most chaotic swirlings of distress and despair, but it was Alliar, somewhere outside the inn. Hauberin fairly leaped down the ladder, landing noiselessly on the earthen floor, and raced to the door, thinking wildly, *If it's bolted, how do I get out? How do I handle an iron bolt?*

But the door was unbarred. Of course, Alliar had opened it. Hauberin safely slipped the latch with a fold of his tunic and rushed out into the storm. The wind nearly knocked him off his feet. Staggering and breathless, the prince stood with head down, trying to orient himself.

"*Alliar!*"

Again he felt that terrible, despairing swirl of emotion, and looked up, shivering, half-blinded by flailing strands of hair, staring with night-sighted eyes.... There! Alliar, outlined sharply against the turbulent sky, had abandoned human form and—oh, the anguish in that slender, alien shape with its upthrust, yearning arms!

"Ae, Alliar," the prince breathed, and struggled to his

friend's side. The luminous eyes were wild and sightless, not truly conscious. "Li? Can you hear me? Li!"

Carefully, he opened his mind to the being, only to be stunned by the wave of raw emotion suddenly surging over him. Staggering with grief not his, Hauberin reached out to blindly catch Alliar in his arms. The being crumpled bonelessly against him and they both fell, Hauberin gasping for breath, helpless against that terrible, so much more than flesh-and-blood sorrow, clinging desperately to his friend, afraid to let go lest he lose Alliar over the edge into madness. Image after image assaulted his mind, alien, incomprehensible, anguished memories of freedom forever lost to this solid, fleshy prison—

No! These aren't my memories! "Li, stop it! Break the contact!"

But the torment, the torment, the long, long years of slavery. . . . The sorcerer, the master, the one to be feared— Ae, ae, no!

"It's over, Li, over. He's dead. I killed him. I freed you. You're safe— Ae, Li, you'll tear my mind in two!"

Desperate for his own safety now, the prince fought back, struggling like a man fighting the sea, painfully building up wall after wall of will, pulling free from the anguish that wasn't his own till suddenly he was alone in his mind, shaking, but still slinging to an Alliar gone chill and rigid as a dull golden statue.

"Alliar?"

Not the slightest quiver of an eyelid. *Shock,* Hauberin thought. Or what passed for shock in such as Li. The prince shuddered, knowing what he must do, then very delicately began to let down the walls of his mental barricade. At once he was engulfed again in the turbulence of Alliar's mindless panic. But this time he was prepared. As much for his own sanity as that of his friend, Hauberin pictured a field, a quiet field somewhere in the midst of his lands. Ignoring the physical and psychic storms that lashed at him, the prince threw every fiber of his will into seeing that field, only that field, tranquil in the clear light of Faerie. . . . Nothing large was happening there, nothing ever had. There was only the gentle rustling of the silky grass. . . . He could smell the sweetness of that grass, hear the sleepy buzzing of insects half-drugged by warmth. . . . There was no storm, no wind, only the peace, the endless, soothing peace. . . .

Half-hypnotized himself, Hauberin started violently when Alliar stirred in his arms. Quickly he reassured the being, *"It's all right, Li. You're safe, you're here, in the present. Come with me, back to the present."*

Life flared abruptly in the blankly staring eyes. For a time the being could do nothing but huddle helplessly against Hauberin, trying with sudden little spasms to regain control over mind and body. The prince waited, shivering in the wind. Alliar's body, cool-fleshed at the best of times, was almost as cold as that wind right now, but Hauberin dared not let go. But his teeth were beginning to chatter, and at last the prince could wait no longer and asked tentatively:

"Li?"

"Yes. I'm . . . I'm here." The being pulled away, sitting with head down, shuddering. "Forgive me. I—didn't expect—I—I don't know these mortal winds, and they—called to me, and— Oh, how I ached to go with them!"

The anguish in the hopeless words trembled in the air between them. Hauberin hesitated, aching with his friend's pain, hating with every nerve what he was going to say. "I could free you. You know that. I could free you if you can no longer bear—"

"By killing this mortal shell?" Alliar gave him a soft, weary smile, eyes suddenly infinitely old, infinitely sad. "Oh my friend, do you think I would ever place such a burden on you?" Then the being added, almost lightly "I never was one of the High Ones, after all, even when I was . . . in that other way of being. None of the High Winds would ever have been snared into flesh."

"Don't belittle yourself."

"Ach, who better? But what I'm trying to tell you is that I . . . don't know any more if I could ever be what

I once was." There was a brittle edge to Alliar's words that was very close to hysteria. "I've been in this flesh-and-blood shape for so long and long, thinking flesh-and-blood thoughts, feeling flesh-and-blood emotions none of my kin would comprehend. Why, I might even have acquired a flesh-and-blood soul! Do you think that's possible?"

Hauberin fought to control his shivering. "Li, if we're g-going to debate theology, can't we get back indoors first? No matter what you say, you're obviously s-still a wind spirit if you don't feel this cold, but I— Look you, if we stay here much longer, the humans are going to find me frozen in the morning."

Alliar gave him a contrite glance. "And you without even your cloak in this wind."

"There was hardly time to search for it."

With what was plainly a great effort, Alliar stood, swaying slightly. Hauberin scrambled to his feet, feeling bruised in body and mind both. "Come, back to the inn."

Stumbling with weariness, Alliar staggered forward, just barely reshaping into human form, the taller, heavier body sagging in Hauberin's supporting arms. "Please, Li, don't collapse, not just yet. I don't think I could carry you."

The short way back seemed an endless journey through cold and wind and worry. Shivering, struggling beneath Alliar's weight, Hauberin prodded himself on with thoughts of a warm hearth, warm blankets. . . .

But the door to the inn was bolted fast.

"No!" It was a cry of princely fury. "You'll not shut us out!" Hauberin forgot all his intentions of avoiding magic in this Power-poor Realm, and sent out a blazing surge of will to catch a human mind, set a human body to working the bolt. The door swung open, and the prince forced his way inside, slamming it shut again behind himself and the sagging Alliar with a deft foot. Surrounded suddenly by stale, beer-and-human scented but wondrously warm air, he dropped his psychic hold, staring fiercely into the eyes of the innkeeper.

"I can manage the rest of the way," came Alliar's weary thought. *"I suspect you'll have to pacify our good host. I'm sorry, I . . . just can't do any more."*

"It's all right, Li," Hauberin soothed. *"Just go and get some rest. I can handle this alone."*

He watched his friend struggle safely up to the loft, then turned regally to the human. "Why did you bolt the door?"

The man didn't flinch. "Didn't know what might be tryin' to get in, what with the storm 'n all." He frowned, plainly not remembering what had made him reopen the door. "What happened out there, m'lord? You look like a man who's been battlin' devils."

Hauberin laughed wearily, feeling the close air stealing the strength from him. "You're not that far from wrong. Oh, no, I didn't mean that literally! None of your cloven-hoofed monsters were out for a stroll. Look you," he added evasively, "have you never heard of folk walking in their sleep?"

"Is that what happened? Your friend was walkin' in his sleep, out in the storm?"

It sounded unlikely to Hauberin, too. "You've said it," he replied vaguely, foot on the lowest rung of the ladder to the loft. It would have been lovely to sit before a roaring fire for a time, preferably with mulled wine in hand, but not at the price of further interrogation. "Once more, good host, good night."

"One question more, m'lord." The human's voice was taut with sudden tension. "How did you get past the iron?"

Hauberin froze. "Why, whatever can you mean?"

"Forgive me if I'm wrong. But I'm not wrong, am I?"

The prince turned, stalking forward a step, wary, menacing. The human's hand closed about something, an amulet or crucifix, no doubt, but he held his ground. "They told me iron over the door'd be enough."

" 'They' would seem to have been mistaken. Tell me, when did you first suspect?"

"Not suspect, m'lord, not exactly. Wondered. The

youngster bein' with you fooled me a bit. Then . . . well,
first, you didn't know a' Saracens. I told myself that might
a' just been that you were a foreigner. But then I saw
you 'n your friend lookin' at each other and plainly talkin'
to each other—but you never said a word aloud."

Oh, damn. "I see. Careless of us."

"And just before, when you two were out in the storm,
I saw— As God is my witness, I saw your friend change
shape. And that's why I bolted the door. There's the
truth of it, and you can do what you want. Only don't
hurt my wife 'n son, because they know nothin' a' this."

Hauberin let out his breath in a long sigh. *Brave little
man. Brave, foolish little man whom I could destroy with
three well-chosen Words.* "I never yet did harm to the
innocent, nor punished courage in human or other."

The man swallowed. "It's true, then. You be a noble-
man of—of—"

"Faerie?" Hauberin smiled faintly, correcting with
reflexive truthfulness. "I am a prince of Faerie."

There came twin gasps of amazement, one from the
innkeeper, one from—

"So, Aimery. How long have you been awake and
listening?"

The boy staggered to his side, using a staff as a cane.
"Not very long, my lord—ah—Your Grace."

Long enough, obviously. "Why, how composed you
are, Aimery! I'm impressed."

"It's n-not composure, Your Grace, it's shock." The
boy's grin was quick and nervous. "I knew you were
foreign to these lands, but I never dreamed just *how*
foreign."

"And here I was callin' him a Saracen," the innkeeper
muttered.

Aimery's eyes widened. "Then . . . it's true, that night,
the robbers—what I thought I saw— It really *was*
magic. . . ."

"That doesn't frighten you?"

"Oh, it does," the boy admitted, face red. "You m-must
know this, Your Grace: We're forbidden to have anything

at all to do with the Black Arts—I—I beg your pardon,
I mean the magical arts. But I . . ." He straightened
proudly. "You saved my life, Your Grace, for whatever
your reasons, and so I cannot be afraid of you." The
quick grin came and went again. "Overawed, I admit.
Your Grace, no matter what the facts, I am in your debt."

Hauberin forced back a smile. "Nobly said." He looked
from one wide-eyed human to the other, and sighed. The
last thing he wanted to do right now was work any mind-
spells. But he could hardly leave these folk with the
knowledge of who and what he was. "This will not hurt
you in any way."

He hadn't thought it possible for Aimery to become
even more wide-eyed. "Please, Your Grace," the boy
whispered, "might I speak to you alone? For j-just a
moment?"

Curious, Hauberin nodded, drawing the boy aside.
"What?"

"You—you're going to take away our memories of this,
aren't you?"

"Am I?"

"Please, leave me mine."

"Ah? Why?"

"Because I . . . you . . . Oh please, Your Grace, I've
never seen any true wonder in my life before, not even
the smallest of magics. And this is so very splendid! I—
I don't want to lose it." The boy drew himself up proudly.
"I give you my word on my honor as a squire and a—a
good Christian: I shall not betray your secret."

He fell silent, staring at Hauberin with pleading eyes.
Wounded wood-sprite eyes, thought the prince, remembering how Alliar looked at him in just the same plaintive
way when the being wanted something from him. It usually worked.

Ah well, there was no reason to doubt the boy's sincer-
ity. "So be it. Stay here and wait."

Gently, carefully, Hauberin wove a mind-spell about
the innkeeper and—since she was almost certainly awake
and aware—his wife as well, *feeling* their essences sturdy

and unshakable as the stone walls about them. No dream-
ers, these. They were quite willing to believe only in
whatever they could see or touch, and the prince silently
thanked them for that lack of imagination; it made his
work so much simpler.

"*We are harmless travellers,*" he sent, "*stopped here
merely for the comfort of a roof over our heads. Believe.*

"*You saw nothing outré this night, nothing. If you
think at all of Faerie or magic, know that you dream.
Believe.*

"*We will be gone with morning. Till then, we mean no
harm to you or yours. Believe.*"

To his relief, Hauberin saw the innkeeper blankly
return to bed, and knew his message had been heard.
Delicately he retreated from the humans' minds and sank
gladly to a bench near the banked fire, wondering if he
had enough energy left to prod it into life magically—he
certainly couldn't touch those iron pokers—and clenching
his hands to hide their trembling. What should have been
effortless had been anything but!

I should just be thankful the spell worked at all.

But then the prince remembered Aimery, and looked
up in resignation. "Come here, boy. Prod that fire up a
bit, if you would. Ahh, yes. . . ." He baked blissfully for
a time, eyes closed, feeling the last residue of chill leaving his bones, then glanced up at the wide-eyed boy.
"Sit, before you collapse from the weight of wonder."

Aimery bit his lip, then blurted out, "You—you don't
have to worry, Your Grace. I mean, about them."

"Are you telling me my craft?"

"Oh, no!"

"Hush. You'll wake them."

"Ah. Yes." In a fierce whisper, the boy continued, "I
only meant—I owe you my life, Your Grace! If any wish
to harm you, they must deal with me first."

Hauberin just barely bit back a laugh. "Thank you,"
he said solemnly, and started to get to his feet. The boy
jumped up, too, in hasty courtesy.

"Uh . . . Your Grace?"

"Yes, Aimery. What is it?"

"You're going on in the morning, aren't you?"

"Yes. Why?"

"I only . . . You were travelling today, too, by daylight . . . I mean—"

"Most of my race can't endure mortal sunlight. I can. Does that answer your question?"

"One of them," Aimery said with a flash of spirit. "I've got dozens more."

Hauberin laughed softly. "I'm sure you have. But the rest of them can wait till morning. No . . . wait. Now you can answer a question for me."

"If I'm able, Your Grace," the boy said cautiously.

"It's nothing distressing. I wish to enter your baron's castle tomorrow. How should I do this?"

Aimery hesitated. "You . . . don't mean my lord baron any harm, do you? I'm sorry, Your Grace, but I have to ask."

"No. I mean him no harm. You *do* know my people's reputation for honesty?"

The boy nodded. Very softly, he said, "I can understand the need to keep your—your race a secret. I guess you'd want to keep your royal title a secret, too."

"Exactly."

"Ah. Well. I don't know why the story of this . . . Melusine is so important to you— Wait, Your Grace, I didn't mean to pry, truly! But I would think the best thing to do would be . . . just to enter as a guest. We all love new faces at the castle; we see so few of them. And a mysterious noble stranger . . . Oh, my lord baron does love a mystery!" Aimery's eyes were bright with excitement. "I'll have a story ready, Your Grace, never fear." The boy glanced at him apologetically. "I . . . may have to embroider the truth a bit."

"Lie, you mean. I would rather you didn't. But these are human ways. If you must. . . ."

"Trust me, Your Grace. I shan't betray you."

Hauberin held the boy's gaze for a long moment, reading a confused tangle of human emotions, many of them beyond Faerie comprehension. But honesty, Hauberin knew. And honesty seemed uppermost. The prince nodded, stifling a sudden yawn. "So be it. Best bank the fire again before we burn down the inn. Aimery, I bid you a good night—or at least what's left of the night."

He was up the ladder and back to his pallet before the boy could reply.

IX
OLD FRIENDS AND NEW

Hauberin woke this time amid silence and stray rays of early morning sunlight stealing through cracks in the walls, and found Alliar sitting at his side in human guise, studying him with almost parental warmth. But then Alliar realized Hauberin was awake, and scrambled up in embarrassment, making much of brushing stray bits of straw from clothing and hair.

"Li? Are you all right?"

"Why shouldn't I be?"

"Stop that." Hauberin got to his feet, catching his friend's gaze before Alliar could glance away. "*Are* you all right?"

"Yes. Truly." The being hesitated, then added softly, "Thank you."

"I only did—"

"Hush. I shall not forget." For an instant the familiar golden eyes were alien, filled with cool, elemental power. . . . Then Alliar grinned. "Enough solemnity. It's a bright morning out there. Shall we see how Squire Aimery is doing and go out on the road again?"

Hauberin smiled. "We shall, indeed."

But when Hauberin, Alliar, and the limping Aimery stepped outside to a chilly morning and a sky full of sunlight and speeding clouds, they found themselves no longer alone.

"Now, wasn't this a stroke of good fortune, Your—ah—my lord?" Aimery asked cheerfully. "Meeting up with these my Lord Baron's men, I mean, and them with spare horses so you need no longer be afoot. A stroke of good fortune, indeed." But then the boy's eyes widened. "Or . . . did you . . . ?"

"Did we what?" murmured an amused Alliar.

"Oh, my lords, you know!" Aimery surreptitiously sketched what presumably was meant to be an arcane gesture in the air. Alliar chuckled.

"Whatever gave you that idea?"

"But—I—"

"Enough, Li," Hauberin cut in, adding silently, *"You're alarming the boy. We don't want these other humans wondering about us, either."* He hesitated, then added warily, *"You are feeling well?"*

"Oh, my friend, I thought I'd already assured you: Yes. I am."

The tender, wry, amused little mind-touch that accompanied the words reassured Hauberin more than any declarations. "Aimery," he said to the boy, "I hate to disillusion you, but all I did was wave the party down." *"Couldn't do much else,"* he commented silently, *"not with this Realm's damnable lack of Power."*

"Nervous, are we?" Alliar teased.

"No. Yes. How should I not be nervous?"

The castle was looming up before them, a great mass of walls and towers. Hauberin, casting a speculative eye over the heavy, narrow-windowed fortifications, heard Alliar's soft, "Impressive. A fortress truly meant for war, eh, Aimery?"

"It was in the past, my lord. And should God will it, it certainly could be again." The boy's light voice was suddenly more mature, the voice of a squire trained to arms. "Even if matters should ever come again to siege, well, with the grace of God, we should be able to hold it far longer than forty days."

"Forty days?" Hauberin, who had just been deciding he wouldn't care to attack those walls without magic, raised a curious eyebrow. "Is that some ritual time span?"

"Oh no, my lord." Aimery flashed his quick grin. "Well, yes, in a way I suppose it is. After forty days' service to their liege lord, common men-at-arms are free to go home to their fields."

"Then after forty days, there's peace, perforce?"

"Ah . . . no. If the attacker hires mercenaries—those Godless men—the siege can go on till the castle falls or is relieved."

"Or the attacker runs out of gold. Why such contempt in your voice?"

"For mercenaries?" Aimery regarded Hauberin with horror. "To fight for your liege lord, the man to whom you've sworn homage, is right and honorable. But to soil your knightly vows by fighting, killing, for nothing but gold . . ."

"I see. But why are you looking questions at me?"

"Your pardon, but I was just wondering . . . Don't you have siegecraft in—your native land?"

Hauberin laughed, remembering his brief non-attack on Serein's estate. "In my native land battles seldom last long enough to warrant a siege. Remember, we have other weapons than swords at our disposal."

As the boy stared at him, plainly imagining who-knew-what arcane terrors, Alliar cut in, "Even at this range, I can't make out the device on that banner. Aimery?"

"That's the baron's personal standard, showing he's in residence. The device is his own, of course: azure, an antelope reguardant, argent."

"A what?"

"A silver antelope—it's white, really—looking over its shoulder, the field—that's the background—blue."

"Then why didn't you just—"

"Ae." It was a soft, involuntary cry from Hauberin.

"My lord?"

"It's . . . nothing to worry you."

"Not the right design, my Prince?"

"No." Hauberin fought down a sudden keen despair. *"I was so certain this was the right fortress. If we have to begin anew . . ."*

"It could have changed hands, you know, through marriage or— The boy did mention war."

Hauberin sighed. "Let us see what we shall see," he said aloud. Standing in the stirrups, he added, "There seem to be travellers ahead of us."

"Oh, yes, my lord." Aimery was settling happily into the role of guide. "In these times of peace, there are always merchants and victuallers and the like. See? The drawbridge is down and the portcullis is up."

"And the gates," Alliar commented, "are closed."

"Not completely. There's a door in one, do you see it, to let people in and out without risking the danger of an unexpected attack."

"And whose eyes are those, peering at us from that window by the gates?"

Aimery gave Alliar an admiring glance. "You're sharp-sighted, my lord! That's the chief porter, the fellow who keeps watch on everyone coming and going, and who decides who gets to enter." As Hauberin thoughtfully began to gather a persuasion-spell in his mind, the boy continued lightly, "He'll recognize my livery, of course, even if it is . . . ah . . . somewhat the worse for wear, and let us pass." He smiled confidently at Hauberin and Alliar. "Don't worry, my lords. You're with me. No one will stop you."

"Thank you, Squire Aimery," Hauberin replied somberly. "That is most reassuring."

They were in the shadow of the walls now, and the prince shifted uneasily in the saddle, his good humor fading. The castle reeked of damp, of chill stone and old death—

Nonsense.

The damp and chill were real enough, but as for anything else: that was only overwrought nerves complaining.

But the sheer mass of the fortress weighed down on him, silently hostile. This outer defense was so thick it was like riding into the mouth of a cavern, or a monster. . . .

Don't be a fool! It's just a place, a thing; it has no life of its own.

Aimery was giving the all but unseen porter a self-confident little wave. But Hauberin hardly noticed. He felt a new darkness pressing down on him, the cold burning of iron overhead. . . . The prince glanced up as they passed under the weight of the portcullis, the cruelly spiked iron gate, and flinched. If it should start to slide downward . . .

"It's securely fastened, my lord," Aimery had seen. "No danger, never fear." But then the boy stopped short, blinking. "It's the—the iron, isn't it?" he whispered. "Just as the old tales say: Your people can't endure iron."

Hauberin frowned, not happy at having a weakness exposed, even to a friendly human. But before he could speak, Aimery added:

"Don't worry. I'll keep your secret, by my faith. Oh, but my lord, you'll have to be very careful here!"

"Just what I've been telling him," Alliar murmured.

Hauberin glanced at the being as they rode on. *"You look as uncomfortable as I feel."*

"So much stone. . . . No winds could ever find their way through all of it."

"We have castles in Faerie, too, Li."

"Made of air and light."

"Poetic. If hardly accurate."

Hauberin hesitated, remembering last night's hysteria. Maybe he should tell Alliar the being need not continue; surely he could go on alone. But . . . Powers, he really didn't want to be alone, not in this cold, iron-haunted place. . . .

Ashamed of his weakness, the prince said, a bit too briskly, *"Cheer up, Li. I see sunlight ahead of us."*

Alliar straightened. *"And a new line of walls beyond that. Winds, what a suspicious folk!"*

"You'd be suspicious, too, if you didn't have magic to shield you."

Hauberin glanced up at the two guard towers flanking the entrance, vaguely sensing the presence of wary humans, eyeing narrow openings in the stone that could only have been arrow slits. Oh, he definitely wouldn't like to attack this place without magic!

Suddenly they were coming out into the sunlight and the great open area between the outer and inner rings of walls, and the shock of light and life and noise hit Hauberin like a psychic blow.

"There's an entire town in here!"

Aimery chuckled. "Just about. This is the Outer Ward, where we keep the kitchen and storehouses. The workshops, too. Oh, and the stables and the animal pens."

"I've noticed." The barnyard smells were staggering.

So was the number of people crowded into the Ward. There were folk feeding animals, carving wood, tending forges, folk gossiping and arguing and shouting, and packs of busy, noise, dirty children running everywhere— For a moment, the sheer weight of all those active, teeming, alien human minds nearly overcame him until the prince hastily raised mental barriers to shut them out, or at least mute their roar.

He glanced at Alliar. The being didn't look particularly happy, glancing longingly up at the free sky, but otherwise, perversely, seemed to be enduring much more successfully than he.

Of course. Not having any human blood, Alliar wasn't as distressingly easily attuned.

Aimery was eyeing them both warily. Hauberin forced a smile. "It *is* a bit overwhelming, isn't it?"

"I suppose it must be, to a stranger." The boy resumed his busy, matter-of-fact guide's voice. "The barracks of the castle men-at-arms are out here, and the families of craftsmen and servants and other such dependents. Here, I believe, our escort will be leaving us— Yes? Yes. But we'll go on." Aimery rode boldly forward, seemingly affected neither by the noise nor the smells. Hauberin and Alliar exchanged rueful glances and followed, trying not to breathe too deeply.

"Powers above," the prince murmured in his native tongue as they passed a well right in the middle of everything. He hoped the human wine would be drinkable, because he certainly wasn't going to drink any of that water!

And had his mother, his clean, quiet mother, really grown up amid all this? "I suppose the baron's actual living quarters lie within this second ring of walls?" the prince asked. *"And I trust they'll be more . . . civilized,"* he added silently to Alliar, who gave him a wry shrug.

Aimery missed it. "Yes, my lord, within the Inner Ward."

"What," murmured the being, "not another armed gateway?"

"And another portcullis as well." Fighting a growing urge to turn and run like an animal in a trap about to close, Hauberin forced himself to consider these new defenses with a critical eye. The walls and towers were even more massive than those of the outer ring, and the prince nodded grim approval. "Even should your baron fail to defend the Outer Ward, he would still have a fair chance of holding the Inner."

"Yes, my lord," Aimery said dutifully as they rode under the portcullis and into a new courtyard. There was not one sign of green life here, only a sweep of stone cobblestones, a jumble of stone outbuildings, and a large, square-sided stone building, several stories high, facing them across the yard. At least, though, the yard was reasonably clean and empty, with only a few servants going their silent way. It was also blessedly quiet by comparison with what Hauberin had already seen. But as Aimery reined up at the inner edge of the massive gateway, the prince frowned, once more uncomfortably aware of watchful eyes upon him.

"Now what?"

"Now I formally announce your presence, my lords." Aimery stopped, regarding the prince in dismay. "I'm sorry, Your Grace," he whispered. "I don't know what to call you."

"My name: Hauberin."

To his surprise, the boy drew back, eyes astonished. "Not *the* Auberon?" he asked in a voice that quavered.

"Hauberin," the prince corrected, enunciating precisely.

"Oh. Of course." Aimery reddened. "T-That other is supposed to be the King of Fairyland." His blush deepened. "But you'd know more about that than I."

Hauberin shrugged. Auberon wasn't the name of either the High King or Queen, but he certainly wasn't going to mention their correct use-names to a human.

Aimery was quick to recover his composure, if not quite his normal color. "Were you come here alone, without one of us squires escorting you, someone would have sounded a trumpet from one of the towers. But since you're with me . . . See, here's the gong to call someone to meet us."

The boy stood in the stirrups, one-legged, protecting his ankle, and struck the gong a heroic blow. The heavy metallic clang rang painfully on keen Faerie ears, and both Hauberin and Alliar winced. Aimery looked at them in dismay.

"Did—did the sound of iron hurt you, Your Grace?"

"Not exactly. And it's not 'Your Grace,' remember, just 'my lord.' Here comes someone."

"That's . . . mm . . . Bertran. One of my fellow squires."

The newcomer was dark-haired and taller by half a head than the stocky Aimery, more lean and gangling of build, the boy's senior by a year or so. He stared. "Aimery! What in God's name happened to you? And why . . ."

His voice trailed into silence at Aimery's frantic little hand gestures. Bertran tensed at the sight of the two strangers. For a second, surprise danced in his eyes at the sight of Hauberin's exotic features. Then a mask of formal, well-schooled politeness fell into place. Bertran bowed.

"God give you good day, my lords." Rules of human (at least, noble human) etiquette were presumably keeping the squire from asking questions; if they had come with Aimery, obviously they couldn't be enemies. "May I bid you welcome? And will it please you to follow me?"

Their horses' hoofs clattered against the smooth, well-swept cobblestones. *"At least it's cleaner here,"* Alliar commented. *"And the folk look more orderly."*

"Servants of a higher order," Hauberin said. *"See how many of them are wearing the baron's livery."* "Aimery? What's this great hall of a building we're approaching?"

Aimery grinned daringly. "Why, just that, my lord: the Great Hall. And above it, my Lord Baron's private and guest chambers."

"My lords?" Bertran wasn't approving of his fellow squire's levity. "Will it please you to dismount?"

"It will." Hauberin, amused, sprang lithely down, followed by Alliar, who turned to see if Aimery needed help. But the boy managed skillfully enough, though once down, he had to gesture desperately to Bertran for aid. As servants led the horses away, Hauberin's sharp ears caught the two squires' whisperings:

"Your leg, too?"

"Wrenched my ankle, that's all. Bertran, hurry! Believe me, these are hardly folk to be left standing here for long."

The urgency in Aimery's voice made Bertran's eyes widen. "But .. Ah ..." He bowed to Hauberin and Alliar once more, clearly stalling for time while he marshalled his thoughts. "May I," he said at last, "take the liberty of greeting you in my Lord Baron's name in his absence?"

"What's this?" Aimery's voice was sharp. "The baron's away?"

"For the day only." Bertran had regained his self-control; the boy would make a disgustingly self-possessed adult some day. "Baron Gilbert has gone a-hunting, my lords, he and his lady wife and many of their retainers."

"Well and good," interrupted Aimery again, "but who's to formally welcome these lords?"

Bertran frowned at him, annoyed. "Do you think the

inner gates would have been left open if none of the baron's family were home?"

"Oh."

"These gentles," he bowed to Hauberin and Alliar yet again, "will be formally welcomed by my Lord Baron's brother, of course."

"Of course," echoed a smooth voice from the doorway of the Great Hall. Both squires whirled, Bertran just barely keeping Aimery from going sprawling, and bowed deeply, giving Hauberin and Alliar a clear view of the newcomer.

And the prince felt the shocked touch of Alliar's mind against his: *"That's the man who nearly ran us down in the forest! That's the man who tried to kill us!"*

The young man was handsome enough, Hauberin thought sourly, well-made in form and clean-featured face, his dark gold hair and beard neatly trimmed, his height more apparent now that he was afoot. The prince, who hadn't moved a muscle for all Alliar's silent outrage, smiled thinly.

"Whatever happened in the forest, Li, this . . . Raimond is now our host." The exquisite irony of it tickled his Faerie sense of humor. *"And we will be polite."*

"As you will it, my Prince." The emotion behind the thought was anything but polite. *"Eh, but look at him, standing there so arrogantly."*

"Arrogance can be corrected. This is not the place for it." Hauberin was very well aware of the castle folk all watching them. His set smile didn't waver. *"We will be polite."*

But the human's attention wasn't truly on him, not yet. "Aimery! What is the meaning of this?"

"My—my lord?"

"What happened to you?"

"I—"

"I thought I could trust you to return in good speed and in good order! How dare you appear before me late—and in such disarray?"

The boy stared, plainly too taken aback by the unexpected

attack to defend himself. *It's not my affair,* Hauberin told himself, *it's really not my affair.* But he found himself interjecting, "Aimery is hardly to blame for his appearance. He was attacked by bandits in the forest, and very narrowly escaped with his life."

Hot brown eyes flashed to him. Hauberin could practically hear the thought behind them: Who's this? A threat? "And how would you know that?"

What, no words of courtesy? "I was there," Hauberin said flatly.

"Oh, my lord, he saved my life! He—"

"I have not given you leave to speak, squire." Tall Sir Raimond moved one sly step forward, just enough to force the prince to look up at him. But Hauberin was well used to looking up at taller folk; Hauberin was not impressed.

"As you can see, Sir Raimond, the boy is injured. Give him leave to retire if you won't let him speak."

"So now! You give orders freely for a stranger."

Why, Chaos take you, you insolent . . . "No order. Merely a suggestion."

Behind those words glimmered the subtlest of persuasion-spells, reaching gently out to ensnare—

Nothing!

But that was impossible, the man was human, no sorcerer, he couldn't be blocking—

Off guard in his astonishment, the prince heard himself finishing, "A better idea by far than abandoning a boy placed in your charge."

Damn! He hadn't meant to say that. And oh, the delighted buzzing from their audience.

"Polite?" came Alliar's wry comment as the human's eyes blazed up in fury. "This boy, as you call him, is a full squire. And if he cannot defend himself, why then, he has no right to that rank!"

He locked glances with Hauberin, plainly intending to put this insolent stranger in his place. But the cold, alien anger glinting in those slanting black eyes would have shaken any human. The young man turned away, not without a muttered, "You go too far—"

The sudden blare of trumpets cut into whatever else he might have said. Sir Raimond froze. "The hunting party. You are my brother's guest, not mine."

With that, he whirled with a melodramatic snap of cloak, and vanished back into the Great Hall, followed by a small swarm of worried, excited retainers.

"Why, what a spoiled child it is!" Hauberin murmured. And just then his smile held nothing at all of humanity.

Aimery was staring at him in horror. "Oh, my lord, please forgive him, he's s-so quick to anger sometimes, but he means nothing by it. He doesn't know who you are, he didn't mean . . ."

The prince glanced at Bertran, who was wild-eyed with confusion, bewildered by his fellow squire's panic, wondering just how powerful these strangers might be. And there was still that fascinated audience of castle folk, delighted at the chance of watching their betters' quarrel.

Your entertainment is over, Hauberin told them silently. "No, Aimery. The man is in no danger from me. Yet," he added softly. The prince turned at a wild clamor of voices and hoofbeats against stone and dogs whining and yelping till his head rang. "Here, I would think, comes your baron."

Ae, what a confused tangle! Servants hurried here and there, holding bridles or stirrups or running off on mysterious errands. The richly dressed hunting party dismounted, laughing, the men in their tunics and hose and swinging cloaks slapping dust off their clothing, the women in their long, full gowns—wide enough to drape decorously over both legs as they rode, like their men, astride—slipping to the ground so neatly they showed not the faintest hint of ankle, men and women both butterfly-bright in reds, blues, yellows. The cheerful hounds, tails wagging, panting, intrigued by the alien scents of Hauberin and Alliar (or non-scents, in the wind spirit's case) swirled about in parti-colored canine circles, yapping, thrusting cold noses into Hauberin's hands, darting off,

getting underfoot and sworn at by the humans till taken
in hand at last by their keepers.

The prince drew back, overwhelmed by the noise, the
sheer number of lives, the new assault on his psychic
senses, and met by chance the deep brown eyes of the
man who, judging from the aura of matter-of-fact power
surrounding him, must surely be Baron Gilbert himself.

A boy in livery—Denis, presumably, the third squire—
leaped from his own horse to hold his lord's stirrup. The
man dismounted with practiced ease, still studying Hauberin with those somber, humorless eyes. No longer
young, this baron; there were no drastic signs of human
aging as there had been with the innkeeper, but the dark
gold of hair and beard that seemed to be a baronial
family trait was faded and streaked with gray. And there
was a certain . . . brittleness about the man that reminded
Hauberin of the ancient Faerie sage, Sharailan. The
baron was as tall at least as his hot-tempered younger
brother (Hauberin couldn't resist a plaintive: *Is every
adult I meet in this Realm going to be tall?*), but with a
hundred times the cool self-control evident in every
proud line of him.

Too much self-control, perhaps?

"A man who doesn't laugh very often," Alliar summarized neatly. *"Now, what? Does their custom demand we
speak first, or must we wait for him?"*

Hauberin hadn't the faintest idea. But Aimery was
already limping determinedly forward, leaning on Bertran's arm, to bow before his lord, who was staring at
him in astonishment.

"Aimery! God's name, lad, are you all right?"

At least someone cared about the boy's well-being!

"Yes, my lord," Aimery said quickly. "A broken arm,
a wrenched ankle, nothing worse. (*"'Nothing worse,'"*
mimicked Hauberin. *"The little hero!"* and felt Alliar's
silent laugh.) "I was set upon by bandits in the forest."

"Bandits," the baron muttered. "My Lord Thibault
sends all his sweepings to us. We shall need to do some

serious hunting by and by! But how is it that you escaped?"

"That's due to these two gentles." Aimery gave them a smile radiant with hero worship. "They saved my life."

The baron regarded Hauberin and Alliar with new interest. "My gratitude, my lords. It would have been a sorrowful thing had the good squire been slain."

"Indeed." Hauberin was bemused by the calm, precise voice. *If someone told the man his castle was burning, he'd probably just murmur, "A pity."*

"Aimery," the baron said, "go to your quarters. You may join us in the Great Hall after, but you are excused from waiting at table. Bertran, go with him; I see he needs your help." The man turned back to his unexpected guests, inclining his head a polite fraction. "Your pardon for this delay, my lords. My lady wife will see that you are rested and given clean clothing." A hint of curiosity was struggling to surface in the cool brown eyes, but the baron's smile was quite formal and proper. "In God's name," he said without any real warmth, "welcome."

X

GUESTS

Hauberin eyed the Baroness Matilde in some delight. At last: an adult human who wasn't so ridiculously tall! She was his own height, perhaps even a touch shorter, a lithe, slim young woman in quiet blue, her long braids wound about with so much ribbon he couldn't be sure of their color.

A handsome woman, too, at least to Faerie eyes. Despite the ruddy skin that seemed a human characteristic (the result, no doubt, of living under that garish sun), her face was nicely high of cheekbone, with an intriguing slant to those intelligent dark eyes, though for all he knew, human standards of beauty were different enough to find her too exotic to be attractive.

But . . . odd. After her first open glance at him, honest curiosity in her eyes, the baroness had looked hastily away, never quite meeting his gaze again, almost as though he somehow frightened her, or at least made her uneasy. Puzzled, the prince sent out a delicate mind-touch, but met nothing save the blank wall of the totally magickless.

"Welcome in my husband's name," the woman said, and there was the warmth of courtesy, if nothing more, in her voice. "Forgive me. I must go now to oversee the dinner." Hauberin thought the glimpse of weary harassment that flickered in her eyes was genuine; the lady of the household, if he remembered his mother correctly, was in charge of every aspect of castle life. "My ladies and servants will see to your comfort."

With that, the baroness fled.

*   *   *

"I don't understand it," Alliar said plaintively in the Faerie tongue. "We've been bathed—"

"Our feet, at least."

"—and fussed over and pampered by those pretty little servants—"

"Ladies, Li. The baroness' ladies-in-waiting."

They hadn't made too much of an impression on him, other than a faint, easily ignored sensual stirring at their blatant flirtations; Hauberin preferred intelligence to bland prettiness and vapid giggling. Besides, he didn't find their round eyes and silly little human shells of ears particularly appealing.

But he had quite liked what little he'd seen of the Baroness Matilde. A pity she was so unnerved by strangers. And human. And, for that matter, married; Hauberin had never considered adultery a sport.

Ach, stupid. This ridiculous quest was taking long enough as it was. He had no intention of endangering it with any human complications.

"Ah, my Prince . . . ?"

"Oh. Sorry, Li. You were saying?"

"Only that I think some of those ladies had more than a polite interest in you."

Hauberin laughed. "And in you, my so apparently human friend."

Alliar shot him a look of sheer, stunned disbelief. "You mean . . . for those . . . gendered sports?"

"Exactly."

"Ae." The being grinned ruefully. "The poor things are in for a sad surprise if they think they could—I could— There's a limit to what I can imitate, after all! But what I started to say was: with all the attention that's been showered on us, no one has so much as asked our business here. Now we're about to sit down to dine with the baron—and he doesn't even know our names! Oh, my Prince, I don't understand your humans at all. Don't they have any curiosity?"

"Curiosity has nothing to do with it, Li. Don't you

remember what Aimery told us earlier? Noble manners forbid the asking of questions before guests have had a chance to refresh themselves. After dinner, we'll probably face more questions than we can answer. I just wish I knew what story our Aimery has concocted."

"Indeed." Alliar eyed Hauberin's small harp in dismay. "You don't expect us to sing for our suppers?"

Hauberin grinned. "Hardly. I only thought music might make a pleasant thank you gift for this hospitality." The prince glanced down at himself. The deep red, ankle-length, richly embroidered tunic seemed proper enough (it had better be; he was rapidly running out of changes of clothing), particularly after he had added to it a simple coronet of Faerie silver and an intricate silver neck-chain of dwarven craft. "Well? Do I look convincingly human?"

"Convincingly, if a touch exotically." Alliar glanced at him in sudden sympathy. "You're nervous all over again, aren't you, my friend?"

Hauberin sighed. "Nervous. And impatient. And eager to be done with this charade." Switching to the human tongue, he added, "Come, my friend. The Great Hall awaits."

As they entered the Hall, Hauberin froze, stunned by a combination of smell—smoke, cooking, and too many not too clean humans—and a wall of noise so thick it was nearly tangible.

Can I possibly get away with saying, "Thank you, I'll eat in my room"?

But of course there wasn't any such easy way out, so Hauberin, feeling the equally shocked Alliar gritting mental teeth beside him, marched forward with desperate regal courage. They were seated at the linen-covered High Table on its dais, as guests of obvious—if still unspecified—rank. The steward must have noted Alliar's subtle deference to the prince, because he gave Hauberin the place of honor to the right of Baron Gilbert, who sat straight-backed and dignified in his canopied chair.

To the baron's left was the Baroness Matilde, of whom all Hauberin could see without rudely leaning around his host, was a hint of that high-cheekboned face framed by braids so thickly wound with metallic thread he still had no idea of their color. But seeing her beside her husband for the first time, the prince realized with a small shock just how young she was, possibly his own age or even less. These weren't his own Faerie folk, to whom the concept of time was all but meaningless; he couldn't help but wonder at seeing human youth wed to age, even if the baroness' mien was every bit as sober as her husband's.

But then, married to that grave, proper man, with such a gap of mortal years between them, how could she be anything but weighed down by his sobriety. Odd, odd, that she should have chosen such a mate. . . .

It wasn't his business, Hauberin reminded himself.

To the baroness' left sat her brother-in-law, the silently brooding Raimond, and Hauberin frowned slightly. Matters between them had hardly been improved by their formal introduction. When the baron had learned how they'd already met, he had subjected his furious younger brother to a lecture on courtesy all the more painful for its lack of temper.

And in front of everyone, as well. Hardly tactful. Hardly a way to ensure brotherly love, either.

"My Prince? Our Raimond's not at all happy about your occupying his rightful place, is he?"

"He's not happy about anything to do with me."

Hauberin grinned, enjoying what he admitted was a petty satisfaction. But the baron's cousin, Lisette, very young, very pretty, and very, very shy, sat between him and Alliar, and the prince quickly softened his grin to a polite smile, and received the faintest smile and small dip of the head in return. The lady, it seemed, wasn't much of a conversationalist.

Hauberin turned to look about the vastness of the hall again, trying in vain to inure himself to the noise and smell. The windows, set high in the thick walls, were little more than the usual arrow-slits, but the wide fire-place and many torches fought off some of the stone building's chill and provided, along with clouds of smoke, more than enough light for even human eyes—and there were a good many human eyes in that hall. All the folk of the castle seemed to be crowded in there, seated at trestle tables (easily assembled, easily removed), gossip-ing and joking and calling to each other, and the prince hastily raised a psychic mind-wall in self-defense, won-dering how long it would be before his mental strength gave way.

He was not at all happy with the way the humans kept staring at him. *As though I were some bizarre creature in a cage.*

Eh, but wait . . . he had suddenly sensed—vaguely, through his protective barriers—a most curious aura. Hauberin looked over the throng more slowly, hunting. . . . There: The tantalizing emanations seemed to be coming from that dark-robed little man at the back of the hall.

Well now, a human magician!

A petty one. One without even enough Power to react to Hauberin's presence. A conjurer, nothing more, proba-bly here to entertain the nobles. It might prove amusing to see his tricks, the prince decided, and dismissed him.

Denis and Bertran were serving those at the High Table (an odd custom, to turn nobly born youngsters into servants), but the temporarily disabled Aimery was seated at a table just below the baronial dais. Hauberin watched him a moment, then chuckled.

"I see our Aimery has already found himself a young lady to fuss over him," he murmured to Lisette.

"Of course, my lord," Her pretty blue eyes were wide and innocent. "Even a page must have a lady to revere."

"And to revere him, eh? Have you a lad, then?"

How the girl was blushing! "My lord, I am betrothed."

"What, a child like you?"

"I am fifteen, my lord. Next spring I shall be a wedded wife."

Powers, they wed young in this land! Hauberin bowed from the waist. "I stand corrected."

Lisette seemed to shrink into herself. "I m-meant no offense, my lord."

"None taken, my lady." Studying her, he had to smile. "And you're looking forward to next spring, aren't you?"

"Yes, my lord," she murmured so softly that even Faerie ears had to strain, blushing an even deeper pink. Lisette looked in confusion down at the table before her, and would say no more. Hauberin honored her embarrassment and glanced instead down the white linen length of the High Table.

No forks, of course. He hadn't expected any; he could remember his mother describing her surprise at the Faerie folk's use of such "effete and luxurious" tools. Well, the lack of forks wasn't a true handicap, not if one's hands were clean and one was a neat feeder. There weren't any plates either, save for thick and presumably impervious slabs of hard bread. The rest of the setting was elegant enough: heavy linen napkins and wrought silver drinking cups; the baron was making a good showing for his guests. The floor was thickly covered with rushes—Hauberin had expected that, too, from his mother's tales—and if they weren't exactly fresh, at least some considerate servant had strewn the area about the High Table with armfuls of fresh flowers and herbs, which mercifully masked unpleasant aromas. Hauberin grimly shut his mind to thoughts of what might be living in the layers underneath, and turned his mind instead to finding an explanation of his presence.

Just in time. During the second course of venison, rabbit, and pork, the baron turned to Hauberin with his precise, formal smile, and asked, "You've come far, my lord Hauberin?"

Aimery, it seemed, had already spoken with the baron. "Far indeed," the prince agreed.

"From your words earlier, you would seem to have travelled up from the south. Would you chance to have news of Arle or Tramount?"

"Alas, my good lord," Hauberin said, "we've been wandering through so much forest of late . . . When I look back, all I seem to remember are branches and leaves and that dusty, dusty road." He smiled charmingly. "We are not, of course, used to foot-travel."

"Of course not. What did happen to your horses?"

The prince hesitated a moment, feigning discomfort. "We lost them," he said at last. Which was true enough, in a way.

"Humph. To bandits, you mean. No shame in that, my lord. Though if I might suggest that two young gentles not travel alone . . . ?"

"At the time, we saw no peril in it. Foolish, perhaps, but . . ."

"My lord, can you tell me anything about these bandits?"

"Only that they were vermin. They gave no sign of being in someone's employ, if that's what you're asking, or of coming from this—this Baron Thibault." Faerie curiosity aroused, the prince asked, "My Lord Baron, who is he?"

The cold eyes glittered. "A treacherous man. A sly, treacherous man who holds the lands on the eastern border of my own only through the mercy of good Duke Alain, our liege lord. Bah! He holds them despite Touranne."

That name again. "Ah, Touranne?"

Baron Gilbert glanced at him in surprise. "Ah, of course," the man said after a tiny pause. "How could a stranger possibly know?" He hesitated a moment more, as though mentally summarizing a familiar story, then began, "In brief, the old Duke Blaise has been dead these two years and more." The man paused to piously cross himself, a flicker of surprise in his eyes when Hauberin didn't follow suit. "Alas, he left no legitimate sons. Only Rogier. His bastard."

Hauberin blinked. "I'm sorry. The word escapes me."

"Bastard? An . . . ah . . . unnatural child."

Feeling hopelessly lost in human illogic, the prince protested, "How can a child be unnatural?"

"What my lord husband means," Baroness Matilde murmured tactfully, leaning forward, "is that the son was not born to his wife."

Her lord husband did not approve of her interruption. At his stern glare, she shrank back with the smallest of sighs. Hauberin shook his head.

"I still don't understand. Wouldn't this Rogier, being his father's son, still be the heir?"

Baron Gilbert looked at him in horror. "No, my lord! A bastard cannot inherit. The old Duke had quite properly designated his young cousin as heir."

"Rogier, I take it, disagreed?"

"Indeed. Matters were settled at Touranne, just outside the city walls, right at the river's edge. The bastard's forces were defeated, and Duke Alain was triumphant."

Raimond supported Rogier! Hauberin realized suddenly. *Of course. That explains why he's still in disgrace.* "What happened to Rogier?"

"Though his body was never recovered—the river is deep and swift—there's no doubt he died; I, myself, witnessed him tumbling into the water after he'd received a terrible blow to the head."

Hauberin was intrigued by this glimpse into human politics. "And Baron Thibault was backing Rogier?"

He had obviously struck a sore point. "Oh no!" Baron Gilbert said drily. "The turncoat promised himself to both sides, then held back his men from the fighting till he knew for sure which would be the winning side. And didn't he play the loyal vassal at Duke Alain's feet!" The baron broke off abruptly. "But that is the past." His smile was a polite thing. "Young Aimery came to us after his first lord was slain at Touranne, when the lad was yet a page."

"So he told me."

"Yes. The good squire is easy with his words. My lord, Aimery has told me an intriguing tale."

It almost caught Hauberin off guard. "Has he?"

"The squire said you are under an oath not to reveal your true rank or native land. Nor, in fact, to reveal anything of yourself save your name and the fact that you are on a quest." The brown eyes were cool, neither believing nor disbelieving, for all that there was a fierce little flickering of curiosity deep within them. It seemed that, just as Aimery had promised, the baron did enjoy a mystery. "But Aimery has sworn to me you are of high rank, indeed."

"Yes." Hauberin evasively let the one word answer all. "My Lord Baron, I would truly prefer not to discuss my reasons for being in this land. But those reasons have nothing of dishonor about them, nor of danger to you or your Realm, my word and will upon it."

Did that sound convincing enough? Or should he try to back up his words a touch? The simple persuasion-spell had worked well enough so far (save, of course, on Raimond . . .). It was difficult for Hauberin to focus his will with all the countless janglings of human auras crowding in about him, so he tried nothing more than the gentlest enhancement of his words: *nothing of dishonor, nor of danger . . .* And, to his relief, there was no resistance; the baron smiled his formal little smile and relaxed in his canopied chair.

But . . . why had the baroness tensed suddenly? For an instant, Hauberin could almost have sworn she'd sensed— Ridiculous. If ever he had met a human with no feel for magic, it was she.

Nerves, the prince decided.

Now that the third and final course of marzipan and fruit had been served, it was time for an entertainer. Hauberin, who had been expecting the conjurer, watched a minstrel step forward instead, carrying a stringed instrument (after a moment, Hauberin put a name to it: a lute). The prince smiled, putting thoughts of magic from his mind for the moment, and leaned forward slightly in anticipation.

His pleasure faded after the first note. For one thing, the clamor from the people at the lower tables continued

undiminished. For another, the minstrel's voice was . . .
adequate. Worst of all, his lute was ever so slightly mis-
tuned. Maybe these humans couldn't notice it, but the
slight wrongness was exquisitely painful to Faerie ears.

"*Doesn't he hear?*" came Alliar's plaintive cry. "*Doesn't
he realize?*"

Hauberin grit his teeth, waiting. "*He's only human. He
has to finish eventually.*"

Wonderful. The man was finally coming to the end of
that seemingly interminable ballad. He . . . wasn't going
to sing again, was he?

No. Powers be praised, he was being dutifully
rewarded by the emotionless baron, and returning to a
place at the lower tables. Hauberin overheard Baron Gilbert mutter to his wife, "That was your idea, my dear,"
and turned sharply to his host, determined to wipe out
the insult to the name of music.

"My lord, my lady, now *I* will sing for you."

It sounded, he thought wryly, more like a royal command than a courtesy. Aware of the humans staring, the
prince shouldered his harp and strode boldly forward to
the chair a serving man hastily brought for him. With a
quick, sharp glance at the offending minstrel, Hauberin
tuned his harp with care, running his hands experimentally over the strings, picking out a few random chords,
aware of the clamor slowly dying about him. While noble
musicians, he knew, weren't unknown, these castle folk
plainly weren't used to having someone of rank perform.
Particularly someone with such an aura of mystery surrounding him.

So now, he told them silently, *if you stir so much as
a finger till I'm done, then I've been in this Realm too
long.*

He sang the tale of Thiuran and Elenfal, which his
mother had translated into the human tongue one Faerie
winter long past. And from the plaintive opening chords
marking the first meeting of the tragic lovers, there was
heavy silence within the Hall. Hauberin smiled faintly,
glancing slyly at his audience, seeing noble and common

alike held like so many wide-eyed children by the keen, alien, magical beauty of his song. Only the Baroness Matilde showed more than passive wonder. Her young face was so filled with joy and a desperate, aching hunger that it was nearly painful to watch.

The tale sang its way to the inevitable tragic end, to Elenfal's bittersweet farewell to life and her collapse at the side of the treacherously magic-slain Thiuran. Hauberin looked up from the harp to silence and not a few tears from his audience. Ha, even surly Sir Raimond was suspiciously red of face! Wryly amused, the prince returned to his place, Alliar's congratulations warm in his mind.

"Was that a tale from your native land, my lord?"

"Yes, my Lord Baron." Hauberin saw the baroness lean forward ever so slightly at that, studying him with so wondering an eye that he almost raised a hand to be sure his hair still covered the telltale ears.

"Beautifully sung," the baron said shortly. "Beautifully sung."

That was high praise from that unemotional man. Hauberin laughed lightly, bowing from the waist. "Thank you, my lord. And since my song has pleased you, I shall ask for my reward. Oh no, my lord," he added hastily, seeing the baron's eyebrows shoot up in astonishment, "I didn't mean in coin! You see," the prince continued, picking his words with care, "I know little of the tales of this land. Since I've given you one from mine, I think a fitting exchange would be a tale from yours."

That actually struck a small spark of humor in those sober eyes. "To select only one . . ."

"I've heard an intriguing hint of one." Hauberin's casual tone sounded incredibly forced to him. "I would like to learn the whole of it, if possible. It concerns a witch-woman. A noble woman."

The baron tensed, almost imperceptibly. "Her name?"

"Melusine."

Oh, he wasn't at all prepared for the reaction: the wave of shock, almost terror, from the baroness, the swirling of hatred and disgust from the baron, the sudden rigid wall of denial. As Hauberin stared, feeling Alliar's mind touch his in bewilderment, Baron Gilbert said, "I fear I must disappoint you."

"I—I don't understand. Have I somehow offended—"

"No, no, nothing like that." The man smiled faintly, but his eyes were chill. "It's only that—we know of no such tale. I'm sorry, my lord, We know of no such woman."

XI

REVELATIONS

Baron Gilbert, as was his wont, had retired early, soon after sunset and an evening prayer, and now slept soundly in the baronial featherbed. Beside him, forgotten, lay his young wife, wide awake and painfully alone.

After a fruitless time of trying to compose her mind to sleep, Matilde glanced at her husband. He was sleeping on his back, face perfectly composed even in slumber, arms perfectly straight at his sides. And for a moment she battled a wicked urge to slap him, scream at him, do anything that would break that cool perfection. God help her, the man didn't even snore!

Matilde sighed silently and turned away. What right had she to complain? Secure in her husband's castle, she never lacked for food or drink or any of the comforts of life. And what if that husband was nearly twice her age? Everyone knew a girl must be wed to an older man to steady her.

Steady me. As though I was nothing more than a mare, or maybe a hawk being broken to slavery—

No. That wasn't fair. Baron Gilbert might not be the hero from a minstrel's romance, but he had always been kind to her in his own remote way. He had never once beat her, never even raised a hand to her, never condemned her openly for having failed after these four years of marriage to give him an heir. (Was that it all her fault, though? Most men the baron's age had sired a bastard or two, yet he had none. Surely a son could only be made from passion, not some impassive sense of duty.) But then, he had Raimond for an heir.

Poor, spoiled, frustrated Raimond. Raimond who, Matilde didn't doubt, must throughly hate his precise, unforgiving brother by now.

It was difficult living up to perfection.

Matilde stirred restlessly. Dear God, what was wrong with her tonight? Why couldn't she be content? Why must she feel this secret aching for ... Ah, she didn't even know what she wanted.

Freedom?

Nonsense. She was a woman of nearly three-and-twenty, not some callow little girl; as her husband was always lecturing her, life couldn't be all song and light and laughter. Besides, what was freedom to a noblewoman? If she ran away to live her own life, she would end up dying of starvation, exposure, or worse. Matilde was only too aware her training was limited to what a woman of her rank might need to oversee a castle's affairs: she couldn't do anything truly practical in the outside world, not cook, nor clean, nor (God help her) play the strumpet. And for all her husband's riches she had no wealth of her own; the king and his court, so far away in Paris, had ruled that a noblewoman legally owned nothing, not even the clothes she wore.

Enough of this, Matilde scolded herself. The good Lord knew many a poor woman would envy her position. This ridiculous discontent she felt could only have been roused by their so-exotic guest, with his hint of mystery, his foreign face and ways, his music—

His music. Remembering, Matilde frantically stifled an unexpected sob. Oh, dear God! The achingly pure beauty of that music had cut like a sword, joy so sharp it was very close to pain. She had almost called out to him to stop. And yet every note had fallen like rain on a parched plain, feeding a deep inner hunger she'd never known was there. Listening, she could have wept, knowing that soon the music would be gone, but the desert remain.

Matilde shivered suddenly, and pulled the bedclothes

more closely about herself. Who was he, this . . . Hauberin? There was an air of wildness to him, of careless, perilous power, enticing and terrifying, almost reminding her of—

No! Wide-eyed, heart pounding, Matilde struggled with the forbidden, terrible memories that all at once were fighting to surface. She would not remember! She must not!

Why did you come here? Matilde cried out to the stranger in silent despair. *Curse you, oh curse you, why have you upset my life?*

"But I don't need a body-servant!" Hauberin was in no mood for diplomacy. "I don't *want* a body-servant!"

"Of course, m'lord." The human was neither young nor old, short nor tall, ugly nor— Ach, Hugh was a perfect cipher of a man, and quite unflappable. "Here we are, m'lord."

The room was small and chill, and Hauberin thought it would definitely have benefited from a fireplace. But it looked comfortable enough in all else, even if the one window was—as usual—nothing more than an arrow-slit. The newly white-washed walls were prettily painted with flowers and leaves, and the large canopied bed was rich with furs and heavily embroidered curtains. There wasn't space for much else: a three-legged chair, a clothes chest of heavy wood, a little table in one corner with a small painting upon it (some manner of shrine?) and an unlit candle before the painting. . . .

"So!" Hauberin snapped. "And just where were you proposing to sleep?"

The servant looked at him in surprise, flinching a little from those angry, alien eyes. "Why, right here, m'lord. On this pallet right at the foot of the bed. So as if you need anything in the night, you can wake me."

"There's no stopping you, is there?"

"M'lord?" Hugh paused. "Is it *me* you don't want? Would you prefer some other servant?"

"What? Oh, no, no. Look you, it's nothing personal, but— You're here on the baron's orders, aren't you?"

"Why, yes, m'lord. Of course. Said it wasn't proper, a gentle like you being without a man-servant."

All this was being said while the human was neatly and efficiently unpacking the contents of Hauberin's pack. The prince sighed in surrender. Whether Baron Gilbert really was only being polite, or whether—more likely—he wanted someone to keep a watchful eye on this stranger with the awkward questions, there was no way to be rid of Hugh. Short of magic.

Hauberin told himself he should feel flattered; he *could* be sleeping on a pallet down in the Great Hall like almost everybody else, obnoxious thought! Fortunate that the baron wanted to show off to his visitors, offering Hauberin and Alliar each one of these precious new guest chambers.

"Alliar?"

"Ach, my Prince, I can't stay here!" The panic trembling in the thought was all unchecked by the intervening walls. *"This—this is like the prison cell, the sorcerer's cellar, the—"*

"Softly," Hauberin soothed. *"You need endure it for only a little, little while, only till the night-blind humans sleep. Then you may wander as you will."*

There was a pause. Then: *"Ah. Of course."* Relief mingled with embarrassment. *"I should have realized— Thank you."*

"Ah . . . m'lord?"

Hauberin started. "What is it, Hugh?"

"Will you be wanting anything else, m'lord?"

"No. Yes. Just tie those bed-curtains back all the way."

"But—m'lord, it isn't safe! Night air is dangerous!"

"Oh, come now. You're planning to sleep without being encased."

"But I'm—I mean, you're—"

"Enough!" Hauberin's frustrated anger flared up anew. "No, I do not need help in undressing. Yes, you've put everything away. Now, good night!"

He lay in darkness for a while, trying to forget the nagging intrusion of the human presence, trying to plot his next course of action for all that he was truly weary now. And despite the fact that some thoughtful servant—Hugh?—had warmed the bed in advance with a hot brick wrapped in cloth, he was shivering with an inner chill.

Although Hauberin had never encountered deliberate falsehood before, there wasn't the slightest doubt that the baron had been lying.

But why? What harm could Mother possibly have done to make him deny her very existence?

What if it hadn't been her fault? What if the memory of who and what her father had been was so very terrible—

No! This was as bad as his old childhood fears—and just about as useless.

Hauberin sighed. As soon as the castle was safely asleep, the prince would pay Baron Gilbert a visit. And no matter how difficult it might be to work true magic in this Realm, he would find a way to persuade the man's sleeping mind to tell him the truth.

But he couldn't do anything till Hugh slept. And, judging from the tension radiating from the man, that wasn't going to be for some time. Hauberin sighed again.

"Hugh."

"M'lord?"

"Look you, I . . . know you mean well."

"Please, m'lord." Hugh's tone was embarrassed. There was a long silence, then he added softly, "Heard you sing in the Hall."

"Ah?"

"It . . . isn't my place, and all, but I just wanted to say . . . it was beautiful, m'lord. Made me think of . . . oh, I don't know. Springtime, maybe. Moonlight."

"Did it?" Hauberin smiled into the darkness. "Good night, Hugh."

"M'lord?" The quelled tension swirled up anew.

"What now, Hugh?"

"Heard you talking to m'lord baron. M'lord, I . . . know something of the Lady Melusine."

"What!" Hauberin sat bolt upright.

"Ah . . . yes, m'lord. Please, you'll not be telling anyone, they don't like folk talking about her—"

"No, no, I won't tell anyone! Come, out with it!"

"Well, I don't know too much. But it seems she's an ancestor of the family, some three, four generations back. She's supposed to have been a witch." A rustling of the pallet indicated Hugh had probably just crossed himself. "And they say one night she was carried off by a d-devil in the shape of a tall, fair man."

My father! "Go on, Hugh! What else?"

"I'm sorry, m'lord. That's all I know." He added apologetically, "I told you, they don't like to talk about her."

"So you did. Thank you." Hauberin slid wearily back down onto the bed. An ancestor of the family. Powers above, that made Baron Gilbert his kinsman. All the more reason to pay the man a visit!

But he still couldn't act until Hugh was asleep. With the tension eased, that shouldn't take too long. . . .

Not long at all. . . .

All he had to do was wait. . . .

Once again he was walking down a chill, all too familiar corridor, further now than he had ever been. Once again he was forced to go on and on, sick with horror and his own helplessness. And soon he would have to see—

"No! Ae, no!"

"Wh-what? M'lord?"

Hauberin blinked, dazed, suddenly aware that he was clinging to the room's narrow window—though how he'd gotten there, he didn't know—as though he had been clawing for fresh air, shuddering with cold but drenched with perspiration.

"M'lord?" Hugh was sitting up on his pallet, staring. "Are you all right?"

The prince couldn't answer, the darkness still held him, he could feel nothing. . . .

After an uneasy moment, Hugh got to his feet, fumbling with flint and steel till he had gotten the oil lamp burning. "There, now. That's better. M'lord?"

"Yes," Hauberin gasped. "Yes, I'm here."

"It was only a dream, m'lord." The human shook his head. "Must have been one hell of one, begging your pardon."

"Ah, yes."

"Uh . . . m'lord? It's cold out here. Don't you think you'd better get back to bed before you take a chill?"

Hauberin agreed, glad to huddle under the warmth of the fur coverings. Hugh eyed him warily.

"Shall I . . . uh . . . leave the lamp burning, m'lord?"

"No. I'm well enough now. Truly. It was, as you say, only a dream. Go back to your own bed."

Still shivering, Hauberin waited in silence for the man to settle down, thinking, two nights of peace and now this! Oh, fool, to dare believe he was free!

But at last the dream's grue was forced away by anger at this stolid, nearly magickless Realm and the weariness it gave him, anger at himself for having yielded to it. Hauberin turned his head, listening. Hugh's breathing had slowed to a gentle snoring. Asleep again, no doubt of it.

The night, by the feel of it, was very late, somewhere near the dawn. At least, Hauberin thought darkly, Serein's timing had been off, allowing him a fair amount of sleep before the dream. And there was still some time in which to act.

Softly the prince got to his feet and dressed, making a good job of it since he doubted he would return to bed this night, softly stepped over Hugh, who never stirred, and left. He found himself standing on the edge of a narrow, curved stairway in darkness deep enough to tax even Faerie sight, but he was reluctant to start a light lest it attract suspicious guards.

Now to locate the baron's chambers. Thanks to Hugh's

solicitations, Hauberin hadn't been able to watch which
way the man had gone after leaving his guests. He was
fairly certain the baronial rooms weren't in this quarter,
but to be positive, touched a cautious hand to the chill
stones of the wall, relaxing his senses, and received scattered and confusing hints of practically everyone who had
recently passed this way. There wasn't much trace of
baron or baroness. Silently Hauberin descended, planning to return to the Great Hall and track his quarry
from there.

Wait ... the light up ahead might be muffled and
uncertain, but it was beacon-bright to his darkness-
adjusted eyes. Guards? No ... surely someone who
didn't want to be seen. A thief, perhaps. Or thieves, from
the sound of their careful whispers, two of them.

They were blocking his way. Hauberin stole carefully
forward, wondering if he could slip past the two cloak-
shrouded humans. . . . No. The hallway was too narrow.
The prince frowned. Could one of them be the baron?

It couldn't. The voice belonged to a younger man, and
the wisps of dark blond hair escaping the cloak's hood
were untouched by gray. Raimond, then. And his partner
was surely that little human sorcerer! Now, what mischief
might be here?

". . . but he mustn't be slain!" That was Raimond's
fierce hiss. "I don't want his blood on me."

"It won't be, my lord." The other voice was calm.

"But will it work?"

"Yes, my lord."

"Are you *sure*? If you fail, and he learns I'm behind
this— Can I trust you?"

"Well, that's for you to decide, my lord, isn't it?"

"Damn you, don't get bold with me! I'm paying you
good gold, and you'll not trick me or I'll turn you over
to the Church!"

"Oh, I don't think so, my lord. You don't want the holy
fathers"—mockery dripped from the words—"to know
you've been calling on the Dark Powers. Not even your
loving brother could save you then."

The frustrated fury blazing from Sir Raimond was daz-zlingly plain to the watching Hauberin, but the little sorcerer was unmoved. "My lord, we're wasting time. Anyone might stumble on us here. What you will shall be done, but I must have time."

"Time, time! All right, then: two days. No more."

"That should be sufficient." The sorcerer paused. "But, my lord . . ."

"What now?"

"Those strangers, in particular that small, dark young man . . ." For the first time, a touch of uncertainty quivered in the human's voice. "My lord, there's something about him . . . While he was singing, I sensed . . . I'm not sure what I sensed. My lord, watch him."

"Never fear." Raimond's voice was suddenly cool and quiet, tinged with such bitter hatred that Hauberin stared. "I shall see to him."

"My . . . lord?"

"No, man, don't touch me!" It was Raimond's normal, hot-tempered voice once more. "Just see that you do your part. Now, get back to the Hall before you're missed!"

As the two humans went their separate ways, Raimond passed so close to the shadow-hidden prince the folds of the dark cloak brushed against him. *And what was that all about?* Hauberin wondered. *Are you plotting against Duke Alain, or your brother? Either way, my dear Raimond, you'll "see to me" at your cost!*

But these dark human plots had nothing to do with him. The corridor was once again open, and Hauberin put the conspirators from his mind and started forward—

Only to stop short with a silent oath because here came footsteps behind him, and the wavering light of a torch.

"Following me, Hugh?"

"Sweet Jesu!" The human nearly dropped the torch. "I— M'lord, I didn't see you standing there in the dark!"

"And *were* you following me?"

"Well, I . . . uh . . . woke up and found you weren't in

your bed— Thought you'd gone to answer a call of nature
or something, and gotten lost."

The baron's creature, no doubt about it, keeping a
watchful eye on the stranger-guest. "I wasn't lost. Why
don't you go back to bed, Hugh?"

He was all set to focus more than a little will behind
the words, but— Ae, what now? Guards. A whole troop
of them, evidently the predawn patrol preparing to go
on duty, laughing and joking softly. A happy lot. And in
his frustration, Hauberin could have cheerfully blasted
the lot. He clearly wasn't going to reach Baron Gilbert
this night. But if not now, when? He would have no
excuse for lingering past the morning.

"It *is* nearly morning, isn't it?"

Hugh blinked at him. "Lacking less than an hour to
sunrise, I would guess, m'lord."

Sunrise. Ah, there was something. How could he stay
angry when there was such an alien wonder to come?

Hauberin accepted what he could of the situation.
"I've a whim to watch the sunrise. This stair will take
me to the ramparts?"

"Uh, yes, m'lord, but—"

"I shall go alone."

"But—"

"Alone."

He stared into Hugh's merely human eyes. And all at
once there was no argument at all.

It was cold and damp up here. He should have thought
to bring a cloak. The sky was heavy with the promise of
yet more rain—

Hauberin bit back a laugh. By all means, let it rain! A
downpour would give him a perfect excuse for lingering
here another day.

But the east was slowly brightening from gray into
color, and the prince forgot everything else to stand,
silent and wondering, at the ever-growing radiance. The
eastern clouds were blossoming, shell-pink, rose-pink,
carmine, gold—beautiful, so beautiful with the patches

of vibrant blue behind them! Ah, and the terrible, wonderful splendor of the rising sun! Helpless with awe, Hauberin gasped and nearly wept for beauty, and at the last turned away only because the fierce, brave light had grown too painful.

He wasn't alone. Tense, sun-dazzled, Hauberin blinked blindly at a vague, dark outline. "Alliar?" he said doubtfully.

"No, my lord."

A woman's voice . . . "Ah, my Lady Baroness. What, were you up here all this time?"

"Yes. I dared not speak. You . . . looked like a man seeing his first sunrise."

"Did I?"

"Please, don't be embarrassed. I often come up here at dawn myself. There's a—newness to the air then, a freedom." For an instant, staring out at the morning, she looked so young and fierce that Hauberin wondered. "At times," the woman continued, so softly it was almost only to herself, "I think there's more of God out here than behind all the cold chapel walls—"

She broke off, plainly shocked at herself, finishing lamely, "My lord husband tolerates my whims."

Hauberin wasn't interested in her lord husband just then. He was far too intrigued by that almost Faerie cast to her features, all the more clearly revealed in open sunlight. And what a pleasure for once not to have to stare up at someone! They really were almost exactly of a height; humans, he guessed, probably considered her short. Her braids were bright in the morning light, not yet masked by ribbons, and the prince exclaimed in sudden delight:

"You shouldn't hide your hair! It's lovely, like the very soul of flame."

"My hair," she said flatly, "is red."

"Why, what's the matter?"

"Please. Don't mock."

He stared amazed at the hurt in her eyes. "Believe me, I meant no mockery. Did I just overstep one of your customs?" When she hesitated, the prince continued with a touch of impatience, "Come now, I really don't understand."

"I don't know how it is in your land, but here everyone knows red hair is unlucky. Ugly. Sir Judas' hair, they say, was red."

Hauberin had no idea who this "Sir Judas" might be. But he knew the pain his so-different coloring and lack of height had caused him, and in sudden understanding said gently, "In my land, such hair is a wonder, the rarest and most precious of shades." An image of Ereledan flashed through his mind—yes, curse him, Ereledan's hair was the very same hue.

"Your people are all dark, then, my lord?"

"No. They're fair. Golden-haired. And tall."

"Oh. I know how that feels, being the odd one out, believe me." Her smile was a brief, lovely thing. "You miss your folk, though, don't you?"

Was it that obvious? Hauberin drew back slightly. "I have my reasons for being here."

The smile faded slightly. "And you've sworn an oath not to speak of them."

"Why, lady, you heard our good Aimery. Are you doubting him?"

"We both know Aimery's good-heartedness. And his gift for clever words."

The prince tensed ever so slightly. "I've sworn I mean no harm to any here. Are you doubting my word as well?"

"Oh, no." If she had heard the faint purr of warning in his voice, she chose to ignore it. "But you must admit, my lord, it does all sound like something out of a minstrel's romance."

"It does," Hauberin agreed, and left it at that. He met her stare, and saw the dark gaze drop.

"Forgive me," the woman said. "It's not my place to question what my lord husband has accepted." She glanced back over her shoulder as though expecting to find the baron waiting. "I shall be late to chapel. I must go."

"Ah, wait."

"My lord?"

"Why are you so ashamed of your kinswoman the Lady Melusine?"

"Oh, again!" Sharp terror flared up in her eyes. "Didn't you hear my husband? We don't know—"

"Forgive me, but you do."

The woman stared at him. "Why is it so important to you? A stranger, a foreigner— Why should it be so very important to you?"

How could he answer? Because the lady was my mother, long years before you were born. Because I am of Faerie, and there's a curse on me. "I . . . cannot say."

"Your oath again?" But she couldn't help but be aware of his very real distress. And at last the baroness sighed. "I do owe you a debt for that wondrous music last night."

"I wasn't looking for reward."

"I know that." She hesitated, as though all at once torn between laughter and tears. "You wouldn't understand. How could you, since song comes so easily to you? I . . . I can play the harp, somewhat, and sing, somewhat. So can little Lisette. But my husband has no ear for music at all, and so we seldom . . ." She turned aside, looking out into space. "Thank you, my lord." It was barely more than a murmur. "Your music was food and drink to a starving soul, and— Ah, I sound like a fool."

"No."

"As for telling you what you want to know . . . what harm can there possibly be in it?" She glanced nervously over her shoulder again. "But I can't speak now, not here."

"Where, then?"

The baroness smiled, a little too brightly: Two of her ladies had appeared, hunting their mistress. "I must go

now, to chapel, with my husband. Will it please you
to join us?" When Hauberin hesitated, unsure of her
meaning, the woman added, "The chapel is a quiet,
tranquil place. After mass, I might linger there alone
in the holy silence for a few moments."

She gave him a charming curtsey. He bowed, then
straightened slowly, watching her retreating back.

So be it, lady.

"Li?"

*"I'm here, my Prince, just outside the door. You . . .
don't want me to go in there, do you?"*

*"No. I wouldn't inflict that on you. Just stand watch.
The last thing I want is to be surprised by a suspicious
human."*

Hauberin glanced about at the chapel. Its ceiling was
high and arched, its walls richly painted with scenes
that meant little to him. And it reeked of hatred for
any such as the Faerie kind, sharp as the scent of iron.
The prince winced at the tormented wooden figure on
its cross, fighting down a fit of coughing from the not
quite dissipated swirlings of incense, his spirit bur-
dened by the weight of humorless human piety.

"My lord." The baroness was standing half in
shadow, half in candlelight, nervous as a cat.

"Don't be afraid," the prince told her. "I won't hurt
you. And I'm not planning to use"—with a wry glance
about the chapel—"the . . . ah . . . Black Arts."

"God's mercy, I should hope not!" She licked dry
lips. "We have only a few moments. What would you
know?"

"Whatever you can tell me." He hesitated. "I already
know the Lady Melusine was called a witch."

"She *was* a witch. At least, she had . . . certain
powers."

"You couldn't have met her."

"Oh, no, that was some three generations back!
Besides, the lady vanished while she was still a young
woman." She added with a defiant flash of dark eyes,

"But I've never heard she used her powers for ill. I can't believe it was a devil that carried her off, either."

"It wasn't," Hauberin muttered, and the woman stared at him.

"How could you—"

"Lady, please." The lack of free air was beginning to wear at his patience. "What of her parents? That's what I really want to know."

She drew back, alarmed by his intensity. "I can only tell you of her mother, the Baroness Alianor, wife to Baron Gautier, who built the first stone keep on this site."

Hauberin sighed. Pleasant though it might have been under other circumstances to hear about his grandmother, this was hardly the information he needed. "I already know the Lady Melusine wasn't the baron's child." He fought to keep his voice level. "Who was her father?"

"I don't know."

"Impossible!"

"I'm not lying, my lord!"

"Ah, I'm sorry. I must sound like a madman to you. But believe me, I'm not insane."

"No," she murmured. "But what you may be, my lord, I'm not sure."

"Lady . . ."

"All right. Baroness Alianor bore her husband two fine children, fair-haired like their father, a son first, from whom my lord husband is descended, then a daughter, my great-grandmother. You didn't know my husband and I are related? We're cousins. Oh yes," she added sourly, "we received proper dispensation for our marriage, you needn't look at me like that."

Hauberin, who hadn't the vaguest idea what she meant, nodded politely. "Of course you did. Please, go on."

"Baron Gautier, like so many other nobles, left for the Holy Land on crusade. He never returned." The baroness hesitated. "Some months after news of her husband's death reached her, Baroness Alianor was said to have been visited by a strange darkness. Some said it was a devil, some called it a pagan spirit the baron had roused in his travels. There was talk linking the baroness with witchcraft, but she was of high enough rank for it to come to naught." Matilde swallowed. "And then, well over a year after the baron's death, Baroness Alianor bore a child, a girl, small, dark and wild, they say, as any changeling."

She paused again, so obviously unhappy that the rest of the tale could only be tragic. Yet Hauberin had to prod, "Please, continue."

"There . . . isn't much more. The baroness . . . died not long after. Her brother was a strict, stern man. He . . ."

"Slew her?"

"There . . . are always rumors. She died. Her daughter was raised as a noblewoman, of course, but must have had a harsh time of it, poor thing, always being reminded of her shameful birth, always . . . different, even before her—powers developed."

Hauberin winced. No wonder his mother had refused to discuss her childhood! And no wonder she'd been so understanding of his.

"At any rate," the baroness continued softly, "after her disappearance, outraged members of the family had the door to the chambers she'd inherited from her mother bolted fast, the window barred, lest the darkness that had sired her ever try to return. You may have noted that window when you arrived; it's the topmost one in the western tower. But—"

"This 'darkness,'" Hauberin cut in sharply. "Who— what—was he?"

"I told you, my lord, I don't know. Baroness Alianor never spoke of him. Even under threat from her brother, even though he . . . beat her, she never, never named the father of her child."

"Ah, no, I can't accept that! Somebody must know."

"I—I'm sorry. That's all there is." She hesitated, bewildered and torn by his distress. "I'm afraid even my lord husband couldn't tell you more. If he would talk of it at all. He considers it a family shame— My lord? What is it?"

Hauberin had caught a sudden silent warning from Alliar. "I believe your husband is waiting, my lady," he said in quiet resignation. "Shall we join him?"

XII
LESSONS

Baron Gilbert's well-schooled face, as ever, revealed little outward emotion, but his stance as Hauberin and the baroness left the chapel together spoke worlds of disapproval. The fixed stare he gave the prince was decidedly icy.

Is it that he doesn't want me in his chapel, Hauberin wondered. *Or doesn't he approve of me being alone with his wife?*

The baroness seemed not to notice any coldness on her husband's part. Greeting him with a charming smile, she took his arm and turned to go, without so much as a glance back at Hauberin. After a heartbeat's resistance, Baron Gilbert yielded and let her lead him away. As they left, unaware of the keenness of Faerie hearing, Hauberin caught first the baron's baritone grumble, then his wife's indignant:

"In a *chapel*? Credit me with better judgment than that! No, my lord husband, nothing untoward happened in there, I swear it by my faith. Our guest was curious about our ways, that's all."

"I noticed he wasn't curious enough to attend Mass."

"Ah. Well. I . . . don't think he's exactly of our beliefs."

"A pagan?" the baron blurted.

"No, I don't think so. What he is, though . . ."

Is a good deal stranger than pagan, the prince finished wryly.

He turned to rejoin the uneasy Alliar, who asked him volumes in one brief brush of mind against mind. Hauberin shook his head.

"Too many servants watching us," he said in the Faerie tongue. "Come, let's walk."

As they ambled on at random down a castle corridor, discreetly trailed by servants who "just happened" to be going the same way, Hauberin quickly repeated the story the baroness had told him. "There's just no help for it, Li. I must see whatever's left of my mother's chambers. If those rooms really haven't been disturbed for . . . what? . . . some three human generations, there may still be traces of auras—"

"And you mean to tap them?" Alliar stopped short. "Do you have any idea how dangerous that is?"

"Temporal distortions, you mean?"

"Among other things! Such as—"

"I'll risk it." Hauberin started forward again. After a moment, Alliar followed, protesting:

"But you can't— Besides, the baron isn't going to just let you walk into rooms his family has kept bolted!"

"Ah, but that's where you can help, my friend. If you can sufficiently distract the baron and his entourage, you'll give me my chance."

Alliar hesitated for a long while. "There's no dissuading you, is there?"

"No."

"Then . . . done," the being agreed reluctantly. "But I still think you're risking—"

"I know. But there's no other choice." At the sound of hurrying footsteps behind them, Hauberin glanced back over his shoulder. "Now, what?"

A nervous little wisp of a man-servant was scurrying up to them, stopping with a quick little birdlike dip of a bow.

"Yes?" the prince asked.

"My lords, my Lord Baron sends you word that he will be engaged in castle affairs this morning. He thought that rather than sitting with him in the Hall, you might wish to visit the tilting yard instead."

Alliar grimaced. "Our good host was very right."

And perhaps, while everyone else is occupied, Hauberin

added to himself, *I'll have my chance at those locked chambers*. He waved a regal hand at the servant. "Lead on."

The servant brought them to the top of a stairway curving down the outside of a castle tower, bowed his avian bow once more, and scurried away.

"Probably off to hunt worms," Alliar muttered, and Hauberin laughed.

Below them, the yard was already busy despite the still early hour and the chill, damp air. On one side, some of the baron's knights in full mail were working with sword and shield. On the other, a few of the common men-at-arms were practicing wrestling holds. And just at the foot of the stairs, the two squires, Denis and Bertran, were studiously duelling with blunted swords under the keen eye of the solid, scarred, sergeant-at-arms. Aimery, arm in sling, sat on the steps and watched glumly. Hauberin, descending lightly, chuckled.

"Don't despair. You'll be able to earn new bruises soon enough."

"What— My lord!" The boy's face brightened. "God give you a good morning."

"And you. Eh, sit."

"Oh, but my ankle's much improved."

"Good. Don't abuse it."

They watched the activities in silence for a time. Then Alliar, who had been studying the sword and shield combats, said, "Now, I think I'd like to try that."

As Hauberin stared at his friend in astonishment, Aimery agreed cheerfully, "Oh, of course. As my lord baron's guest you'd be welcome. And they're always glad of new blood—" He winced. "I didn't mean spilled."

"I should hope not," Hauberin muttered, watching the being swagger—there was no other word for it—over to the knights, looking the very image of the world-weary human noble. "And I sincerely hope Li knows what's what."

"He's donning iron!" whispered Aimery in horror.

"That *is* what composes mail in this Realm."

"But—iron! I thought you couldn't—"

"I can't. Alliar can. Hush, now. Watch."

Alliar had, over the years, learned to handle a sword with considerable expertise, having often been pushed by the boy-Hauberin into being his duelling companion. The pseudo-human shape was strong enough to bear the weight of the borrowed mail shirt with ease. But the being wasn't at all familiar with the foreign idea of a shield. Hauberin watched Alliar make several experimental passes, evidently throwing off an occasional jest that made the watching men laugh aloud. There now, Li seemed to be ready. As ready as Li was likely to be.

It wasn't too painful. The being was too inhumanly graceful and quick to be in any real danger. And Alliar actually managed to get in a few solid blows to the slower human opponent. But of course experience told in the end, as the human used his shield to hook Alliar's and force it out of line. The being frantically tried to recover, but in Li's haste, let the borrowed sword go out of line as well.

"Ae, look out," Hauberin muttered, seeing what was coming.

Too late. In the next moment, Alliar was at sword's edge and laughingly conceding defeat. Slithering out of the mail shirt, the being returned to Hauberin's side with a rueful smile.

"That is not, by any means, as simple as it looked!"

The prince shrugged. "You're not hurt?"

"Only . . . ah . . . winded a bit."

Hauberin winced at the pun, then grinned at Aimery. "We don't fight with shields in my land. As Alliar has just proven."

"No shields?" The sergeant-at-arms had overheard, and waved Denis and Bertran to stillness. "Your pardon, m'lord, but—no shields?"

Damn. I had to go and draw attention to myself. There went any hope of slipping away unnoticed. "None,"

Hauberin answered, a touch amused, in spite of his impatience, by the man's blatant curiosity. "Our stances are
different, too. We— Ach, I can't show you properly from
up here." He stepped down to the yard. "Let me have
one of your practice swords."

The prince could afford to be daring: The hilts
weren't iron, but mere wood wrapped with leather. He
was as safe as a man carrying a hot poker by a cool
handle.

"Too heavy. A lighter one . . . Yes, this will do. No,
I don't want armor!" He fought down a shudder at
the thought of iron encasing him and added honestly
enough, "I haven't the height or breadth to carry all
that weight." *Even if it wouldn't fry me at a touch.*
Hauberin glanced at the human. "Put down your
shield."

"But, m'lord, this leaves a man's whole front
unprotected!"

"Not if you turn, so."

"What, nearly sideways? Does present less of a target,
but . . ."

"Come, try it. Skill's the thing, not brute force."

He demonstrated a few supple passes and saw the
sergeant's eyes widen. Eh, a mistake: he was moving too
swiftly for a human, and a human's slower reaction time.
Before anyone could begin to wonder, Hauberin subtly
slackened speed, aware that he was attracting a crowd.
The sergeant was following his lead fairly well being,
after all, a professional weapons-master. But the human
was still awkward in this new pose and the fear of hurting
his unarmored opponent, and after a few leery passes,
he drew back with a nervous grin, scarred face red with
the strain.

"Int'resting, m'lord. Most int'resting. But, begging
your pardon, m'lord, this is all well and good in a courtyard. If a man's in the middle of battle, he's going to
want all the shielding he can get."

"My people do have other defenses," Hauberin agreed,

and heard a smothered little gasp of laughter from Aimery.

But then the boy was saying, "Oh, my lord," and Hauberin glanced up to see Sir Raimond descending the stair, Aimery hastily crowding himself out of the way against the wall. Raimond was dressed for travel, a thick cloak over heavy riding clothes, and Hauberin, wondering where the young man might be going in such a rush, commented, "Better put a hood to that cloak."

"My clothing is my own concern."

"Tsk, just trying to spare you wetting your hair." Now, what was in those troubled eyes? Fear? Guilt? Just what had that secret midnight meeting been about?

"Spare me your worry," Raimond muttered as he swept by. But then he stopped short, almost as though a sudden voice had called to him, and turned to the prince with a thin smile. "That was an unusual style of handling a sword. But you seem to be teaching it easily enough."

"What does that mean?"

"Perhaps your mysterious secret isn't so mysterious at all."

"My . . . secret."

"Why, who and what you really are! Perhaps it's all been a clever masquerade. Perhaps underneath it all, you are no more than you seemed just now: a duelling instructor."

It was so clumsy an attempt at insult that Hauberin hesitated, torn between rage and an urge to laugh in the human's face. "Sir Raimond," he said at last, his voice soft and firm as though speaking to a not quite bright child. "You were clearly in a rush to be away from here. Don't let me stop you."

But Raimond had taken up one of the practice swords. He made a few tentative passes with it, then looked down its length at the prince, smiling. "I think I just might try my hand at this bizarre style of yours. Show me how it's done."

It was an order. Hauberin raised an eyebrow. "I am not, despite your jest, a teacher."

"What's this? Afraid, my lord?"

He seemed to be aching for a quarrel as surely—and as artlessly—as ever one child taunted another. Hauberin thought again of that secret meeting, and of that scornful, "I'll see to him." *But I'll not play your little game, my lord!* He raked the human with one brief, contemptuous glance and turned away.

"Alliar, shall we—"

"Don't you turn your back on me!"

A hand closed savagely on his arm, pulling him about. Hauberin cried out in sudden rage and tore free, eyes blazing. Just for a moment, his hand raised to strike— with Power. But then, regretfully, he remembered where he was. "Very well, my lord. If you wish a lesson, by the Powers, you've just earned the right to one."

"No!" Alliar thrust between them with a quick, *"Are you insane? Those swords are iron! You can't fight him!"*

"If there's a lesson, I'll gladly teach it."

"Step aside, lackey!" the human snapped.

"Lackey!"

"Li, no! Stand aside."

"But—iron! This won't be a friendly demonstration with a cautious sergeant. The blades may be blunted, but if he so much as scratches you—"

"He won't. *He'll be too handicapped by those bulky clothes—ha, and by the weight of that mail shirt under the tunic—and by an unfamiliar sword style. Don't worry."*

"Don't worry! I'd be mad not to— This *is* madness!"

Of course it was: the wild, proud, illogical Faerie madness. And just now, Hauberin was wholly of Faerie. "Step aside, Li. You wanted this, my lord Raimond. Come."

The human threw off his cloak and attacked.

It was a jest almost from the start. Raimond was a good swordsman; the brother of a baron could scarcely be anything else. But he stood little chance against this slim, dark flame of an opponent who darted in and out, mocking, comfortable in what to Raimond was a stance against every rule of swordplay, teasing the young human's blade a little more out of line with every taunting feint. In his desperate attempts to block that supple speed, Raimond slipped bit by bit back into the frontal attack that had been drilled into him since boyhood. Hauberin laughed aloud and lunged, stabbing the blunted point of his sword against his opponent's mail-protected chest, then lightly springing back, blade at rest.

"Lesson's over, my lord. You're dead."

But it wasn't over. Furious at having looked the fool in front of underlings, Raimond attacked again, and this time there was nothing of a jest about it. The horrified cries of the onlookers ringing in his ears, Hauberin found himself being driven back and back, too engaged in avoiding that perilous iron blade to counterattack. As Raimond swung at him, he parried, two-handed. The shock of impact as the two blades *skreed* together echoed through every nerve, nearly staggering him— Ae! The swords had locked at the hilt, and he hadn't a chance in a battle of raw strength, any more than he'd had in the death-duel with Serein.

Serein? Why think of Serein now?

Hauberin did the only thing he could: He gave way suddenly, slipping under Raimond's arm as though falling, freeing his snared sword with one quick, desperate twist of his wrist. The prince landed on one knee and one outflung hand, off balance, but Raimond was just as much off balance, stumbling forward, nearly going headlong. He recovered quickly, but Hauberin was already scrambling up, ready to—

Something tangled itself about his ankles, and before Hauberin could catch himself, he fell full length. And Serein was— *No, no, not Serein: Raimond!*—Raimond was raising his sword in both hands, high over his head, ready to stab savagely down, his eyes glinting green—

"No!" Alliar sprang forward, dragging the human away even as Hauberin fought free of the encumbrance—Raimond's fallen cloak—and rolled aside, sword in hand.

"Let go of me!" Raimond gasped in fury. "Let go, damn you!" He tore free to face an equally furious Alliar, who was showing every sign of losing control and human shape, and Hauberin shot to his feet with a savage:

"*Enough!*"

The sheer force of that cry made them both turn to stare. Hauberin saw nothing at all of Serein in Raimond's eyes, nothing but very human rage, and thought with relief that the sea-green glint had been only a trick of the darkening sky or his own nerves. "Alliar, step back. And you, Sir Raimond, you wished to leave. The lesson is over. Leave!"

It wasn't the voice of guest or servant. It was the voice of unquestioned royalty. Raimond, for all his fury, flinched. Without another word, he swept up his discarded cloak, flung it dramatically about himself, and stalked off, attendants hurrying frantically after him, leaving stunned silence behind.

"Mad," Alliar breathed at last. "Utterly mad."

"Just thoroughly childish." Hauberin paused to catch his breath, reflecting sourly that if the baron was his distant relative, then so was Raimond. Every family had some bad blood. "Li, thank you for the rescue."

"What did you expect me to do? Watch him spit you?"

"I doubt he could have— What is it, Aimery?"

The boy was hobbling to his side, eyes troubled. "My lord . . ." He glanced warily about. The others were all returning, somewhat obviously, to what they had been doing before the duel, but he still kept his voice low. "You've never met Sir Raimond before yesterday, have you?"

"You know that. Only in passing, as it were, that day in the forest. Why?"

"Because . . ." Aimery shook his head. "Because it doesn't make sense. Why should he hate you?"

"Why, indeed?" Hauberin glanced in the direction Raimond had taken. "I really don't— Eh, but here comes the rain! Come, let's get inside."

XIII
CHECKMATE

Courtesy insisted Hauberin and Alliar pay their respects once more to Baron Gilbert, who was still in the Great Hall in his canopied chair. But the last of the castle folk with whom he'd been meeting were trailing out, and the baron himself was getting to his feet, straightening with the delicate care of someone who has been sitting in one position too long.

"Ah, my lords." His eyes brightened at the sight of his guests; apparently he had forgiven Hauberin for his . . . indiscreet meeting in the chapel. "A foul day for travelling. You will, of course, stay with us one more night."

The prince bowed. "We should be honored."

"But," Baron Gilbert continued in a cautious tone, "there is something I must know of you first, my lord."

Maybe he hadn't quite forgiven, after all. Hauberin said warily, "If I'm able to tell you, I shall."

The baron's severe face was all at once aglow. "Do you," he said with barely controlled fervor, "play chess?"

Hauberin laughed in relief. "Play it, my Lord Baron? My people invented the game!"

"Ah, splendid! What better pastime for gentlefolk who are, perforce, kept within? Come, follow me, my lords. We shall try our hand at it right now."

Hauberin mused idly that he would have loved to follow Raimond and find out what that spoiled child was about. If the weather wasn't quite so foul.

But much more important than the scratching of any mere itch of curiosity, there were his mother's chambers to investigate. The steps to the western tower were right beyond that far wall. If only he could puzzle out a way to reach them without—

"My lord? Your move."

The prince started. He studied the chessboard for a time, then moved a beautifully carved little ivory knight forward, settling back to watch the baron from hooded eyes. This human version of what they called chess was far less complex than the intricate Faerie game—which frequently involved magic and the use of more than one dimension—but it was challenging enough even so to be amusing.

Or it would have been, had Baron Gilbert not been such an extraordinarily cautious player. There he went again, deliberating over a piece, touching it, then withdrawing his hand with a grunt, only to start the whole thing over again with a new piece. Hauberin sighed soundlessly, exchanging a quick, rueful glance with the watching Alliar. The prince gazed about the small room yet again, for all that he had noted everything in it already: Besides the chairs on which they sat and the table at which they played, he could look at the wide fireplace, its comfortable blaze welcome on such a cold, wet day, the one tapestry, new enough for the colors of the hunting scene to be almost garish, or the smooth floor, kept clear of rushes to show off the luxury of patterned tiles.

Even here in the baron's solar, there was nothing of true privacy. The Baroness Matilde was present with her ladies, all of them apparently absorbed in their needlework, save for the baroness herself, who was radiating the same quiet boredom Hauberin felt, and shy, pretty little Lisette, the prince's dinner companion of the night before, who was playing a harp, and making a fair job of it, too, for a human amateur.

But now she was stumbling over the same chord three times in a row. Hauberin silently went to her side, wordlessly moving her compliant, chilly little hands into the proper fingering till the girl, blushing with confusion, managed it by herself. Hauberin glanced at the baroness, whose eyes flickered with amusement.

"Thank you," she mouthed, and the prince gave her a little bow and returned to the chessboard.

The baron glanced up at him. "You are restless, my lord. Surely you're not planning to leave us after all. That torrent is hardly weather for travel."

"Sir Raimond is out in it," Hauberin murmured, testing.

"I am not," the baron returned, "my brother's keeper, to quote the Holy Word." Something hinted in the cool eyes: anger? pain? "I heard how he virtually forced you into a duel, my lord."

And nearly killed me. "A . . . childish prank."

"Raimond is no longer a child." For one startling instant, very real pain blazed out from the man. Then, as suddenly as though a veil had dropped, it was gone, and the baron was adding stiffly, "But I will not trouble you with such matters." Not a trace of emotion creased the elegant, somber face. "You *will* be staying with us, then?"

Human self-control. Almost inhuman self-control. Hauberin forced a smile, suddenly pitying the young baroness very much. "I fear we must indeed impose on your hospitality."

"No imposition at all."

"Ah . . . your king's in danger, you know."

"What—" The man's glance dropped to the chessboard. "Mm." That lost him in thought for a good span of time, and Hauberin suddenly grinned to himself.

"Alliar."

"My Prince?"

"How's your game?"

"Good enough, you know that."

"Good enough to keep our kind host occupied for a bit?"

A flame of understanding. *"Oh, indeed. We should be able to play out one of the most complex and slowest*

*games in human history! Certainly long enough for some-
one to go . . . exploring."*

The baron at last made his move. Hauberin shook his
head, and pounced. "Check, my lord baron. And mate."

"Indeed, indeed." It was a mutter. "You will, I trust,
give me a return game?"

"Oh, but my lords!" Alliar cut in, smiling. "Am I not
to have this game?"

The baron, out of courtesy, could hardly refuse. Hauberin switched places with his friend and waited, watching
till he saw the human totally engrossed. Then he quietly
got to his feet and moved across the small chamber, so
slowly and smoothly that no one glanced up at him. Subtle as a stalking cat, he slipped out and onto the landing
that led onto the spiral stairway down to the Great Hall
and up to the western tower.

He found himself facing two guards. Coolly, Hauberin
nodded to them, stepped onto the spiral, and began his
climb, radiating the confidence of a man who knew
exactly where he was going and had every right to be
going there.

It worked. He wasn't so much as challenged.

Though the lower stair had been brightly lit, the light
grew vague as the prince climbed. No one, after all, was
going to waste good torches on a stairway that would
rarely be used by the baron. Darkness, of course, was
hardly a problem for someone of Faerie. But the stairs
grew increasingly slick as he climbed, rain slithering
down the slick stone from the tower's open top like so
many reed-thin snakes. Hauberin moved warily, picturing
himself slipping and falling all the ignominious and painful way down to the bottom. The prince suspected there
should have been another guard up there on the tower
top, but presumably that extra touch of security was
being neglected on such a foul day. That was fine with
Hauberin; he would be running that much less of a risk
of being surprised.

A brief, straight flight of stairs branched off from the
main spiral, up into darkness. The prince paused for a

moment, letting his eyes adjust to even less light, then
smiled grimly as he saw that the stair ended at a bolted
door. Beyond it were the rooms he sought. Hauberin
climbed his careful way up to stand pondering. He could
have removed the bolt without risking the touch of iron
by snaring it in a loop of clothing and pulling. Unfortunately, the door was also secured by a masive iron monster of a lock.

Can't have things too easy, now, can we?

It was just possible that the baroness kept the key on
her chatelaine's ring, along with all the other keys to the
castle. Then again, from everything he'd seen so far,
these human folk were just melodramatic enough to have
hurled the key into the moat.

Still, the prince told himself firmly, this was only a
lock, no matter what the material. There were unlocking
spells, conveniently fueled only by mind and will; they
should, at least in theory, work.

Hauberin glanced about, making absolutely certain
he was alone, then took a deep breath and stared at the
lock. Bit by bit he shut out the world around him, the
rain, the dank, heavy walls, shut out everything save
the lock. He saw and felt and smelled nothing but the
lock, the inner shape of it, the design of it. The coldness
of iron ached in his mind (*No, reject that*), the red raw-
ness of rust burned like a smoldering fire (*No, reject that,
too*). The pattern of locking was there, heavy from age
and disuse, rejecting him by simply being what it was: a
creation meant to resist. Delicately, he began unravelling
its essence, picking at it with his will *here,* pressing at it
there and *there* even though his head was beginning to
ache (*No! There was no pain, there was only the spell,
building, building*) ... A little more pressure and he
would ... a little more—

With a sudden anguished shriek, the lock burst apart.
Hauberin threw himself aside as a hail of deadly iron
shards smashed against the wall, missing his face by a
handsbreadth.

"Powers ..."

For a long while, Hauberin couldn't do anything but lean against the clammy wall and listen to his racing heart. That would have been an ugly, ugly way to die.

Ae, but had anyone heard the lock explode?

No. He was surrounded by silence broken only by the muted sound of rain on stone. After a time, the prince recovered his breath, and began struggling with the rusted bolt, looping it as he'd planned in a fold of his full sleeve. It was a clumsy way to work, made all the clumsier by the bolt being heavy and rusted shut for so many years.

Would it never move . . . ? Would it . . . never . . . move— The bolt slid free with a horrible metallic squeal, but a roll of thunder drowned out the noise. Hauberin silently thanked whatever Powers might be in this human Realm, and warily pushed at the heavy oaken door. The dampness, fortunately, must have gotten into the hinges, because the door moved almost noiselessly, creeping nearly halfway open before jamming. Hauberin bit his lip in sudden sharp tension, and slipped through the narrow opening, wondering what he would find.

Nothing. The castle folk might have been too superstitious to use rooms associated in their minds with sorcery, but that hadn't stopped them from stripping those rooms of furnishings. They might even have burned everything.

But he didn't need much physical residue, no more than a scrap of fabric, a splinter of wood. He didn't have to give up hope just yet.

The prince prowled silently through the two small, barren, musty chambers, leaving light footprints in the dust of three generations, uncomfortably aware of the burning cold of the iron bars at the one narrow window. Nothing, nothing . . .

Hauberin stopped short. Closing his eyes, he began searching again, senses this time going beyond the physical. Almost at once he felt something pulling at him, and opened his eyes to find himself fallen to his knees in a corner of the room, amid a small mound of rubble where mortar had cracked and fallen away from stone.

Wondering, the prince closed his eyes again, following the impulse that made him sweep his hands out over the rubble.

Something burned him!

But even as the prince's eyes shot open, he realized the shock had been psychic, not physical. Warily Hauberin reached into the cracked mortar again, withdrawing: What was it? A scrap of parchment? Ha, yes, and with a fragment of writing on it as well!

Hauberin shot to his feet, heart pounding so wildly it nearly staggered him, knowing with every psychic sense this scrap of parchment far too small to be read was what he sought, one fragile little link with the past.

If—if I don't calm myself I'll never learn anything.

Even the simplest mind-quieting disciplines he'd learned as a child seemed far beyond his abilities right now, but Hauberin kept at them and kept at them, and at last his excitement, his fear and hope, faded to calm. He let out his breath in a soft, relaxed sigh, holding the scrap of parchment with both hands, eyes focused not on the realities of the empty room, but on the past. . . . Hauberin's breathing slowed. His senses seemed to expand, spinning out and out, far beyond the limits of the room, beyond the limits of time.

And there was a room, this room, no longer barren and gray with dust. A chair stood within it, a chest, a lovely canopied bed, and warm-hued tapestries covered the starkness of the walls. A cradle stood by the bed, with a small, sleeping form within.

His mother as a babe! Huaberin *knew* it all at once with psychic certainty, just as he *knew* he was seeing her through another's eyes, and the shock of it was almost enough to hurl himself away—

No! He hadn't learned anything yet, he dared not lose control. Hauberin forced emotion aside, relaxing his hold on real time, letting it slip away. . . .

Once more he saw that room as it had been, and the babe, and suddenly realized he was watching through a woman's eyes (glimpse of long, graceful hands, glimpse of thick golden braids being thrown impatiently back over velvet-clad shoulders).

Lady Alianor. It could only be she: his human grandmother.

Now those graceful hands were putting pen to parchment. She could read, the Lady Alianor, she could write, rare skill among nobility, and as Hauberin watched, she blotted the ink with sand and sealed the parchment with her signet ring, saying to someone, *"She's already safely baptized, my dear little witch-child, and now I'll protect her against mortal harm as well."* Straightening, the woman handed the small parchment roll to a young, plain human servant, his eyes liquid with devotion, telling him, *"I will keep one copy. Take this other. Leave it safely in the treasury of St. Denis, this record of my dear little one's birth, there and in no place else."* And in her mind as the young man bowed and left was the image of a noble building of spires and light, colored light, a great glowing circle of red, blue, gold.

Hauberin wondered, *A temple?* But the thought was vague, sliding away like smoke. A flood of memories rushed in to drown his mind, memories that weren't his own: the thoughts and hopes and fears of a warm and vital human woman. With that part of consciousness still his own, Hauberin ached with the terrible knowledge of the tragedy to come. And even though there was no hope for it, he struggled to scream out to her, *"Run, run from your brother!"* But he was helpless, and the last awareness of his separate self was fading. . . .

No, ae, no! One small corner of Hauberin's mind knew he had linked too closely with the past, with the Lady Alianor herself who, human though she was, was still flesh of his flesh. He must remember who he was, what he was, when he was! He was being torn, not *here*, not *then*—Powers help him, *no!*

Despairing, Hauberin fought with all his ebbing strength, striking out frantically to find something, anything of his own time. There, ah, there, he had brushed

another mind! Whose it was— No matter! It was someone of the present, it was a focus.

With a last savage rush of will, Hauberin tore himself
from the past and hurled himself at reality. He lost contact with that other mind, but now he knew which way
to turn and—

As spirit shot back into flesh, Hauberin dimly heard
himself scream aloud. And then the psychic impact
hurled him into darkness.

Damn his brother, and damn Duke Alain, and damn,
damn, *damn* this weather!

Bent nearly double over his horse's wet mane, Raimond continued to mutter oath after futile oath. He
hadn't ridden more than a few bow-lengths down from
the baronial castle before the rain had started. Now it
was pouring fiercely enough to warrant Sir Noah out of
the Scriptures building a second ark.

Raimond broke off his cursing to grab frantically at the
hood of his riding cloak. Though he had pulled the hood
as far forward as it would go, the wind kept pushing it
back, slapping him in the face with watery flails. At this
point it hardly mattered whether he covered his head or
not. He was already nearly as wet in this downpour as
though he had gone swimming fully clad, and the thick
wool of his cloak was so rain-sodden it flapped heavily at
his back with each stride of his unhappy horse.

I should go back, Raimond thought yet again. *I should
abandon this whole miserable business and go home.*

For a moment he was tormented by an image of himself sprawled before a roaring fire, warm and dry, a flagon
of mulled wine in hand.

With dear brother Gilbert lecturing him on noble pro-
priety and the sin of sloth— No, thank you.

Raimond's teeth flashed in a silent snarl. Ever since
they'd both been children, Gilbert the older by a good
many years and Raimond so sickly a boy he'd seemed fit
for nothing but the Church, Gilbert had taken it on himself to protect his younger sibling. Oversee his brother's

moral education, whether Raimond willed it or not. For
a time, the young man really had considered taking holy
orders just to escape. After all, a clever man of noble
birth could rise through the churchly ranks to a position
of true temporal power; there were churchmen in Chris-
tendom who were the real power behind many a throne.
But acquiring power took time. And the thought of a life
filled with even more restrictions than his brother could
place upon him— Raimond spat.

Forget the past. And rain or no, it was too late to turn
back. What he'd set in motion could hardly be stopped
now.

Besides, he owed Rogier this much.

Ah, Rogier . . . Now *there* had been a man truly meant
for power. For all his discomfort, Raimond smiled,
remembering. When he, desperate for something *he*
could achieve, something that had nothing of his brother
about it, had tentatively tried dabbling in other men's
politics, Rogier had made him welcome. And, oh God,
it had been a genuine welcome, for *him*, not for the
baron's younger brother, the baron's landless shadow.
For the first time in his life, someone was actually willing
to accept him simply as himself.

If only Rogier hadn't been born on the wrong side of
the proverbial blanket. If only he had managed to oust
his cousin, thrice-damned Alain, Raimond knew his own
life would be different. Instead of riding through the
rain, imperiling himself, he would be warm and dry and
happy in Touranne, his own master, dependent on his
brother for nothing. He would stand at *Duke* Rogier's
right hand, serving him willingly as vassal and friend.

But there had been that final battle. And now Rogier
was dead, God rest his soul, and that arrogant, mealy-
mouthed cousin ruled the duchy: Duke Alain.

Raimond sneezed. God's mercy, he'd be lucky if he
got out of this without lung sickness. He bent even lower
over the neck of his straining horse, hearing it panting.
He knew the proper way to ride a distance was to

alternate gaits: canter, walk, trot, canter. But he couldn't waste time, he had too much ground to cover!

Yes, but a horse couldn't run full out for very long. Rain or no rain, the animal had needed one rest already and was going to need another very soon.

Raimond sneezed again, and swore. They were rapidly leaving his brother's fields; the forest encroached more closely on the baronial demesne here to the north.

"Come on, horse," he urged. "Just a little further. Just till we reach the forest's shelter."

Off to the right curved the broad road that led to Touranne (*"broad as the road to Hell,"* raced through his mind), but Raimond forced the horse straight ahead, even though it was fighting him and slowing to a heavy-limbed, weary trot, down a narrow path that wound its way into the first stands of trees. As the forest thickened, the young man dodged this way and that in the saddle, swearing as a bush nearly pulled his cloak from his back, narrowly avoiding low branches that seemed all thorns, hunting for relative dryness. To one side loomed an ancient oak, broad of trunk and so thick with leaves the circle beneath them was almost dry.

"So be it," he told the animal, reining it in under the broad branches. "Now you can stop."

He dismounted, boots squelching into mud, and wrapped his arms about himself, wincing at the touch of clammy cloth, trying to get warm, clenching his fists with impatience. It was impossible to judge the time of day from the heavy sky, but he knew there was still a way to ride.

God's mercy, it was dark as the Pit under these branches. Dark and eerily silent, with nothing to be heard but his horse's heavy breath and the rattling of rain on leaves. Raimond shivered, and told himself it was merely from cold.

But this enforced stop was giving him too much time to think. Oh, yes, he had disliked that . . . Hauberin at sight, the dark, haughty little foreigner. And he should have done what he always did with disliked guests:

ignored the man and gone about his own affairs. But
Raimond was only too well aware how he had deliberately confronted the man, wasting precious time with that
ridiculous challenge in the tilting yard— He might have
killed the little fool.

Might? God's mercy, he had *wanted* to kill him!
Drowning in waves of total, mindless hatred, there had
been room in his brain for nothing but blood lust, almost
as though someone else had been controlling him. Yes,
and the night before, when he'd met with that scum of
a magician, there had been that time of blankness, almost
as though that someone else had spoken with his
voice. . . .

Possession, Raimond thought in terror. Dear God, possession, or the result of tampering with the . . . Black
Arts— No, God, please, no . . .

But he could hardly back out now. Wearily Raimond
climbed back into the saddle and gathered up the reins.
The forces he'd set into action must be allowed to play
their game through. And, for the sake of his honor and
perhaps even his soul, he dare not be late.

XIV
TEMPESTS

"My lord! Oh, please, my lord, wake up!"

A voice was calling him, hands were shaking him, and Hauberin groaned and opened his eyes, too dizzy and sick to focus on reality at first.

"My lord!" the voice insisted. "Come, hurry, get up! They mustn't find you here."

He blinked, vision already clearing. A woman . . . a glint of red hair . . . With a great rush of relief, he recognized her, and knew he was back in his right self, in his proper time. "My . . . lady baroness . . ."

If only she would stop pulling at him! The danger he'd escaped so narrowly had been very real, but he hadn't been hurt in mind or body; there wasn't a magician born who hadn't fainted at one time or another from sheer psychic exhaustion. Hauberin struggled to tell the woman that if she'd only give him a chance to catch his breath, he would be fine, but the words just wouldn't come out right.

"At l-least you recognize me," Baroness Matilde was stammering. "Can you stand? Hurry, please, can you stand?"

"Don't . . ." Trying to elude her insistent tugging on his arm, Hauberin managed to get to his knees, head swimming. "Lady . . . please . . . don't tug . . . I just . . . may faint."

"No!"

She held something sharp-scented under his nose. Hauberin coughed and angrily tried to push her hand away, but the sharpness did seem to be clearing his head. With a great effort, he staggered to his feet.

"Can you walk yet? Please, my lord, they mustn't find you here!"

"They? Who? Lady, let be! You can't carry me." He stared into her panicked face, fighting to control his senses. "What is this? What's wrong?"

"Don't you know? Dear God, if my husband finds you here—Sorcery— They'll burn you!"

If only she would be quiet for a moment, give him a chance to think— But now she had slipped his arm about her shoulders and was half supporting, half dragging him out of there. Hauberin struggled through the doorway, then pulled away from her, falling back against a dank wall, gasping. But the frantic Matilde was battling with the heavy door, and he clenched his teeth against dizziness and stumbled forward to help her.

"Be careful, my lord! There . . . that's it. I'll just slide the bolt in . . . place . . . again." She froze, staring at the shattered lock. "What . . . did you do to it?"

"Too much enthusiasm."

She gave him a wild glance, eyes white-rimmed like those of a frightened pony. "No matter. We'll just have to leave it like that and hope no one notices— Oh, be careful, you'll fall!"

Still too dizzy to manage that slick stairway alone, he'd had no intention of trying it just yet. But somehow his overly determined guardian was forcing him down the spiral steps whether he would or not.

"My lady wife! What means this?"

This time Hauberin almost did fall. *Wonderful*, he thought wearily. *The outraged husband. Just what every good farce needs.* The prince could picture the scene from the baron's viewpoint: himself disheveled and vague in the baroness' close embrace. *Just wonderful.*

"Ae!" That was Alliar, rushing up past Baron Gilbert, almost knocking the man out of the way in haste.

Hauberin sagged gladly against his friend, wishing heartily that everyone would simply leave him alone, and tried to muster his thoughts into a coherent explanation. The baroness was quicker.

"Please, my lord husband, don't shout." There wasn't a trace of her former near-hysteria. "I thought I heard a noise, so—"

"So you went to look, up an isolated tower, all by yourself!"

"You're right, husband, of course, I should have taken someone with me. I wasn't thinking. But see, I *did* hear something. Our guest— These steps are so slippery! The poor man must have fallen and stunned himself."

That was one way of putting it. The baron, whatever he might have been thinking, could hardly have argued the point, and after a flurry of activity Hauberin found himself back in his little guest chamber, the baroness busily shooing out servants, ladies and, with the reasonably credible explanation that there just wasn't enough room, her husband. Only Alliar, who refused to be ousted, and wide-eyed little Lisette remained.

Hauberin's mind had at last cleared, and he would have loved to be left alone to shudder and come to terms with how close he had come to mind-death. But for all his protests, Baroness Matilde insisted on efficiently examining his head. Alliar hovered nervously in the background, anxious thoughts quivering around the prince like so many frightened birds.

"*Stop that!*" Hauberin said silently. "*I'm all right, Li. I only—*"

The prince winced as Baroness Matilde touched a sore spot on his forehead. "*So!*" Alliar exclaimed. "*You're all right, are you?*"

"*It's nothing. I must have bumped my head against the wall when I collapsed—*"

"*Collapsed!*"

"*It's nothing. I'm fine. Alliar, please, I'll tell you the whole story later.*"

Judging from the twin frowns on being and baroness,

a rather spectacular bruise was starting to form on his forehead, but neither of his determined nurses would accept that he really wasn't hurt.

"Are you dizzy?" Baroness Matilde asked briskly.

"Not any more. I—"

"Sleepy?"

"No. My lady—"

"Is your vision at all blurred?"

"No. But—"

"A moment more, if you would, my lord. Lisette, dear, send someone for my herbals."

"The wormwood for headache?" The girl was stealing shy, sympathetic glances at Hauberin. "And comfrey for the bruise?"

"And the lavender and— Lisette! Where are you going?"

As she scurried off, the girl flashed a quick smile. "To fetch it myself, my lady. A servant would take so long— I know where everything is kept."

"Lisette!"

She was already gone. The baroness sighed, flicking a glance at Hauberin. "I do think the maid is taken with you, my lord."

"She's very young."

"Yes. Marriage will settle her down." The woman glanced up at the nervous Alliar. "Until Lisette returns, I trust you will serve as sufficent chaperon. At least as far as my lord husband is concerned." Just the faintest hint of sarcasm edged the words. "Oh, and you, my lord," she added to Hauberin, who was chuckling softly, "should be in bed."

An undercurrent of panic still raced beneath the woman's apparent calm, and Hauberin glanced up from his chair, noting how she shied from meeting his gaze. "I'll be all right where I am," he said shortly, all at once totally weary of the endless fussing. "Truly."

He felt Alliar's thoughts brush his again, and added for the sake of both worriers, "Look. I can stand, turn, bend; I'm quite myself again."

The baroness had been nervously biting her lip. "Whatever that self may be."

"What—"

"No, my lord, I—I don't want to know. I don't want to know why you're here, or what you want, but I will trust your word that you mean us no harm."

"You weren't so frightened of me up on the ramparts, or in the chapel. Why now?"

"I . . . worry over the safety of my husband's guests."

"Commendable. But, lady: How did you know where I was?"

"You heard what I told my husband. I heard the sound of your fall."

"Over the roar of the storm? And through all those stone walls?" Hauberin paused, thinking of the mind that had pulled him back to true time, wondering . . . Oh no, that was ridiculous! Surely there had never been a human less attuned to magic than this woman. Bemused, the prince asked softly, "Can there be more to you, I wonder, than you seem?"

"What manner of question is this?"

"And what was all that panic about 'They mustn't find you here'?"

She turned away. "That's for you to answer, my lord."

"Don't play games, lady."

"The bolted door thrown ajar, my lord, the shattered lock—"

"The lock," Hauberin said, delicately skirting falsehood, "was ancient. Any pressure might have broken it." He moved to face her again, blocking her path. "Whatever you may think, I assure you, I am no sorcerer."

That hardly seemed to comfort her. "I . . ." she began, but then her face brightened with relief. "Ah, Lisette!"

Wordlessly, the baroness began to tend Hauberin's bruise, her chilly fingers never flinching from the touch of his skin, her face impassive. Wordlessly, Hauberin submitted.

"My Lady Baroness," he said at last, when she seemed

done, "is there a building of . . ." Aie, what was the name the Lady Alianora had mentioned? It was there at the edge of memory, if only he could snare it. "St. Denis," Hauberin burst out in triumph, "near this castle? Soft golden stone, twin spires, a glowing circle of color set between them?"

The baroness frowned slightly. Lisette cut in, shy and eager, "That sounds like the church of St. Denis in Touranne, our good duke's city."

"It does." The woman's voice was carefully toneless, but she could hardly have missed Hauberin's start. "If that is where you wish to travel, my lord, I'm sure my lord husband will happy to provide a guide for you tomorrow."

The prince was hard put not to laugh aloud in sudden hope. It was real, this church, no fancy of an overtaxed brain, and it still existed in the here-and-now! Gambling his life, his sanity, had been worth the risk. For if his grandmother's letter was still safe in the church treasury (Powers grant it be so!), this outlandish name-quest was almost over. "Ah, yes, lady, that would be wonderfully kind."

"For today, though," the baroness added, getting to her feet, box of herbs tucked under her arm, "you must do nothing strenuous. Tell me at once if you feel dizzy or overwhelmingly sleepy. Now I—I must rejoin my husband."

Trailed by the bewildered Lisette, she all but ran from the room.

Halfway down the stair from the guest chamber, Matilde brought herself to a determined halt. Though her heart was still racing with panic, she managed to force her face into its customary mask of calm. Ignoring the terrified child-she'd-been sobbing in her mind, the young woman descended the rest of the stairway with careful dignity, to be met at the bottom by a nervous manservant: the Baron Gilbert was waiting in their solar.

From one crisis to the next, she thought, and obeyed the implicit summons.

As Matilde entered the solar, steeling her nerves to quiet, she found her husband seated in a high-backed chair by the fire, staring into the flames. She cleared her throat, and he glanced up. "Well? How does he?"

The steadiness of the baron's gaze would have stared down a basilisk. Matilde forced a smile and moved to sit across from him, fighting to keep her voice light. "Well enough, husband. He has a nasty bruise on his forehead, but I don't think any serious harm was done."

"You must be glad of that." His voice was just too carefully neutral, and Matilde tensed in sudden anger.

"Of course I am. He's our guest."

"Ah."

"My lord husband, we've been wed now for four years." The words exploded from her. "Have I ever in all that time, given you one moment's cause for jealousy? Well? Have I?"

"Don't be foolish."

"Then surely you know I wouldn't think of—of staining your honor with a . . . foreigner. . . ."

Her voice faltered. Foreign. Dear God, just *how* foreign . . . ?

The baron's steady gaze dropped beneath the heat of her fury. He muttered something placating, then added, "He will be healthy enough to leave us tomorrow?"

"I don't doubt it." Matilde took a steadying breath. "My lord husband, he wishes to travel to Touranne. To the church of St. Denis."

The man's eyebrows shot up. "I thought he wasn't of our faith."

"So did I. Maybe he—he's planning to convert, or—" Ach, she was starting to babble. Matilde cut herself off in mid-sentence, suddenly overwhelmed. If she had to spend one more moment sitting here trading platitudes while all the time her heart was racing like a panicky rabbit, she was going to scream. "At any rate," Matilde said, very carefully, "all is well. And now, my lord husband, if you will excuse me, I . . . must go and see to the restocking of our larder."

It hadn't been a false excuse; as baroness, she was the castle's overseer. As she met with her husband's steward, checking the supply of bread and meat and wine, as she spoke with butler or pantler or maidservant, Matilde forced herself to act the perfect, competent chatelaine, and prayed that no one guessed the emotions surging behind the mask.

Saints, oh saints, how could she tell anyone? It wasn't as though Hauberin had actually done or said anything wrong. It wasn't even so much what he was, or . . . might be.

Matilde stifled a humorless laugh. Despite what Baron Gilbert might think, what Hauberin roused in her wasn't anything as blatant, as relatively safe, as lust (though, God help her, she did find him attractive). It was terror, pure and uncomplicated.

Terror of herself.

All at once Matilde had to turn aside into a shadowy corner of the kitchen, away from the bustle of cook and underlings, clenching her teeth in anguish, remembering . . .

The child-Matilde had had no idea why all the folk had gathered in the town square that market day, or why her parents were arguing as to whether or not she should be with them; whether it was right for a child of noble blood to watch. Adults were always sending children away whenever there was something really interesting to watch. Angry at her parents, she had insisted, "I want to stay."

Her father had nodded approval. "Be good for her. Teach her the way of Right."

When she'd complained she couldn't see, he had cleared a space before her. And then she had been able to see too clearly that open stretch of cobblestones, that ominous pile of wood with the stake set cruel in its midst.

She had seen the poor captive—a thin-faced, desperate woman—bound to that stake by iron chains.

And then it had happened. All at once she was no longer in her own small self. All at once she was feeling the prisoner's terror, the eager, hating hunger in the crowd around her like one giant, pitiless animal. Stricken, she had screamed to be taken away. But it was too late for escape, too late to do anything but see the flames and hear the screams, and feel the agony that licked at her flesh—

With a strangled gasp, Matilde thrust herself back into the present, trembling. It couldn't have happened like that. She had fallen ill soon after; she must have been already burning with fever. Of course she hadn't felt those flames. Only a witch could have sensed another's pain so stronger, and she wasn't a witch, never that!

She glanced about guiltily. Startled servants were making self-conscious efforts not to look her way. With a mighty effort, Matilde shut out the past, retreating back behind her mask of calm. The perfect chatelaine gave them all an almost convincingly serene smile.

At least, Raimond thought, dismounting and shaking out his sodden clothes as best he could, it had finally stopped raining. And he'd reached his destination in all good time.

This ... *was* the right place, wasn't it? The hour couldn't be anywhere near nightfall, but between the heaviness of the sky and the screen of leaves overhead, it was nearly black as midnight in this dank little glade.

As his eyes gradually adjusted to the dim light, Raimond peered warily about. An involuntary shudder shook him. As a boy he had explored here in defiance of his brother and the church ban on such heathen sites. The place had frightened him even in full sunlight, though of course he had never said anything about it to Gilbert. Up to this moment he had thought those fears only a child's foolishness. But now he felt not at all advanced from the boy he'd been. Surrounded by heavy silence and the looming black shapes of gnarled, ancient trees dripping rags of moss, he had to struggle not to sign himself.

In the midst of the twisted trees, in what must have once, ages past, been a cleared circle of earth, was the heart of his childhood terror: a broken ring of weathered stones rising out of a savage tangle of underbrush like so many pale, pagan ghosts. Hating ghosts. Ghosts to rend a Christian soul. . . .

Raimond spat. God, how it stank here! The rain should have washed away the stench, or at least deadened it, but no matter how he turned, the reek of wet stone and rotten vegetation caught in his throat and made him cough. And ah, would he never be warm again?

Something shoved him. Raimond got out a strangled "God's blood!" and whirled to see—

His horse. Raimond let out a shaky laugh. At least the animal didn't seem to be bothered by its surroundings, foraging with apparent calm for bits of greenery. Though what it could find palatable . . .

The horse flung its head up, ears pricked, and rumbled deep in its throat. Raimond's hand flew to his sword as something large and dark crashed its way through the underbrush. He waited tensely, clutching the hilt, heart racing, as that Something resolved itself into a second horse that stopped at the far side of the stones, on its back a figure shrouded in a plain, dark cloak.

Silence. The rider sat motionless, a black, featureless mass in the darkness, head turned to Raimond. Raimond clenched his jaw, determined not to be the first one to yield. But the blank stare of that hood was unnerving, like something out of a priest's lectures on Hell, and all at once he burst out:

"Well? Who are you?"

There was the faintest of chuckles. "So, my lord. You came."

Raimond straightened angrily. "I said, who are you?"

The figure chuckled again and pushed back its hood, revealing the face of the little sorcerer with whom he'd plotted the night before. "Now do you recognize me, my lord?"

Raimond nodded tersely, staring into the shadows behind the sorcerer, hand tightening on his sword hilt. "I thought you said to come alone."

"I did."

Raimond shifted so that his back was to a tree, thinking, *treachery.* . . . "Then who is that lurking behind you?"

"No one to frighten you, my young lord," murmured a deep, amused voice, and after a moment, Raimond placed it.

"Baron Thibault. You trespass on my lands, my lord."

"*Your* lands?" the baron murmured. "I thought they belonged to your brother. No, man, don't bristle at me. I didn't mean any insult." Baron Thibault kneed his horse forward a few steps, and sat, a clean-shaven, brown-haired man of middle years and stocky build, studying Raimond, a faint smile on his fleshy lips. Gold glinted about his neck, and an elegant golden ring flashed from a glove hand as he dismounted. "After all, my young lord Raimond, despite past . . . unpleasantness, we are allies just now."

"Allies," Raimond echoed skeptically.

Baron Thibault flicked a glance in the sorcerer's direction. "You didn't tell him?"

"I didn't think it my place, my Lord Baron."

"Tell me what?" Raimond cut in.

"That I am here as well." The new voice was so soft Raimond had to strain to hear it. "That I still live."

Tall and lean, the stranger moved noiselessly forward to stand beside the baron, face completely hidden beneath the shadow of a deep hood.

Does everyone have to be so damned mysterious?

There was nothing at all to be seen beneath that hood, and Raimond snapped, "Enough games! Tell me who you are and why you're here, or I'm leaving."

"You never did have patience, my young Hotblood."

Raimond froze. No man had ever called him by that name save one, and he . . .

"Who are you?" he asked, half fearful of the answer.

The stranger pushed back the hood of his cloak, revealing a fine-boned aristocratic face: too thin, too finely drawn, pale and etched with lines of suffering till it seemed more the face of a saint than that of the fierce and vibrant man who— No, this couldn't be! Raimond stared, pierced by hope so sharp it was nearly terror. Swaying with shock, struggling not to swoon like a stupid woman, he managed to gasp out only, "My . . . lord Rogier! But you're—".

"Dead?" the other murmured. "Not quite."

"But— No! Touranne— I saw—"

"You saw a man take a blow to the head. You saw him fall into the river. What you didn't see was his body dragged, nearly lifeless, from that river by the men of good Baron Thibault."

"But it's been so long. . . ."

"A head wound is no simple thing to heal," the man said gently. "Baron Thibault kept me hidden, safe, all this time. Out of, no doubt, the pure goodness of his heart." Rogier's eyes glinted (*Green*, thought the dazed Raimond, *green as the eyes of a beast at night; his eyes were never green* . . .) as they glanced sideways at the baron in cynical humor. "Perhaps he harbored some plan of using my sleeping mind but living body as his puppet in some power scheme—"

"Oh no, my lord!" the baron protested, and received a sharp, ironic smile in return.

"No matter, my Lord Baron. For whatever motive, you did keep me safe till the moment when my scattered wits so suddenly returned. Come now, Hotblood, stop staring! Do I look like a dead man to you?"

Overwhelmed, Raimond fell to one knee. "No, my lord Rogier," he said in wonder. "You most surely do not." Dizzy and terrified at this sudden change in his plans, his life, Raimond added fervently, "My lord, I—I am your loyal vassal, as before. What do you ask of me?"

Rogier hesitated. For a moment his eyes were terribly sad, terribly alone. "I fear I must ask much, my little Hotblood. As much as you can give me."

Raimond blinked, feeling a small shiver steal its way up his spine. "Why, anything, my lord, you know that. I only . . ."

Raimond stumbled to a stop, mouth gone dry. Rogier was glancing at the little sorcerer. And a quick, secret smile flashed between them, sly and cruel. That smile . . . those green-glinting eyes . . . All at once Raimond realized he was afraid, though he couldn't have said exactly why. All at once he wanted nothing so much as to be safely back in his brother's castle, even if it meant putting up with Gilbert's lectures.

But before he could move, Rogier, still smiling faintly, turned back to him, eyes clear and chill as ice. As Raimond stared up, helplessly fascinated as a bird before a snake, he heard the man say gently, "I don't think you quite understand. What we need, my young Hotblood, is nothing less than your life."

For an instant, Raimond was too stunned to even gasp, his mind screaming that Rogier would never harm him, that surely the man had been speaking in metaphors—

Not with those cold, cold eyes. A surge of pure self-preservation made Raimond leap up with a horrified, "No!" If he could only get to his horse—

But it was three to his one. He closed one hand about a stirrup, but the startled horse danced away, dragging him. Before he could catch at the dangling reins, strong arms pulled him back. The frightened horse shrilled its alarm as someone slapped it, and rushed off in a storm of broken branches.

Damn, oh damn!

Raimond twisted savagely, struggling to free himself, to get enough room to draw his sword. Before he could draw the blade halfway from its sheath, his captors fell on him, forcing him to the ground, the smell of mold rank in his nostrils. As he tried to writhe free, gasping, someone tore the blade from his hand, sending it flying out of his reach. His body was crushed against the earth, his arms pinned to his sides.

"Bind him, curse you!" Baron Thibault hissed. "I can't hold him forever!"

Wild with terror, Raimond fought the triple weight restraining him, forgetting nobility, kicking and biting like any peasant in sheer animal panic. Despite his struggles, he felt the sorcerer easily snare his wrists, binding them deftly (*As though I was a felon, damn him!*). Suddenly released, Raimond tried to struggle to his feet, only to lose his balance and fall again. The sorcerer was upon him again before he could so much as kick, binding his legs as well. Raimond managed to gasp out, "You filthy little traitor!" before he was gagged with a scrap of cloth. Helpless, he twisted about to glare up at his captors.

"That does it." It was a satisfied mutter from Baron Thibault. "Get him onto your horse, sorcerer, and we'll take him back to my castle. His brother will pay us well for—"

"No," Rogier interrupted. "He must not be taken from this circle."

"What nonsense is this?" The baron stared at Rogier. And as he stared, the color slowly drained from his florid face. "God's mercy," Thibault breathed at last. "Those words about needing his life—you meant it literally, didn't you?"

Raimond stiffened in horror, fighting against the gag choking him, pleading silently, *No, dear God, no, Rogier, you can't—*

But Rogier was saying calmly, "I'm afraid I did."

"Exactly," purred the sorcerer, looking from one man to the other. "This is a place of ancient Power, lacking only blood to free it from the stones." He glanced down, gloating, at Raimond. "Human blood."

"Have you both gone insane?" Baron Thibault exploded. "I only went along with this farce because I

thought you meant to hold the boy for ransom. But murder—"

"Not murder," the sorcerer corrected. "Sacrifice."

"Murder, I say! And I will not be a party to such
blasphemy!"

That's right, Raimond thought eagerly, *argue with
them, please, please, change their minds before* . . .

"No, my lord?" Rogier asked. "And what are you planning to do? Tell someone what we mean to do here—
and have my dear cousin the duke, your liege lord, learn
you harbored me? Do you fancy a traitor's death, my
lord?"

The baron floundered, speechless, turning away from
Raimond's pleading eyes. "No," he muttered at last. "I'll
keep my mouth shut. But I'll not be a witness to this
foulness, either."

No! Don't go! Raimond screamed at him silently.

But without another backward glance, Baron Thibault
threw himself into the saddle and rode away, leaving
Raimond alone and despairing with his killers to be. He
tried not to flinch as the sorcerer approached, knife glinting in hand. But, oh God, he was about to die! Raimond
squeezed his eyes shut, trying to pray, but the only thing
that came to mind was a childish wondering if his brother
would mourn him at all. In another moment he would
feel the bite of the blade—

"No," Rogier said, and Raimond's eyes snapped open.
"The ritual must not be performed just yet."

The sorcerer straightened, frowning. "But, my lord—"

"What's this? Are you questioning me?"

"N-no, my lord. But we should never have let his horse
escape. It's sure to run home. And *that* is sure to bring
Baron Gilbert after us."

Rogier—or, Raimond thought in terror, whoever was
wearing Rogier's body—smiled thinly. "What of it? Look
you, you're the one familiar with the Power here. You're
the one who insisted that all the signs of sky and earth
say the ritual must be performed tomorrow eve—or not
at all."

The sorcerer sighed in submission. "So be it, my lord."
Raimond shut his eyes in shaken relief. He wasn't
going to die.

Not just yet.

XV
POWER PLAYS

Hauberin shivered. Even with a fire blazing in the deep hearth, the baronial solar was still abysmally chilly and dank, reeking of damp stone. The prince's temper was growing shorter by the moment, while his nerves fairly quivered with impatience to be off, to be doing something, to be away from these ... humans who couldn't even manage to heat a room properly. A flash of memory brought to mind himself in his own palace study, curled up in a moment's snug privacy in a deep window seat, watching the rain, a goblet of spiced wine in his hand, the downpour outside heightening the pleasure of being warm and dry and at his ease—now *that* was how it should be in a civilized home!

Powers, would this endless day never be done?

Hauberin straightened his chair, listening to sudden not-sound: It had finally stopped raining. Not that it mattered. Even if Alliar and he could make their way over the morass those primitive, unpaved roads must be by now, he could hardly suggest leaving at this late hour, not if he wished any human guidance— Damn!

Aside from the equally impatient Alliar, seated across the chess table from him, the prince reflected that he might as well have been alone. Baroness Matilde was off seeing to castle provisions or laundry or the like. Baron Gilbert sat by the fire, puzzling over a parchment with his seneschal (neither of them, the prince guessed with a spark of contempt, particularly literate) and tacitly ignoring his troublesome guests.

The morning's excitement—the duel with Raimond,

the discovery of that crucial parchment (*"And,"* Alliar cut
in severely, catching the edge of his thought, *"that too-
close brush with mind-death."*)—could have belonged to
another world.

The prince bit back an oath, fighting the impulse to
pace. If only there was something he could *do*! Aside
from concentrating all this long afternoon on total innocence, total harmlessness— Harmlessness! The last thing
he felt right now was harmless, curse the humans for
their narrow minds! Powers, how he would love to work
some sharp, mischief-making spell just to see what would
happen.

"What would happen," Hauberin said to Alliar, who
had been following his thoughts, *'is that the baron would
toss us out into the mud."*

The fastidious being winced. *"After we've been so meek
and mild, too."* The wind spirit stirred restlessly, outline
blurring slightly then returning to sharp focus again at
Hauberin's warning glance. *"Besides,"* Alliar added, *"we
need his escort, or at least accurate directions, to get us
to Touranne."*

*"I know it. But if I sit staring at this chessboard much
longer, waiting on a human's pleasure . . ."* Alliar tactfully
didn't bring up the subject of his own human blood, and
Hauberin got to his feet, stretching. *"It must nearly be
time for my Lord Baron's dinner. One more round of
courtesy before bedtime. And then—"*

He broke off at a sudden clamor outside the keep.
The baron looked up, frowning, then shot to his feet,
eyes wild with alarm as he caught some of the words.
"Raimond," he muttered, and swept out of the room.
Hauberin and Alliar exchanged curious glances and
followed.

There in the courtyard, a ghostly figure in the darkness
but completely undisturbed by the fuss surrounding it,
stood Raimond's horse.

If Hauberin had harbored any doubts about the baron's love for his brother, they vanished there and then
as he watched that cool, self-possessed man dissolve into

near-hysteria, cursing and worrying over Raimond in the same breath.

"You, you, and you." The man's finger stabbed at startled guards. "Mount up and search to the north—yes, *now*, you louts! And you three will search to the—don't give me those insolent stares! Mount up, I say, and—"

"My lord husband." Baroness Matilde had come hurrying out of the Great Hall to the baron's side. "Please, my lord husband, you know the men can't be sent out now, when it's all but night."

"They must! Raimond is out there somewhere, injured, or s-slain."

"It's already too dark. Even with torches, the men aren't going to be able to see, particularly if they have to enter the forest." The woman glanced quickly up at the sky. "I don't think there's to be any more rain; God willing, we'll be able to follow Raimond's trail in the morning."

"We can't wait that long!"

"We really don't have a choice. If your men ride blindly out into the darkness now, their horse's hoofs are going to destroy any hope we have of finding Raimond." The baron glared at her, eyes fierce as those of a cornered predator, but she never flinched. "Please. You know I'm right. I don't like the thought of your poor brother out there alone either, but there truly is nothing we can do till morning."

Baron Gilbert shuddered, then straightened with a shadow of his usual pride, a man desperately struggling to recover self-control. "Save pray," he said softly. "So be it. We will begin our search at daybreak."

As he turned to reenter the Hall, his tormented glance caught Hauberin and Alliar. The baron hesitated, very blatantly reluctant to call on them for anything. Worry overwhelmed pride, and he burst out, "My lords, I know you planned to leave on the morrow. But will you not first help us on our search?"

Why should I care what happens to a man who tried to kill me? But he could hardly say that to his host.

Instead, working his delicate way around untruth, the prince answered evasively, "We ... will do what we can," and left it at that.

Dinner had been a grim ordeal, what with the baron and his wife lost in their thoughts, the empty chair at the baroness' side reminding them painfully of the missing Raimond. Even the usually ebullient castle folk had been subdued and somber, reflecting their master's mood, and Hauberin and Alliar were honestly glad when they could make their excuses and escape to relative privacy.

But now, alone in his guest chamber with the wary Hugh, Hauberin found himself chattering like an idiot and setting himself ridiculous little tasks, seeing to the fold of this tunic or the dusting of that pair of shoes until, with a little hiss of disgust at his cowardice, the prince realized he'd been trying like a frightened child to put off going to sleep. Hauberin settled into bed and grimly awaited his ordeal-by-nightmare. Maybe the curse, or enchantment, or whatever it was would simply fail to attack him this one night.

Of course. And maybe Raimond would fly home on butterfly wings.

At last, inevitably, Hauberin slept ...

... and the dreams began. That terrible, featureless corridor tried to form itself around him—but this once it seemed dim and unreal, its Power muted, overlaid instead by quick flashes of visions that, for all their confused brevity, had nothing of hallucination about them. Hauberin's dreaming sight caught clear glimpses of undeniably real forest, of an undeniably real Raimond alive, unharmed but powerless.

Another figure stood over Raimond, tall and thin, wrapped in a hooded cloak. As the visions continued their flickering, illogical progression, Hauberin lost track of Raimond and saw only that mysterious cloaked figure: a human, surely, a stranger, and yet somehow so teasingly familiar. ... The prince stirred restlessly in his sleep, certain he must recognize this figure, certain that he dared not fail. If only he could see beneath that concealing hood, if only he could see—

Hauberin woke with a start, sitting bolt upright in astonishment, knowing exactly who he'd sensed. Though that truly had been a human's body, the *feel* of him, the essence, had been unmistakably that of:

"Serein!"

Oh, ridiculous! Serein was dead.

But the visions had been far too clear. Hauberin knew with a magician's conviction he couldn't shrug the whole thing off with "just a dream."

"*Alliar,*" he called, mind to mind, and felt the wind spirit's senses brush his own. "*Li, you know I've never been much of a seer. But this once I . . . think I may have dreamed truly. Used far-sight. And if so . . .*"

Hauberin paused, rubbing the sleep from his eyes, trying to focus his thoughts. True enough, he never had shown much ability at far-sight, save for when there was a psychic linking to the one he sensed, some tie of blood or strong emotion—

Such as hatred—

No! How could Serein possibly still be alive?

When he was growing up, the prince had heard fanciful tales of a spell known as Free-of-Death, which, those tales said, cast a spirit safely from a dying body. No sage had ever been able to prove any such spell actually existed. But . . . what if, in the last moment of his life Serein really had thrown his spirit free?

Hauberin snorted. Not *that* again! He'd toyed with the idea often enough during those long, dream-tormented nights. And come up with the same conclusion each time: impossible. Free-of-Death, assuming it wasn't just a fable, could only be cast when a host body waited nearby, mind-dead or so weak of mind it could easily be possessed. There'd been no such host anywhere on that mountain! If Serein *had* cast such a spell, his bodiless essence would have blown to dust upon the wind.

Besides, how in the name of all the Powers could

Serein have thrown his spirit into a Realm he didn't even know existed?

"*My Prince?*" Alliar prodded warily.

"*Yes.*" Hauberin let out his breath in a long, weary sigh. "*Li, I may be mistaken. But until I know for sure whether or not I saw Serein—*"

"*Serein!*"

"*—I'm afraid we must definitely be a part of tomorrow's search party.*"

A nervous groom had sworn he'd last seen Sir Raimond heading full-tilt due north. And so, north, the party rode: Baron Gilbert and his wife, Hauberin and Alliar, with the baron's finest trackers, huntsmen and dogs.

But after nearly a full day of fruitless searching, with the night swiftly approaching, only those dogs remained cheerful, wagging their tails, sniffing the cooling air with every indication of canine delight—and showing no sign that they were following a trail.

How could they? the prince thought. *After all that rain, there can hardly be any scent left for them to follow.*

The humans weren't doing much better, picking out what *might* have been a hoofprint here or a crushed bush that *might* have been trodden by a galloping horse there, and Hauberin, nerves taut with the aftermath of his warning dream, struggled with the impulse to kick his horse into a gallop and leave the rest of them behind, because by now he knew, he *felt*, the way they must go, yet couldn't share that arcane knowledge with anyone but Alliar.

Baron Gilbert was taking out his frustration and worry on the "hopeless trackers" and their "hopeless dogs" and "this whole God-forsaken day." In a burst of fury, he finally banished the dogs and their handlers back to the castle, ignoring his wife's patient, weary attempts to soothe him.

"My Lord Baron," Hauberin broke in, "your brother could hardly have been riding cross-country, not in that downpour. This is the only northbound road on your demesne, am I right?"

"Yes, but—"

"Then we must keep going."

Ignoring the baron's frown, Hauberin urged his horse on. After a moment, he heard the others following him. But as they approached the dark green line of forest, the prince ignored the humans. Straightening in the saddle, he stared rigidly ahead, every arcane sense alert and prickling with the faintest teasing hint of . . . what? He almost had it. . . . Ae, no. Something else was in there, confusing the psychic trace, something . . . odd, decidedly Powerful. . . .

Baron Gilbert was muttering angrily to himself. Hauberin, lost in his frustrating pyschic search, cut in without even realizing he was interrupting:

"This *is* the road."

"I told you it was!" the baron snapped, then tempered that with a more restrained, "Yes. But it forks just at the forest's verge, the main branch leading to Touranne—" He broke off with a muttered oath. "If Raimond's ridden that way, out in the open, his tracks will have been washed away, and we'll never—"

"He didn't."

Baron Gilbert shot him a sharp, suspicious glance. "How could you know that?"

Hauberin blinked, brought abruptly back to caution. How, indeed? Alliar came to his aid with a smooth, "Because we've both noticed that horse-high mass of broken branches in the forest ahead, as though a weary horse had crashed through them fairly recently: Sir Raimond's horse, I don't doubt."

Hope blazed up in Baron Gilbert's eyes. Without another word, heedless of the coming darkness, he urged the party on into the looming mass of trees.

The delighted trackers were babbling about something in the cold, clear light of the full, rising moon—hoof-prints, a scrap of cloth that might have been torn from

Raimond's cloak—but the prince hardly heard them. The *feel* of Power, alien, primal, perilous, had grown so strong now it blazed like a beacon in his mind.

"Raimond *did* pass this way." Baron Gilbert's eyes were so fierce with mixed fear and hope their fire cut through Hauberin's trance. Startled by a surge of pity for this man who—too severe, too human though he was— was still his kinsman, the prince exclaimed:

"You mustn't go on. The danger—"

"What danger? To me? To Raimond?"

"I'm not—"

"Come, my lord, tell me." The baron's voice was cold with suspicion. "How could you know there's danger?"

"I . . . can't tell you. I can only warn—"

"Warning taken." Baron Gilbert reached out to catch Hauberin's arm in a painful grip. Before the angry prince could pull free, the baron murmured, "You knew we'd find traces of Raimond here. You know danger lies ahead. What else might you know about this matter, my lord?"

Hauberin jerked his arm away. "I'm not trying to trap you!"

"Indeed." Baron Gilbert's hand dropped, none too subtly, to the hilt of his sword. "Since you seem so wise, my lord, I think you must serve as our guide."

The prince glared. "So be it, my Lord Baron."

Hauberin and Alliar slipped from their horses and slid into the forest, Faerie eyes already adjusted to the night, intending with one accord to elude the inconvenient humans. They did escape most of the night-blind humans who, despite the moonlight, were blundering and crashing about, muttering curses and fumbling for the makings of torches. But, amazingly, baron and baroness kept pace, and when Hauberin glanced back over his shoulder, his gaze was met by Matilde's intent stare. It was she who was following him, leading her stumbling husband; the woman must have astonishingly keen night vision for a human.

Hauberin turned away. Enough. He had warned them. He could do no more. Particularly not now, when the *feel* of alien Power was becoming so painful a throbbing in the air he could hardly think.

But behind that Power hid— What? A darkness that might be only an occult echo. And there was still something else. . . . Heart racing, Hauberin fought to focus·on that one elusive aura, praying, *No, it can't be, it can't* . . .

Ach, the overwrought humans were making so much psychic noise he could barely think! The prince signalled sharply to them to wait and be silent, hoping they'd seen and would obey, then stole forward, Alliar a shadow at his side, to crouch hidden amid the bushes. Warily, Hauberin parted branches, Power surging before him. . . .

For one confused instant he could only stare. Could *that* be its source? That crude circle of undeniably human-worked stones?

Ae, no. Whoever had placed the stones, however many ages past, had certainly been of arcane wisdom, and a circle was a potent Symbol in itself, but the true Power lay in the land beneath. In this magic-poor Realm, Hauberin realized, the Earth-force wasn't evenly distributed. Instead, it surfaced only rarely, in dazzling, perilous upthrusts of Power like this one, calling and calling to him to draw its endless strength into his being. . . .

Hauberin came back to himself with a gasp, shaking. No, oh no, he wasn't going to try controlling something like that! This wasn't the easy magic of Faerie, but raw, primal Power strong enough to blast him to the heart. Unstable Power that could all too easily erupt into—

The prince froze, thoughts trailing to silence. A tall, lean figure was stepping out from behind a stone, shrouded in night and the same dark echo of Power Hauberin had sensed earlier. But beneath the darkness was an all-too-familiar aura. . . . Dimly, the prince heard the humans behind him gasping out, "Rogier!" But though the body facing him was human, the spirit animating it was unmistakably, undeniably:

"Serein!"

Haubering shot to his feet, quivering with horror. "Powers above, how many times must I kill you?"

"Ah, you *do* recognize me." The voice was alien, the words pure Serein. "Never again, little cousin." The man's teeth flashed in a quick smile. "I set an elaborate trap, didn't I, luring Raimond, luring you? Elaborate, but it worked."

Hauberin blocked out the terrified inner voice screaming that all this was impossible, unnatural, Serein couldn't possibly be here; it *was* possible, he *was* here, and the prince ignored his horror as best he could, thinking of Raimond's irrational attack, the flash of sea-green eyes— "I wasn't hallucinating. You really were possessing Raimond, weren't you?"

Serein's human body shrugged. "Briefly. Long enough."

But Hauberin caught a hint of disquiet behind the words. He *felt* the trace of darkness lingering about Serein and fought down a sudden shudder, wondering aloud, "Now, what could be frightening you?"

"Nothing!" Serein snapped, a bit too quickly. "Look you, this is hardly the time for a leisurely chat." His smile was cold. "I'm tired of this feeble human shell, cousin. Yours will suit me far, far better."

Hauberin just barely managed to keep from starting. "Is *that* your plan? To go home in my place? The Dark you will!"

"How can you stop me? You can't wield your pretty magicks here. And the body I wear is far more attuned to this Realm than yours, and— What do *you* want?"

A second figure—that little human sorcerer, by the Powers—had stolen out of shadow to tug at Serein's sleeve, hissing, "My lord, wait, what about me? The moon and time are right; you promised me Power."

Without taking his gaze from Hauberin, Serein shoved the sorcerer aside, so roughly the man nearly fell. "Yes, yes, do what you will. Just stay out of my way. And now, cousin, no more wasted time."

What happened next happened in a blur of confusion.

Out of the corner of his eye, Hauberin glimpsed the sorcerer dragging a bound but savagely struggling Raimond into the circle, saw a knife flash in the little man's hand even as—

—Baron Gilbert cried out "Raimond!" and rushed forward, sword drawn, to slash at the sorcerer who was about to stab his sacrifice even as—

—Serein, eyes wild, drew Power up from the land in great waves of white hot flame surrounding him that—

—engulfed Hauberin's own magic, drowning caution. His world all at once full of nothing but that Power, there was nothing he could do but pull it to him, ecstasy blazing along every nerve as the Earth-force responded to his magic and his human, native blood, surrounding him with more and yet more wild, glorious strength—

Too wild! That part of his mind clinging frantically to sanity knew neither he nor Serein could ever control so much force. Panicked, Hauberin struggled to draw free. But there was no longer any way to quiet what they'd called up, and the unstable Power was cresting—

In the instant of reason left to him, Hauberin seized the only escape he could find. Holding the wildfire at bay with all his strength of will, gasping with the strain, he caught Alliar by the arm (feeling Li catch his hair in a powerful grip at the same time), then abruptly dropped all resistance. As earth and sky erupted into one blaze of force, he let the unleashed Power recoil, hurling them out and away from peril—

Into darkness.

XVI
NOWHERE

Pain woke Hauberin. For a moment he lay sprawled where he'd fallen, eyes shut, feeling every nerve in his body protesting, and couldn't remember what he might have been doing to make him hurt like this. Power . . . it had something to do with wild torrents of Power. . . .

Oh, indeed! As memory returned in a rush, the prince swallowed drily, shaken by What Might Have Been. How lucky, how incredibly lucky, to have escaped that eruption of Earth-force with nothing worse than an aching mind and body!

Gradually Hauberin regained enough self-control to will pain down to a muted throbbing. The last thing he could remember clearly was snatching Alliar's arm and feeling the two of them being hurled aside like chips of wood on the crest of a wave. Obviously they'd survived, and landed here—

Here? Where? The prince opened his eyes a cautious crack, and looked up at a canopy of perfectly ordinary-seeming leaves far overhead, and beyond that, glimpses of luminous sky that might have been sunless or simply overcast. The air was warm and soft, smelling of sweet vegetation. The light was the clear, pale blue of mortal twilight, but there was a . . . *feel* . . . to it all that reminded him almost of Faerie. For the first time in however many days, the sense of *heaviness* weighing down his spirit was nearly gone. This was never the human Realm; there was magic here.

"Alliar?" the prince asked in wary mind-speech. *"Are you all right?"*

"*Mm*," came the groggy response, and then a more coherent, "*Yes. I think so.*" After an instant, the being added laconically, "*That was* not *the way I would have chosen to travel.*"

"*Better than staying to be crushed.*"

"*Oh, agreed! But where are we?*"

"*I haven't the slightest . . .*" Hauberin broke off as he felt a hand still clamped tightly on his hair. "Ah, Li, you can let go now."

"*?*"

The prince opened his eyes fully to see the being looking at him—from the other side of a small glade. With a startled yelp, Hauberin twisted aside, jerking his hair painfully free of the unknown, and sprang to his feet, staring down at:

"Baroness Matilde!"

The young woman, hair and riding dress disheveled, moaned faintly in protest. Her eyelids fluttered open and she looked up at him, gaze soft and unfocused. But that gaze quickly sharpened in alarm, and Matilde struggled to sit up (Hauberin winced as strands of black hair fell from her hands). "My lord! Where is everyone?" Her voice rose, sharp with panic. "Where are *we*? It was full night a moment ago, yet now— What is this place?"

"Gently, now," the prince soothed, "gently. You're in no danger." He waited till she seemed to have regained most of her composure, then continued carefully, " 'Where,' I don't know yet. As to 'what . . .' " He hesitated, remembering her fear of things arcane. "That's not going to be easy to explain."

Matilde impatiently tossed a tangled red braid back over her shoulder, fixing him with a rigid stare. "I'm not a frightened child. Be honest."

"How much of what you saw back in the stone circle did you understand?"

"You and Rogier— But . . . that . . . wasn't really Rogier, was it?"

"No."

Her fierce gaze faltered. "Possession . . . ? A . . . demon?"

"A kinsman," Hauberin said drily.

"What—"

"Look you, I'll be blunt and try not to alarm you too much: That circle marked a site of Power, magical Power. Between us, my cousin and I loosed more of that Power than we could control. The eruption threw me, Alliar and—since you were clinging to me—you here."

Her eyes were very wide. "Magic . . ."

But Hauberin abruptly waved her to silence. Both he and Alliar stiffened, listening. *"We're not alone,"* the being said.

"I know." Strolling casually to the thick, glossy green foliage surrounding the glade, Hauberin toyed idly with a leaf, then pounced with Faerie speed. There was a squeal, a thrashing, and then the prince was straightening with his squirming catch. Small and thin, nearly light as a bird in his hands, the creature was wizened and brown as bark, clad in bright scraps of cloth, sharply slanted of wild green eyes, sharply pointed of face and ears. It— he—could only be some manner of forest sprite— Ah, of course. Hauberin identified him from his mother's tales: a *lutin,* a mischievous, chaotic little being. The *lutin* writhed feverishly in Hauberin's grip, blurring, shifting hastily from sprite to snake to giant spider and back again, trying to pull free, trying to bite, and the prince gave him a shake and a stern:

"Stop that!"

He'd said it without thinking in the Faerie tongue. The *lutin* froze, feral eyes widening, and twisted about to stare up at his captor. "One o' tha High Ones!" The dialect was strange, but unmistakably of Faerie. "Forgive me, Lord. I didna know you."

Stunned, Hauberin said, "This isn't a Faerie Realm. How can you know the language?"

"Sa, sa, tha High One sports wi' me. Surely he knows where he is." The creature smiled ingratiatingly up at

Hauberin. "Let me go, High One. I sha' na run, na till you gi' me leave."

Seeing the mischief darting in those bright eyes, Hauberin had his doubts, but he let the *lutin* slip to the ground. The little being stared boldly up at him, hands on hips, head to one side, then glanced at Alliar and the wide-eyed Matilde and grinned impudently. "Faerie Lord, wind-thing, human, all t'gether—what a fine confusion!"

"Indeed. Now tell me how it is you speak a Faerie tongue."

"Why, surely tha High One knows this is Nulle Part."

"Nowhere." Hauberin repeated the human word flatly. "Small one, if this is a jest . . ."

The creature shook his head impatiently. "We stand in Nulle Part: na mortal land, na Faerie, but so-close to both. Clever folk"—the *lutin's* grin left no doubt he was including himself in that category—"travel there and here again whenever we find tha paths."

Matilde got slowly to her feet, never taking her gaze from the *lutin*. "Nowhere?" She'd caught that one human word. "Is he saying this isn't a real land at all?"

"So it would seem." Hauberin glanced at the *lutin*, who was beaming at Matilde with honest, earthy enjoyment. "You speak the human tongue, small one, don't you? Then answer the lady."

The *lutin* shrugged and easily switched languages. "We had tha mortal lands once," he told her, his alien accent thick. "Then came ye, tha human-ones, and brought tha bitter metal wi' ye." He spat.

Matilde glanced helplessly at Hauberin. " 'Bitter metal' . . . ?"

"Iron." The prince couldn't quite keep the distaste from his voice. "And so the magical beings retreated, eh, sprite?" As the creature nodded, Hauberin mused, "They evidently couldn't find their way into true Faerie; maybe they were too closely tied to mortal lands for that. But they could reach this little not-land." He smiled, savoring the *feel* of the air. "This little pocket of magic."

The baroness has gone very pale. "You knew, didn't you, my lord?" she murmured. "You knew about the magic from the start."

Hauberin sighed. "Lady, I think we're past the point of pretense. If you know what I am—"

"A High One," the *lutin* cut in, eyes alive with mischief, and dodged Alliar's swat. "One a' tha Faerie-kin," he called out, suddenly scampering away.

"Wait," Hauberin commanded, "I haven't given you leave— Stop!" But the little thing only laughed. The prince swore under his breath: *Trust a lutin* . . . "He's headed your way, Li! Stop him!"

Hampered by pseudo-human form, Alliar was still almost as quick as the sprite—almost. For a time it looked very much like a tall, two-legged cat trying to trap a particularly elusive mouse. But then Alliar made one desperate, full-length lunge. The giggling *lutin* wriggled out from under the being's outstretched arms, and vanished into the forest. Alliar disappeared with a crash into a mass of bushes, only to emerge again after a stunned moment, scratched and empty-handed, brushing off leaves and twigs. "I missed. He's gone."

"Damn." The Realm-travelling little creature could have shown them a path back to mortal lands. But as he glanced at his panting, rumpled friend, the prince forgot his frustration, cherishing the thought of that leafy dive: one of the few times he'd caught Alliar being flesh-and-blood clumsy. "You gave it a gallant try," Hauberin said, struggling not to laugh.

Alliar's bow dripped sarcasm.

"My lords?" asked the bewildered Matilde, and Hauberin turned to her with what he hoped was a reassuring smile. She didn't look at all comforted. "What was that . . . being?"

"A *lutin*. A small, sentient fragment of the forest's life-force. Nothing to frighten you, for all his strangeness. Those little ones are mischief incarnate, but there's no real harm to any of them."

"Wh-What he said about you wasn't a lie, was it? The old tales say magic creatures can't lie."

"They can't," Hauberin admitted, then paused, considering her. "But you didn't need the *lutin's* help, did you? You already knew the truth about me."

"I'd guessed." Matilde's voice was very soft. "I just didn't believe. Not really. Till now."

"But you never said a word to your husband."

"Oh, God! Do you really think he would have believed me? 'My lord husband, our guest isn't human, but a—a being out of—" She gave a strangled little laugh. "I didn't want to be locked away as a madwoman, or b-burned as a witch." Matilde's eyes were wild, but she continued resolutely, "Don't worry, my lord, I'm not about to collapse into hysterics. If I started screaming now, I d-don't think I'd be able to stop. But that wouldn't get me back to husband and home. You're the only one who can return me, and you . . . you . . ." She shivered suddenly, hugging her arms about herself. "You truly are of Faerie. You aren't human."

"Yes to the first, not exactly to the second. Lady," Hauberin said gently, "even as truthfulness binds the sprite, so it binds me. I never lied to you or your husband. I mean no harm to you or any of your kin. My name really is Hauberin. And my rank is . . . high enough."

"High enough," Alliar muttered. "He's a prince, lady, the ruler of his land."

Matilde's eyes widened even more. "But what in the name of all that's holy were you doing in our castle?"

Hauberin glanced a warning to Alliar. "I thought I was merely . . . tracing my ancestry. It would seem I was hunting my cousin as well." He paused, listening to the forest about them, suddenly uneasy. The dim blue twilight hadn't darkened and the air remained mild, but there was the scent of approaching night to it. The things that might walk Nulle Part after dark wouldn't be as harmless as a forest sprite, and he wasn't quite sure how much of this non-land's Power he could wield. "Much as

I'd love to answer the rest of your questions, I think we'd better find a secure spot to make camp first, and start gathering firewood."

Matilde bit her lip. "Is that necessary? Can't you just use your . . . Art to take us home?"

Hauberin hesitated. His travel-spell would surely work well enough even from . . . Nowhere to transport them safely to Faerie. But what was he to do with Matilde? He supposed a true Faerie Lord—pitilesss and practical—would simply keep her there, whether she willed it or not. That was certainly the simplest solution, because if he didn't return her from Faerie to her precise time, if he made the slightest error, she would die of sudden old age.

And yet, the thought of keeping this brave, bright lady a virtual prisoner . . . Nulle Part, for all its magic, was a direct offshoot of the mortal Realm; it existed in very nearly the same time-frame. If they traveled back to Matilde's land from here, there wouldn't be any temporal problems.

Oh yes, if.

The prince sighed. "I could take you home," he said honestly, "if only I knew exactly where we are. Ah lady, don't worry! Either Alliar or I will puzzle it out soon enough."

"*Optimist.*"

"*Hush.*" Hauberin looked about him. "I think this is as safe a site for a camp as we're likely to find; with empty space on all sides, nothing can steal up on us. Let's gather our firewood before night falls." He paused. "I don't think I have to warn anyone about taking only dead branches?"

The trees, like the rest of Nulle Part, were an intriguing mixture of Earthly and Other. As they foraged in the underbrush, Hauberin keeping a protective eye on the human woman, the prince's attention was caught by a bush of bright red berries that looked very much like *ailaitha,* native to his own lands. Hauberin knelt by the bush, murmuring the words of an identification spell, then sat back on his heels with a pleased smile. Not only had the spell worked—almost as easily as it would have in Faerie—but this was indeed an *ailaitha* bush, the seeds presumably scattered by one of the Realm-wandering sprites. Alliar probably didn't need food yet, but he and Matilde did. At least they wouldn't have to fast this night.

Now, what could he use to hold the berries? A basket magicked out of leaves? If Matilde had a scarf or kerchief, that would be much simpler.

"Ah, lady," Hauberin began, then froze. "Lady!"

"Oh come, look." The woman's voice was soft and crooning. "I've found a puppy, and I think the poor thing's hurt."

A puppy? Here? Warily, Hauberin moved to where Matilde crouched in the underbrush. Something whimpered and wriggled at his approach, staring up at him with big, frightened eyes. The prince raised a surprised brow. This funny, snub-nosed little creature really *was* a pup, looking very much like those baby hounds-to-be he'd seen tumbling about the baron's castle, all awkward paws and scraggly fur.

But . . . what was a blatantly mortal pup doing here? Hauberin glanced up at Matilde, and saw her normal keen eyes clouded over with softness—or enchantment. And all at once the prince remembered that human inn, and the innkeeper mentioning, too lightly, tales of magical creatures:

"*. . . like the* galipote, *who can make himself look like your favorite hound, just waitin' for you to turn your back.*"

"Matilde, no!" As she reached down to the puppy, Hauberin snatched her aside. The pup glared up at him in cheated rage, hungry green fire blazing in suddenly far from innocent eyes, and the prince shouted out in the Faerie language, "You've lost to me, creature! By all the Power of my blood, I command you, take your rightful form!"

He put a surging of will behind the words. The puppy form cringed, snarling, then submitted, obediently blurring, growing . . . puppy no longer but a long, sleek canine shape, pale as moonlight, angry intelligence in its tapering green eyes. It made one defiant rush at Matilde— only to spring back with a startled yelp as she lunged at it with her suddenly drawn belt-knife.

The *galipote* glanced from the threatening iron on one side to the equally threatening Faerie lord on the other. And all at once all its defiance broke. Tail between its legs like a frightened hound, the creature turned and raced wildly away, yipping. As its cried died away, Hauberin and Matilde stared after it in amazement, then, as one, burst into laughter.

"What—what was that?" Matilde gasped. "A g-*galipote* out of the—the tales?'"

The prince nodded. "A—hungry one."

"But it looked so silly! Not like a—a demon, l-like a frightened puppy running for its life!"

Hauberin took a deep, steadying breath. "Ach, lady," he began. But as Matilde, wiping her eyes, turned to him, he saw only the knife glinting in her hand, and instinctively flinched away from iron. The woman stared at him, then glanced down at the blade.

"Oh. Of course." She hastily resheathed it. "You . . . really *are* of Faerie."

"Did you still have any doubts?"

"What was it you shouted at the *galipote*? A—a spell?"

"Not really. I simply commanded the creature to reveal its true form. It had enough awe of things Faerie to obey. Lady, come. I've found us some berries for dinner."

But she stopped him with a gentle hand on his arm. "You saved my life. Thank you."

That simple touch seemed to blaze through him. He froze, stunned, thinking, *Oh no, not here, not now. . . .* Matilde's eyes, their delicate slant so like those of a Faerie woman, were soft and wondering, for this brief time totally unshadowed by fear. Her lips held the faintest trace of a smile, so sweet . . . All at once Hauberin realized how very much aware he was of the feminine warmth and scent of her. Time seemed to still as they stared at each other, hardly daring to breathe. . . .

But then the prince flinched away as though she'd burned him, reminding himself angrily, *She's human. And another man's wife.* "I could hardly have let you be eaten," he said belatedly.

"No. Of course not." She was struggling to match his brusque tone, refusing to meet his gaze, busily smoothing her disheveled hair. "Ach, the tangles . . ."

Tangles. "Matilde, I . . ."

"Are you two all right?" It was Alliar, appearing in the wind spirit's usual silent fashion. "I heard you shout—"

"Fine. Everything's fine." This once, Hauberin could cheerfully have throttled his friend. "My lady," he added, voice rigidly neutral, "if you will gather these berries, Alliar and I will take care of the firewood."

By the time the three of them were kneeling before their newly acquired pile of wood, the prince had almost convinced himself that warm, disconcerting moment had meant nothing.

Matilde certainly seemed to think so. Judging from her unembarrassed manner, she hadn't meant to express anything more than honest gratitude. Now, eyeing the wood with a doubtful glance, she said, "I *think* there's enough to see us through the night. If nights here are anything like mortal nights. I don't know what we're going to do for flint, but at least I have the steel."

She hesitantly touched her little knife, but Hauberin shook his head. "No need."

He sparked the fire into life with an extravagant flash of will, showing off; having flinched from a lady's dainty dagger still rankled. But her reaction wasn't at all what he'd expected: a wave of such undeniable terror that the prince said, abashed:

"Here now, I'm sorry. I didn't mean to frighten you."

She shook her head. "It wasn't you, or—that. It was . . . I . . ."

"Lady?"

"I—Oh, God help me, *I can do that, too!*"

Hauberin and Alliar stared. "But what's so terrible about that?" the being asked.

"Don't you see? I'm *human! Humans* aren't supposed to be able to do things like that!"

"Why ever not? Hauberin's own mother—"

But the prince waved his friend to silence. "Ah, so *that* explains it," he murmured. "All along I thought you almost unnaturally magickless, even if you did so miraculously know I was in trouble in the tower room—"

"I told you, I heard your fall."

"Through the rainstorm. Of course. And you just happened to flee here with me—"

"I didn't think about it, I just— It only—"

"Seemed like the right choice at the time," Hauberin completed. "You weren't magickless at all. Instead, you were hiding your gifts so completely—even, I'd guess, from yourself—that I couldn't sense—"

"No!" It was a cry of pain. "I don't have any gifts! I'm not a witch, or—or—"

"Lady," Alliar soothed, "we'd be the last to accuse you."

She glanced from one Faerie being to the other. "Of . . . course. But," the woman insisted stubbornly, "I'm not a witch."

Hauberin sighed. "If it's any comfort, it's true that my own mother was called a witch. It's not such a terrible name."

"Isn't it?" Matilde's voice was savage. "They *burn* witches, my lord, they chain them to stakes, and light the fire under their feet, and there's no escape, only the smoke and the flames and the pain—"

She broke off with a strangled little sob. As Hauberin and Alliar watched her in helpless astonishment, she gradually fought herself back under control, wiping her eyes with an angry hand. "Forgive me. I didn't mean to do that."

"Nonsense," the prince murmured. "After all you've been through this day, you're entitled to a little collapse."

"No. I mustn't. My husband . . ."

Wouldn't allow such weakness, Hauberin finished silently. "You must love him very much."

Matilde glanced at him in surprise. "What has love to do with it?"

"Ah . . . well . . ." the prince floundered, "you married him."

Her eyes narrowed. "I don't know how things stand in Faerie, but women in my land don't have much say in the matter. A noblewoman must be wed."

"Why?"

"Because there's no other choice!" Matilde erupted. "She's not allowed to own property, so His Gracious Majesty off in Paris has decreed. She isn't trained to—to run a farm or a business like her common-born sisters. It's wed, or enter a nunnery."

"And you didn't want that," Hauberin said, feeling his way through unknown territory. Matilde eyed him uneasily.

"You . . . wouldn't know about such things as nunneries, would you? They're walled retreats, behind which holy woman live and pray, shut away from the distractions of the world."

Alliar made a tiny sound of distress. "A prison."

"No. Not for those with a true calling. But I . . . oh, dear Lord, I—I think I would have smothered behind those walls."

"Ae, yes," the being murmured in sympathy. "So you wed to escape confinement."

"I . . . wouldn't have put it quite that way, but . . . yes. My parents warned me that not many men would want a . . . willful . . . wife, one who wantonly spoke her own mind. Particularly one with 'unlucky' hair." She gave a red braid a sharp tug. "Of course they were right. But my lord husband made a most gracious offer for me. And he's been good to me. Oh, come," she added desperately, "you're both staring at me as though I've been speaking a foreign tongue!"

"In Faerie," Hauberin murmured, "we wed for love."

That earned him an astonished stare. "What, even you, a prince?"

"Even me. My people can't lie, remember? And a forced marriage would certainly be a lie."

"But you can't dare wait till you fall in love! I mean, if your people follow any laws of succession—"

"I must produce an heir? Well yes, everyone would be much happier if said heir came from a wife; it's . . . tidier." Hauberin hesitated, trying to avoid shocking her human sensibilities. "But the first child I sire, in wedlock or without, becomes my legal heir."

"But . . ."

"We are not a fertile race. We can't afford to worry about that ridiculous 'legitimate' or 'illegitimate.'" He shook his head, bemused, "I never realized how large the gap is between our two peoples' ways. No wonder my mother— Ah, enough of this. Let's eat the *ailaitha* berries before they spoil." When he saw Matilde hesitate, Hauberin added wryly, "I assure you, no matter what the stories say, tasting Faerie food won't enslave you."

'Oh, I didn't think it would," she lied boldly, and bit into a berry, hastily leaning forward to keep the spurt of juice from her clothes. "Mm, sweet!"

"And nourishing," Hauberin added. "They should keep us healthy till we get out of Nulle Part. Which hopefully won't take too long."

"Amen."

They were silent for a time, munching. Suddenly Matilde gave a brittle little laugh.

"Lady?"

"Here my husband is forever worrying about my honor. If he could see me now, alone with two strange men . . ."

"?" Alliar asked silently.

"*Gendered games,*" Hauberin explained, and saw comprehension dawn.

"'Strange,' indeed," the being murmured. "No danger from me, lady, believe me. Even if I . . . could desire, I . . . ah, couldn't."

Matilde's eyes were suddenly fully of pity. "Oh, I'm sorry. I didn't realize . . . Was it a . . . war wound, my lord?"

Hauberin nearly choked. "*She means to the male anatomy, Li.*"

"*Oh. Oh!*" "No!" the being cried aloud. "What I meant was, I literally can't—I don't have— Oh, Winds! What I am isn't a man, but a wind spirit. Yes, I know this disguise is convincing, but— Here. Look."

Alliar smoothly slid into one of the being's more usual forms: lithe and sleekly golden of skin and mane, face and body fiercely planed, lovely and sexless as stone. Matilde drew in her breath in astonishment, and Alliar asked uneasily, "Am I so frightening?"

"So beautiful. I've . . . seen your likeness on church walls, my lord. You lack only the wings to be an angel."

As Hauberin explained the concept in a flash of thought, the being's eyes widened in embarrassment. "Oh, hardly that! But thank you, my lady."

Alliar and Matilde smiled shyly, lost for an instant in their own world. To his amazement, Hauberin felt a sharp twinge of jealousy. Of *Alliar*? Oh, how utterly ridiculous! But the prince heard himself saying, a touch too sharply, "I think you've been asked to accept too many wonders this day, lady. You must be weary."

Matilde, still staring at Alliar, started to protest, only to hastily stifle a yawn. Hauberin laughed shortly. "You see? Your body is living by mortal time, which must be somewhere in the small hours of the night. I wish I could conjure an angelic blanket for you"—he shot a wry glance at Alliar—"but I'm not an angel, either. Let's try to get some sleep, regardless."

The night was very dark; this little pocket of Nowhere lacked stars. Matilde, deep in exhausted slumber, was curled up against the chill like a child, red hair a tangled mass, face looking very young, very innocent. Hauberin sat starkly awake, not daring to gaze her way, staring moodily into the fire. All at once aware of eyes upon him, the prince glanced up to see Alliar, quiet as a golden statue, watching him.

"*What?*" Hauberin asked shortly.

"*She's human.*"

"*I know that.*"

"*Only human.*" Alliar's eyes were glowing orbs in the darkness. "*You already carry human blood enough in your veins. You dare not mate with a human woman, and risk creating a magickless heir.*"

Hauberin stirred impatiently. "*What would you know about such things?*"

"*Oh, please. Maybe I can't really understand flesh-and-blood mating games, but I can still recognize them. I've seen you play them with women before this.*"

"*I wasn't playing any mating games. And stay out of my affairs.*"

I can't. Not if I'm truly your friend. Hauberin, you cannot let it happen."

"*Dammit, I know! Nothing happened. Nothing's going to happen. Now, leave me alone!*"

Feeling Alliar's insulted anger like a door slamming shut against his mind, the prince stared into the fire with renewed intensity. Powers, the sooner he found the way out of this ridiculous Nulle Part . . .

Oh, idiot! He wasn't likely to get a better chance to try than right now, with the fire to serve as focus. Staring into it, not attempting to see pictures in the flickering flames, Hauberin instead let them soothe him, half hypnotize his conscious self. . . . Whispering calming Words, relaxing his mind still further, the prince let his inner self roam free, hunting . . . hunting . . .

Yes. The sprite hadn't tricked him. All at once he *felt* the arcane paths tangling through Nulle Part like so many silvery threads, each leading to a different possibility, a Realm, a place, a time—or, unpredictably, to the emptiness beyond time and space. He shuddered away from that terrible nothingness, hunting anew. . . .

There. He could see it as a pattern in his mind, the one path they needed, that twisting puzzle of a psychic

ribbon: the one path that would take them safely back
to the stone circle in the human Realm. He knew it, he
felt it, and sent his senses soaring along the path to mem-
orize its every devious turn. It was no easy thing; the
path seemed to squirm under his touch like a living thing
consciously trying to escape, but Hauberin dared not let
go or he might never find it again. Straining, he sent his
mind twisting with it, following its every move, struggling
with it till every convolution was set into his memory—

Ah, Powers be praised, he was done. Hauberin slid
back into himself and, before he could move or even
think, into exhausted sleep as well.

XVII

THE TANGLED WAY

Matilde woke slowly, in stages, first aware that her bed seemed unusually hard and lumpy, then realizing it wasn't a bed at all, then blinking in confusion, unable to think why she had been sleeping on bare ground, in her clothes, with only her riding cloak for blanket. The world about her was dim with twilight—

But that couldn't be! She couldn't have slept the night and day around, could she?

No. Of course not. This wasn't the mortal world, but Nulle Part, Nowhere.

Matilde sat up carefully, stiff muscles complaining, and brushed wild hair back from her face, wishing irrelevantly (amid all the alien surroundings) for a comb, then froze, looking across the embers of the dying fire to where the . . . being that called himself—itself?—Alliar watched her.

Itself. A *spirit*, she thought, *a wind-spirit*, and then, wildly: *How can a spirit be in physical form?*

She didn't quite have the nerve to ask.

A small, prim voice within her was scolding faintly that no, she shouldn't merely be nervous, she should surely be terrified. Surrounded by strangeness, by heathen creatures, she should be lost in prayer, begging Heaven to protect her soul.

And yet, for all that a priest would thunder at her that this place was un-Godly, that *she* was un-Godly, Matilde knew she wasn't afraid. She hadn't truly been afraid since that first alarming moment of arrival. After all, she thought with a flash of dark humor, the creatures of

Nulle Part only wanted to eat her, not condemn her or burn her at the stake—

But she wasn't going to start babbling to herself like this. Matilde began to greet Alliar politely, but was hastily waved to silence. The being pointed, and she looked down to find Hauberin still curled in sleep, sleek black hair fallen forward to half-hide his face.

A pang almost of pain shot through her at the sight of the sharp, proud features now relaxed and defenseless. He had seemed so human back in her husband's castle, dazzling them all with clever words and charming manners so they'd never really had a chance to study him at rest. Now there could be no mistaking the alien cast of his face: ever so slightly too high of cheekbone, too narrow of chin and pointed of ear for true humanity. And yet, she thought, he didn't look overly exotic; at the moment, even with those elegant ears, he seemed more like any weary, travel-stained young man than a Faerie prince.

And here I always thought a Faerie prince would be all tall and fair and golden-haired!

But his black hair was beautiful, smooth and straight as a fall of water, so dark it had gleamed blue-purple in the sunlight. It must be silk-soft to the touch. Hardly aware of what she was doing, Matilde reached out a gentle hand to brush the wild strands back from his face, only to freeze at Alliar's steady gaze. The golden face was expressionless, and yet she felt such a weight of quiet disapproval that she drew back.

"I wasn't going to hurt him," she mouthed indignantly.

But a moan from Hauberin caught her attention. Ah, poor man, his dreams seemed to have turned dark, because he was fighting them, murmuring broken phrases in what surely must be his native tongue, struggling to escape. Matilde was just about to wake him when he woke himself, starting up with a wild cry, face to face with her, dark eyes blazing into her own, wild and blank with terror. Helpless, Matilde stammered for words of comfort, but sanity returned with a rush to those slanted eyes, and the prince sat back with a weary sigh, head in hands.

Matilde hadn't seen or heard the being move, but Alliar was there at her side, so suddenly she started.

"The dream?" the being asked softly, and Hauberin nodded, adding with weary humor, "I think I'm growing used to it; I wasn't much further down the corridor. And at least this time I got some sleep."

Matilde looked from one to the other in open confusion. "A recurring dream?" she asked hesitantly. "A . . . prophetic one?"

Hauberin rubbed a hand over his eyes. "Powers, I hope not. Ah, it's too complicated to explain. Let's just say my cousin cursed me with what I thought was his dying breath, and leave it at that."

"The cousin who's . . . wearing . . . Rogier's body."

"Yes." The prince got to his feet, stretching, managing somehow, Matilde thought enviously, to look elegant despite rumpled tunic and dirt-stained cloak. Feeling suddenly hopelessly grubby, she tried to do *something* with her impossible hair, rebraiding it hastily into two tight plaits, muttering over the tangles, very much aware of Hauberin's glance on her. Last night . . . No. She wouldn't think of that; she was a married woman, and human, while he— No, again. That moment of—of whatever had almost happened between them was gone as though it had never been, and Matilde wasn't sure if she was disappointed or relieved.

But Hauberin was grinning. "Ah, I *do* remember!" he said with such evident relief that both Matilde and Alliar stared at him in bewilderment. He laughed. "No, I haven't lost my mind. Last night I used the fire to find the way out of Nowhere for us, and it's still set in my memory. Come, let's take care of . . . ah . . . necessaries, and be on our way."

Did she really want to go back . . . ? Back to hiding and pretending . . . ?

Oh, nonsense. Her husband was back there, and her

good, safe, mortal life. She certainly didn't want to stay in this gloomy twilight Nowhere forever!

A flicker of motion caught her eye. Matilde glanced at Alliar in time to see the being shimmer and change back into man-shape. Alliar shrugged. "It makes a better defensive form, don't you think?"

"Doesn't that hurt?" Matilde burst out before she could guard her tongue. "Changing shape like that, isn't it . . . uncomfortable?"

Alliar chuckled, but Matilde surprised something unthinkably old and sad in the golden eyes. For a moment she saw the endless sweep of sky reflected there, the endless sweep of freedom. . . . Freedom lost. Dizzy, she staggered, and the moment was past. "You understand," the being murmured. "Why should one shape be more difficult than another, when all are forced?"

Bewildered, Matilde stammered over a deluge of questions, but Alliar only smiled and held up a hand. "I don't want to be trapped in Nulle Part any more than you do. Let's follow Hauberin, shall we?"

Faerie prince and wind-spirit moved as smoothly through the tangled underbrush as fish through water. Panting, stumbling over roots, snagging clothes and skin on thorns, Matilde struggled after them, fighting back oaths she'd never realized she knew. The path (nothing as clear as a physical one) might be leading them back to the human world, but it was a Godforsakenly difficult one to follow.

Be thankful for small mercies, she told herself. At least the weather remained clear and warm, and nothing was actively menacing them; even whatever birds might be in the forest were keeping still, unnerved by human or Faerie strangers.

Hauberin stopped short for perhaps the hundredth time, evidently questing for whatever psychic ribbon they were following. Matilde, head down, crashed right into his back, and recoiled with an embarrassed mutter of apology. Eyes opaque and alien enough to make her shiver, focused on something beyond the physical, he never noticed, only started forward again. With a great sigh, she followed.

What an unpredictable thing this forest was, now a dense tangle of underbrush, now an open progression of trees orderly enough to be part of some noble's park.

It was in the midst of such an orderly stretch that Matilde gave up. "You may be of Faerie, my lords—Your Grace—"

Jarred back to the real world, the prince stared at her as though seeing her for the first time. (*And what a sight I must be*, she thought, *red-faced and sweaty as a farmer.*) He blinked.

"Hauberin," he said belatedly. "Forget the formal titles. We're hardly in a proper court now."

She dipped her head to him. "Hauberin, then. You may be of Faerie, but remember I'm only human. I . . . must rest."

"Ae, of course." The olive-dark skin flushed slightly. "Forgive us."

She sank gladly to a rock, content for a time just to steady her breathing, then glanced about at the twilight-dim light that was beginning to wear on her nerves. Was this Nowhere always so gloomy? A flash of memory made her quote, " 'A land that seemed always afternoon . . .' " and add, "The stories say Faerie has no sun, either. Is your own land like this?"

Hauberin had perched on the opposite side of the rock. He shook his head. "Nothing even half so dreary. It's true we have nothing like your mortal sun. But our very air is alive with light during the day, so beautiful. And at night—oh, at night a thousand, thousand stars light the sky—they blaze with color, red and blue and green, not like your simple Earthly stars—and the moonlight spilling down is pure, unstained silver."

Such longing ached in his voice that Matilde turned with a faint, sympathetic smile, thinking that Faerie or human, homesickness was the same. "That morning on the castle wall," she murmured, "when I said you looked like a man seeing his first sunrise . . . It really *was* your first, wasn't it?"

He smiled in return. "It was. And oh, what a splendid sight. . . ."

But he was looking full at her as he said that, and his eyes were dark as night . . . a warm, wonderful night. . . .

A cough from Alliar jarred them both back to reality. Hauberin snapped something short and sharp to the being who, not at all discomforted by the princely rebuke, raised a shoulder in the slightest of shrugs, as though to say, *someone* has to be sensible. Matilde bit back a little laugh, seeing the easy warmth behind the sharpness, reminded of the comfortable, friendly joshing she'd seen between some of her husband's men-at-arms, astonishing herself by the envy she felt.

"You *are* friends, aren't you?" she asked unnecessarily.

Hauberin raised a wry eyebrow, eyes alight with humor. "Would I suffer such insolence from anyone else?"

But something he had mentioned earlier was nagging at her memory. Carefully Matilde began, "Would you . . . be offended if I asked you a question?"

"Probably not. Ask."

"Yesterday you told me you were in my husband's castle tracing your ancestry. And later, you mentioned that your own mother was—was called a witch. Are you . . .? Was she . . . ?"

"Human?" The dark eyes blazed with such sudden anger that Matilde realized too late she'd broken a rule of Faerie etiquette: asking one of his ever-truthful race a question he couldn't avoid answering. But then the prince sighed and moved a hand in an odd, ritualistic little gesture, murmuring, "*Athenial ne thenial:* you shared thoughts with me, I share with you. Ae, yes. I am my father's rightful heir, but my mother was of your people. Now, are you rested enough to go on?"

"I did offend you, didn't I?"

Hauberin glanced sharply at her. "You didn't mean to.

And I'll admit I'm not always comfortable about my mixed blood."

"But your subjects accept you, don't they? and—"

His laugh interrupted her. "Believe me, if I hadn't inherited magic, I doubt I would have reached my majority, let alone ruled."

"I—I didn't realize . . ."

"Ach no, it wasn't as bad as I'm making it sound. What royal court—including, I've no doubt, human ones—isn't full of intrigues? Of course I had—and have—enemies."

"Including," Matilde added daringly, "your cousin?"

"Including my cousin. Serein. Whom I intend to oust from his stolen home as soon as we return."

"He . . . killed Rogier, didn't he?"

"Oh, probably. Any man who would stoop to child-murder—" he said it as though it was the foulest obscenity (which, thought Matilde, it was) "—wouldn't shrink from killing a grown man. A . . . mere human, to boot."

Matilde bit her lip. "I shouldn't want him for a foe."

Hauberin shrugged. "One can't, as the saying goes, pick one's relatives. Serein only once dared attack me openly, and I—thought I'd put an end to him. Look you, I did have—what shall I say?—friendlier family, too, and friends. I still do have my friends," he added with a quick grin at Alliar, who made him an elegant little bow. The prince stretched restlessly, then got to his feet. "Enough of this. No, it's not easy being part-other-than-Faerie, no, I'm not really bitter about what I can't change, and yes, I do love my land and people very much and most of them seem quite content with their prince, human blood or no. Now, let's do something about getting out of Nulle Part."

Wearily Matilde got to her feet and followed. The open progression of trees narrowed all too soon for her comfort, the way becoming overgrown once more. At last she found herself trailing the others down a narrow corridor lined with a maze of intertwined bushes taller than her head: walls of heavy, dark green leaves looming over her on both sides, so close they brushed her arms like so many moist, chilly hands. Matilde shuddered, pulling her cloak about her, and the leaves left damp streaks on the thick wool. The air was heavy with the odor of dank, overripe growth, and she could swear the ground squelched faintly beneath her feet. Dear saints, did Hauberin really know where he was going? Was he deliberately leading them into a swamp? Or maybe even into a trap . . . ? He was a Faerie man, after all, not really human. . . . Soulless, the priests would say. As if priests knew anything about Faerie.

The thick, dank air was wearing on her nerves. Matilde all at once could have sworn that something was watching them, keeping pace with every step. The *galipote*? Something worse? But when the young woman glanced wildly about, she saw nothing but the heavy vegetation and heard nothing but her own squelching footsteps.

Don't be a fool, she snapped at herself. *I'm with two magical beings. If there was any real danger, they'd know it.*

It wasn't too comforting to see that both Hauberin and Alliar were alert as two wild things. Something disconcertingly close emitted a sobbing cry, and Matilde jumped violently, barely biting back a cry of her own, vaguely gratified to see prince and wind spirit start, too.

"Bird?" suggested Hauberin after a taut moment, but Alliar hesitated a long, nerve-racking while, searching with some arcane wind-spirit sense before reluctantly nodding and murmuring:

"Maybe. At least it doesn't mean us any harm. I think."

Hauberin flicked his gaze warningly to Matilde, and Alliar switched to a melodious language that could only be the Faerie tongue. Insulted, Matilde murmured, "I'm not a child, gentles. You don't have to shield me.'

The prince, Faerie-truthful, took her words at face value, saying frankly, "We were agreeing that we're being watched by something or someone hostile."

Did he have to be *quite* so honest? Matilde looked into the fierce, wary eyes and swallowed drily. "Then it

wasn't just my fancy," she managed, struggling to keep
her voice level. "Are we in peril?"

"No. Not yet, as far as Alliar or I can sense. But it
might be wise for you to keep close."

"No fear," she muttered, hand closing firmly about the
hilt of her little belt-knife.

To Matilde's immense relief, the claustrophobic path
gradually began to widen, then suddenly opened up onto
a wide, mossy glade verging on a lake that lay still as
gray mist under the gray mist sky. There wasn't a sound,
not the slightest chirp of bird or rustle of reed, there
wasn't the slightest sign of life, and yet she found herself
struggling not to cringe beneath the weight of unseen
eyes. Hauberin glanced her way.

"You feel it too, don't you?" he murmured.

Matilde nodded almost absently. There was something
about this scene . . . something nagging at her memory.
A story she had once heard. . . . If only she could
remember. . . .

"Why, look at this!" Alliar exclaimed, and Matilde
turned to see a gleam of silver, glint of gem: a small
goblet bobbing on the water, half-hidden in the reeds at
the lake's edge.

"Now, how did this get here?" the being wondered,
and stooped to scoop it up—

The elusive memory returned to Matilde with a shock.
"No, don't!" she screamed, and pulled Alliar away with
a strength born of panic. The astonished being went
sprawling—and the silvery-green arm snaking up out of
the water closed on empty air.

In the next moment, the lake-being was upon them,
sleek and lithe, thick silver hair swirling about a fine-
boned, elegant face, the tapering eyes fiercely green as
he stared at Matilde in implacable hunger (for food, or
for something more?), the whole close enough to handsome man-form to send a little shiver racing through her.
But the teeth bared in an angry smile were pointed, and
scales shimmered along the too-limber arms. And the

hands that reached for her as the being lunged ended in
gleaming claws. For one terrifying moment, deathly chill
fingers closed with implacable strength about her wrist
and she saw nothing but death by drowning in the green-
flame eyes.

But then Hauberin was shouting out a sharp, commanding spell in the Faerie tongue. The words seemed
to blaze for an instant in the air, and the creature
released Matilde with a hiss, as though her flesh had all
at once burned him.

"D-Drac," Matilde cried out, stumbling over her
words, "dragon-man—"

"Drac," the being agreed, and the smile he gave her,
sharp teeth hidden, was urbane and sensual, so sensual
it sent a little prickle shivering through her even as she
recoiled. "Lovely thing, lovely human woman ... how
long since I've touched soft woman-flesh. . . ." he purred,
voice as mellifluous as water flowing smoothly over stone.
"You fear me. Am I so monstrous to you?"

Oh, no. He was fair, inhumanly fair, and the light in
his green eyes promised such wonders. . . .

Dazed, Matilde felt a hand close about her arm, dig-
ging into her flesh till she gasped in startled pain and
turned to stare at Hauberin—and only then realized the
drac had nearly charmed her right into the water: Drac,
dragon-man in one, stalker of woman, eater of human
flesh—

"You shall not have this woman." Hauberin's voice was
cold with command.

"Shan't I?" The drac smiled again, stare never leaving
Matilde's face. "I saw the *galipote* running in fear, I
laughed at it and followed you, waiting, waiting till you
came to my very doorway. I am no foolish *galipote*, my
friends, to abandon food and sport."

For answer, Hauberin snapped out a ringing Faerie
phrase that made the drac start. The sharp green gaze
shot from Matilde to Hauberin, as though the being was
only now fully aware of the prince. The drac's eyes narrowed warily, but his smile never wavered.

"Faerie-man," he purred. "Silly little Faerie-man. Your spells will barely work here; you have no true power over Nulle Part."

"No? Then dare come closer," Hauberin retorted.

Instead, the drac stalked sideways, circling. Hauberin turned with him, dark eyes fierce, keeping Matilde always behind him. Alliar fell into place behind her, guarding her back, and Matilde heard the drac give the softest hiss of frustration.

"Long and long has it been since I've touched woman-skin, long since I've tasted the sweetness of human-flesh. I shall not be defeated now."

There was no warning, no betraying tensing of muscles. Suddenly the drac was at her side, swifter even than Faerie speed. There wasn't any time to plan, to think. Faced with a blur of fangs, green-flame eyes, flashing claws, Matilde did the only thing she could, and lunged with her belt-knife. She felt the little blade graze flesh, heard the drac scream—a high, alien shrilling that burned at her ears and went on and on and on. Green eyes, wide and hating, stared into her own, sharp teeth flashed for her throat—

But then Hauberin shoved the drac aside. Still keen-ing, the dragon-man fell, crumpling bonelessly. Heart racing, Matilde stared, expecting a trick, expecting him to leap up again. But after an eternity of watching, the crumpled figure remained still. Alliar stuck out a wary foot and pushed the body onto its back, and Matilde drew in her breath in a sharp gasp of horror.

The green eyes stared sightlessly up at the sky, their fierceness fled. The flesh had fallen away from the con-torted, finely-planed face, rigid with agony, leaving it lit-tle more than skin stretched tightly over bone.

"Dead . . ." Alliar murmured, and:

"Iron-poison," Hauberin said flatly.

Matilde couldn't bear to look at that agonized mask any longer. "But . . . I only scratched him. . . ."

The prince was rigid with horror, eyes wide, dusky skin pale. "It was enough."

His terror was only just held in check. Matilde swallowed drily, all at once understanding: iron-death was a nightmare of his people—a nightmare come all too real. And such a death could just as easily have been his if her knife had slipped. . . . Dear God.

Without warning, Hauberin snagged her wrist with a cold hand, voice taut. "Come, we must go on."

He led them away so swiftly Matilde and even Alliar could hardly keep up. After a time of being half-dragged through dense underbrush that scratched her skin and tugged painfully at her hair, Matilde gasped out, "Wait! I— You— Stop it!" and planted her feet firmly, pulling the prince to a halt with her. As he stared at her, wild-eyed, she said flatly, "I don't blame you for being frightened of—of iron-death, it looks like a truly foul thing. But I don't want to be towed like a reluctant puppy, either!"

Sanity flooded back into the stark eyes. He reddened. "Of course not. Forgive me." Glancing around, the prince added cajolingly, "Ah, but we're so close to our goal now. Just a little further."

It wasn't quite as close as Matilde would have liked. But all at once the three of them were bursting through a final snarl of bushes to find—

"But this can't be right!" she protested. "This is where we started!"

To her astonishment, she heard Alliar chuckle. Hauberin grinned at her; though his hair was as wild a tangle as her own, his clothing disheveled, he'd managed to totally regain his self-possession. "Exactly. Or, not quite exactly. Don't you feel the difference?"

Blinking, Matilde listened to nothing, looked at trees that seemed perfectly the same. But . . . they weren't. There was the faintest golden haze, the slightest out-of-focus shimmering to everything, as though this wasn't quite the same world, and she turned back to Hauberin in alarm.

"Ah, you do feel it!" he said. "There's more Power in you than you want to admit. But what you're sensing is that Nulle Part is as convoluted as Faerie and as devious as human Realms."

Alliar nodded. "We couldn't return to the Gate by which we entered without all that circling about to place us on the . . . mm, the proper arcane level of existence."

A shrilling of high-pitched laughter sounded from the forest, and Hauberin's grin broadened. "See? Even the *lutin* agrees. My, how that little trickster must have enjoyed watching our struggle. It *was* a ridiculous journey, wasn't it?"

His smile was infectious. Glancing from prince to wind spirit, Matilde found herself grinning back. "The most ridiculous I've ever known. Though I've never had such unusual travelling companions. Or such . . . ah . . . entertaining ones!"

"Or I such a brave lady." Alliar made her a sweeping bow. "You saved my life. Though I doubt," the being added dryly, "the drac would have actually eaten me. One taste of this pseudo-stuff, and he probably would have spat me out!"

It was too silly a picture. Laughter welled up within her, and Matilde gave up and let it explode. Dear God, dear God, all at once she understood the warmth men felt after a battle, when they found themselves still alive and unharmed: comrades in arms, all differences of rank or gender or race forgotten in the surge of relief and sheer camaraderie. For this one bright moment she was included in the shining circle of the friendship she had so envied.

But it couldn't last. Abruptly sobered, Matilde knew she would lose this strange, joyous sense of friendship as soon as she returned home. Home to husband. To respectability. To the proper order and way of doing things, with never anything half so dangerous as a mad dash through magical forest with Faerie folk. And for a moment she could have cried aloud for the impending loss of freedom, and shriek like a spoiled child, "No! I don't want to go back!"

But she could hardly stay here in Nowhere. Engulfed

in a sudden flood of guilt, Matilde reminded herself
sharply she wasn't some light, soulless Faerie creature.
She was human, and married, and a lady of rank, and
there must be no more foolishness.

"You can return us?" she asked quietly, fighting to
keep the pain from her voice. "To the exact spot and
time we left?"

Hauberin shrugged. "Close enough."

"Then . . . please, take me home," Matilde said, and
closed her mind to regret.

XVIII

RETURNS AND DEPARTURES

Raimond groaned, aching equally in head, legs and wrists. And he was cold, too, shudderingly cold, and damp. A dank, sour smell filled his nostrils, and after a long, bewildered moment he identified it as that of leaf mold, and opened his eyes to find himself lying in underbrush in a world gone pale gray with morning.

Underbrush? Forest?

Oh, God! All at once he remembered the sorcerer and that glinting sacrificial knife— Biting back a whimper, Raimond shrank back into the shielding bushes, heart pounding painfully, expecting to feel a blade come plunging down. . . .

But after what seemed an endless wait, nothing happened. No one came looking for him, and Raimond dared straighten, realizing for the first time the gag that had been choking him was down around his neck, leaving his mouth sore but free.

Not that he was about to shout, God's blood, no, with who knew what foes still lurking. Maybe they were watching him right now! Maybe they were just waiting to see what he would do before they pounced on him and—

No, no, there wasn't anyone around, he could almost swear it. Raimond swallowed dryly—God, what he wouldn't have given for a drink!—then touched a cautious tongue to the sore corners of his mouth, wincing at the sharp tang of blood. Warily, he tested the ropes holding his arms and legs, and barely bit back a cry of triumph: the bindings about his arms had come loose. After a time of desperate contortion, he managed to work his wrists free, trying to ignore the slickness that was almost certainly blood. Ugh, yes, blood it was, as though some great force had torn the skin from them.

Raimond froze, staring wild-eyed into space, suddenly remembering that force, that night gone mad: devil's work, sorcery flaming into the sky, tearing the darkness asunder, revealing the very heart of Hell— Oh, God, God, the devils had been loose this night, and foremost among them had been the one who'd passed as a man, Hauberin, and the other, the demon that dared wear the shape of Rogier. . . .

He wouldn't let himself think of that just yet. Instead, Raimond busied himself with freeing his legs. As the last of the ropes fell away, he staggered to his feet, wiping his bloody mouth with a bloody hand, glancing wildly around for enemies. The forest about him was torn and battered, tree limbs strewn about as though there had been some terrible storm. A storm of sorcery. . . .

But now not a leaf stirred. Raimond licked sore lips again. Maybe, oh maybe all that sorcery had chased everyone away and left him safe. . . .

But in those last confused seconds before the world had been torn open, he had heard his brother's voice, yes, and others with him.

"Gilbert . . ."

Surely, no matter what had happened, his brother would have searched for him. Gilbert wouldn't have just left him here, bound and alone.

Unless Gilbert . . . had been slain . . . ?

God, what if *everyone* had been slain? What if Hell had won and the whole world was dead and he was the only one left?

No! That's impossible!

But what if it *was* true? Frantic, Raimond burst out into the open, only to stop short at the sight of the looming gray stones.

"Oh, God!"

Human bodies lay crumpled gracelessly askew about the stones as though tossed there by some demonic child. Hands trembling so badly he could barely use them, Raimond forced himself to turn them over, one by one, biting back a whimpering that threatened to turn itself into pure hysterical sobbing. One dead man, two, three . . . Not a one was his brother, not a one—

The sorcerer!

Raimond was halfway back to the shelter of the bushes before he realized that last body had lain just as still as the others. He edged cautiously forward to prod it with a toe. Dead . . . ? Yes. Quite dead.

"You tried to kill me, you treacherous, base-born little son of a whore! And I'm still alive, and you're dead!"

All the terror he'd undergone, all the pain, for this! Raimond rained a sudden frenzy of kicks upon the body, then turned, panting, to snatch a sword from one of the others. He would cut the sorcerer's treacherous head from his treacherous body!

But without warning the world crashed open before him. A sudden sharp blast of wind forced him stumbling back, gasping, frantically clawing strands of hair from his eyes. And he saw the devil step forth from empty space, the devil named Hauberin, and with him, his consort: Matilde, his brother's wife!

It was beyond bearing. With a shout of terror and rage, Raimond lowered his sword and charged.

Hauberin stepped forward out of Nowhere into dazzlingly bright daylight and the sudden, shocking loss of Power the human Realm imposed. Half blinded, aching from the loss, he heard Alliar's gasp, blinked frantically to clear his vision—and saw a madman charging him, sword aimed right at his heart!

The prince threw himself aside, kicking out as he fell, putting all his magic-lost fury into the blow. His foot struck bone; there was a grunt of pain and a crash. He landed, rolled, sprang back to his feet, raging, and found the human struggling back to his, sword clenched in shaking hand. He stumbled towards the prince, and Hauberin laughed savagely. Iron or no, this fool would learn what it meant to attack a prince of—

But then Matilde cried out, "Raimond!"

The madman—it *was* Raimond, by the Powers!—hesitated ever so slightly at the sound of his name, long enough for Alliar to catch him from behind, pinning his arms to his body.

"No, damn you! Let me go!"

But Alliar's hand closed with implacable force about Raimond's wrist, ignoring the man's furious oaths. The sword fell with a soft thump to the ground, and the being quickly kicked it away. Gasping, swearing, Raimond fought and squirmed, but Alliar held him helpless as a child in a parent's arms. Hauberin smiled thinly. Li's apparently human forms, with their apparently human limitations, were deceptive; the strength of the winds was in those arms. Pinioned, Raimond stared savagely at the prince, gasping out:

"Devil! Demon!"

"He's not—" Matilde began.

"And you!" Wild eyes blazed. "You witch! Whore! Lying with—"

But a firm golden hand over his mouth muffled whatever else Raimond had been about to shriek. Alliar gave the man a stern shake, murmuring as though to a child, "Softly, now. Softly, if you would stay conscious."

Raimond tensed, eyes frantic, then all at once sagged submissively in his captor's grasp.

Matilde, riding cloak wrapped tightly about herself, was gazing about the glen in horror. "Oh, Hugh . . ." she murmured, almost to herself, "and Jerome, Phillip . . . dead, God rest their souls. But where are the others? And I d-don't see my lord husband here, either."

Barely aware of the baroness's words, Hauberin said absently, "They probably fled." How could he think of human matters now? How, when every psychic sense was shouting to him that Serein was gone from here, Serein had escaped?

But escaped to where? Hauberin knew he should be proud of having returned himself, Alliar and Matilde from Nulle Part without having lost more than a few hours of mortal night and morning. But during those lost hours, who knew how far Serein might have run?

Raimond was squirming about distractingly, trying to shout out something from behind Alliar's hand.

"Let him speak, Li."

The being obligingly dropped the gagging hand to let the young man gasp out, "It's not true, Gilbert wouldn't have fled! He knew I was here, he—he wouldn't have abandoned me!"

"No," the prince agreed, remembering that meticulous man. "But then, where is he?" He caught Raimond's sudden start. "You know what happened to your brother, don't you?"

"I think . . . dammit, I can't talk like this. I . . . can't even breathe."

"Don't crush the man, Li; it isn't courteous. Raimond, if we let you go, will you speak to us like a civilized man? And not try to cut out my heart?"

Raimond hesitated, then nodded. Alliar glanced at Hauberin for confirmation, then shrugged and let go.

For a moment Raimond stood motionless, as though too cowed to move, but Hauberin surprised a sly little sideways glance: the man was trying to find his sword without being too blatant about it.

"No," the prince said shortly, and Raimond started guiltily. "You can hunt out your weapon later."

The young man glared at that, then suddenly, melodramatically, signed himself, boldly defiant. Hauberin blinked in confusion, then got the point and laughed. "I'm not a Thing; your holy signs don't hurt me. Now forget this nonsense and tell me what happened here after we . . . ah . . . left. Where is Baron Gilbert? And . . . Rogier?"

"I don't know. D-dammit, don't stare at me like that! I really don't know! *You're* the demon, *you* should know!"

The prince sighed. "I repeat, I'm not a Thing. And if I knew everything, I'd hardly be wasting time like this, would I? Come, at least tell me if Rogier was acting alone."

Raimond hesitated. "No. He wasn't."

"So? Continue."

"I . . . didn't mean for anyone to die. But when the sorcerer gave me a chance to avenge my lord Rogier . . ."

As Hauberin listened to the tale of petty sorcery and betrayal, Matilde stiffened.

"Thibault!" she spat. "Of course. If anyone would shelter a traitor for personal gain, it would be he. And if ever there was a man who'd jump at the chance of holding a rival for ransom— He has my husband, my lords, I'm sure of it."

"I didn't see all that happened," Raimond murmured. "But . . . after Rogier . . . after he betrayed me . . . Yes. He and Baron Thibault almost certainly captured my brother."

Matilde glanced from Raimond to Hauberin. "It's not so bad, Thibault won't dare harm him, not if it means risking the ransom!"

"Thibault," Hauberin reminded her quietly, "has already declared himself a traitor to his liege lord. He was in league with a sorcerer—which dealing, I believe, is what you people call a mortal sin—and with a . . . with Rogier. By now, he's hardly likely to care about chivalry. The sooner we snatch Gilbert back, the better."

He felt Alliar's confused, "?"

"What?"

"You can't possibly be worrying about the baron!"

"Now what do you think?" Hauberin threw back his head, questing with more than physical senses, wondering, *Serein, kinsman-who-was-dead, where are you . . . ?*

He froze. There was something . . . the faintest of intangible threads . . . "*But where the baron is,*" the prince continued silently, "*Serein almost certainly is, too.*

And oh, my friend, my cousin is not going to escape me again."

Hauberin straightened in sudden alarm. "Hoofbeats."

He melted into the underbrush, closely followed by Matilde and Alliar, the later pulling the wild-eyed Raimond along. They waited in tense silence till the riders, disheveled men-at-arms, broke into the open, horses picking their way over the fallen branches with delicate care. Matilde stared at the riders for a moment then exclaimed, "It's all right, they're our men."

She stepped out of hiding before Hauberin—thinking of treachery—could stop her. To his relief, the guards hastily dismounted, bowing to her. "My lady! Now God be praised, you're safe."

"What of my husband? Is the baron . . . ?"

The guards exchanged nervous glances. "Lady," one began reluctantly, "we haven't seen him since . . . since that terrible sorcery hurled us all away." The man flinched at the sight of the dead and hastily crossed himself, correcting softly, "Almost all of us, God rest 'em. After a long chase, we managed to catch our horses—poor beasts were maddened with fright—and hurried back here. . . ." His voice trailed off, his eyes widening as Hauberin moved to join Matilde. "My lord." The tone was almost reverential. "Forgive me, my lord, we had no idea who you were."

"And that is . . . ?"

"Why, a wizard, my lord! Battling the evil sorcerer who'd attacked us."

Hauberin just barely managed to turn his astonished laugh into a cough. Was *that* what they'd thought they'd seen? If so, he wasn't about to dissuade them! "It seems that this Thibault really does have your baron. Eh, wait! The man's certainly had time to get back to his castle by now. Were you planning on storming the battlements with only the . . . ah . . . ten of you?"

And in the process alerting Serein— Damn. There had to be a way into that castle without Serein's knowledge . . .

Of course, there was this advantage: no matter what

weird ability the man might have learned to let him
switch bodies, in this Realm his Faerie magics—particularly now that it was a human body he wore—could only
be as weakened as Hauberin's own. Especially if he was
in Thibault's castle, virtually ringed round with iron. . . .

The prince paused thoughtfully, glancing about at the
company, then smiled. "Now, of course you, Raimond,
must go home— No, don't argue, man! Think: If Thibault captures you, he has both Gilbert *and* Gilbert's
only heir. Go home and wait. And take these men with
you to make sure you get there."

"First," murmured Matilde, "we must bury the dead."

"Not here, lady, surely!" a guard protested. "This is a
heathen place."

Hauberin stirred impatiently. "What difference can it
possibly make to the dead?" He frowned at the horrified
looks he received and added sharply, "Take them with
you, then. Only go!"

"Well and good," Raimond snapped, "but what about
you? What are you planning to do?"

"Why, meet with Thibault, of course—"

"And betray us!"

"And remind him," Hauberin continued smoothly,
"that we—particularly you—know all about his treasonous connivings. With you safely out of his hands, why,
what can he do but yield as gracefully as possible? Come,
two of you ride double. We'll need the mounts."

A burst of panicky thought from Alliar: "*You can't be
meaning to rush boldly into the enemy camp!*"

"*Oh Li, think. A chance to cut off both Serein* and *his
curse in one—how can I not risk it?*"

"You aren't doing this strictly from chivalry, are you?"
Matilde murmured, and Hauberin flashed her a quick,
sardonic smile and an honest, "Hardly. Thibault's castle
lies in that direction, I'd guess?"

"How would you know . . . ah, yes. Your cousin must
be there, too." The woman bit her lip. "You'll take Alliar
with you, of course. And—me."

"No!"

"Yes. What, are you worried about my reputation?" she mocked. "Surely that's been damaged enough already. Look you, maybe it wasn't one of your wondrous Faerie love-matches, but Gilbert is my husband! I'm not going to wait home like some poor little creature out of the songs to find out if I've become a widow. Besides," Matilde added fiercely, eyes glinting with pain, "I'm not an heir, only a wife, and possibly a—a barren one, too. Thibault won't dare harm me, but I don't make much of a bargaining counter, either. Oh come, we've delayed long enough!"

Hauberin had been thinking more of Serein than the merely human Thibault. But Matilde was a free, rational being. And Serein would be just as dangerous whether or not she was there. The prince held up a hand in surrender. "So be it."

They rode that day into night, hardly speaking, and made such camp as they could, hardly speaking. Sitting before their small fire, Hauberin glanced at Matilde, who was huddled into herself, eyes shadowed and remote.

"Lady? Are you well?"

She nodded curtly.

"Ah come, what is it? You've not spoken more than a word all day. This is surely more than mere worry for your husband."

She looked at him. "They didn't mean a thing to you, did they?"

"They? Who? Ah, those dead men?" Hauberin held up a helpless hand. "What should they mean? I never knew them."

"You killed them!"

"Oh, I did not! Look you, don't try to make me into one of your guilt-ridden human knights. Yes, I am sorry for the waste of life, but those three were merely unfortunate enough to be in the way of erupting Power, and there's the end of it."

"You would have had them buried in unhallowed ground."

"Unhallowed." Hauberin considered the word for a time, rolling it about in his mind, hunting its meaning. "Unclean, you mean?" He paused again, considering. "Unsacred, because it wasn't within the boundaries of one of your churches? How absurd!"

"Absurd!"

"Lady, the earth is itself incredibly Powerful, far and far removed from any petty little mortal ideas of good or evil. Whatever foulness humans work may leave a shadow on the surface, may even stain the soil, but they cannot possibly change its inner nature. The earth cannot be unclean."

Matilde was studying him quizzically. "You really *are* alien, aren't you?" she murmured, and shuddered.

At a loss, Hauberin glanced at Alliar, who sat half in shadow, a golden statue with glowing golden eyes, and asked, *"You're not going to help me out of this, are you?"*

"How? If you're alien to her right now, then I am doubly so."

Hauberin sighed and turned back to Matilde. "Poor lady. You're very weary, aren't you?"

"How should I not be?"

"I . . . know a simple spell to banish fatigue; I've just used it on myself and—"

"No!" she erupted. "No spells! No magic!"

"But—"

"It's magic killed those men, magic that trapped my husband, magic that—that might even have already slain— Oh *God!*" Matilde sat for a long time with head buried in hands, then slowly straightened, eyes haunted. "No magic," she repeated softly. "Just . . . let me be."

Matilde turned her back on him, curling up in her cloak. Hauberin looked across her huddled form, and started.

There, barely to be seen in shadow, stood a *lutin.* Whether it was the same sprite from Nulle Part, Hauberin had no way of knowing; the creatures had as many shapes as whims.

"Small one?" he murmured in the Faerie tongue. "What would you?"

The *lutin* blinked at the sound of the language, but said nothing and did nothing but study him a long, silent while, eyes glittering in the night. Then, without warning, small, sharp teeth flashed in a quick smile and the *lutin* was gone.

"*Now, what was* that *all about?*" Alliar asked silently.

Hauberin shrugged. "*Who knows? Maybe it was planning a prank. Or maybe the thing was simply curious.*" The prince glanced down at the sleeping Matilde and laughed without sound. *No magic, eh?* he thought. *I'm sorry, lady, but that hardly seems likely.*

XIX

DISCOVERIES

The morning brought no strangeness with it; the *lutin* apparently had been nothing worse than curious. They ate and smoothed out their dress as best as possible, and rode on their way, and if Matilde remained remote, Hauberin told himself she had, after all, undergone a good deal recently, particularly for a human, and let it pass.

Baron Thibault's lands looked, Hauberin mused, unkept, the hedges just a bit too overgrown, the growing crops just a little too weed-filled. What few peasants they passed in the full day of riding were sullen, barely glancing at them.

Not that we're such elegant creatures by now. What I'd give for a change of clothing. And a long, long bath.

As much wish for a swift, happy return to Faerie. And an equally swift end to Serein and his curse.

Thibault's squat gray castle, an ugly, unpoetic thing outlined against the golden afternoon light, was every bit as sloppy as his lands. Frowning, Hauberin noted vines on the outer walls—a lovely ladder for invaders—and hints of crumbling mortar and chipped stone. Unlike Baron Gilbert's fortress, which had depended on its hilltop setting for additional security, this castle's entranceway was protected by a drawn-up wooden bridge flanked by heavy watchtowers and surrounded by a stagnant ring of water (Hauberin's memory suddenly supplied the missing word, "moat") half-hidden by a mass of waterlilies; when the wind shifted, such a reek of decaying vegetation rolled out from it the prince nearly gagged.

"Lazy housekeeping," Alliar murmured.

Also, Hauberin thought fastidiously, an effective barrier: who would want to swim across that foulness? He sat his horse in silence for a time, sending out a delicate thread of psychic sense, searching . . . wondering if his cousin might not be doing the exact same thing. There . . . no . . . yes . . . ah, he couldn't be sure, not with all that stone and iron interfering. At least it meant Serein couldn't sense him, either.

"Time to raise our treaty flag," he said.

With a wry grin, Alliar lifted the sorry thing—a scrap of a not-very white surcoat impaled on a branch—and called out in a voice mighty as a storm wind: "Ho, the castle!"

A startled face appeared in a watchtower window. A voice called down, predictably, "Who goes there?"

Before Alliar could answer, Matilde stood in the stirrups and shouted, clear as a war trumpet, "I am Baroness Matilde, wife to Baron Gilbert de Bouvain. Tell your master I have come to speak with him."

"My lady—"

"*Now!*"

The face hastily vanished.

And, a short time later, the drawbridge came creaking its slow way down. As an obsequious man-servant ushered them into the castle, Hauberin glanced admiringly at Matilde. Even in this human Realm, honesty could sometimes prove a most effective tool!

To Hauberin's mild surprise, they weren't ushered into the Great Hall, but led directly to Baron Thibault's private solar, a room as slovenly as everything else they'd seen so far, crammed full of glittering gold plate and hunting trophies with little regard for taste. Heavy, smoke-darkened tapestries lined the walls, and chipped, elegantly patterned tiles covered the unswept floor.

Baron Thibault sat overflowing a cushioned chair beside the fireplace, gilded cup in hand.

The baron, Hauberin thought wryly, matched his surroundings: overfed, overripe, just a shade too soft for handsomeness, just a shade too richly dressed for elegance. Gold dripped from neck and fingers, and the smile he offered his visitors was equally as rich: charming and, the prince didn't doubt, totally insincere. The slightest glaze to his eyes implied that the cup he held had been refilled more than once, but despite the wine, the faintest trace of fear still encircled him, thin as mist.

"My Lady Baroness. And gentles. Please, be seated."

There wasn't the slightest trace of drunkenness in Thibault's steady voice. At his gesture, servants scuttled forward with three chairs. Matilde sat, the heart of dignity despite her by now sadly soiled riding clothes. Hauberin and Alliar perched, not at all at ease, the being watching the baron closely, the prince questing warily with his mind for traces of his cousin, finding none.

"Will you not drink with me, lady, gentles?"

Hauberin shot back to the here and now. Powers, no, he wasn't going to share drink with this *nilethen-nichal*, this shelterer-of-an-enemy; that would be as dark as a lie—and probably more perilous. But he could hardly refuse. The prince took the proffered cup, but did not drink. Nor, he noticed, did Matilde.

"Enough courtesies, my lord," she said. "You know why I am here."

Baron Thibault raised a bushy brow. "No, my lady, I do not."

"Oh, come! You have my husband."

"I . . . what?" It was a cry of pure astonishment. And, Hauberin thought in uneasy surprise, it was far too realistic to have been feigned. "No, lady," the baron exclaimed, still amazed, "I most certainly do not!"

"Please. Don't lie."

"I'm not lying! On my honor as a noble, lady, I am not lying. I do not have your husband, and I'll swear to that on whatever holy relics you wish."

"But—"

"I'm sorry."

"Perhaps you don't actually have the man," Hauberin interjected, knowing how smoothly truth could be sidestepped, "but surely you know where he can be found."

"No, I—" Thibault froze in mid-speech, staring at the prince as though only now really seeing him. "God's blood. The wizard."

There was a startled hiss from Alliar. "And how would you know what I am?" Hauberin asked warily, and received a nervous flash of a smile from the baron in return. The *feel* of the human's fear hung heavily in the air between them.

"I will be honest, Sir Wizard," Thibault said in a rush, "I had my spies at those heathen stones. They hurried back here to tell me what had happened. And I . . ." The man's tongue swiped quickly, uneasily, across his lips, and his voice sank to a harsh whisper. "I must speak with you, my lord. Alone."

"I think not."

"Oh please, you don't understand." The baron lurched to his feet. "My lady, if you will excuse us for just a moment?"

Curious despite himself, Hauberin allowed himself to be herded to the far side of the solar, fighting not to show his distaste at the man's wine-scented breath. After an apprehensive glance back at the staring Alliar, Thibault whispered urgently, "It's about that . . . about him. Rogier."

"Go on."

"About Rogier, and the—the demon possessing him." The baron mopped his brow with a precious square of silk, apparently not noticing Hauberin's involuntary start. "My lord," Thibault continued, "you would know more about such matters than I. But he—the demon—tried to control me, too. Believe me, I never would have done what I did, allied myself with that—with the sorcerer and— Look you, Gilbert and I have never been friends, but I would never sink so low as to use sorcery . . ."

"Please, my lord baron. Get to your point."

"Ah. Yes. I—couldn't help myself, I found myself agreeing to things. . . ."

"You seem to have free will now." As free as the wine would allow, at any rate.

"Y-Yes. The demon lost his hold on me when I, all accidentally, was splashed with holy water by my priest."

"Convenient."

"Please, my lord, I'm not lying! It wasn't an easy thing, but—my lord, I tricked the demon in Rogier's body, I trapped him behind cold iron bars."

"What!"

"Yes, it's true, but I d-don't know how much longer I can hold him there!" Thibault seemed virtually at the edge of tears, desperation quivering in his voice. "Oh please, you must help me, you can't let him get loose again!"

Powers. It was just barely possible. Oh, not the nonsense about the holy water, of course, Serein was no demon. But he also was no skilled plotter, either; he never had been. If he really had made some mistake, if the human really had imprisoned him . . .

"What proof can you offer me?" Hauberin asked.

"Proof, proof! God's blood, man, what do you want from me? The demon's head?"

That would be nice, the prince thought drily. But Thibault was continuing:

"I know his name; he—he let it slip when he thought I was still under his control. And it's a devilish name, all right, not a good Christian name at all: Serein. That's right, and when he realized I had trapped him, he started railing to me about my not being able to hold him, because he was such a powerful demon even a prince of Faerie on a Faerie hill couldn't kill him." Thibault stopped, blinking owlishly. "Is that good enough?"

"*Hauberin*." Alliar's wind-keen ears had overheard. "*You can't believe him.*"

"*Serein would never have given his name to a human. Not unless he was under great strain. And who else but*

Serein would boast about my not having killed him? Li, I don't dare not believe."

"I'm going with you."

"No. Right now Matilde is in greater need. Stay with her, my friend." After a moment, he felt Alliar's reluctant agreement, and nodded. "Come, my Lord Baron," Hauberin said. "Show me your captive demon."

The baron led him down the winding stair to the Great Hall, steps just slightly befuddled by wine. "There. The demon's down there, down that other stairway." The words seemed to delight him, because he added in a singsong voice, "The dungeon's down there, and the demon's down there, and—"

"And you're going down there, too," Hauberin told him.

"No, I don't want to—"

"Yes, you do." The prince gave him a not-quite gentle shove in the right direction. "That's right, my lord. You first."

Hauberin, thinking of what little he knew of human dungeons, had been expecting a row of dank, cramped, ugly little cells. But at the bottom of the stair, a vast vaulted area lay below the Hall: the castle cellars, somewhat dank, but smelling more of dust than cruelty. They were piled high with mysterious crates and casks, dimly lit by flickering torchlight.

The prince stopped short. "Now, who lit those torches, my lord?" he asked softly.

Thibault blinked at him, face guileless. "Why, my servants, of course. They're always coming and going down here, getting supplies, replacing tools, and so the torches are almost always lit."

At the far end of the open vault, a section of the cellar had been screened off by a huge iron gate. Thibault saw Hauberin stare at it, and the color faded from the human's face. "Yes," he whispered. "The demon's locked behind there. You sense him, don't you?"

No, Hauberin didn't, not with a virtual wall of iron

blocking him. But as he stalked forward at the baron's side, every arcane sense sprang alert. And in one wild rush of awareness he knew, "Everything you've told me was a lie!" Furious at himself for having been so gullible, for being so of Faerie he hadn't recognized falsehood, he spat out, "There's no lock on that gate, he's not your prisoner. And you— Damn you!"

He backhanded the man across the face with all his strength. Baron Thibault stumbled away from him, crumpling to the floor, whimpering, "I couldn't help it, I couldn't think, he—he was in my mind, he made me do it."

But Hauberin wasn't listening. Thibault's men were rushing at him, no innocent servants but fully armed men-at-arms, ringing him around with their swords.

I can't use Power here, not with all this iron!

But the guards couldn't know true magic from simple illusion, and when a bolt of fire flashed out from him to them, they believed what their eyes told them. Yelling in alarm, they staggered back, and Hauberin darted through the opened circle for the stairway— Damn! They had him cut off.

Glancing feverishly about, the prince laughed suddenly, scrambling up and up a rickety pile of crates. One guard tried climbing up after him, and Hauberin whirled, bracing himself, and kicked out, catching the man squarely in the chest and sending him crashing back to the floor. The crates swayed wildly, and Hauberin nearly fell, caught his balance, and hurriedly reached up to where a pair of torches burned smokily in their holders. Tearing them free, he hurled them down into the pile of crates, which caught with a gratifying rush of flame. He heard the baron's frantic yelps to his men:

"The fire! Put out the fire, curse you, before the whole cellar takes!"

Hauberin leaped down into a cloud of smoke and a swirl of confusion, kicking at feet that tried to trip him, punching at hands that grabbed at him. He sprang for the stairway and started to climb, only too well aware of how painfully exposed he was just now, hearing behind him an all-too-familiar voice, Serein's voice, shouting:

"Never mind the fire, idiots! Stop him!"

Panting, the prince glanced back over his shoulder and saw an archer taking aim. He twisted frantically aside even as Serein screamed out, "No! Not iron!" knowing even as he did that there wasn't enough time, enough room—

Hauberin felt the arrow slamming into his arm as a whitehot flash so overwhelming his mind couldn't even interpret it as pain—

And then he was tumbling helplessly down into darkness.

Alliar sprang up with a cry of anguish: "Hauberin!"

Matilde scrambled to her feet, heart pounding. "What is it? What—"

"Treachery!" The being's eyes were wild and unfocused. "I felt his mind cry out, then there was nothing— and now I can't sense him at all!" Golden fingers clamped painfully about her wrist. "We have to find him!"

Matilde struggled futilely against the being's strength as she was dragged along. "Alliar, wait, you're hurting me. Alliar . . ."

But then she was crashing into the being as Alliar stopped dead at the head of the stair, faced by a solid wall of guards. "That's right," gasped Thibault's voice from below. "Hold them there." And then, to Matilde's horror, "They know. They must die. *He* told me: there— there must be no witnesses."

He'd gone mad, Matilde thought. And, being mad, he meant to kill them.

"The devil he will!" Matilde slapped the leading guard across the face (thankful he wasn't helmeted), and as he staggered back in sheer surprise, she and Alliar turned as smoothly as though they'd rehearsed it and raced back into the solar.

"No other way out!" the being gasped, eyes wild and blank. "No other door, no window—"

"Alliar, stop it." She could understand a wind spirit's claustrophobic terror of closed spaces, but now, with guards rushing in to seize them was hardly the time—

Closed spaces! Of course! Matilde snatched at Alliar's arm, barely noting its inhuman chill. "Come on!"

"The fireplace?"

"Don't argue." Matilde was glancing up its smokey chimney, praising Heaven it was too warm for a fire to have been lit. Ah, yes! Dimly seen against the square of sky far overhead were the recesses for smoking meat, the iron rungs set into the chimney wall to facilitate cleaning. Hastily she shed her encumbering riding cloak. "Just climb."

Of course it didn't take the guards long to follow them. But a grunt from Alliar, a stifled cry of pain and a most gratifying crash told Matilde that the being had kicked the lead guard back down on top of the others.

Grinning fiercely, the woman continued to climb, half choked on the reek of old smoke, hands and feet slipping on the greasy rungs (*Saints above, doesn't Thibault ever clean up here?*). After one glance up at that tantalizing blue square that never seemed to get any larger, Matilde clenched her teeth and refused to look again. The weight of her riding skirt pulled at her, growing heavier with every passing moment, and one shin was aching savagely where she kept banging it against the rungs again and again. By now every muscle was complaining, burning as though there really was a fire surrounding her, and her lungs ached with strain. God, for one clear, clean breath of air! Now trickles of perspiration were working their tickling way down her face, but she couldn't spare the time or a hand to wipe them away, and this ordeal would never be over, but she simply refused to just give up and die. . . .

It took her a long moment to realize there was light all about her. With a gasp and a wriggle, Matilde was out of the chimney, clinging to its rim, Alliar, disheveled and dirty, beside her. They exchanged fierce, conspiratorial grins. But then the sound of panting from within the chimney made them both start and look back down.

"The guards!" Matilde glanced about and found no escape from this chimney, because the one clear spot of roof they could have safely jumped down to was swarming with more of Thibault's men. She groaned. It had all been useless. They were trapped.

But Alliar, a clear, cold, alien light in the golden eyes, was pulling off the filthy tunic, standing on the chimney's narrow rim in linen hose alone. Matilde caught a brief glimpse of a smooth, hairless, sleekly muscled chest, disconcertingly nippleless, then Alliar was pulling her to her feet. She swayed, dizzied by the vast expanse around her.

"I can't—"

"Don't argue! Just hold fast!"

She didn't have a choice. A guard was snatching at her skirts, so Matilde seized Alliar in a deathgrip. She felt powerful muscles tense. And then they were plunging out into space.

XX
FLIGHTS

But they weren't falling, they were flying, soaring out into empty air, and Matilde gasped to see that the golden shape to which she clung, lying atop the sleek, chilly back, had all at once become even more alien, flattened, just barely recognizable, wide sheets of golden skin stretched between outstretched arms and body catching the wind.

It wasn't flight at that. It was a long, straining glide, and after the first moment of sheer terrified exhilaration, Matilde realized that Alliar, tiring rapidly, was struggling just to bring them down safely inside the forest, so tantalizingly near.

A little further, she pleaded silently, *only a little further*. . . .

But they were losing height so rapidly. . . .

"I can't!" It was a cry of pure despair.

And then they hit a tree. Torn from Alliar, Matilde was bruised, scratched, terrified, a whirlwind of leaves spinning before her eyes as she grabbed frantically at branches, catching, falling, catching again. Her hands closed on a slippery branch. For an instant it held and she dared think she was safe. . . .

Then, with a horrifying crack, something gave. The branch whipped out then down, hurling her off. Falling once more, Matilde shrieked, sure she was going to break her leg, or her arm, or her neck—

Instead she landed, winded but unbroken, in the middle of a thick, springy bush.

For a time, Matilde was too shaken to move, lying in

her prickly bed while the world continued to whirl dizzily about her. But at last it stilled and, aching, more and more aware of every bruise, every scrape, she managed to roll her weary way down onto the nice, solid, unmoving ground.

But what had happened to Alliar? Matilde struggled to her feet, half afraid of what she might find. A glint of golden skin . . . The being lay prone, incredible wings vanished back into the malleable form, so flat against the earth that for a heart-stopping moment she was sure Alliar was dead. But then she saw the sleek chest rising and falling, and at last the being rolled over to stare blankly up at the leaves overhead.

"Alliar . . . ? Are you . . . all right?"

The being hesitated as though considering the question very carefully, then nodded. "Aching." Alliar's voice was a whisper, but a hint of humor quivered in it. "More weary than ever I recall. But otherwise all right." The being sat up with immense care. "I wasn't sure we were going to make it. The wind was fading out from under me; didn't recognize a distant cousin, I suppose," wryly. "And if some of those guards had thought to loose arrows at us while we were still in range—"

"They were all too stunned. So," Matilde added, "was I. I . . . didn't know you could do that."

"Neither did I. Desperation does amazing things." Alliar staggered upright. "What of you? You aren't hurt, are you?"

"Nothing worse than scrapes and bruises." Matilde scrambled up, trying not to wince. "They didn't even try to come after us. Probably thought you were a demon."

But Alliar had stopped listening, looking out over the brush to where Baron Thibault's castle squatted grimly in the fading light.

"He's still in there. Hauberin is still in there. Alive. I'd *feel* it were he . . . dead. But something terrible has happened to him."

"Oh, surely not," Matilde said feebly. "I don't think Thibault would dare hurt him," and the being whirled

on her savagely. "You think not? After the man tried to
kill us?"

"It must have been the wine ruling him, or—or—"

"Or magic-madness from Serein having weakened his
mind. Ae, it doesn't matter now! You think Hauberin's
safe? When he could be tortured through sheer human
ignorance? When the slightest touch of iron sears Faerie
skin? If they try to chain him . . . ah, winds!"

Alliar turned away, shuddering. Matilde put a tentative
hand on a bare golden shoulder, then withdrew it with
a gasp. "You're so cold!"

"The flesh, not me," the being said absently. "I don't
feel the cold. And if that magic-maddened human doesn't
torment him, what of Serein? Winds, winds, what will
Serein do to him?" Eyes wild with despair blazed into
her own. "I must get him out of there!"

"And so we will," Matilde soothed. "As soon as it's
fully night, we'll find a way in there."

"We?"

"You didn't expect me to abandon him, did you? We'll
rescue him," the woman said firmly.

Oh God, but how?

"Can do't," said a small voice near her feet, and she
started, looking sharply down. A child? What was a child
doing here? Particularly one so sharp-featured, so
pointed of face and feral of eye— "The *lutin*!" Matilde
gasped.

"A *lutin*, at any rate," Alliar corrected. "What would
you, small one?"

"Where be tha third one?" the *lutin* asked, small hands
on hips. "Tha Faerie-man?"

"I think you know."

The *lutin* nodded sharply. "In tha cold, bitter place.
The human place." He spat. "Not good for Faerie-kin."

"No, but—"

"Can get ya into tha' cold place. No one t'see ya,
either."

Alliar knelt at the *lutin*'s side so swiftly the little creature jumped back. "Are you telling us the truth, small one? Or is this just another of your tricks?"

"Tricks? Tricks?" The feral eyes were bright with sudden mischief. "What're tricks?"

"Please. If you betray us, the humans and their . . . bitter metal will kill the Faerie-man. Do you want that?"

"Na, na!" Suddenly the *lutin*'s light voice was perfectly serious. "Humans shallna take another a' us. No tricks. Come."

He scuttled surefootedly forward through the near-darkness, out of the forest into the open, and Alliar and Matilde hurried after, to stop short nearly at the edge of the moat. Feeling suddenly painfully exposed with no sheltering trees about her, even in that moonless night, Matilde looked nervously up at the dark mass of the watchtowers, where she could see torchlight flickering, sure she was about to be spotted, but Alliar, unconcerned, stood with head thrown back like a questing beast, then gave a soft, fierce laugh.

"Where the master is lax, the servants are lazy. What guards may still be alert after dining and drinking aren't the ones in those watchtowers. No one's awake in there." Alliar studied the castle for one more long, careful moment, then grinned. "I don't think anyone's patrolling the ramparts, either. My Lord Baron really does keep a sloppy watch."

Matilde glanced at the being, amazed at Alliar's sharp sight (though, she reminded herself, this *was* a spirit; she shouldn't be surprised at anything). "Or else this . . . Serein . . . has everyone bespelled?"

The being waved that off. "He never had that much Power."

The *lutin* hissed in impatience. "Pay attention, ya!" he scolded. "Tha way ya want is there."

"In the moat . . . ?" Matilde asked doubtfully.

"Na, na, *there!*"

"The drawbridge? But it's up; we can't possibly—"

"The vines!" Alliar exclaimed. "Once we get across

the moat, we can climb right up them into one of the windows."

Matilde's merely human vision saw nothing but a solid black mass of wall, but she remembered those vines from before. "Assuming they'll hold our weight," she added doubtfully. "And that nobody's waiting on the other side of that window."

Alliar shrugged. "There's only one way to find out."

"Indeed." Matilde glanced down at the moat, a mass of smelly blackness in the night, and tried not to think about what might be living in that swampy water. "I used to swim. Before I grew too old for such ... childish things; I suppose I can still manage. But what about you?"

"Think the water won't let me in because I'm of a different element? Oh, I can swim. Hauberin insisted I learn, once upon a time. Eh, come, let's try it."

But Matilde looked down at their small benefactor. "Thank you, my ... ah ... my lord *lutin*."

There was a sharp, delighted laugh from the *lutin*, an equally sharp tug at one of her braids, and then she and Alliar were alone. The being, clad only in lightweight linen hose, slipped silently into the moat. Matilde hesitated, knowing it was absurd to feel embarrassed in front of a genderless spirit yet not quite having the courage to strip. But if she didn't get rid of her bedraggled riding gown, its weight was going to drown her, so Matilde abandoned foolishness and struggled out of the dress, kicking off her low boots, feeling incredibly light and free in just her simple chemise.

Her white chemise that glowed like a beacon even by starlight. Hastily Matilde held her breath, and jumped into the shelter of the water.

Ugh, it felt almost thick and slippery as oil, and she didn't even want to think about what might be in there with her. At least she could remember how to keep herself afloat. The water didn't seem to splash like normal water, either; she could paddle her way through it without raising more than a ripple. But swimming wasn't as easy as she recalled; her muscles were definitely out of practice for such exercise. Trying not to breath too deeply, Matilde struggled determinedly after Alliar—a sleek golden knife slicing the water—to the small, artificial island on which the castle stood. Treading water, the being paused for a moment, then scrambled onto land.

But the first vine the being seized tore free and tumbled Alliar in an arc back into the water. This time there definitely was a splash, and Matilde caught her breath, expecting an outcry from the castle. But there wasn't a sound, and after an anxious moment, the being surfaced, festooned with water lilies and spitting out a short, sharp, alien exclamation that needed no translation. As Matilde bit back a near-hysterical giggle, Alliar swept off the plants, scrambled back up onto the island and began to climb again.

The second vine held. Halfway up the castle wall, Alliar paused to signal to Matilde. She tried to pull herself up onto land, only to sink back into the water, panting. She tried again and yet again, scraping her knee against rock yet unable to get a purchase, the weight of herself and the water an insufferable burden.

"Alliar!" she whispered, and the being came slithering down the vine. A cool golden hand reached impatiently down to grasp hers, and Matilde had a new chance to be amazed at the wind spirit's strength as she was raised against the water's pull. Her flailing feet struck solid ground, and she whispered up, "I'm all right now. You can let go."

Maybe Alliar's strength wasn't quite inexhaustible. The grin she received was decidedly weary, and she could have sworn she heard the being panting. But Alliar swarmed back up the vine, signalling to her to follow.

At least her feet had something to push against. From what her questing fingers could find, the vines were spread up and out across the wall like a tracery of iron, each tendril sunk deep into the mortar between the stones. In fact, judging from what she felt, the main reason for eradicating such vines wouldn't be so much to repel invaders as to keep the castle intact; there were some definite gaps in the wall where the tenacious plants had pulled out whole chunks of mortar and brought down several blocks of stone.

Climbing things seems to be my fate, she thought wryly, remembering the frantic scrabble up the chimney.

Matilde's groping toes found a fork in the vine, and she managed to raise herself, slowly and carefully, hunting for a second foothold, her mind unexpectedly casting back to childhood days. She'd been a confirmed climber of trees and walls back then, at least until her father had found out and forced her back into the proper behavior for a girl of gentle breeding.

Gentle! He should see me now!

Matilde found a small hole in the stone with one foot, raised herself again, memory prompting her to take her time till she'd found sure places to grip where the mortar was missing. She took another torturous step upward, then another, flattening herself against the cold stone like a lizard she'd seen on a rock, took yet another step, and yet another, not sure how high she'd climbed, not daring to look down to find out. Now, if she could just reach high enough to close her hand about the next twist of vine. . . .

Without warning, her feet slipped free. For what seemed an eternity, Matilde hung by her arms alone, terrified, hunting desperately for a new foothold, fighting not to sob with the effort. Then, just before she knew she would have had to let go and fall, she managed to wedge the toes of one foot between wall and vine, praying she wouldn't tear the whole thing—vine and crumbling stones and all—free. As though mocking her, telling her she wasn't miserable enough, the breeze began to rise, sweeping across her wet chemise, which wrapped itself lovingly about her body, till Matilde was shivering helplessly. Her bare feet were so cold she could hardly feel her toes. Oh saints, and how her muscles ached! She wasn't a lithe little girl any more, and this wasn't a harmless man-high wall off which she could safely jump, and

in another moment her arms and legs were going to give
way and let her fall.

I can't do this, I can't.

And yet . . . Hauberin was almost certainly undergoing
a worse ordeal. One without any hope at all of escape.
"Something terrible has happened to him," Alliar had
cried, and *"The very touch of iron sears Faerie skin."*
Matilde remembered the drac, slain by one small scratch
from her knife, and thought, against her will, of Hauberin
lying in the creature's place, face contorted with agony,
the beautiful dark eyes blank and empty . . . dear God,
no.

But for a long moment, heart aching or not, she just
couldn't move, clinging to vine and wall, eyes shut, thinking that if ever she got out of this, she would never, ever
complain about her lot again. And if anyone ever dared
lecture her about women being the weaker vessel, he
would regret it!

Teeth clenched, Matilde gathered what was left of
strength and courage, and began the painful climb after
Alliar who, after glancing back to make sure she was all
right, was scampering up the wall with disgusting ease.
Lost in her fog of exhaustion, Matilde continued to
climb, silently raging at beings who seemed to think
human bodies could do anything spirits could do—and
nearly shrieked as a hand shot out of the wall to close
about her arm.

"It's me," whispered Alliar, "we're here," and pulled.
After that first terrified moment, she realized the being
wasn't trying to drag her through solid stone; they'd
reached a window at last. But even though a stone had
crumbled away here, too—Matilde had a wild mental
image of Baron Thibault giving a procrastinating wave of
the hand when faced with needed repair—what remained
was barely wider than the standard arrow-slit.

*I'll never fit. They'll find me hanging here in the
morning.*

But then Alliar whispered, "Exhale."

She did, flattening herself as much as possible. The

being pulled, and Matilde was abruptly tumbling through and down in a heap onto a stone floor, elbows and one knee scraped, hair dripping and chemise bunched up in most unseemly fashion about her thighs. Hastily pushing the sodden cloth back down about her legs (feeling it outlining her body so closely she wondered why she bothered), Matilde blinked about at darkness. "Where . . . ?"

"A guardroom, I think," Alliar murmured. "Yes. There's the guards' torch, burned out. And there are the guards, sound asleep!"

"But . . . so heavily," Matilde breathed, scrambling to her feet and staring as her eyes grew accustomed to the gloom. "Almost as though . . ."

"As though they were bespelled?" Alliar sighed. "Forgive me. You were right earlier and I was wrong. There's definitely the *feel* of enchanted sleep about these men."

"I know . . ."

"So now! Sense it, do you?"

"No, I only meant . . ." Matilde hastily dropped her voice to a whisper. "We shouldn't talk so loudly!"

"You don't have to worry; nothing short of time will unravel that spell. And," the being added thoughtfully, "I wonder if perhaps it lies about everyone else in the castle, too."

Matilde shivered, flinging her wet hair over her shoulder, wincing as the cold weight of it slapped against her back. "That would explain why no one at all was on guard."

"It has to be Serein's doing. Serein's spell, to ensure no human would disturb him." Neither of them wanted to say why he wouldn't want to be disturbed, but the being's eyes glinted with cold anger. "It's true that he never could wield such Power before. But then, he never could switch bodies before, either." Alliar grinned, a fierce flash of teeth in the darkness. "We should thank him. By being so human-wary and eliminating all the guards, our dear little Serein has made our task so much the easier."

Easier. All they had to do was find Hauberin before

the sleep-spell wore off or they shattered it, rescue him, and escape out through a castle full of enemies, one of whom was a renegade Faerie sorcerer.

Is that all? Matilde wondered wryly. *Why, after all we've done so far, it seems almost too easy!*

Not, dear Lord understand, that she was complaining.

How long had he been huddling here, arm and mind aflame? All the stories said iron-poisoning was an agonizing but quick death, and he had seen the drac's death as proof, and yet, perversely, despite the endless pain, his body seemed to be refusing to leave that pain behind. He ached for water, and for the simple chance to just lie down. But the last remnants of pride kept him from begging. And the rope looped about his wrists kept him tethered to the iron ring set into the wall, so that the best he could do was sprawl like this, leaning his feverish head and body against the dank, wondrously cool stone of the wall, and wish whoever was babbling on and on would stop.

"Hauberin! Damn you, you can't die! Hauberin, answer me!"

Serein. The prince peered through the fever-haze at the anxious, furious human face and Faerie aura and managed a faint, rusty laugh. "Too bad, cousin. You don't . . . get my body after all. Have to . . . have to stay a human."

Serein was raging at him, warning, "Don't you mock me!" Hauberin sagged against the wall, letting the surging of blood in his ears drown out his cousin's fury. But he was still conscious enough to be dimly aware that underneath the bluster, Serein was terrified. And with the sudden brittle clarity of fever, Hauberin knew why, and cut across his cousin's words with:

"You're trapped, aren't you? It wasn't *you* made the transfer from body to body." He saw Serein start, eyes widening, and continued, hearing the words tumble out beyond his control, fascinated at what they were saying as though they weren't his. "It was someone, something else that pulled your spirit across realms. Ha, yes, something else. Maybe not even something of Faerie."

"No, that's ridiculous—"

"But now, your ally, whatever, whoever, your ally has betrayed you. Betrayed the traitor. Abandoned you. Left you here caught in your helpless little human self."

"No!"

"You *can't* get out of that body, can you? It dies, you die, for good this time."

"Damn you, Hauberin, I'll—"

"What? Kill me?" The prince laughed, then broke off with a choked cry as he jarred his wounded arm, sending new fire blazing through him. For a time Hauberin could do nothing but wait, teeth clenched, until at last the pain had ebbed to a more endurable level and he could gasp out, "I'm already dead, Serein. Body just hasn't gotten the message yet. . . ."

The prince sank wearily back against the wall, eyes closed, ignoring his cousin's frantic noise, feeling the rising fever-flames sweeping him further and further from lucidity, welcoming them. Soon it wouldn't matter what Serein said.

Soon nothing at all would matter.

Alliar hesitated, lips tight in distaste. *Phaugh*, these humans were like animals, flopping down to sleep here in the Great Hall wherever they could crowd in their pallets. The air was equally crowded with the none-too cleanly smells of them. The being glanced about the dark Hall, plotting the best path—stepping on someone certainly *would* break the sleep-spell—and listening with every sense for any trace of Hauberin. . . .

Ae, was *that* Hauberin's aura, that poor, distorted, fever-bright thing? Horrified, Alliar started forward, Matilde stepping hesitantly after, only to stop short at the head of a downward-leading flight of stairs.

"The cellars?" Alliar wondered softly, unsure of human architecture.

"Or the dungeons," Matilde murmured. "If Hauberin is down there—"

"He is." The being stared at arcane flames, faintly blue, crossing and recrossing the stairway. "Serein has set Wards."

"Spells to keep everyone out? You ... can't get through them?"

"I don't know." For all that Alliar shivered with impatience, there was nothing to do but relax as best as possible, clear the senses, study the Wards on all their levels, *feeling* their form, the Power behind them. . . . The being straightened in triumph. "I have it! They were set for flesh-and-blood reality—*not* for such as I." Alliar glanced at the woman. "I'm sorry. I can't take you with me. But I'll be back as swiftly as I can. With Hauberin!"

Hidden in shadow, golden skin darkened almost to black, Alliar stood in helpless silence at the head of the stairs, just out of sight of the human woman, shaking under the sudden assault of panic.
How can I go down there? *Ae, how?*

Swimming the moat had been simple by comparison; the water had been foul, lifeless, an alien thing to a spirit, the virtue choked from it by human misuse, human neglect, but at least it had encouraged swift action. This cellar, this ... tomb had been gouged from the living earth, then walled off from it, from all life, from even the hint of sky and free, open air. . . . Ah, the harsh cold stone, cruel as Ysilar's prison. . . .

But there at the far end of the vast chamber, where the darkness should be at its deepest, torches flickered where none should be. Hauberin was down there. And Serein. And, with Serein, who knew what torment?

Ah, winds, winds!

Teeth and fists clenched, the being forced a trembling body step by step down the stairway to the bottom. Alliar took a deep, steadying breath, then hurried forward, keeping to shadow, refusing to think of the cold stone weight pressing in on all sides, refusing to think of—

The being stopped dead, barely holding back a gasp. There, slumped against a wall, wrists bound to an iron ring (by rope, winds be praised, only by rope), lay Hauberin, limp as a child's broken doll, tangled hair fallen forward over his face. Over him crouched a form. . . .

Serein. Serein in his stolen human body, shouting at the prince, shaking him without effect. With a soft, frantic oath, the man snatched something from his belt and slapped at Hauberin's arm with it. The prince jerked upright at the brief contact, crying out in hoarse anguish, struggling for an instant against his bonds, then going limp once more. Alliar smelled the faintest stench of burning— Iron! Serein had struck Hauberin with an iron knife!

The being lunged. The startled Serein had no time to do more than yell in pain as a golden hand closed so savagely about his wrist that bones cracked. The knife fell from lifeless fingers, and Alliar hurled it aside with all the fury of the wind, then backhanded Serein with such force the man crumpled.

Glancing about, Alliar grinned sharply at the sight of iron manacles hanging from a second ring. Iron wouldn't burn the man's human shell, but it would certainly hold him. Quickly the being fastened the chains about Serein's wrists, then turned to the prince.

"Hauberin . . . ? Can you hear me?"

The knife blade had blistered a small patch on the prince's forearm, Alliar could see that clearly. But if that was the worst of it, well, Hauberin had survived an iron burn before this, and this one wasn't so terrible a wound. . . .

But there was worse. The prince's sleeve was torn above the elbow, and the stains darkening it were surely blood. Hauberin's face, as he looked weakly up at the being, was flushed, his eyes glazed with pain and fever. "Li . . . ?"

"Yes, I—I'm here."

"The fire . . . Li, we must put out the fire . . . castle will burn. . . ."

"Oh, my friend, no." Alliar knelt by Hauberin's side, tearing at the ropes holding him. "There's no fire here."

"Yes . . . feel it . . . fire . . ."

As the last strands parted, the prince slumped helplessly forward into the being's arms, and Alliar winced. Flesh-and-blood folk were always amazingly warm to the touch, but this terrible fever-heat was so much greater than normal warmth— "Hauberin! What did he do to you?"

At first Alliar thought the prince too far gone into fever to answer. But then Hauberin murmured in the weariest of whispers, "Not he. Arrow." And then, though the being prayed to all the Powers not to hear the word, "Iron."

"No. Ah, no, no, no."

For what felt an eternity, Alliar could find no way to move, to do anything but hold the prince with arms that seemed to have lost all their strength and sit staring into space, heart and mind empty, save for the one bitter thought that kept repeating itself: *Iron-poisoning, iron-death . . .*

"No, ah, no . . ."

But Hauberin still breathed. And damned if he was going to die in this dark prison! Despairing, Alliar stood, gathering Hauberin up, trying not to jar the prince's wounds, and began climbing the stairway. Something clinked underfoot— The knife, Serein's iron knife. Alliar hissed, about to kick the cursed thing away, when a frantic voice called out:

"Wait!" It was Serein, wild-eyed, struggling against his chains. "You—Alliar! You c-can't leave me here!"

"Can't I?"

"Damn you—"

"No, traitor. Damn *you*."

Alliar turned away, but Serein screamed, "No, *please*! You don't understand, the Wards are still set, and I can't lower them, not while I'm chained. No one will come down here, no one *can* come down here, n-not while I live. This body is strong, it might last for days before—

Alliar, no, please, you can't just leave me like this! Hauberin would never do it, Hauberin would never be so cruel!"

Alliar glanced down at the feverish, dying prince. "I'm not Hauberin."

"Oh, Powers, wait. . . ."

Serein, traitor, murderer, could not be allowed to live. But such anguish quivered in that moan that the being turned back involuntarily. Serein, all defiance gone, huddled in piteous terror in the flickering light of torches that would soon burn out. And memory stabbed at Alliar's mind:

Ysilar's prison, and the slow, slow torment of merciless stone all around, lifeless stone and lifeless darkness forever. . . .

"Winds."

Carefully the being put Hauberin's limp body down and picked up the knife. And, in one quick, accurate, deadly movement, hurled it.

"Alliar!"

Nearly at the top of the stair, the being froze, astonished. A slim white ghost-form stood outlined against the darkness: Matilde in her simple chemise. "Matilde! How did you—"

"The—the Wards, are gone, I . . . uh . . . I felt them fall, and— Oh . . ." Her bare feet made no sound as she hurried down to Alliar's side. The woman touched a gentle hand to Hauberin's cheek. "So hot! What—"

"He was wounded." Alliar forced out the words painfully. "With iron."

Horror flashed in Matilde's eyes. "But—but he's alive, surely there's hope that— We have to get him out of here!"

A sudden surge of noise from above told Alliar that not only the Wards had fallen with Serein's death; the sleep-spell had shattered, too. And Thibault and his men were going to come rushing down in the next moment, trapping them.

"No, I can't!" the being cried out in pain. "I won't let him die here!" Arms tightly about Hauberin, Alliar told Matilde shortly, "Hold my arm. Hold fast! Don't let go no matter what you see or hear!" She wasn't one to waste time with questions; she gripped with almost inhuman force. Eyes shut, concentrating fiercely, the being hunted for the Spell of Return Hauberin had taught when they were first setting out on this misguided journey (ae, how long ago that seemed!), then called out the Words. For one endless, terrifying moment, nothing seemed to happen. Quivering with panic, the being knew it wasn't going to work, the proper Power was never going to build, they were going to be trapped here in darkness forever. . . .

But a Gate was shimmering into being, and Alliar laughed in relief. No time to be sure it was exactly the right time and place:

As the first men-at-arms came hurrying down the stairway, Alliar and Matilde, the prince held securely between them, stepped through and left the human Realm behind.

XXI
DEATHWATCH

Helping Alliar cradle the unconscious Hauberin, Matilde at first was too absorbed to notice her surroundings, save to note absently that the light in this spacious new room into which they'd arrived was bright, oh most wondrously bright and luminous, daylight when it had been full night an instant before. But ... luminous light, a part of her mind wondered uneasily, not sunlight at all. *Faerie* light?

But before she could ask aloud, even before the floor was steady under her shaky feet, Alliar was shouting out what could only be a cry for help—in what she'd come to recognize as the Faerie tongue.

And in the next moment the room was full of people who were never human: tall, elegant, fierce-eyed men and women in exquisite, rainbow-bright robes, their hair like finest gold or spun silver, their faces—ah, she'd never seen anything quite so proud or wild-thing beautiful as those sharp-planed faces, more alien than that of Hauberin, with his tempering of human blood.

But for all their splendor, these wondrous creatures were crowding in just like any other panic-stricken courtiers, crying out their alarm, patently ignoring her (the dirty little human in her ragged chemise, with her bare feet and wild hair) as they pressed in around their prince, and Matilde stiffened indignantly. Oh, she didn't doubt she looked like a beggar woman. But damned if she'd let them cow her, not after all she had gone through so far for their prince's sake! All this panicky crowding wasn't helping Hauberin any, either, so she pushed her way rudely forward to where the prince lay in the cornered, crouching Alliar's arms and shouted out with true baronial ferocity:

"That's enough!"

Glittering eyes, green or blue or silver like so many uncanny gems, focused on her for the first time, radiating such Power, such hostility, that she had to lick suddenly dry lips before she could ask, "D-do any of you speak the human tongue?"

"No," murmured Alliar, shooting her a grateful glance for keeping the horde at bay, "but I'll translate for you."

"Fine. Tell them—tell them their prince is wounded. *Don't* tell them it was iron, or we'll have true panic. Have them get the royal physicians or surgeons or whatever the term is here—and tell them to hurry!"

Matilde hovered nervously in the doorway of the royal bedchamber: far larger than any bedchamber she'd ever seen, spacious even with the reserved crowd of Faerie nobles standing to one side; much more elegant, too, with its ivory-and-silver bed and graceful tables and chairs.

The nobles hadn't wanted her here, shooting her glances of genuine distaste even though someone (more out of aesthetic reasons than sympathy, she guessed) had thrown her a glamorous blue silk cloak to cover her disreputable chemise. Even now silvery-eyed dark-clad servants were still trying to convince her to leave, murmuring their disapproval, but she angrily shook them off, watching Hauberin. He had been lying still as death in that princely bed, but now, without warning, he began thrashing wildly in his fever, seeing who knew what foes, calling out words that made no sense to her, his eyes fierce and blank. The nobles stirred nervously, but none of them made a move. Alliar, at the prince's side, murmured soothingly to him but, lost in the terror of his delirium, Hauberin fought all Alliar's attempts to hold him still.

Matilde couldn't stand it. Ignoring the nobles' gasps,

she ran to the bedside, just as Hauberin tore free of his friend's arms. For a moment the savage, fever-hot eyes blazed into her own, the prince's hand raised to gesture, insane Power swirling about him. Since she could hardly outrun a spell, Matilde said, as sensibly as she could:

"You don't want to do that. It's only me, Matilde. You know I'm not going to hurt you. Now, why don't you just lie down and rest?"

And to her unutterable relief, she saw sanity flicker behind the fever. "Matilde," Hauberin said, quite reasonably. "I trust you are being treated well?"

With that, his eyelids slid down, and he sank limply back against the pillows. Alliar and Matilde sighed simultaneously in relief and exchanged quick, thankful glances. But before the woman could say anything, three others were suddenly at the bedside, wise-eyed folk who bore an air of quiet competency about them. These could only be the royal physicians, two slender, golden-haired men and an ageless woman whose hair was a soft, definite blue, and Matilde hastily moved out of their way.

As they leaned over him, Hauberin's eyelids fluttered open again. He moaned, stirring in restless pain, and the blue-haired woman put a gentle, professional hand on his forehead, murmuring what Matilde guessed must be a calming spell in his ear. Yet Hauberin remained awake, uncomfortable. The physician tensed, her face too well-schooled to show alarm, then snapped out a few commanding words.

Matilde gulped. The woman *couldn't* have conjured that goblet out of the air; she must have simply transported it. (*Oh, is* that *all?* her mind gibbered.) Hauberin drank the contents without quarrel, and after a moment sank back into drugged sleep. The physician straightened again, face still impassive, but Matilde, shaken, slowly realized she was feeling the woman's worry as clearly as her own.

How can I . . . ?

One of the men asked Alliar brisk questions, which the being answered with increasing reluctance, and Matilde, frustrated by her lack of the Faerie language, could only guess from the shock and terror on the physicians' faces that the being was mentioning that iron arrowhead. The three drew back from the bedside, glancing over their shoulders at the uneasy nobles, then set to work, but even as they efficiently cleaned and dressed the prince's wounds, Matilde, with her bewildering new sensitivity, *felt* a frightening air of hopelessness already about them. They joined hands and began to murmur over him, and she just barely choked back a startled cry, seeing magic shimmer from each to each, *feeling* it echoing through every nerve. Power surged up in a glowing blue wave till Matilde could have screamed from the tension, thinking wildly that it would heal him, iron-wound or no, so much magic *must* heal him, praying for tension's release.

But there was no release. The Power, maddeningly, simply . . . faded. Matilde knew, even before the physicians staggered back, faces drawn and eyes despairing, that their spell had failed. One of the men murmured to Alliar, who gave a fierce cry of denial, echoed involuntarily by Matilde. Startled, they turned to look at her, and she, just as startled, said defiantly:

"W-well, you can't just give up on him!"

The physicians studied her silently for a moment, so intently her heart began to pound, then the blue-haired woman moved to her side, drawing her aside with a cool hand on her arm, asking her a sharp question. Matilde, held by the sharply slanted blue-green eyes, alien and unreadable, shook her head.

"I'm sorry, I can't understand you."

The woman sighed impatiently, studied Matilde a moment more as though judging endurance, then moved so that her palms lay flat against the sides of Matilde's head. The unfathomable eyes burned into hers till there was nothing to the world but those blue-green depths. Power encircled them in a swift, dazzling, dizzying wave. . . . When the physician suddenly removed her hands, Matilde staggered and nearly fell, head aching fiercely.

"The effect will pass quickly."

Matilde straightened in shock. "I . . . understood that." And then she stopped in renewed shock at the once-alien now-familiar sounds coming from her own mouth.

"Of course. Now tell me: You are Matilde?"

"Yes, but what has that to do with—"

"Our prince has called your name, his mind to mine."

"But—"

"An *ainathanach* must know something of our language." Unspoken was: human though you are. "We had no time for standard teaching. But you, with your seeds of Power, absorbed enough."

Seeds of . . . Power? "What is an . . . uh . . . *aina* . . . *ainathanach*?"

The woman hesitated, then said evasively, "The language spell is not all-powerful. But you've learned as much of our tongue as you need."

"Uh . . . thank you, but—wait, where are you—"

The three physicians had already faded back into the shimmer of glamor from which they'd come. Matilde hurried back to the bed. "They *can't* have given up!" she began.

Alliar wasn't seeing or hearing her. Head thrown back, the being keened in anguish, the sound high and shrill as the wind, eerie enough to send the hair prickling up on Matilde's arms, echoing on and on till she, too, could have screamed, till at last Alliar collapsed at the bedside, panting. "What more can they do," the being murmured in a soft, broken voice, "save dull his pain? There is no cure for iron-poisoning." Alliar reached out to smooth disheveled locks of hair back from Hauberin's face with such a tender hand the sight nearly broke Matilde's control.

"Alliar . . . ?" she asked uneasily, because if she didn't say something, she'd weep. "What does . . . *ainathanach* mean?"

The being glanced sharply at her, eyes too bright. "You are one. I am the other."

"Yes, but what does it *mean*?"

"It's a ritual position. Though others will come and go, the two *ainathanachi'al* must stay till . . . till they are no longer needed. The word means death-watcher."

"B-but he's still alive!"

"Ae-yi, what more do you want of me? I've told you: there is no cure." The being sank back to the bedside. "There is nothing left, nothing but . . . waiting."

Alliar's total surrender terrified her. "I can't accept that! I saw the wound when they were cleaning it— Oh yes, there was infection, but if he had to be hit by an arrow, he couldn't have been more fortunate about it: no veins torn, no damage to the bone; in a human, we would call it a flesh wound, nothing that can't heal—"

The being roused at that, glaring at her so savagely she flinched. "He is not a human. And iron-wounds do not heal. You saw how the drac died from your knife's cut. Or had you forgotten?"

"Alliar, please. I couldn't forget. It was a terrible thing. But it took only a few moments."

"Iron-poisoning is swift."

"That's exactly my point! Hauberin isn't dead!"

The being gave a long, infinitely weary sigh. "Ah, Matilde . . . you mean well, all human-hopeful. I wish I could hope with you. I don't know why Hauberin's mind picked you of all people as *ainathanach*— Ach, no, I didn't mean that the way it sounded; I'm just . . . fragile enough to break right now. Matilde, we can only do this one thing, serve him this one final time: as loving *ainathanachi'al*. Accept."

Looking at Hauberin's too-quiet face, Matilde was suddenly overwhelmed by such sheer weariness of body and spirit together she sank to the floor. Oh God, God, they'd undergone so much together; she could not accept his death.

But . . . what else could she do?

* * *

The vase was an ancient, delicate, lovely thing, so finely carved the light shone through its gleaming white sides. But Charailis, noble lady, ambitious lady, let it fall, unheeding, standing in stunned silence: lovely pale stone woman with pale silver hair.

Dying . . . Hauberin, dying . . .

She broke suddenly into frenzied life, catching the reed-slim servant (not-man, not-cat, finely carved and fragile as the vase) in so sharp a grip her nails cut into the thin arm and the servant hissed in pain. Charailis loosed her grip only slightly, insisting, "Are you sure of this?"

"Ah, lady, so very sure. All the royal castle mourning is, even while the poor, ill prince still breathes. Please, lady, if you break me, I cannot serve."

Charailis absently released it. A thin pink tongue briefly caressed the nail marks, then the servant added thoughtfully, "Iron-poisoning, they say."

The woman tensed, dismissing the servant with an autocratic wave.

Iron-poisoning. She shuddered delicately. Now, how could Hauberin have managed that? From wandering in other Realms like his fool of a father? If he knew his father's travel-spell, he could have been gone countless mortal days within a single Faerie afternoon. Long enough to find that fatal metal and— No matter. He had named no heir. And with Serein already dead . . .

Charailis stooped to pick up the shards of vase, then paused. Slowly, languorously, she smiled, and began plans for a visit. A royal visit.

Ereledan, strong form clad in plain leather armor, red hair swirling about his face as he stamped and fought his way across the smooth rooftop, froze in the middle of a parry, so abruptly his sleekly muscled fencing partner— who was also his bedmate of the moment—only barely managed not to stab him with the unbated swords they were using.

"Dammit, man, I nearly gutted you just then!"

Ereledan ignored her. Normally he rather enjoyed
their game of common soldier, common mate, particularly since their fencing bouts usually ended with equally
violent bouts of another kind (powerful Listel with her
crown of bright blonde braids had such a fine command
of human profanity he suspected she'd once actually
taken a human soldier for lover), but now he absently
waved her away, barely hearing Listel's anger at being
dismissed like a servant, and summoned the man-slave
he'd just heard gossiping to a fellow.

"Speak," he commanded and listened impassively, then
sent the slave on his way with a Power-enhanced blow
as punishment for gossiping. And only the clenching of
Ereledan's fists revealed his shock.

Hauberin dying of iron-poisoning. And leaving no heir.

Ereledan turned sharply to command his slaves to
ready their master for his journey—

Powers, no! He dare not visit the royal palace, not just
yet. His mind had been reassuringly clear of late, but he
still didn't know what had caused those frightening mental lapses: attacking the prince, acting the fool before his
cousins . . . Ereledan swore. What if he went empty-
witted before all that noble company? Worse, what if he
suddenly, helplessly, turned violent?

Besides, Ereledan told himself hastily, to appear too
suddenly was to cast doubts in noble minds. It wasn't as
though he was afraid, of course not, it was just that they
trusted him little enough as it was. If they thought he'd
had a hand in their prince's death . . .

No, indeed. He would wait. Hauberin could not possibly live much longer. And when he died, when it came
down to a choice between hot-blooded Ereledan or chill,
passionless, boring Charailis, well, there was no doubt at
all which one of them would wind up on the throne!

Ah, he burned, he burned . . .
Someone was calling him, mocking him, and Hauberin,
wandering blindly through the red-mist corridors of his

*fever-dreams, turned this way and that, aching with
every move, yet saw no one.*

"Who are you?" he called out at last. "Where?"

"Where? Here. Who? Your enemy."

*Serein? the prince wondered vaguely. No. That could
never be Serein's voice, no matter what shape he wore.
There was a strangeness behind it, an eerie, hating,
chaos-wild feel of the Outer Dark—"Who are you?"
Hauberin shouted. "Show yourself!"*

*"Oh, no," the voice taunted. "You shall never see me.
None of your family ever has. Not your mother, not
even your father. They never knew the shape of their
slayer."*

*And in the fever-dream, it seemed very easy to accept:
"You killed them!"*

*"Why, what a clever little thing it is." Mockery hot as
the fever-flames echoed in the words. "Oh, yes. Yes. They
are dead, and you shall die, and the last of your line
with you."*

"Murderer! Coward!"

"Brave names, little one, helpless, dying little one."

*"I will not die! Hear me, murderer, you shall not kill
me! You shall not kill me!"*

"You shall not kill me!"

Matilde awoke with a start from where she'd fallen at
one side of the bed, staring across at the equally startled
Alliar, wondering wildly who had shouted.

Ah, no. It hadn't been a shout, only a fevered murmur,
magnified by her groggy mind. Hauberin was still alive,
still fighting. But how much longer could he endure,
poor, exhausted, fever-racked man? Matilde had lost all
track of time: now and again she'd seen the physicians
drain and cleanse the iron-wound (dead tissue sloughing
away at every treatment till at last only healthy flesh
remained); now and again quiet nobles had filed in and
out, honoring their prince with intricate little bows, blatantly ignoring the human at his bedside; now and again
servants had brought her food, and she'd eaten without

tasting a thing, clean clothing, and she'd dressed without noting what she wore. There had been brief times away from the bedside for bathing and tending her body's needs, but they'd hardly seemed significant. Matilde accepted dully that the glamor in Faerie's very air might have enchanted her, or mere human shock overwhelmed her mind, but for all she knew Hauberin's ordeal could already have lasted a day or a week.

Ah well, she was hardly going to complain. Hauberin's state was far worse than hers. Matilde reached out a hand to stroke his cheek with weary tenderness, feeling the unabated heat, and winced. If he was a human, she would be worrying by now that such intense fever would damage his mind—

Wait. Matilde prodded her groggy mind, knowing she was missing something vital. . . . *If he was a human . . .*

"Oh, God, of course!" Matilde struggled to her feet, calling out, "Physicians! Where are you?"

They were almost instantly at her side, hissing at her to be quiet.

"I can't be quiet! You're killing him!"

"The human has gone mad," one of the men muttered, such contempt dripping in his words that Matilde had to clamp down on her lip with her teeth to keep from retorting; losing her temper wasn't going to help Hauberin.

"Look you," she said as carefully as she could, "I'm not blaming you for being so terrified of iron-death; I've seen it happen, and it's a . . . a horrible thing. But I *am* blaming you for being so frightened you forgot basic medicine!"

"Had we, indeed?" the blue-haired woman purred, very softly. "And how would the so-wise human child tutor us?"

"Ah, well . . ." Matilde stared into the chill, alien eyes, then hastily looked away. "The trouble is that you're forgetting something. We're all tired; *I* nearly forgot it. I'm . . . not trying to belittle your prince. But he has two . . . ah . . . heritages, not just one: he's half human—"

"What a clever little girl it is."

"—and it's the human blood you so despise," Matilde finished hotly, "that's resisting the iron-poisoning!"

She saw the faintest shock of surprise cross the elegant faces. They plainly hadn't even considered it; the court had, after all, had years to put the embarrassment of Hauberin's mixed blood out of their minds.

Almost too successfully. Matilde hurried on before anyone could stop her, "But even human blood isn't going to save him if you don't break that fever quickly."

No human could have accepted a new situation so swiftly, without a word of insulted argument. "Exactly," the blue-haired woman agreed. And if she raged at Matilde, the mere human, for pointing out her error, nothing of it showed in voice or face.

The physicians waved Matilde and Alliar away, then murmured a series of twisting spell-syllables. A rush of Power followed, filling the room with blue-white light and cold, such sudden cold that Matilde gasped, then coughed as the chill air bit at her lungs.

Dear God, they're going to freeze him alive!

Shuddering, she huddled next to Alliar—whose naturally chill skin wasn't much shelter. Surely the physicians had lost control of their magic. Surely this ordeal-by-cold was never going to end. . . .

But then the blue-haired woman was snapping out sharp Words, and almost as suddenly as they'd been conjured, the intense cold and blue-white glare were gone. Half-frozen, Matilde winced to see Hauberin lying deathly still, hardly seeming to breathe. Dear God, had the sudden shock of cold stopped his heart . . . ?

"No . . ." Alliar moaned, rushing forward to snatch up the prince's hand. But then the being sank down on the edge of the bed with a small, shaken laugh. Matilde warily followed, touching a hand to Hauberin's face, letting out her breath in a long sigh to find his forehead normally cool and damp.

"It worked," the being murmured. "The fever's broken."

Suddenly Matilde's legs wouldn't hold her. Barely noticing the physicians' grudging but genuine bows, she collapsed on the bed's other edge.

There between Matilde and Alliar, unaware of their giddy, exhausted grins, Hauberin had fallen into a deep, healing sleep.

XXII
ROYAL EXECUTION

How word of their prince's survival had reached so many people so quickly, Matilde couldn't even begin to guess. But as Hauberin, no longer plagued by even the slightest touch of fever, slept, not even stirring when wary servants changed the perspiration-soaked bedding about him, a crowd of nobles came swarming in, silent as so many sleek cats but with their mood changing with Faerie swiftness from deepest dejection to wildest joy. Though they had the sense and good taste not to press in on the royal bed itself (there were guards among that crowd to keep things that way), Matilde found herself engulfed in a whirlwind of color, catching quick, dizzying glimpses of narrow, elegant faces, glinting green eyes, of tall, supple figures in robes of more fabrics and in more shades than she could name. Bits of dialogue filled her ears:

"Who would have thought it: a human *ainathanach*."

"Why, she looks almost . . . civilized."

"Only a human. But that flame-hair is lovely."

"Red as Ereledan's hair."

"Ah, Ereledan. Where is he?"

"Home. All bluster, no action, our brave flame-hair."

And, "Flame-hair," purred a voice behind Matilde.

It took her a moment to realize that it was she being addressed, not the mysterious Ereledan. A hand on her shoulder made her turn, staring up in startled wonder into a pair of lazy green eyes set aslant in a narrow, sensual male face, ageless as were all the faces there, exquisitely framed by straight, sleek hair of the palest gold. But a touch of careless cruelty hinted in the slight smile, a hint of *What amuses me, I take* in those glowing eyes, enough to destroy any desire his exotic beauty might have roused.

"Pretty human," he murmured, reaching out a long-fingered hand to caress her hair, and Matilde hastily pulled back, saying, "Your pardon, my lord."

She turned away as quickly as she could without seeming rude, trying to find her way through the crowd—only to find her way blocked by a second man, tall, golden, glorious. His slanted, sapphire-dark eyes were just as casually ruthless as the first man's had been, and when he whispered, "Pretty flame-hair, come and play with me," she could only stammer out, "N-No!" and turn to flee without thinking of rudeness. A chuckle sounded behind her, and a hand brushed her hair. Without looking back, Matilde knocked it away, panic churning within her. Dear God, she had to get out of here!

A cool hand closed about her own. At the end of endurance, she whirled to fight.

"Ah, the children have been pestering you," said a quiet, amused voice.

"Alliar!"

"Don't let the idle creatures frighten you; they would never dare harm someone under the prince's protection. Don't courtiers in your own Realm play such games?"

Matilde remembered her one brief visit to the royal court in Paris, and suddenly she didn't know if she wanted to curse or simply sit down and weep like a too-weary child. "Yes."

"Well, then. Hauberin isn't likely to wake for some time, even with this crowd here. Want to escape?"

She gave the being a heartfelt nod. But as they started forward, Matilde came face to face with so exquisite a woman she stopped short, staring openly. Faerie-ageless, coolly elegant in a simple gown of somber blue, the woman was tall and slim just to the point

of gauntness, with the clear, pale, flawless skin that
seemed a Faerie characteristic, her long, straight fall
of silvery hair held back from the high, fine bones of
her face by a thin lapis coronet. Eyes pale blue as
shadowed ice studied Matilde, analyzing this interlop-
ing human, and Matilde, determined not to be out-
done, stared right back.

And for an instant she saw behind the cool facade . . .
for an instant she, too, ached with the sudden emptiness,
the endless tedium of long, long life with nothing of
purpose to fill it. . . . Terrified, Matilde began to stammer
out something, she didn't know what, words of pity,
perhaps—

But then Alliar stepped smoothly between them, the
very essence of courtesy in silken tunic and hose, and
the spell was broken. "My lady Charailis," the being said
with a slight, formal bow.

"Alliar." The woman's dip of the head was just as
formal.

"Now, what brings you here, lady?" Though the
being's tone was casual, Alliar's smile was dagger-sharp.
"Hope, perhaps, of finding our good prince dead?"

"Iron-poisoning is a cruel death," the lady answered
smoothly, eyes shadowed by long, pale lashes. "I would
not wish it on anyone."

"Even someone who stood between you and the
throne?"

"Even so."

The tension between them was a very real thing. Matilde said uneasily, "Alliar . . ."

"Ah, yes." Alliar bowed shortly to Lady Charailis and
took Matilde's arm. "Let us leave this lady to her
thoughts."

"Who *was* that?" Matilde whispered as they made
their way through the crowd.

"A challenger. One who, out of boredom, no doubt,
has recently discovered royal ambition. One who," the
being added with quiet anger, "had Hauberin not survived, just might have legally gained the throne. Though

she shall not have Hauberin *or* his throne if I have any
say in the matter."

As though by accident, their path had brought them
to the side of a tall, sharp-faced man, eyes and hair radiant blue; Matilde would have named him for a warrior,
and a leader of warriors, even without the silver-hilted
sword at his side.

"Ah, Kerlaias," Alliar said cheerfully, "allow me to
introduce my former fellow-*ainathanach*. Matilde, this is
Kerlaias, Captain of the Royal Guard."

Puzzled, Matilde curtseyed politely, and received Kerlaias' curt bow in return. "What do you want, Alliar?"
the warrior asked bluntly, the slightest hint of contempt
for this not-Faerie being in his eyes.

"Oh wise Kerlaias, so quick to come to the point."
The slightest touch of mockery tinged Alliar's voice in
return. "Have you seen our lovely Charailis wandering
about, my friend? Are you keeping a careful eye on
the lady?"

"I'm not a fool, spirit. Of course I am."

"Of course you are," echoed Alliar, smiling sweetly.
Taking Matilde's arm once more, the being led her away.
But once they were out of Kerlaias' sight, Alliar let out
pent-up breath in a gusty sigh. "I hate playing these
idiotic court games," the being muttered. "Ae, I've done
all I can for now. Hauberin will be safe with this crowd
to guard him. Come, let us, by all means, get away from
here."

But Matilde winced when she saw where she was
being led. "Oh no, Alliar, not out a window. Not more
climbing."

Poised on the windowsill like a misplaced angelic
statue, the being smiled sympathetically. "Just a bit,
brave lady. And then nobody will bother us for a time.
Come, trust me. Don't look out or down."

Her green silk gown and slippers were hardly meant
for climbing, but . . . ah well, she'd risk it. Alliar's grip
was reassuringly firm as the being murmured, "That's

right, out on this ledge. Now, turn to your left and jump. Don't fear; I'll catch you."

She did, blindly, Alliar did, confidently, and Matilde found herself in a flat little stone rectangle, formed by the meeting of two walls and a tower on three sides and a low edging of balustrade on the fourth. It was just wide and deep enough for two people—or beings—to sit in comfort, and Matilde gratefully sat.

"This is one of my hiding places," the being said lightly. "I have about a dozen scattered here and there. The various royal architects who worked on the palace over the eons, bless their devious minds, built it full of odd angles and niches."

"Why would you need to hide ..." But then Matilde glimpsed the wise, wild, sad eyes. "Oh. We ... ah ... flesh-and-blood people must madden you."

A shrug, a smile. "Sometimes."

"You ... can't be freed?"

"Why lady," Alliar said, a touch too brightly, "do you see any chains binding me? Surely I *am* free."

"I'm sorry. I didn't mean to hurt you."

"Ach, I know. And no, the spell on me seems totally, irrevocably unbreakable. Ysilar—damn his mad self to the Outer Dark—would probably be delighted if he knew."

"Ysilar?"

"My original captor. The sorcerer who dragged me down from the skies and imposed shape on me." Quickly, staring off into space, Alliar summarized the tale of enslavement and release. "And there you have it," the being concluded, voice just a bit too casual to be convincing. "It was Hauberin who rescued me, who gave me his friendship and taught me to take joy in what I must be. You know, don't you, that I'll never be able to thank you properly for the saving of his life."

Shaken by the sudden intensity of the fierce golden gaze, Matilde cried, "Oh, what else could I do?"

There was a long pause. "Lady ... Matilde ..." the being said quietly, "please. Do not love him."

"I . . . don't," she murmured, and then, more strongly, "Of course I don't."

"Ah." Alliar leaned back against a wall with a weary sigh, and Matilde glanced at the being in surprise. "I wasn't sure you ever got tired. Not exhausted, just plain tired."

"Oh, I do. Not," Alliar added, a touch smugly, "as easily as you flesh-and-blood types, of course."

Knowing when she was being teased, Matilde kept silent, looking up at the luminous, achingly blue sky. Suddenly overwhelmed with the need to see where she was—in all that time at Hauberin's bedside, there'd never once been the chance to simply glance out a window—she straightened enough to look over the low railing. And gasped at the beauty before her, the wild, lovely sweep of green fields and forest, the fierce blue towers of distant mountains, all so wondrously radiant with the clear, sunless Faerie light every leaf seemed caught in the very moment of Creation.

And to Matilde's utter astonishment, a fierce, terrifying surge of *belonging* shook her. Somewhere down there was land that was *hers*, and she ached to find it, to sink her fingers into the soil and feel its Power and make it truly her own—

God, no, that's impossible! I'm human, only human!

Matilde shrank hastily back against the wall, heart pounding so painfully she thought Alliar surely must hear. But the being was watching her, curious, so she babbled out the first thing that came to mind, an inane:

"It's beautiful. But not as strange as I expected."

Alliar gave a startled shout of laughter. "Strange! This land of Hauberin's lies only on the outskirts of 'strange.' There are places further into Faerie, or further out, near the Edges, that would satisfy any craving for 'strange.' Places where rocks float and trees melt and the sky sinks beneath your feet."

Matilde shuddered. "No, thank you."

"I don't like that sort of thing, either. Oh, and don't give me that surprised glance. I'm Air, not Chaos."

She really didn't want that reminder of Alliar's total alienness just then. Matilde squirmed on the hard stone, trying to get more comfortable, wishing the being had stocked some cushions.

"Cushions!" she erupted, bursting into laughter as Alliar stared in astonishment. "I'm sitting next to a—a wind spirit on a palace in the middle of Faerie, speaking a language that was put in my brain by magic, I'm feeling ties to the land I can't possibly have and bearing the seeds of Power I don't want, and I'm worried about *cushions*?" The laughter was jarring her, a painful, wracking thing, and Matilde struggled to stop. But there was no stopping, and gradually laughter turned to tears. "I'm a human woman, a married woman," she gasped out, "married, and my husband's missing, and I haven't even spared him a thought! That—that other life d-doesn't seem real, and I—I—I don't even know who I am anymore! I don't even know if I'm still *me*, or—or—"

Silently Alliar reached out to enfold her in cool, comforting arms. And if the sleekly muscled chest against which she pressed her face didn't feel at all human and smelled of nothing but air, just then Matilde didn't care, sobbing with absolute abandon.

But after a time, the worst of the storm passed. She realized Alliar was stroking her hair with gentle, asexual, care, sniffed, gulped, and managed to say:

"That feels n-nice."

"Mm. Hauberin likes it, too."

That startled her. She straightened, wiping futilely at her eyes with a hand, and Alliar chuckled. With the air of a conjuror, the being produced a square of cloth from out of a sleeve. Matilde hastily accepted it, drying eyes and nose, embarrassed. "I'm sorry."

Alliar waved a casual hand. "Ah, don't be. If I could weep, I'd would have been even soggier back there in the bedchamber. Besides, I've been expecting something like this from you sooner or later; you're a brave young woman, my dear Matilde, but you've been through an amazing amount of adventure recently."

She couldn't talk about that just yet. Instead, somewhat to her horror, Matilde heard herself say hesitantly, "I . . . uh . . . it's not really my business, but . . . what you said about stroking Hauberin's hair—"

"Oh, Winds, woman, I meant back when he was still a boy. What did you think I meant?"

Matilde glanced at the sexless figure, remembering how it had seemed perfectly humanly male, wondering if it might also sometimes look perfectly female as well. . . . "That . . . you . . . loved him."

Alliar blinked in confusion. "I thought we'd established that."

"No, I mean . . ."

She couldn't quite find a tactful way to word it. There was a long, awkward pause, during which Matilde could feel her cheeks reddening. Then, to her embarrassed horror, Alliar burst into laughter.

"You mean, are we lovers in the flesh-games way? Oh my dear, sweet, confused Matilde: how? Can you smell yellow? Or hear blue?"

"I don't see what— Oh. It's that foreign to you?"

"It's that foreign." The being straightened, head to one side, then grinned. "Well now, Hauberin's awakening." Springing up, Alliar offered Matilde a hand. "Come, my fellow former-*ainathanach*, let's go greet him."

Charailis moved quietly among the swirl of celebrating courtiers at nightfall, a lovely, tranquil figure in somber blue, moon-silver fall of hair still in its thin lapis circlet. If that circlet chanced to remind some of a crown, remind them how close she stood to the throne, why, so be it.

But the mind behind the tranquil mask was seething.

How could Hauberin still be alive? How could that . . . half-blood be actually surviving iron-poisoning? Ae, she had come so close, she had almost felt the silver crown upon her brow. . . . Charailis silently chastised herself for foolish hope, foolish anticipation, but the anger remained.

And if he lives, no, since *he lives, where does that leave me?*

As hopeless as Ereledan— No, the woman thought wryly, not quite. Braggart Ereledan hadn't even the courage to come this far.

Ah well. The game was lost, at least for now.

Or perhaps it wasn't. Charailis smiled slightly, decided at last, subtly pulling Power to her, setting an aura of calm about herself so not even the most skillful could catch the way of her thoughts.

Hauberin was still weak, after all. It was just possible the fever, no matter what the physicians swore, had damaged his mind. It was just possible that, drained as he must be, he would be unable to wield Power enough to defend himself. Should he, by some strange mischance, have need to do so.

The bedroom was larger than any she'd had back in the human Realm, the walls curved and faintly pink, softly luminescent: *like sleeping in a giant pink pearl,* Matilde mused sleepily. The large arch of a window looked out over land turned coolly mysterious beneath a sky radiant and crowded with stars—the brilliant, many-colored stars of Faerie, glittering with Power and set in patterns strange to her. She should have been afraid, there beneath that alien sky, but there comes a limit to everything, and right now Matilde was just too tired to care about anything much other than that the bed in which she lay (after having been bathed and groomed and cooed over by three friendly little wisps of silver-eyed women-things) was wonderfully soft. And she didn't have to share it with anyone . . . most particularly not with a husband who had all the warmth and compassion of a log. . . .

*   *   *

Curled up in a cushioned alcove, Alliar quietly watched the night, golden eyes glazed. More weary of mind and body both than the being would ever have admitted, Alliar was truly glad there wasn't anything to be done right now. Matilde was tucked away in a cozy bedroom, drifting into dreams. Hauberin, after his brief but blessedly rational waking, was safely asleep once more in the royal chambers, a servant watching over him.

The being sighed. It would have been nice to be that watcher, just in case; one couldn't be too careful when Charailis was concerned, now that she'd found royal ambition. But for all that this golden pseudo-body was amazingly resilient, there *were* limits. Right now, after all that had happened in the past few Faerie-and-mortal days, there was no strength left to it at all.

The being sagged in the alcove, losing the struggle with awareness. Sighing in surrender, Alliar sank into mind-quiet trance.

Hauberin struggled slowly up out of sleep, now nearly awake, now snared by eerie wisps of dream, a nameless sense of peril weighing down his consciousness. Somehow he found his way to the surface, forcing open impossibly heavy eyelids, too drained of strength by that simple act to do more than lie still and try to clear his mind.

Surely there had been an awakening before this? He thought he could remember Alliar's face, radiant with joy, and another beside it . . . Matilde? Oh no, surely not. Surely the being wouldn't have brought her here, out of her rightful Realm.

Hauberin's eyelids slid slowly closed again. But that nameless weight of disaster remained. His arm ached, and his throat was uncomfortably dry, and he forced his eyes open once more, looking about for the servant who must surely be nearby.

A figure stood at the foot of his bed, tall, slim, wrapped in a hooded blue cloak: never a servant. Hauberin made one abortive attempt to rise, then sank back, gasping out, "Who . . . ?"

"You weren't meant to wake." A woman's voice, so teasingly familiar. . . .

"Charailis," Hauberin breathed.

"Charailis," she agreed quietly, pushing back her hood. "It might be best if you simply drifted back to sleep. There's no need for you to suffer."

"Don't . . . be so . . . melodramatic," Hauberin gasped, angry at his voice for betraying his weakness. "How did you . . ."

"Get in here? Oh, my dear, it was simple. Your people have been celebrating your most miraculous recovery. Their resistance is low: not even your so-proud Kerlaias felt my suggestion-spell; not even he suspected the woman he saw leaving the palace was only air and ice, illusion; not even he suspected the woman who entered here was anyone other than a servant. Enough delay, Hauberin. You haven't the strength to fight me, or simply call for help."

True enough, Hauberin thought darkly.

In the next instant, he felt the surge of Charailis' Power, and knew he hadn't a chance of defending himself.

Jarred from sleep, Matilde found herself on her feet, heart pounding painfully, without the faintest idea of where she was or what had awakened her. Hauberin! Hauberin was in dire danger, and as Matilde was surrounded by startled servants crooning at her, trying to coax this bewildering human back to her proper place, she saw and heard and felt nothing but the prince:

Oh, I won't let you die, not now, not after all this! I will not let you die!

Alliar uncoiled with serpentine speed and strength, landing lightly on the other side of the room in the one bound, spirit-mind instantly cleared of trance. *Matilde?*

Was that Matilde in such fierce distress? And—ae, Hauberin!

The being raced grimly for the royal chambers.

As Charailis' Power engulfed him, crushing at mind and heart, Hauberin fought back as best he could. The magic was there in his blood, the defensive spells were whole in his brain—but he just didn't have the strength to use them, and so, struggling for breath, he was going to die. . . .

But a sudden, lightning-sharp touch against his mind roused him, sending new Power, new strength, new life surging into him: borrowed Power, unshaped and raw, from some unknown source, but right then he hardly cared. Too dazed for subtlety, Hauberin hurled magic up about himself in blue fire, Shielding himself with all his renewed will just as Charailis hurled her Power, cold and gray as despair—

Magics crashed together in one white-hot blast so fierce it destroyed every shadow in the room and blazed out into the night. Terrified, half-blinded, Hauberin lost the edge of his will and felt the Shielding slip.

But it had held just long enough. Uncontrolled Power surged back like a wave against a rock, recoiling upon the one other living target in the room.

Charailis stood transfixed for an endless moment, head thrown back, mouth open in a silent scream as her own Power destroyed her. Then, graceful to the last, her elegant, lifeless body sank slowly to the floor.

Borrowed strength vanished, Hauberin collapsed back against the pillows, shaking with shock. Whatever Warding spells Charailis had placed upon the room had shattered with her death, and guards came rushing in.

"You're . . . a bit . . . late." Hauberin managed to put enough sarcasm into the gasp to make the abashed Kerlaias wince.

"My Prince!"

That was Alliar, brusquely shoving guards aside. Supported in the circle of the being's arms, a slight figure sagged in total exhaustion. Hauberin caught a trace of familiar aura and stared in weary wonder.

This was the one who had sent him that incredible surge of Power, the one who had saved him once and yet again:

Matilde.

XXIII

PUZZLES AND PROBLEMS

Still dazed and uncertain after nearly two days of healing sleep, Matilde stopped in the wide doorway, staring. Beyond lay what could only be the royal study, a light, airy room lined with intricately wrought shelves of wood and silver like branches of a delicate, fantastic forest. A priceless forest: In her Realm only the wealthy owned more than two or three books—the costly, hand-copied things—but here were so many volumes (copied, no doubt, by magic) she ached with frustration at not being able to read.

Hauberin, clad in a wine-red robe, a thin silver coronet holding back sleek black hair from a still almost gaunt face, and a silken sling supporting his wounded arm, was perched in one of the two arched windows, examining a scroll as best he could with only one free hand. He looked so unquestionably *royal* that Matilde hesitated, suddenly feeling absurdly shy.

Idiot. He *hasn't changed, even if he's wearing a crown now.*

Besides, she could hardly go on just standing here like a silly little girl, so Matilde gave a polite cough.

"Don't hover in the doorway," Hauberin said without looking up. "Enter."

"Ah . . . it's me. Matilde. You asked to see me."

The dark head jerked up in surprise. Hauberin flashed her a quick, embarrassed smile. "Sorry. My psychic senses are still off a bit." His eyebrows rose as the language she'd used registered. "They've taught you our tongue, I see. Magically, of course."

"When I was . . . ah . . . when they thought it was necessary."

"When you were *ainathanach,* you mean. I'm sorry about that; I have no idea why I placed that burden on you."

A long, awkward silence fell. Then Hauberin gave a sharp little laugh.

"This is ridiculous. How can we be wary of each other after all we've been through?"

"I . . . never really had a chance to see you as a prince before."

"Oh, come, the crown doesn't change me into a monster, does it?"

She had to grin. "Hardly. Oh, but how do you feel?"

"Fragile," Hauberin admitted, "but viable. Though yes, the arm does still hurt. Iron-wounds, I'm discovering, take a cursedly long time to heal. But at least they will heal, thanks to you. Matilde, you saved my life twice over."

She could feel her cheeks reddening. "I couldn't very well just let you die, could I?"

"Ah. Well." Hauberin glanced down at the scroll he still held, then gave a small, wry laugh, shaking his head. "I keep forgetting I've only been away a very short time; I'm always expecting to find piles of work waiting for me."

"A short time . . ."

"Oh, yes. Alliar brought us back here the same day Li and I left."

The scroll slipped. Hauberin moved too quickly to catch it, and struck his arm a glancing blow against the wall. Eyes shut, face gone pale, he muttered something short and sharp. "I am forever doing something stupid like that," he said tightly.

Not knowing what else to do, Matilde murmured, "That . . . uh . . . word wasn't part of my language lessons."

"Nor is it going to be." Hauberin opened his eyes, not quite managing a smile. "Forgive me." The words were just a bit clipped with pain. "We're a pampered folk, used to healing wounds with just a concentration of will. This nonsense," he indicated the sling, "is growing . . . tedious. At least Serein had the . . . good taste to wound me twice in the same arm."

Hauberin's voice faltered. Matilde reached out a nervous hand, and the prince deposited the scroll into it. "If you'd just drop this onto the table. . . . Thank you."

"Are you—"

"There's a very pleasant wine in that ewer, with a restorative spell added to it. It might be a nice idea for both of us. If you'd be so kind . . ." He touched his sling. "Pouring is a bit . . . inconvenient just now."

Matilde hastily handed him a filled goblet. Hauberin sipped from it in silence. The color slowly returned to his face; after a bit, he saluted her with the goblet. "Kerlein's potions are a wonder."

"Kerlein?"

"The Lady Kerlein. My physician. Go on, try your wine."

"The blue-haired lady? We've met," Matilde said wryly and took a cautious sip from her own goblet. Oh, wonderful: warm and cool at once, sweet and sharp, sending a surge of strength through her. . . .

"How could you stand to drink what Gilbert and I served?" she burst out, and Hauberin laughed.

"Manners are everything. Ah, but I'm forgetting my own. Come, sit." He added as she settled herself, "I hope you're not finding all this"—the sweep of arm took in the whole land—"too overwhelming."

"Not quite," she retorted. "Bewildering, yes; if I gave you my list of bewildering things we'd be here all day!"

"Oh, really? Name one thing, then."

"Well . . . since this is the royal palace, I expected to see a city around it, or at least a town."

He smiled. "We aren't much for the crowding of cities. Remember that when we feel the need for a market or any other gathering, we can ... ah ... create whatever temporary buildings we need. And the palace *is* the town; you haven't had a chance yet to realize how big it is. My ancestors were a flighty lot, adding a tower here or deleting a walkway there...." His gaze was suddenly abstracted, and Matilde thought with a flash of amusement that he, too, wasn't free of the urge for architectural tamperings. "It was a wonderful place in which to grow up," the prince added, "full of strange nooks and hiding places."

Some of which Alliar had found. "But if there aren't any cities, where does everyone live?"

"Some do live here in the palace. Others have their farms or estates or what-have-you. Forest groves, caves: not all my subjects need or want houses."

"Oh."

Hauberin grinned. "It's not all so amazing. Come, stand up again if you would. See that wisp of smoke, there, to the west?"

Wondering how, with no sun for reference, he could tell west from east (some mystic sense basic to Faerie, she guessed), Matilde obediently leaned out the window. "I see it."

"That's from the chimney of a perfectly human farmer."

"A—what?"

"Oh, yes. As solid and steady a fellow as you'd like. He fell through a rift between Realms one day, saw how fertile the soil was, and settled down. With a pair of buxom woodsprites, I might add. They like his human beard, I'm told. And other things."

She gave a scandalized giggle. "You're inventing all this."

"No, really! He sends me a tribute of vegetables every autumn. A loyal subject. Speaking of which ..." Hauberin's voice was suddenly formal, very regal. "I understand that certain of my courtiers have harassed you."

Matilde remembered those beautiful, casually cruel faces, those lazy, sensual eyes promising delight and pain.

Fighting down a shiver, she murmured, "It was nothing," not wanting to make enemies in this alien land. "It happened right after we knew you were going to live. They were overcome with excitement."

"It will not happen again."

She dipped her head in thanks, then glanced at him skeptically, noticing, now that she was standing this close, the underlying pallor of the olive-dark skin. "Should you really be up and about so soon?"

He started to shrug, then clearly thought better of it. "My arm may be sore—mostly because I keep doing clumsy things to it, as you saw—but I'm no longer ill, thanks to you." Hauberin paused. "Matilde, it was a brave, foolhardy thing you did, feeding me your strength in that burst of Power. Oh, believe me, I appreciate it! But you could have killed yourself, drained the life-energies right out of yourself."

She hadn't realized that. Chilled by what might have been, Matilde slowly sank back into her chair. "I didn't know what else to do! I couldn't just stand back and let that—that traitor murder you."

"Thank you," Hauberin said simply. "Eh, how do *you* feel?"

"Not as weary as before I drank that wine. but I'm— Oh, Hauberin, I'm afraid."

"Surely not of those courtiers. I told you, they won't—"

"You don't understand. I c-cast Power. I *felt* what people were feeling. . . . I looked into Charailis' eyes and saw what she was truly like, inside I mean . . . that poor, treacherous, *empty* woman . . . and I—I didn't kill her, did I?"

The prince shook his head. "All you did was help me Shield myself. The death-magic she loosed recoiled on her. In effect, she killed herself."

"But I don't know how I— What I— Oh God, what's happening to me?"

Hauberin's eyes were gentle. "Don't be frightened, please don't. It's nothing to harm you, only that Faerie is doing what it does to all with latent magic: it's enhancing your innate Power."

Matilde stared in horror, seeing herself as witch, demon, no longer human. . . . "Does that mean I can n-never go home?"

"Why, lady!" the prince exclaimed. "Here you are only newly arrived in my lands, and already you want to leave them?"

"Please. Don't mock me."

He sighed. "No. If you return to human Realms and refuse to use it, your Power will dwindle back into latency."

"Then you can send me home."

"At the moment," Hauberin murmured, "I doubt I could transport you across the room, let alone to another Realm. Stay here as my guest for now, Matilde." His dark eyes were glowing, Powerful. "You will enjoy my lands, I promise."

"But . . ."

Hauberin's face was suddenly closed, alien. "Enough, lady. As for your returning home . . . we shall discuss that at a later time."

The prince held himself regally straight of back till Matilde was gone. Then he sagged in the window seat, furious at his body for its lingering weakness.

"*Alliar.*"

"My Prince."

The being must have been just outside the door, appearing so suddenly Hauberin started, jarring his wounded arm. *Oh,* damn, *not again!* The nagging stab of pain made him snap irritably, "How could you be so thoughtless?"

"I . . . what?"

"Matilde! How could you bring her here?"

"I should think you'd be glad I did," the being drawled. "Without her . . ."

"I wouldn't be here. Yes, I know, but—"

"At the time, there wasn't much of a choice," Alliar

continued. "I had you in my arms—dying, for all I knew—and guards were rushing down the stairs at us. Would you rather I'd abandoned the lady to Baron Thibault's mercies?"

Hauberin held up his free hand in surrender. "No. Of course not. But . . . she wants to go home, Li. When she pressed me, her eyes bright with despair, I couldn't answer her. Instead, I placed the smallest of persuasion-spells on her to keep her here, content, an easy thing now that she's no longer repressing her Power so fiercely. I couldn't bear to tell her the truth."

"Which is?"

"Oh, Li, I *can't* send her home. If I made the slightest miscalculation of time or space—particularly of time—it would kill her!"

The being shrugged. "She seems to like Faerie well enough. Keep her here, then."

"As what? My—pet?"

Alliar's eyes flickered with impatience, but the being said only, "Charailis' estates have reverted to the crown, haven't they? Why not give them to Matilde? She's a capable lady, my friend. She'll make a place for herself."

"I hope so."

Alliar paused, considering, head to one side. "It's not just Matilde's well-being that's worrying you."

"Ae, no. There's the little matter of the succession." Hauberin laughed without humor. "My heirs don't seem to be having much luck, do they? First Serein, then Charailis— And now that the stalemate of Charailis is out of his way, what are we going to do about Ereledan?"

The being snorted. "Ereledan. All brave red-and-bluster, sitting safely at home so no one will think he had anything to do with your poisoning. I don't think we have to worry about him."

"Not worry. Just watch."

"The succession, though . . ." Alliar sighed. "I never was happy with Charailis standing so close to the throne. Now that she's dead . . . I don't know. You must have *some* safe kinsman or kinswoman you could name your heir."

"Who'd be ambitious enough to want the throne, but not so ambitious as to try to take it from me. Ah, I don't know, either."

"Problems of succession are hardly anything new to this land. It manages to survive, regardless. And there's still something else bothering you."

"Yes." Hauberin slid to his feet, leaning back against the wall. "Serein. Can he really be dead this time?"

"As dead as I could arrange." Alliar's eyes glittered. "Hauberin, my aim was good. No one, not even he, recovers from an iron knife through the heart."

"I . . . almost wish you hadn't slain him."

"*What!*"

"Don't shout. The fever hasn't made me soft-minded. But if you could somehow have brought him here—yes, I know, you literally had your hands full—if you *had* been able to bring him, I just might have gotten the truth out of him about his curse. If it really *is* his."

"Eh well, the thing could have died with him. You haven't had the dream since—" The being stopped short. "What do you mean, *if* it was his?"

"When I was down in Thibault's cellars, with Serein doing his best to keep me alert," Hauberin absently touched the iron-burn on his forearm, "he didn't show anger or triumph or any other emotion you'd expect from my dear cousin when he had me in his grasp. He was terrified. And I suddenly realized why: it hadn't been him doing the transferring from body to body at all."

"Oh, but—"

"No, wait. All along it didn't make sense: Serein suddenly wielding magic he couldn't know, placing a curse against the Rules, working a spell previously known only in myth. But when you accept that none of it was his doing, everything fits. Serein, somehow, found himself a powerful, alien ally. But by the time we were in the cellars, that ally, for whatever arcane reason, had decided to totally abandon him. Serein was trapped in human

Realms in the middle of human politics, with nothing but the one fragile human body between him and the unknown— Ha, no wonder he was terrified!"

"Hauberin," Alliar said gently, "you were hardly in any condition to be rational."

"I wasn't imagining it."

"Why should this alien magician-or-whatever hate you?"

"I . . ." Hauberin waved a helpless hand. "I don't know. But I had a strange dream—"

"When?" the being asked skeptically. "While you were delirious?"

"It wasn't just a fever-dream! I spoke with a very real presence, mind to mind, someone or something truly alien, truly hating, that wanted me dead. That . . . had already killed my parents."

"Ach, Hauberin," the being murmured. "Come, sit down."

"Don't patronize me!"

"And don't snap at me. We may never learn how Prince Laherin died, but it was illness that killed your poor mother; there are enough witnesses to swear to that. And it was iron-poisoning that created your dream. Remember when you were feverish from *seralis*? You were convinced an assassin was in the room."

"I'd forgotten." Hauberin stretched, warily. "Ae-yi, maybe you're right," he admitted reluctantly. "Maybe it *was* all in my mind."

"Of course it was."

"Speaking of which, I'll have to do something to reestablish the royal image in the minds of my people."

"Reestablish?" Alliar laughed. "My dear prince, you are the first ruler in recorded history to have survived iron-poisoning. Right now your people are in awe of you!"

"Oh, indeed? We'll see how long that lasts."

But Hauberin couldn't hold back a grin.

Matilde stood in her pink-pearl walled bedchamber

before a mirror rimmed with silver (the royal metal, she knew that now, with its ties to Moon and magic; gold, sun-metal that it was, was unknown here), and stared at the unfamiliar face staring back: pale from the lack of sun, yet as aglow with health as any true Faerie face; red-flame hair unbound save for a band of bright green silk; eyes ... oh, the eyes were the strangest, wild and wide, full of joy and knowledge that had nothing to do with the merely human. . . .

But I am *human,* she remembered with a shock. *Pretend though I might, ache for this land as if it was my homeland though I do, I—am—just—human.*

The image in the mirror was blurring. Matilde turned sharply away, brushing tears from her eyes with a brusque hand. God, how she wanted to stay here. How she wanted to *belong!* But it was impossible, it was foreign (she would *not* say, "Godless," for all that there were no churches here and folk never called on holy names), all foreign.

Ah, but the wonder she'd seen and heard and felt ... magic shining in the very air, waiting to be shaped (shaped like the first illusion she'd cast, hardly knowing what she did, too overcome by Power's demand to be used to be afraid, a flame-red bird, and she standing, head craned back, watching it soar up and up, as delighted as a child); the elegant, fierce, quicksilver-fancied folk, perilous and proud, swift to rage or laugh, to dance, to sing—oh, their music, the wondrous music, sharp as pain, beautiful as joy, feeding the lonely places in her soul, and all of it feeling, somehow, totally *right.* . . .

The one thing she had never dared do was leave the palace grounds; Matilde knew with a strange, calm certainty that once she set foot on Faerie soil, felt the pull of it calling to her *find your heartland, cling to it,* she would never, ever be able to leave.

"Matilde?"

Matilde turned with a start, struggling to keep her face impassive. "Aydris. I didn't hear you enter."

Aydris perched on the edge of an ivory-backed chair like a pretty, slightly plump bird with pastel blue feathers, and Matilde smiled in spite of herself. She liked Aydris, who, for all her Faerie whims and magics, hadn't a drop of malice to her.

But Adyris, like all her race, was swift to catch disturbed emotion. "My dear, what is it? You're not pining for mortal lands?" Her quick smile was bright with mischief. "Or is it Hauberin for whom you pine? Believe me, I'm not a rival; the prince and I have shared joy now and again, yes, but we're friends more than lovers. So if you—"

"No!" Matilde could feel herself blushing; try though she would, she couldn't accept the casual Faerie attitude towards matters sexual. "I'm a married woman, and I— I . . . Aydris, how long have I been here?"

The slanted green eyes all at once were opaque, alien. "Not yet long enough," Aydris replied evasively.

"*How* long? A day? A year?" Horrified, Matilde realized she'd lost all track of time as surely as any poor fool in a fairyland ballad. *And I didn't once have the wit to worry about it!* "Aydris, please! How long?"

"Poor thing. Look in the mirror again. Reassure yourself; you haven't aged."

Even knowing nothing could have changed from a few moments ago, Matilde still had to look, heart racing with the irrational panic she might somehow suddenly find herself hopelessly old. But as she stared into the clear glass, human and Faerie memories overlapped confusingly. Her mind saw Gilbert's face beside her own, her mind heard his voice pleading, *Don't forget your mortal life. You are my wife. Please, please, remember me.*

"Oh, God." Matilde buried her face in her hands as memories of her human life, her human responsibilities, drowned all else. How could she have forgotten . . . ?

She straightened slowly. "It was Hauberin's doing."

Aydris blinked in surprise. "I beg your pardon?"

"That's why I've been so mindlessly content. Hauberin

bespelled me. I've been under his enchantment all this while."

"Why, Matilde! Do you really think he'd do something like that?"

No. Dear saints, no, never.

Yet with her new *feel* for Power, there could be no denying the truth. And that meant everything she'd felt, all the joy and wonder, had been a sham. "Damn him! Oh, d-damn him!"

"Matilde! Wait!"

But Matilde was already storming out into the palace corridors to find the prince, wide-eyed servants scampering out of her way, courtiers staring, whispering after her, "It had to happen eventually. The human's gone mad."

"You, guards!" she snapped. "Where is the prince?"

"Here," murmured a weary voice.

Matilde whirled. Hauberin, clad in somber blue tunic and hose, was watching her quietly, tired eyes deeply shadowed. A corner of her mind rejoiced that not much time had elapsed after all, because even though he'd abandoned the silken sling, he was still treating his arm with obvious care.

"Hauberin, I—"

"You've broken my spell, I see. No, wait, before you explode, come out here into the garden where we can speak in private. And please," he added with wan humor, "don't shout."

The garden was small as a cloister in her own world, open to the sky and heady with the rich scent of the pure white Faerie roses. Hauberin sank to a marble bench and gestured to her to sit. She did, stiffly, beginning, "How could you—"

"Bespell you? Ah, Matilde . . . please believe me, I never meant to hurt you in any way. The only excuse I can offer for what I did is that I wasn't thinking too clearly yet, and I . . . couldn't find any other way to protect you."

"Protect me!"

"I repeat, I didn't want to hurt you."

"But everything I saw and did, everything I felt was a *lie!*"

"Lies are foreign to Faerie," he reminded her softly. "Whatever you felt was real enough; the spell did nothing more than relax your mind."

"To the point of childishness! Hauberin, why? Why in God's name did you think I needed protecting?"

"I wasn't sure I could safely send you home. The times of our two Realms run at different speeds, even as the stories say. I suppose what I was trying to do was make it easier for you to accept living here."

"Are you saying you *can't* send me home?"

"I'm saying it would involve definite risk. But I had no right to make the decision for you."

"Oh. Well." If there was anything more frustrating than having the props of one's anger kicked out from one . . . "Then . . ."

"At any rate," Hauberin continued wearily, "*I* must return to your Realm. It seems that Serein's curse really has outlived him."

"The . . . ah . . . recurring dream?"

"Oh, yes. I must go kin-hunting once more." His gaze was steady. "I give you your choice, lady. If you wish to stay and make a new life here, I will deed you the late Charailis' estates. You shall not want."

"And if I go back?"

The prince shook his head. "I can make no promises."

Matilde clenched her teeth, fighting the urge to burst into tears. *I can't decide, how can I decide . . . ? Now I know what Lady Eve felt when she and Lord Adam were cast out of Eden. . . .* "I . . . can't stay," she said at last. "I can't. Hauberin, while I was bespelled, I didn't need to remember who and what I was. I didn't need to be afraid of magic, or witch-burnings. I only just barely remembered I'm a married woman. I don't want to go back—"

"Why then, stay and—"

"No. I *am* married. And the last thing I recall from

human lands is that my husband is missing. How could I possibly stay here and never know if I was wife or widow?" She took a deep, steadying breath. "Gilbert's been kind to me. I can't abandon him now."

"So be it. I'll just gather Alliar, and some more . . . ah . . . human clothing for us. And then . . ." Hauberin paused, then reached out to quickly touch her cheek. "And then, my brave Matilde, we shall leave."

To her shock, the quick caress sent shivers running through her. She stared deeply into the dark, weary, bemused eyes and thought, *Oh dear God, no, I can't, this can't . . .*

As though aware of her confusion, Hauberin turned sharply away. "My word on it, I will do my best to return us to your rightful time and place."

Whatever that may be, Matilde added in despair.

XXIV
RETURN

Hauberin staggered, dazed by the sudden transition, the sudden loss of Power and—as in his first crossing of Realms—equally sudden rush of strength, feeling free from fatigue for the first time since his wounding. Matilde and Alliar, clad in Faerie approximations of human clothing, had safely made the crossing, too, every bit as dazed, the prince felt, as he. Hauberin glanced warily about, seeing bushes, grass, the dim gray light of early day in a mortal Realm—and directly ahead, the massive bulk of a castle. . . .

Baron Gilbert's castle.

Ae, Matilde! Suddenly totally aware, terrified of what he might see, Hauberin turned to stare at her so fiercely she stared back at him in horror, stammering, "W-What? What is it?"

Giddy with relief, Hauberin grinned. "Nothing. There's not been the slightest change in you. This is your own home Realm and time."

She laughed, stopped, laughed again. "I knew you could do it. I didn't doubt for a moment."

"Now, that," teased Alliar, once more in human-male guise, "is as blatant an example of human falsehood as I've heard."

The being had spoken in the Faerie tongue. Matilde blinked in confusion.

"I—I can't understand you," she said in the human tongue, alarm sharpening her voice. "And I feel . . . odd."

"Ah, don't worry," Hauberin soothed. "The language-spell can only work in Faerie. And the 'odd' sensation is this magic-weak Realm's way of squelching any Power not its own."

He saw from her lonely eyes that she already rued the need to leave Faerie. *Honor and necessity,* he thought, *twin flails to drive us on.* "Come. We've landed close to your husband's castle." *Amazingly close; I probably couldn't do it again in a hundred tries.*

Alliar grinned. "It's nearly morning, too. How charming. We can be the Baron's first callers of the day."

But as they neared the castle in the gradually brightening light, Matilde stopped, eyes widening with shock. "That's not Gilbert's standard, it's Raimond's! No, I'm not mistaken; see, the field is vert instead of azure, green instead of blue. Dear God, where is my husband . . . ?"

The portcullis had not yet been raised. Alliar, hands on hips, bellowed up to the guards in the twin watchtowers, "Ho, you, I know you see us! Let us in!"

Matilde stepped out of shadow. "You know me," she called. "I am Baron Gilbert's wife. Enough of this! Let us enter."

Hauberin could hear the amazed murmurings from where he stood. *Now, what . . . ?* There was a long, long pause, and then the portcullis went clanking up. "About time," Matilde muttered, and strode boldly forward. Hauberin and Alliar followed more slowly, the prince no more comfortable passing under the spiked gate than he had been the first time, half-healed iron-wounds throbbing in response to all that iron.

But then Matilde's brave steps faltered and stopped, and the prince hurried to her side.

Two men stood in the courtyard. One, tall and blond, could only be Raimond . . . but a Raimond strangely changed. The childish wildness was gone from him, and a new maturity was evident in body, stance and eyes. The man beside him was younger, stocky and broad-shouldered, his freckled face pleasant rather than handsome, somehow familiar, yet not quite—

"Aimery!" Hauberin gasped, even as Aimery returned, "My Lord Hauberin! But how—"

"—could you have grown to manhood and—"

"—how," Matilde asked Raimond weakly, "could you have changed so much in only a few days . . . ?"

"A few days!" Raimond echoed. "Matilde, I don't know where you've been and how it is you don't look a moment older, but you weren't vanished for only 'a few days.' You've been gone for ten full years."

". . . and that," Riamond concluded, "was the last time I ever saw my brother, that night when all hell literally seemed to tear loose."

They were sitting in the room that had once been Baron Gilbert's solar, all save the visiting Aimery, who had politely excused himself. Matilde leaned forward to stare at Raimond, eyes fierce. "You can't just have given up!"

"I searched for Gilbert for two years. Two years, Matilde! But the air might as well have swallowed him up for all the traces we found." Riamond gestured helplessly. "A man can only live on hope so long. I can only guess that Thibault, in his madness, murdered my brother."

"Ah, Thibault," Hauberin murmured. "How is he?"

Raimond's brows raised. "Why, dead, my lord, for nearly these ten years. He died quite insane, they say—"

"Ah."

"—and his lands reverted to Duke Alain."

"Who was quick to cede you your brother's lands," Matilde snapped.

"Whom I did not even ask for my brother's lands," Raimond corrected, eyes grim, "till after those two years were past. Dammit, Matilde—your pardon, gentles—I might have been a young idiot back then, but I loved my brother! It . . . wasn't until after I'd lost him that I realized how much I loved him."

"But you don't know Gilbert's dead," Matilde insisted. "You have no proof."

"It's been ten years, Matilde," Raimond said gently. "Ten years without a word. Surely that's proof enough, even in the eyes of the Church."

"Meaning that I'm a widow by default? Because my husband's somehow been—misplaced? I can't accept that."

"I'm sorry. I don't know what else I can say. Look you, you needn't worry; my wife and I—"

"Wife?"

"Ah, you wouldn't know. Margit, Lady Margit of—"

"Duke Alain's cousin?" Matilde asked wryly. "You *have* done well for yourself, haven't you?"

"Yes— No— Never mind that. Matilde, there will always be a place for you here with us."

"As what? A curiosity, not-widow, not-wife? A pensioner, like some poor, witless old crone? No, thank you." But then Matilde's voice softened. "I know you're trying to be kind. But I won't take your charity."

"Well then, if you'd rather enter a nunnery, I could—"

"Oh, please. We both know I don't have the temperament for that."

"But what else is there? You can't just go wandering the roads! Matilde, as your husband's brother I'm responsible for you."

"No. Raimond, don't ask me where I've been, because I won't answer you." The man's glance flicked from her to, disapprovingly, Hauberin and Alliar and back again. "But this I will say: after all I've done and seen, I'm not the woman I was. I've learned no one is responsible for me *but* me."

"But . . . where will you go?"

Matilde turned to Hauberin and Alliar. "My lords, I imagine you are still heading towards Touranne? Yes? Then, if you will have me, I'll go with you." *Don't turn me down,* her eyes pleaded, *I have no other hope.* "Perhaps there I can learn my husband's fate."

Following her formal lead, Hauberin bowed in his chair. "Of course you are welcome, lady."

"But—but you can't!" Raimond stammered. "It isn't right, it isn't proper. . . ." The prince glanced his way but said nothing, and after an awkward moment, the man began carefully, "My Lord Hauberin, when first we met we weren't exactly on amicable terms. If I offended you back then, pray forgive me. I . . . wasn't always myself."

Because Serein had been controlling him? Or was it that Serein's mysterious ally had been controlling him through Serein, supposing that mysterious ally existed— Ach, nonsense, this train of thought was getting far too complicated. Hauberin glanced at Raimond, reminding himself that as far as the human was concerned, it really had been ten years, and dipped his head courteously. "I take it you . . . *are* yourself these days?" he asked, wryly mimicking the man's voice. "Yes? Then let there be peace between us."

Raimond leaned forward in his seat, murmuring so only Hauberin could hear. "Then you . . . won't really let her go with you?"

"Why, my Lord Raimond." Hauberin sat back with a smile. "You heard the lady: I am most certainly not her keeper."

"I hardly expected this," Hauberin murmured to Matilde as they and Alliar rode along the forest road, trailed by half a dozen mounted soldiers.

"I didn't either," she whispered. "The old Raimond would have thrown you into prison and me into a nunnery and tossed the key away. He really has changed in . . . can it really be ten years . . . ?"

But Hauberin turned in the saddle at the sound of rapidly approaching hoofbeats. "Ah, Aimery. And his own escort."

The young man reined his horse in beside them, saluting them cheerfully. "I must follow this road myself if I'm to get home. I didn't think you'd mind if we rode together for a bit."

Hauberin smiled, seeing traces of the friendly boy beneath the man. "Of course not." He glanced at the patently expensive clothing, and added, "No more Squire Aimery, I take it."

"No, my lord. I earned my knighthood some years

back, in service to good Duke Alain after . . . after Baron Gilbert . . . disappeared. I'm sorry, my lady."

"So am I," she murmured.

Aimery glanced warily at Hauberin. "I suspect I know where you've been sheltering," he said softly. "In your homeland, am I right? Ha, I am! That's the only way ten years could have passed by without touching you. Don't worry; I shan't tell anyone. Ah well," Aimery added, a little too loudly, "here's the fork in the road that leads to my own estate. I must say farewell."

But he leaned forward in the saddle as though to adjust a stirrup and murmured, "Be careful, my lord. Baron Raimond isn't ready to give up. The guards are meant to overwhelm you while you sleep and bring you back to his castle as abductors of the lady. He thinks you . . . ah . . . bespelled Baroness Matilde."

"Does he now? How very discourteous of him."

Aimery hesitated. "You . . . didn't . . ." He glanced from Hauberin to the wryly amused Matilde and shook his head. "No. Of course you didn't. My lords, my lady, I must leave now. All will be well with you?"

He looked so much like the earnest boy he'd been that Hauberin said with genuine warmth, "Yes, thanks to you. Aimery, you are something I never thought to find in these lands: a friend. Powers go with you."

"And . . . uh . . . with you."

With a wave of his hand, Aimery and his men rode off.

Hauberin and Alliar exchanged sly glances, touching minds, the same idea occurring to both of them.

"*It seems that our dear Raimond hasn't changed all that much,*" the prince said.

"*And here I was wondering why the guards kept eyeing you nervously, oh great and fearsome sorcerer.*" Alliar laughed. "*What a pity Power is so restricted here; how wonderfully we could entertain them.*"

"*Tsk, Li, you don't want to terrify the poor things; they're only hirelings.*"

"*A shame we must leave them so soon.*"

"Indeed."

"*You're sure you can . . . ?*"

"Oh, yes."

As they rode into the heart of the day, the air warm and soft about them, resonant with the thrumming of insects, six bemused guards found themselves, one by one, overwhelmed by the urge to sleep.

"The weather is so mild," the prince purred, "just right for a nap. Perhaps," he suggested smoothly, "we should stop for a rest."

"Yes," a man murmured. "Rest."

The guards slipped from the saddles, just barely remembering to tie up their horses. As the last of the men drifted off into slumber, Hauberin leaned back against a tree, worn but grinning. Persuasion spells were simple things to manage, even in this Realm—he'd proved that on his last visit—but they did take energy, particularly when they were worked one right after another. Absently rubbing his healing arm over the protective bandages (it must be healing; it itched enough for that), the prince watched as Matilde and Alliar moved softly from horse to horse, cutting the lead ropes.

The guards woke with a start at the sound of hoofbeats. But there wasn't much they could do save watch and swear at the sight of their quarry—and all the horses— galloping off towards Touranne.

Hauberin awoke with a jolt, sitting bolt upright, heart pounding with terror. But after a time it came to him that he *was* awake, safe for the moment, and buried his face in his hands. Powers, Powers, with each repetition of the dream he came just a little closer to the end of that corridor, to that final, terrible revelation. And he knew, with a quiet, dreadful certainty, that if he reached it, he would die.

If he didn't died of exhaustion first. Or frustration. If only there was some swift way to travel in this cursedly magicless Realm! But no, they were limited to a horse's pace. And you couldn't push a horse too hard, or the poor beast would die, and your journey would be even longer—

Oh, Powers!

They had been travelling now towards Touranne for five days, eating whatever small game the predator-quick Alliar could catch and whatever berries the foraging-wise Matilde could find, camping each night around the small fire Hauberin would light with his will. It should have, the prince thought wearily, been a peaceful, almost idyllic time.

At least the dream didn't come every night. Oh no, that would be too simple. Lately, as though a master torturer had devised the curse (too subtle a thing for Serein, surely?), there had been days among the five when he was quite nightmare-free—but anticipation of horror was leaving his sleep increasingly broken and unrefreshing, and his nerves so tight Hauberin thought he would almost have welcomed an attack by tangible foes.

A faint, repetitive sound made him tense. Alliar? No. The being was off somewhere in the forest, hunting or just listening to the wind. Matilde, though, was weeping in her sleep, quietly and hopelessly, and a little pang stabbed through Hauberin. Ah, the poor, brave woman! The prince didn't waste time in self-blame; he knew there hadn't been any way to make the Realm-crossing spell more precise. It was a marvel they'd come as close to time and place as they had, and a mystery still unsolved why Matilde hadn't seemed to age even slightly. But she had lost everything: husband, home, even her proper time. . . .

He crouched at her side, looking down at her help-lessly, aching to comfort her but not knowing how, aching to stroke the long, flame-beautiful hair, aching to touch her. . . .

Ae, Matilde, Hauberin thought hopelessly. *Why do you have to be human?*

Riding on the sixth day at the standard gentle walk,

trot, canter (Hauberin with his still sore arm tucked into his belt for support), they gradually left the forest behind, coming out into gentle rolling countryside dotted with farms. As the day wore down, they crested one last hill and saw a city in the open valley below, an impressive sight there in the twilight, ringed round by tall stone walls broken at regular intervals by watchtowers and bisected by the swift-flowing river that had been the downfall of the late Rogier. Most of the city was hidden behind the stone defenses, but Hauberin, standing in the stirrups, saw the dark mass of the ducal palace rising above the walls and, not too distant from it, the square tops of towers that, he realized with a thrill of excitement, must surely belong to the cathedral.

"Touranne," Matilde said, unnecessarily.

"We'd better get down there before they shut the gates for the night," Hauberin muttered, and kneed his horse forward.

As they neared the city, the walls looming up above them, they passed a collection of ramshackle buildings pressed up against the stones—taverns, the prince guessed, for the poorest or most desperate—and cantered through the deep gateway even as thick, iron-reinforced gates crashed closed behind them, shutting them into Touranne.

Hauberin glanced about in dismay, hardly hearing the guards calling out bored, good-natured comments about, "Just made it," and "Almost had to spend the night out there with the scum." He couldn't see very far in any direction; Touranne seemed to be a crowded maze of narrow, unpaved streets and one- or two-story wood houses set down wherever their owners had seen fit. It stank of too many humans and their animals, and too little sanitation. And, Powers, the cathedral doors were probably shut till the morning, which meant another night wasted, another night of dreaming. . . .

Matilde was looking about almost fiercely, clearly trying to orient herself. "It's changed," she murmured, and Hauberin caught a touch of panic in her voice. "So many

buildings . . . I don't recognize . . ." The woman glanced
his way, eyes wild. "If we can get to the palace, we can
crave shelter from Duke Alain and— No, what am I
saying, it's been ten years but I haven't changed, he'll
think I'm a witch—"

Hauberin reached out to touch her hand. "I know it's
frightening. Just remember you're not alone."

For a fleeting instant her fingers clasped his own.
"Thank you."

Alliar, the essence of human male swagger, came
riding up to them. "It's far too late to visit the cathedral
this night, but our good guards have just given me directions to a genteel inn where, they assure me, we shall
not be set upon by man or bug. Let's be off, shall we?"

Hauberin glanced up at the sign swinging sedately in
the mild night breeze: three swans painted an unlikely
gold swimming in an improbably blue river and labelled,
predictably, The Three Golden Swans. "Here's our inn.
Matilde, you'd best do the bargaining for us; I haven't
the vaguest idea of fair prices."

"You think I do?" she shot back. "After ten years?"
Her voice was edged with fatigue. "We also have a little
problem. I'd just as soon not be taken for a strumpet, if
it's all the same to you."

"Ah . . . what?" asked the bewildered Alliar.

"The innkeep would see two men and a woman sharing a room as immoral," Hauberin explained shortly.
"But Matilde, from what you've told me about city life,
it's not safe for you to stay alone."

"Oh, is *that* the issue?" Alliar slipped lightly to the
ground. "My dear, if you'll let me borrow one of your
gowns. . . . Thank you."

The being disappeared into shadow, only to reappear
as a rather fetching yellow-haired lady's maid. As Matilde
exploded into astonished laughter, Alliar curtseyed with
a flourish. "Problem solved," the being said.

XXV
A MIDNIGHT SWIM

Hauberin tossed wakefully for what seemed an eternity, straw mattress rustling beneath him, telling himself it wasn't that he was afraid of the dream; his nerves were just too tight to let him sleep.

At least the guards had been right: The Three Golden Swans (named, it seemed, after a ballad) *was* a genteel inn by human standards. That meant, Hauberin thought dourly, that it had been actually washed down and swept sometime within the last ten years, there had been chunks of genuine lamb in the stew the travellers had been served, and the straw in the mattress on which he was trying to sleep was reasonably sweet-smelling and free from vermin. It also meant that the innkeeper hardly raised a brow as he accepted enough links of silver to allow his guests the unheard-of luxury of two private rooms and only one to a bed.

By now, Alliar and Matilde must already have settled down for the night; the woman, Hauberin thought enviously, was almost certainly sleeping sweetly, and Li was probably comfortably sunk into a restful trance.

Ah, enough of this. Hauberin rose, pulling on his clothes again, and unbarred the shutters, casting them open to look out into the night. If he ignored the various unclean smells and the uncomfortable *feel* of so many human auras crammed in together, it was pleasant enough out there. A faint sliver of moon hung over the city, and a sudden hint of breeze carried a trace of woodsmoke from someone's cooking fire, more agreeable than most of the underlying scents.

Touranne was very nearly silent. A baby wailed once somewhere in the distance, a thin, high sound of protest, then fell still. A woman in a nearby house laughed briefly with such sensual delight Hauberin's flesh prickled, making him suddenly remember the inn's two serving girls, young, almost pretty in the round-faced human fashion, staring at him, wanton-eyed.

Unfortunately, they'd also been unwashed, smelly, and probably lice-ridden. Ah well.

Hauberin stretched restlessly, impatient with this one small room when the night outside was so warm and clear. He briefly considered going back down through the inn's common room—no. If he didn't wake the innkeeper, he'd certainly wake the innkeeper's loud-mouthed dog.

The prince flexed his bandaged arm experimentally. Still a bit sore, and not as strong yet as it could be, for all his dutiful daily exercising. . . . Still, he had one good arm and two good legs. It should be an easy climb down from the window.

It was.

Hauberin moved silently through the city, aware of the *feel* of sleeping humans on all sides but enjoying the lonely delight of being the only one awake and out on the deserted streets. But he hadn't explored far into the maze of Touranne's narrow streets—stepping delicately around mud and potholes, night-keen sight noting novelties such as the chains strung across alleyways (to slow down thieves, perhaps?)—before he sensed he wasn't the only one out here at all. He was definitely being followed.

Faerie wildness roused. *Well now, just what this night needed: a touch of adventure.*

Mm . . . three . . . no, four louts, armed with clubs and the cold burning that meant iron. For all he knew, Hauberin thought wryly, he might have built up an immunity to the metal by now, but he was hardly about to test the point. The thieves presumably thought him some fool of a human. Let them learn their mistake!

He let them get almost within reach, then darted forward, running surefootedly through the night, not quite so quickly that they'd lose him, laughing to himself as he heard them crashing after him, their merely human vision not up to the task, their merely human feet slipping on the mud he'd avoided, staggering into the potholes he'd dodged. But his arm really wasn't up to all this jarring. Time to end this game and shake his pursuers in darkness. Ah, this shadowed street looked promising, little more than an alley, so narrow the second stories opposite each other were propped apart by beams. He leaped the first of the thief-tripping chains, listening to hear the humans fall—

But they didn't fall. Hauberin froze in horror as he sensed Otherness suddenly settle over them, soft as a falling veil, and knew it in that instant for the same Presence he'd known in his fever-dream: the Presence that wanted him dead.

Alliar was wrong, it wasn't a dream.

Small satisfaction. Outnumbered, unarmed, his Power all but useless in this human Realm, Hauberin turned and ran in earnest through the tangle of streets, hunting for some way to throw these no longer quite human hounds off his trail. If he had the breath to spare, he'd try shouting, and see if that didn't attract a crowd. Unless people were so used to cries for help they didn't even react? Powers, didn't Touranne keep any night watch? Weren't there any guards patrolling?

A beam protruding from a second story caught his eye. Hauberin jumped, missed, frustrated at being too short to do this easily, jumped again and just managed to close his hands around the beam. As the weight of his body pulled at it, his not quite healed arm protested with so sharp a stab of pain he cried out, nearly falling, flailing in vain for a foothold as the first of his pursuers reached him, snatching at his dangling legs.

"If that's what you want," Hauberin gasped, and obligingly let go, landing full on the man, who collapsed with a grunt, striking his head against a wall with a satisfying crack and going still.

One down, Hauberin thought and scrambled to his feet just as the remaining three came storming up. He turned to run— Oh, damn! This was a blind alley, ending in a low wall, beyond and below which rushed Touranne's river. The prince hurried back to his victim and snatched up the club the man had been carrying, hefting the heavy thing experimentally, wishing heartily it was a sword.

A sword—ha, yes. As the thieves charged him, Hauberin lunged with the club with all his strength, punching one of the men full in the stomach. The thief crumpled, curled in breathless agony, but before Hauberin could recover, the other two were on him, taller, stronger than he, knocking the club out of his grasp, bearing him, struggling savagely, to the ground, their unwashed reek choking him. Pinned beneath their weight, the prince felt a rough hand tangle in his hair, jerking his head back, exposing his neck, saw a knife glint in the second man's hand, saw the man's eyes glint just as coldly, and thought, *To the Dark with courage, I'm going to yell like a demon, and maybe someone will—*

As though the Presence had read his thoughts, a hand clamped down over his mouth. Hauberin tensed for the death-blow, feeling nothing but fury that he was going to die so absurdly.

But the blow didn't fall. The prince *felt* a wave of cold, alien delight, saw the corresponding flicker in the entranced eyes and glint of iron blade turned to the flat, and realized it wasn't going to be a quick death. He did the only thing left to him, and bit down on the gagging hand so hard his mouth filled with blood. The thief yelled out an oath, pain breaking the Presence's hold, and jerked his hand free, losing his grip on Hauberin. The prince, not worried about dignity, squirmed and clawed his way free, desperately dodging iron. Someone caught his ankle, and he kicked out, by pure luck connecting with a jaw. The hand fell away, and Hauberin was free, running the only way open to him, towards the river. He glanced back over his shoulder— Damn! They were coming after him. To his astonished relief, though, the sense of Other lifted from them as totally and suddenly as it had come, leaving them only human.

Frightened, raging humans, though, spitting out obscenities that all seemed to end with "witch," or "damned sorcerer!" They were blaming *him* for their troubles! With all the fervor of true witch-burners, they charged him, iron knives forcing the prince up onto the low guarding wall, the river loud behind him. The men stabbed at him savagely, and rather than stay and be spitted, Hauberin turned and dove.

He hit the water cleanly, surfaced gasping; the air might be warm, but the water was cold. The current engulfed him, sweeping him downstream with dizzying speed. Powers, Powers, ridiculous to escape murder only to die in a river! He was a fine swimmer, but not when the cold was sapping the energy from him, not when his injured, overtaxed arm had no strength left in it (he could only pray he hadn't undone all Lady Kerlein's work—not that it was going to matter if he drowned.) There were sheer walls on either side, nothing to cling to, nothing to let him pull himself to safety. Hauberin's eyes widened as an arched bridge loomed up before him. If he grabbed at one of the supports— Ae, no! At the speed he was travelling, that would hurl him against the bridge with enough force to kill him!

Head down, arms forward, praying his aim was good, the prince arrowed through an arch. The river widened on the other side of the bridge, and—oh, Powers be praised—several boats were moored along one embankment. He struck out for them with what was left of his strength, body unresponsive with chill, caught at a rope, missed, caught a second only to be torn free when numbed fingers couldn't grip tightly enough, spun dizzily about, slammed into the side of one of the boats, and started to drown. Dimly he heard someone say, "Now,

what the hell . . ." and thought those were absurd words
to die upon.

But suddenly he wasn't drowning. Something was
snagging his clothes—a fisherman's gaff, tugging his head
above water. Squirming away from the iron hook, he
caught a glimpse of a bearded, weather-beaten face, then
his rescuer had removed the gaff, dragging him out of
the water by hand, and Hauberin recovered enough to
help, struggling against the river's pull till he tumbled
helplessly up onto a wooden deck that stank of fish but
felt most wonderfully solid. He could have lain there all
night, but the man who'd saved him was forcing him to
his feet, half carrying him into the deckhouse, letting him
crumple to a bunk.

"Here." A coarse, heavy woolen cloak came tumbling
down about him. "Wrap that about yerself. I'll just get
the fire burnin' again. And here, take a swallow o' that.
Put some warm in ye."

Too numb to argue, Hauberin caught the leather flask,
needing both trembling hands to hold it, and swallowed
something so strong and raw he nearly choked. But the
rough drink—whatever it was—did send a tide of warmth
rushing through him, enough so he could gasp out,
"Thank you."

The fisherman turned from the brazier he'd been tending and gave a nod. "Not a night for swimmin'," he said
laconically.

"Hardly." Hauberin drew the cloak more tightly about
himself, not caring about the fishy reek. "It was either
that, though, or die."

"Mm. Not a good idea, bein' out alone at night."

"So I learned. I'm . . . a stranger here."

"Figured. Thieves get ye?"

"Almost." Worried, the prince sent his recovering
senses hunting . . . hunting . . .

No. For the moment, at least, he was safe, and Alliar
and Matilde as well. For whatever reason, the Presence
was utterly gone.

Hauberin sneezed, receiving the fisherman's absent

blessing, and took a second swallow, then another and another, drowsy with shock.

"Hey, don't drink it all! Don't wanta clean up after ye puke!"

That struck Hauberin as so absurd he laughed. "Here."

But his wounded arm had awakened from numbness, and the prince gasped as it gave way. The fisherman caught the flask with a deft hand, eyes suddenly somber. "Yer bleedin'," he said quietly. "Hold still."

Dizzy, Hauberin fell back against the bulkhead, eyes closing, hardly feeling the man fumbling with the soaked bandages. But then he sensed the sudden coldness of iron and opened his eyes with a sharp, "No!"

The fisherman, knife in hand, started. "Wasn't goin' ta hurt ye, only cut the wrappin's." But Hauberin was no longer in any condition to hide his fear, and the human's rough face softened slightly. "All right. Don't get in a fit. I'll just use my hands. There, now . . . Ah. Someone got ye good a while back, didn't he? Arrow wound?"

"Mm."

"Burn on the same arm . . . Haven't been too lucky, have ye? And ye've undone a surgeon's good work, too, with all that swimmin' and such. River's not so clean, either." The fisherman paused, then shrugged. "Eh well, best be careful. Ye might wanta bite down on somethin'. This is gonna hurt."

Before Hauberin could stop him, the man had upended the flask over the wound. The prince just had time to clench his teeth—*damned* if he was going to scream before a human—before the tide of pain and weariness and alcohol carried him away.

Someone was shouting, a long way off. Hauberin stirred sleepily in protest.

"Look you, man, we've been searching for him for two days!"

The prince came fully awake. Alliar!

"I know he's down there," the irate being was continuing. "Now let us see him!"

"Maybe." That was the fisherman's drawl. Hauberin heard a scrap of metal on wood; the man had casually picked up the sharply hooked gaff. "Maybe not. All I know is, someone tossed him in the river to drown. Might have been ye."

"Oh, by all the—"

"It wasn't them," Hauberin called up. "Li, I'm all right. Just give me a few moments."

He sat up warily, naked except for the bandage on his arm, expecting weakness, finding, to his surprise, nothing but hunger and a sense of being most wonderfully rested. Even his abused arm no longer ached so foully. The bandage was a rag, but at least it looked clean. Hauberin warily peeked under it, then winced. He really had undone some of Kerlein's work; added to what was left of her neat stitching were heavier, though equally neat, stitches that could only have been the fisherman's work. The scar, Hauberin thought wryly, was going to be an interesting one. The alcohol wash, painful though it had been, had apparently warded off infection; the surrounding flesh looked healthier than it had in days, and the prince chuckled. Crude human treatment had, this once, been more effective than elegant Faerie magics.

As, of course, had his stretch of deep, unbroken sleep for . . . however long it had been.

And why didn't the curse catch up with me? Or the . . . Presence, for that matter? Too much exhaustion for That to track me? Too much alcohol in my system? Hauberin paused, considering. *Or . . . is it that the Presence, like any true creature of the Dark, can't cross running water?*

Ae-yi, even if that was true, he didn't intend to spend his life in hiding on a boat. The fisherman had left Hauberin's clothes spread out on a chest and the prince quickly dressed, the boat subtly rocking under his feet, then hurried out on deck, wincing as the first bright rays of early morning sunlight caught him in the face. Two sets of arms reached out to steady him: Alliar and

Matilde, fairly radiating worry. Hauberin disentangled himself, insisting:

"I'm all right, really. Thanks to this good man who plucked me from the river and gave me hospitality for . . . how long has it been?"

"A day," Alliar said. "You've been missing a full day. During which," the being added with blatant restraint, "the lady and I searched every corner of Touranne for you."

"Ah. I'm sorry." He enhanced that with a heartfelt mental apology, feeling Alliar's angry, reluctant acceptance. "I . . . wasn't in any condition to contact you."

The fisherman shrugged. "Ye slept the rest a' the night I caught you and almost all the next day around. Woke once to eat an' take care of nature, didn't say a thing, then went right back to sleep. Didn't have the heart to wake ye; looked like ye needed it."

"Oh, I did. But I kept you from your fishing. Let me—"

"Na, na, fish aren't runnin' right now; didn't see any crew with me, did ye?"

"At least let me offer you something for your kindness." Alliar held out several links of shining silver chain.

"Didn't do it for reward," the fisherman muttered, insulted.

"Then, why?" Hauberin wondered.

"Oh, I'm always fishin' folk outta the river. Most o' the poor souls already dead. Murdered, suicided, or just plain drowned. Pleasure to catch a live one this time."

But Hauberin drew the man aside. "There's more to it than that. What?"

The rough face reddened. "I really didn't pull ye out for reward; couldn't just stand by an' watch ye drown."

"But . . . ?"

"But after ye fell asleep, I took a good look at ye, at the . . . uh . . . ears an' all, and . . . well . . . ye're one a' Them, ain't ye? One a' the Fair Ones?"

"Ah?"

"The . . . ah . . ."—the man's voice sank to a murmur—
"the Fées out of the Hollow Hills."

Fées? He knew the word from his mother: It was the
local name for his kind. But what were these Hollow
Hills? Were the humans confusing their antique burial
mounds with places of Power? "Surely," Hauberin said
evasively, "such folk are just myth."

"We both know better 'n that, beggin' your pardon.
Someone's in that forest. Watching. Waiting. There's
been too many travellers feelin' eyes on them. Too many
sheep disappearin'—and children, fer that matter."

Hauberin hesitated, wondering what to say. Probably
totally unmagical predators had taken those sheep and
those poor children, too, but at least this once the fisherman was right about what he faced.

*And you want a Faerie blessing on your boat, don't
you? If I had true Power in this Realm, you'd have that
blessing and more, but . . .* "Yes," he said at last, "I am
of Faerie," and the fisherman's world-weary eyes were
all at once open and innocent as a child's.

Inspiration struck. "You must take the silver we offer,"
Hauberin said in his most autocratic voice. "Keep what
you will and spend the rest as honorably as you can, and
it will bring you both good fortune and the good will of
others."

Expecting magic, the fisherman accepted those common sense words *as* magic. Red-faced and grinning, he
clutched the silver links to him as Hauberin scrambled
up onto the dock, followed by Alliar and Matilde.

Neither of them spoke to him for some time, stalking
angrily along at his side. "Look you," the prince said at
last, "I told you I was sorry. I couldn't sleep, the night
was warm, the streets deserted, and I certainly didn't
expect thieves to attack me—"

"What else would you expect?" Matilde snapped.
"Didn't it occur to you the streets might be deserted for
a very good reason?"

"I blamed it on human night-blindness. And those

thieves wouldn't have given me any trouble if it hadn't been for the . . . Presence that suddenly possessed them."

"Not *that* again," Alliar muttered. "I thought we'd established that your so-vicious Presence was only a fever dream."

"I wasn't feverish this time!"

"Oh, no. You were, judging from the smell of you, totally drunk."

"I wasn't drunk!" Hauberin protested. "Oh, maybe I was, a bit, that first night, but after that—"

"After that you were, as the humans say, sleeping it off so thoroughly I couldn't even find your aura. Dreaming up your nebulous Presence—"

"It was real!" But . . . was it? Standing there in the bright sunlight, over a day removed from that nearly fatal night, Hauberin couldn't help a shadow of doubt: those *could* have merely been particularly bloodthirsty thieves; he *might* have been mistaken about any supernatural aspect—a forgivable mistake under the circumstances. But Alliar's attitude infuriated him. "How dare you argue with me! And why won't you believe me?"

"Because you aren't making sense!" the being shouted. "How could that—that Thing have been real when nobody else—not me, not anyone at court—*nobody* has ever so much as *felt* the slightest hint of it?"

"Enough," Matilde cut in coldly. "The two of you sound like little boys quarrelling. Alliar, keep your voice down before someone calls the guards. Hauberin, I don't care whether you were drunk or sober. I'm truly glad you're safe. But if you ever disappear without warning, if you ever frighten me like that again, I swear I'll make you regret it!"

She stalked off. Fuming, Hauberin and Alliar followed her through the awakening city, dodging early-rising servants, children, and dogs. The cool morning air was full of noise: scraps of laughter and quick snatches of whistling, wagons clattering over the rutted streets, church bells clanging from all sides of Touranne. Merchants chatted with each other as they prepared for the day's business, folding the bottom halves of the horizontal shutters that had barricaded their shops at night down and out to form tables for their wares, folding the top halves up to form awnings for their customers. No one seemed to mind that they cut pedestrian space in half in the process. In every open square, food sellers were busy with their stands or braziers, filling the air with the scents of frying meat and fish.

The prince, forcibly reminded that he was famished, stopped to devour two meat pastries from the first seller he saw (bewildering but delighting the woman with a silver link as payment), heedless of grease, gristle, or Alliar. At the being's fastidious insistence, though, he returned to the inn to shed his fishy—and now greasy—clothes and take a quick tub bath.

"Tell me," he asked the burly young servant who was lugging in buckets of hot water for him, "what do you know of the Fées of the Hollow Hills?"

The man put down the buckets so quickly water sloshed over the sides. Hastily crossing himself, he whispered, "Ain't safe ta talk a' them. Never know when they might be listenin'."

"I see. They're all around, then?"

That earned him a nervous glance. "They ... uh ... live in the forest north of here, in the Hills in the forest."

"Ah. You've seen them, then."

"Praise God, no. But they're there, just the same."

Hauberin sighed. Legends were stubborn things. Who knew what some human had seen however long ago to misplace magic in this magickless place? "Never mind," he told the uneasy servant, "that's enough water, thank you," and shooed him out.

Clean once more, Hauberin paused in the middle of toweling dry his hair, all thoughts of mythical Fées replaced by the here and now, suddenly so nervous he trembled. The Presence hadn't resurfaced; maybe the twin barriers of living water and sunlight had banished it; maybe he really had only imagined it. With any luck at all, the thing wouldn't have a chance to resurface. After all this wild adventuring it hardly seemed possible, but very soon now, Hauberin thought, he'd be in the cathedral. Breaking the curse. Learning the truth about his grandsire.

And, Powers help him, about himself.

XXVI

DISTANT COUSINS

Hauberin had not expected to be impressed by any human building; after all, the castles he'd seen so far had struck him more by their massiveness than by any elegance of design. But after travelling through the narrow, crowded streets of Touranne, stepping gingerly around various wet or smelly obstacles, the impact of suddenly coming out into an open square and facing the massive cathedral was strong enough to stop him dead.

The Cathedral of St. Denis was as large as any castle, and still unfinished, one side covered with scaffolding. The smooth stone of the completed walls were palest gold in the sunlight, broken at regular intervals by panels of colored glass, and its twin spires stretched up to the sky. Hauberin guessed that the huge front doors, set in a beautifully carved arched doorway between the spires and thrown open for morning services, were either intricately worked solid bronze, or wood sheathed in bronze.

Then the sun cleared the buildings behind him, and he gasped. In the space above the doorway was set a great round window of colored glass, blazing into life as the light hit it, shards of bright reds and blues and yellows that must be breathtaking when seen from within the cathedral.

It was the window out of his grandmother's memories. Exultant with terror and hope, the prince started forward—only to be blocked by Matilde.

"Not yet," she said shortly. "First I want to know just what it is you're hunting so desperately."

Her eyes were those of someone who has, bit by bit,

come to the edge of endurance. "You've earned an explanation," Hauberin agreed. Quickly, he summarized the
facts of his hunt, leaving Matilde staring.

"Melusine . . . ?" she murmured. "The Lady Melusine
. . . was your mother . . . ? But that was so long ago. . . ."

Hauberin laughed at her expression. "That would
make me . . . what? Over a hundred of your years? No,
believe me, I'm not anywhere near that old! Remember
the tricks we can play with time."

"Oh. Of course." Matilde smiled slightly. "I always felt
a little sorry for the Lady Melusine. I'm glad to learn
she had some happy years."

Hauberin nodded. "She and my father truly loved each
other."

But Matilde was staring anew. "Dear saints. We're
kinfolk."

"Distant kin, yes."

"Ha, and Gilbert's your kin, too! Why, when I tell
him—" She stopped as sharply as though she'd been
struck. "If I can. If he's still alive."

"Surely they'll have some news of him in the cathedral," Hauberin said gently, and took her arm. "Come,
we'll go look."

They found themselves in dim blue light and a haze
of incense in a long central hallway ("The nave," Matilde
whispered to Hauberin and Alliar) flanked on either side
by columns of sleek stone and the walls themselves
beyond that. The vaulted ceiling was dizzyingly far overhead. Windows were set into the walls at regular intervals, some of them still empty or protected by wooden
planking, others filled with pictures worked in the brilliant colored glass these people seemed to favor. "That's
stained glass," Matilde whispered, "and those are scenes
from the Bible. You . . . ah . . . do know about the
Bible?"

"My mother *was* human," Hauberin reminded her,
"and—ah."

The sun had just struck all the windows on one side

of the nave into blazing color. As though that flare had
been a signal, somewhere further into the cathedral the
clear, achingly pure voices of human boys soared up into
song. Dazed by the impact of visual and aural beauty,
Hauberin wandered on, vaguely aware that Matilde, a
solicitous Alliar at her side, had stopped to speak with
one of the cathedral folk: a priest? Ah, no, the proper
term, he thought, was monk, not that it mattered right
now, not with the sunlight and color and song. . . .

At last the young singers fell silent, and the prince
came back to himself to find he'd sunk to a bench without knowing it. A gentle chuckle sounded to his right,
and Hauberin turned to find himself facing a plain-faced
middle-aged monk with the amiable, placid eyes of someone who is totally at home with himself and totally without imagination. "They sometimes strike me that way,
myself," the monk said cheerfully. "The boys do sing
splendidly, don't they? Even when just rehearsing."

Hauberin nodded, too overcome for the moment to
speak. But then, with a sudden tightening of his nerves,
the prince remembered why he was here. The sharp
tension must have shown on his face, because the monk
blinked and asked gently, "Is there anything wrong, my
son?"

Oh, there is, indeed. "I . . . my grandmother left an
important parchment here." *So many generations back
you'd think me—you'd* know me—*for something Other.*
"It . . . uh . . . tells my mother's parentage."

The monk's face lightened with understanding. "Her
father, I take it," he said delicately, "was . . . ah . . . not
married to her mother? Is this a matter of inheritance?
Because if it is, I'm afraid I'm not authorized to—"

"No. I . . ." *Oh, Powers.* "I simply . . . I must know
who he was. Who . . . who I am."

The monk sighed sympathetically. "We are all God's
children," he murmured. "But you've hardly come to
hear me preach to you. Eh well, I can't see the harm. . . .
I can't let you touch anything or take anything from the
Treasury, you understand."

"Of course. I only need to see the parchment."

"Then come, my son. Follow me."

He led Hauberin down the length of the nave. The prince wondered nervously if they were going as far as the altar with its elegant red and gold drapings and canopy, feeling his human disguise growing thin, because he hadn't the vaguest idea of what one did at a human's altar.

But to his relief, the monk, sandaled feet slapping gently against the stone floor, made a sharp right turn into a new hallway, shorter and broader than the first and ending in a second door to the outside. He turned again, this time to the left, and stopped before a ceiling-high iron grill that screened off a stairway leading down. Hauberin, every nerve tightening in response to so much deadly metal, fought such a struggle to keep from flinching away that it was a moment before he realized the monk was studying the narrow door set in the grill and murmuring:

"That's odd. How should the lock be open?"

"You're not the only one who has a key, are you?"

"No, but . . . Ah well, come."

Hauberin dove through the doorway as though through a ring of fire, wincing as his iron-wounds throbbed painfully in response, then followed the monk down to the low, vaulted undercroft, nearly stepping on the man's heels as the monk stopped short on the last step, calling out indignantly:

"Here, now! No one's supposed to be down here!"

A figure in a dark, cowled cloak turned as sharply as a wild thing at bay. Hauberin saw a flash of wild, blank eyes—*bespelled eyes!* the prince realized in shock—then a ringed hand had snatched up a parchment and the figure was rushing at them. It bowled over the monk, who crashed into Hauberin. Hampered by the man's flailing arms, the prince grabbed frantically at the fleeing figure, all at once knowing, *feeling*, that the parchment was his grandmother's record. His hand closed briefly on the edge of the dark cloak, then the figure had pulled free, but not before Hauberin had a fleeting glimpse of the face beneath the cowl:

"Gilbert!"

Oh, no, that was impossible, that was surely impossible. Struggling free of the spluttering monk, Hauberin hurried after the thief—and nearly crashed into the iron door the man had slammed behind him.

Powers, how am I going to—

But of course the thief hadn't had the time to lock it. Hauberin kicked the door open with a safely booted foot and dove out, just in time to see his quarry dashing out the outer door. The prince ran after him, right into a crowd of visitors strolling into the cathedral. Leaving a chorus of indignant cries in his wake, Hauberin fought his way through them, struggling to keep the thief in sight. By the time he reached the outside world, the thief was already crossing the cathedral square, about to vanish into the streets beyond.

Damn you, no!

Hauberin threw all the Power he could summon after the man.

It wasn't enough, not at that range, not with the Realm's interference. The thief staggered, and something small dropped from his hand, but he recovered before Hauberin could reach him, disappearing into the maze of streets. The prince was left standing at the edge of the square, breathless and stunned with despair, blind to the curious crowd gathering about him.

Running footsteps made him turn to see Alliar and Matilde, she looking as hopeless as he felt. "Are you—" the being gasped, "was that—"

"The parchment?" Hauberin waved a hand. "It's out there. Somewhere."

The spectators, realizing the entertainment was over, slowly drifted away. One of them bent to pick up the small object the thief had dropped, but straightened empty-handed at Hauberin's sorcerous glare. Muttering bitterly, "At least I'll get some reward out of this," the prince scooped up the little glinting thing: a signet ring.

In the next moment, he nearly dropped it again. The ring had a faint but very real *feel* to it: the aura of that alien, chaotic, hating Presence. "Here," he said to Alliar. "Touch that. Tell me if *that's* just my imagination, too."

The being warily took the ring, then hastily handed it back, eyes wide. "My pardon. I should never have doubted—Matilde? What's wrong?"

The woman was painfully pale. "Let me—let me see that. Oh, dear saints . . ." She looked up at them, stricken. "This is Gilbert's ring. Don't stare at me like that! It's his signet, it never leaves his hand. I t-told him it was too big for his finger, I warned him he was going to drop it one of these days— Oh, God, he's alive!"

And a thief. And bespelled.

"If so strong an aura's clinging to the ring," Hauberin mused, "that has to mean the . . . ah . . . Other had it," and Gilbert with it, went the unspoken thought, "long enough for a link to have formed."

"And we can use that link to guide us to both Gilbert and That," Alliar continued. "Think it's a trap?"

"Of course it's a trap. But what choice have we?"

They rode out from Touranne in haste, Hauberin with the ring clenched in his fist, trying to ignore the unclean *feel* engulfing the signet, concentrating instead only on the faint psychic pull, like the thinnest of threads, guiding him on.

By midday they had left the open farmland surrounding Touranne behind, riding almost due north up through gently rising scrubland full of tree stumps and saplings, munching in the saddle on bread and cheese (eagerly provided by the innkeeper, glad to be rid of his troublesome guests), pausing only when the horses needed rest. By early afternoon, they were in the midst of true forest once more.

Hauberin dared take his attention from the signet ring enough to glance warily about. Unlike the gentle woodland through which they'd come on their way into the city, this was a rugged place, the land rising and falling sharply, full of rocks and twisting, ancient trees clinging fiercely to the broken ground. The air was cool and damp, rich with the scent of wet earth and vegetation; the steep hillsides glinted with moisture where they weren't blanketed with ferns, and the horses' hoofbeats were muffled by moss. Even though the sun was still almost fully overhead, the light was dim and green, diffused by leaves.

This, the prince realized with a silent laugh, could only be what the humans feared as Fée country. He could easily picture some fearful human traveller riding through this wildness at nightfall, reaching Touranne full of tales of lurking Things.

Matilde shuddered. "I wish it wasn't growing so late. I hope we don't have to stop in this forest for the night."

"What, afraid?" Alliar teased.

"Of squelching," she retorted. "This would be a dank place to camp."

Hauberin silently agreed. But there might not be a choice; as the faint psychic thread led them through a narrow gully, dense forest on the left, an earthen ridge rising on the right, there was no doubt that the already dim light was fading rapidly. While darkness was hardly a problem, neither he nor Matilde nor, for that matter, the horses, were prepared to ride the day and night around, particularly over such broken ground.

And here I'd hoped to be done with this, one way or another, before I had to spend another night's dreaming—

Hauberin came sharply alert as the horses whickered and sidled uneasily, *feeling* a faint, strangely distorted Power brush his own, interfering with his concentration on the signet ring, catching a quick glimpse of glowing green eyes peering out from behind a tree on his left. "Stay between us," he murmured to Matilde, and added with studied calm to Alliar, "Over there. On your side. Watching us."

"I see him. Look to your right."

Hauberin glanced up as though by chance to see a

second slender form stone-still in shadow on the ridge; it would have been totally invisible to human sight. "Well now, it seems they aren't just legends after all."

" 'They?' " Matilde whispered. "Are those Fées?"

Invisible to *Powerless* human sight, Hauberin amended. "Probably. They don't quite *feel* like anyone out of Faerie, though. . . . An interesting problem, eh, Alliar?"

Matilde glanced sharply from being to prince. "This is hardly the time for a discussion! You're not just going to ignore them, are you?"

The prince completely relaxed his concentration on ring and conversation, sending his senses roving delicately out, testing, *feeling* those mysterious other presences, *feeling* that oddly distorted Power of theirs rousing in response to his own before he could count them. He smoothly withdrew back into himself before any of them could accidentally snare him. However many there were—not as many, he sensed, as the Fées would have liked, more, certainly, than he would have liked—they were too many to fight. Nor, judging from the coldness he'd felt, were they in any mood for a parlay.

"Until we're sure how many of them there are," Hauberin said belatedly, "and why they're watching us, ignoring them is all we can do."

He caught up the psychic trail he'd been following, and felt that other Power quiver. As they rode on, the shadowy figures moved with them, and Haubeirn felt the space between his shoulder blades start to prickle. No magical being could handle iron, but that didn't mean the Fées weren't nicely armed with bronze or sharpened stone.

And here we are, neatly caught between forest and ridge.

But the Fées still did nothing more than watch.

"Watch away," the prince told them. "I'm *not going to be the first to yield."*

The night darkened. The horses had long ago accepted the alien scents of the watchers, plodding wearily on like equine sleepwalkers, heads down, ears bobbing limply. Alliar, of course, showed not the slightest sign of fatigue, but Hauberin heard Matilde stifle a yawn and had to fight down one himself.

"Can't we stop . . . ?" the woman complained sleepily. "Don't think I'll ever be able to walk again . . ."

"Sorry," Hauberin murmured. "We don't dare stop. Not here, not now."

No answer. The prince settled as comfortably as he could into the saddle, trying to ignore the complaints of his own tired muscles. . . . The endless ridge continued without a gap on one side, the endless trees continued without a break on the other, featureless walls, hypnotic in their sameness, going on and on like a tunnel . . . a corridor . . . a dark, featureless corridor . . .

. . . *down which he walked, aching with terror, know-ing that this time there would be no escape, this time he was finally close enough to see—*

"No! I won't— *No!*"

His own shout brought the prince jarringly awake, nearly falling, not at all sure where he was, hearing star-tled noises from Alliar and Matilde.

"What's wrong?" the being asked sharply.

Hauberin swallowed dryly, struggling to catch his breath. "Nothing," he rasped out. "I . . . fell asleep in the saddle for a moment, that's all."

At least he hadn't dropped the vital ring. The prince glanced down at it, then clenched his fist about it, cold and sick with the weight of hopelessness. It had all nearly ended here; he had come so painfully close to dying in his sleep. If the dream took him again, it would surely win.

Unless, of course, Hauberin thought grimly, he reached the Other first.

The night up ahead was growing too dark. Something was blocking their path, looming up mysteriously as they approached, making their horses shy and dance nervously—

It was a hill, only a hill, sloping smoothly out of the

surrounding forest, too perfectly round to be natural. Studying it, Hauberin straightened in sudden comprehension. Ah, so *this* was what humans meant by a Hollow Hill! It was an ancient site, so ancient folk had forgotten its purpose as some long-ago chieftain's burial place: dramatic, but perfectly harmless.

Harmless? The psychic thread he followed led, without the slightest deviation, right into the hill.

Impossible. That's a solid mound of earth.

A doorway opened in the hillside, a blacker mouth in the blackness, leading back into a long, narrow cave.

I stand corrected, Hauberin thought wryly.

Green-clad figures moved silently out of the mound to stop, straight-backed and proud, staring coldly at the prince. The prince stared right back in unabashed curiosity. Not much taller than he, these people were thin and lean as hungry hounds, their skin fair almost to unhealthy pallor. Both men and women wore their long, straight white hair in a series of intricate braids woven in multiples of three, six, nine, the magic numbers, a style so old Hauberin had seen it only in history texts; their green robes, though blatantly of human weave, were of an equally antique design. They looked so much alike—the same sharp, narrow, nearly gaunt faces, the same slanted, bitter, green eyes—he could barely tell one from another. And to all of them clung the *feel* of that weak, distorted Power.

And yet, and yet, for all their strangenesses, there could be no doubt: these were Fées, these were folk of Faerie.

Hauberin, amazed, moved one hand in an intricate ceremonial greeting common to most of the magic Peoples.

Not, it seemed, to these. They made not the slightest move in response. save for: "You trespass," one woman said in the human language.

"Not intentionally." In the Faerie tongue, Hauberin began the ritual phrase, "We come without harm, we mean you no harm, we pass on without harm."

Green eyes blinked. "He speaks the ancient tongue," someone murmured.

"Ancient!" the prince echoed in surprise. "It's the language of our homeland!"

"Do not taunt us," the woman replied in so archaic a Faerie dialect the prince had difficulty following her. "You bear the signs of our people," she continued, gesturing to Hauberin's face and ears, "but none of the True Blood have such skin, such hair, such eyes. Be gone from here, half-blooded one." The antiquated word she used, *chaikulai*, held subtle connotations of slavery and shame. "We give no greeting to humankind."

Hauberin fought back a sharp retort, waving the indignantly sputtering Alliar to silence. "No? And yet you let a human pass into your domain."

"No." Her eyes were green ice. "No human has passed this way."

That, Hauberin acknowledged uneasily, might not be quite a lie; what he'd seen in the cathedral might no longer have been truly Gilbert, truly human. Glad that Matilde couldn't have understood the words or the implication behind them, the prince said, "Surely you can't deny you granted someone passage."

The narrow faces were unreadable as stone. "What we did, or did not, is not your concern, *chaikulai*. Now, begone!"

Power glinted in the air. The pale, lean figures were suddenly robed in splendor, tall, proud, terrible in their fury—

Hauberin laughed angrily. "Enough of this!" he cried, and cast his own illusion over himself: a true enough image of himself shining coldly in princely silver robes, the intricate silver crown of High Ceremony gleaming against his black hair. "Half-blood I may be," Hauberin said in the human tongue—he would *not* call himself *chaikulai*—"but I am also a rightful Prince of Faerie, acknowledged by the High King and Queen themselves—and I will *not* be treated like a magickless fool."

Their illusions faltered and fell. Hauberin kept his own

a moment longer, enforcing the image. Then, seeing the bitter envy in the slanted green eyes, he let it fade, knowing better than to push too far, and slipped lightly from the saddle (regally schooled face showing no sign of stiff muscles' protests). Following his lead, Matilde and Alliar also dismounted, Alliar deftly scooping up the three horses' reins. "I must pass through your domain," Hauberin told the Fées. Hunting for the properly archaic turn of phrase, he added, "I hunt a blood-foe, a death-foe. Will you grant me leave?"

Almost reluctantly, the woman who'd first spoken dipped her head. "We grant you leave to enter," she murmured, which wasn't quite what Hauberin was seeking. "We grant you our hospitality. You shall speak with our Lady, and then . . ." She shrugged bonelessly. "It is for you and she to decide what follows. Come, Lord, will you not follow me?" But then the woman turned with a hiss. "Not she! Not the human!"

Hauberin politely held out an arm to Matilde. She, as regal as any Faerie woman, rested her hand upon it. "Yes, she," the prince said mildly, and stared into the Fée's eyes until her gaze fell.

"So be it," she muttered.

"Not me! I can't!" Alliar's silent words were tinged with panic. *"Hauberin, forgive me, I—I can't go into that closeness, I—"*

"Hush," the prince soothed. *"You don't have to enter."*

"But you can't go in there alone, just you and she and the winds know how many of them!"

Hauberin wasn't happy at the idea, either, particularly not when the Presence just might be lurking— No. No one of Faerie kind would tolerate That among them. *"Odd though they are,"* the prince said, wondering if he was comforting Alliar or himself, *"these are still Faerie folk. And as such, since they've offered me hospitality, they cannot break that vow to do me any harm. I repeat, you don't have to come with me."*

The being's relief washed over him. "I'll wait out

here," Alliar said lightly. "After all, somebody has to hold the horses." *"But I'll be ready if you need me,"* the being added silently. *"And . . . laws of hospitality notwithstanding, walk warily, my friend."*

XXVII

NIGHTMARE

At first Hauberin thought the Fées were being deliberately petty to the half-human and the human. Why else leave the passageway into the hill in darkness so thorough even Faerie sight was useless? But after a moment he heard the faintest rasp of palms lightly brushing one stony wall for guidance as though performing a familiar ritual, and realized with a shock of amazement that they either didn't know any light-spells or simply didn't have the Power to use them. For a moment the prince toyed with the idea of trying a spell of his own . . . No. He had accepted their hospitality, no matter how grudgingly it had been given; he was as bound by its rules as they. And pointing out a host's failings was hardly hospitable.

Eh, well, darkness alone never hurt anyone. The floor was smooth under his feet, there didn't seem to be any hidden snares or branching passages, and if they could use a wall for a guide, so could he, touching fingertips to stone as he walked.

An endless time passed in darkness, with no sound other than faint breathing and the now familiar slip of palms against wall. The floor sloped ever so gently beneath his feet, and Hauberin wondered uneasily just how deep into the earth they were going. Matilde hadn't said a word all this while, but her grip on his arm was becoming fierce enough to cut off the circulation.

"You're going to leave bruises," he said.

"Sorry." She loosened her hold ever so slightly. "It's just . . ."

"Don't worry. I won't lose you."

"But how can they live like this? Crowded into darkness— Oh, Hauberin, when I think of the bright light of Faerie . . . How can they stand this?"

Fée hearing was as keen as any of the Faerie peoples. "Because we are not weak, fearful humans," a woman's voice snapped out of nowhere, and both Matilde and Hauberin started.

"I think you hit a sore point," the prince murmured, right in Matilde's ear, and heard her give the ghost of a chuckle.

How *did* they stand it? Or . . . did they? What if the Fées didn't live here at all? What if, despite the ring's insistence that this was the right way, Matilde and he were blithely walking right into a trap—

Impossible. The place had the *feel* of a lived-in fortress. And no Faerie folk ever lied. No matter how long they'd lived in the hated human Realm, the Fées still could be no exception.

"Look," Hauberin soothed Matilde, "there's a glimmer of light up ahead."

"Amen." It was the faintest, most heartfelt whisper.

But now the prince had to wonder, *If they have a source of light, why don't they use it throughout?*

Then they stepped down into a vast chamber, a natural limestone cavern with several smooth passageways leading off into more darkness, and he had his answer: the light came from a few widely spaced glass globes set into the chamber walls and charmed to cast a pale white glow.

"Lilialli'al!"

"Of course," a Fée said condescendingly.

The prince ignored him, staring at the *lilialli'al* in open amazement. He'd never seen one before; nobody in his land used the light-globes any more. The creation of a *lilialli* took tedious, strenuous magic, a foolish waste of time and strength since experiments over the ages had given Faerie simpler, more efficient light-spells.

Just how long have *these folk been here?*

Long enough for many of the nearly everlasting light-globes to have lost their potency. That meant the Fées must have inhabited this land for . . . Powers, for at least since the humans' discovery of iron, probably much longer. The hall must have been a grand thing back then, all magic and splendor. Traces of that splendor remained: silver still glinted here and there from walls intricately carved in archaic designs that meant little to Hauberin, and a few small gems gleamed from the graceful stone throne that sat against the chamber's far side.

"But if the *lilialli'al* are failing," the prince mused aloud, "why don't you simply use candles or torches?"

That earned him a bitter, scornful laugh. "Those are *human* things."

Hauberin shrugged. "They're Faerie things, too, in my land."

The contempt in countless eyes spoke volumes. The prince deliberately turned his back before he said something he'd regret, making much of studying the throne.

Matilde might not have understood the language, but she certainly understood hostility. "If only they didn't all look alike," she whispered unhappily.

Hauberin glanced from the throne and the fading light-globes to the too-pale, too-gaunt, too-similar faces watching him from all sides and felt a sudden uneasy twinge, forcing himself to remember: *These are your hosts, they cannot play you false.*

But he surprised himself with a touch of regret as well for these sad remnants of a once proud race. All too plainly, they had kept themselves aloof from humanity down through the years, scorning to breed the very half-bloods, the despised *chaikulai'al,* that might have given their stock its needed vitality; all too plainly they had mated only among their own small group till what Power this magic-weak Realm allowed them had worn thin and nearly useless. Oh, it would still be enough to frighten a passing human, perhaps even enough to win them such peacekeeping offerings as their green cloth. But he doubted a living child had been born in these caverns within a hundred cycles of the mortal moon. As for the rumor of human children stolen away . . . it was surely that, only rumor. No human child could live for long, shut away from sunlight, from all light. . . .

Why do they stay here? Why didn't they flee to Faerie ages past?

Before he could find a tactful way to ask, there was a stirring among the Fées, a nervous anticipation. The crowd parted, bowing like wheat in the wind to let their Lady pass.

She was old, this Lady, as Sharailan his court sage was old, with something of the same brittleness, but without any of Sharailan's tempering gentleness; in her, the untold ages had worn away any trace of softness, and what was left was sharp as any blade. As she took her place upon the throne, green gown sweeping in stiff folds about her, Hauberin thought of an elegant white hunting hound, all lean, fierce, hungry beauty.

He bowed slightly, arms flat at his sides, the Single Courtesy of ruler to ruler, and she dipped her head in response. But her eyes, oh her fierce green eyes devoured him, as though he were the lover she had awaited all the endless years. Or, perhaps, the savior.

Uneasy, Hauberin said, "Lady? You look at me as though you know me, but I fear I don't know you."

For a moment longer the hungry eyes studied at him. Then the Lady murmured, "I thought it would be simpler, since you are but *chaikulai*. I was not told you are of the High Ones' blood as well. Ay me." Her sigh was soft and infinitely sad.

The vast cavern suddenly seemed chokingly close. Hauberin straightened, trying not to show his growing alarm, all at once very glad of those protecting bonds of hospitality. "Told by whom, Lady?"

"There is no need for you to know. Forgive me."

She raised a weary hand. And the gathered Fées rushed forward. For a few precious moments Hauberin was too stunned by impossibility, by this breaking of unbreakable Faerie Law, to fight back. Then he raised a wild swirling of Power to hurl his attackers away—only to have it smothered by the sheer volume of their weaker magics.

All right then, damn you, we'll do this the human way!

Hearing Matilde's scream of fury and a Fée man's grunt of pain—no delicate flower, she—the prince slammed a foot onto someone's instep (thinking wildly, *I'm getting good at brawling!*), managed to kick back into someone else's shin, but then they were upon him, pinning him back against a wall, grabbing at his limbs. He thought he glimpsed shame in the green eyes, mixed with desperation, but before he could call on their now-tarnished honor, a Fée chanced to catch his arm just above the healing arrow-wound, twisting it, and the prince gasped with the unexpected shock of pain, going submissively limp before the wound could be torn open yet again.

But as soon as he had caught his breath, he shouted to the Lady, "And is *this* how you keep your vows? You lie as well as any human!"

The Fées murmured angrily, tightening their grip on him, but their Lady never stirred. "What I do, I do for my people."

"Even if it means destroying their honor?"

"Ahh," she sighed, "what is honor where a *chaikulai* is concerned?"

"Stop calling him that!" That was Matilde's outraged voice; she might not know the word, but she couldn't have missed the contempt behind it. "He is a prince!"

The Lady smiled faintly, inviting Hauberin to join her bitter humor. "And how can there possibly be honor when humans are involved? Listen to me, *chaikulai*: We are old, far, far older than your few years—ah yes, I can *feel* your youth. These were our lands once."

"No!" Matilde shouted. "They were never yours!"

"Be still." A world of warning was in the simple words. Matilde, no fool, fell silent, and after a moment, the Lady continued softly, "For long and long and long we lived in these lands, shunning only the gaudy sun, glorying in the wonders of mortal night. The humans were as they are now: ugly, foolish things. We ignored them or, if they dared disturb us, toyed with them as the fancy moved us. We lived in peace. But then the iron-wielders came."

"And they drove you back into these caverns," Hauberin continued impatiently, "where you lingered and dwindled. Yes, yes, I can guess the rest of your story. What I don't know is why you stayed."

The Lady raised a languid hand. "These were our lands."

"Oh, please. I don't believe that any more than you. You are of Faerie, not Earth. Why didn't you return?"

The air was suddenly so sharp with tension that Hauberin braced himself, sure his captors were going to strike him. Instead, to his amazement, the Fées keened softly in anguish. The Lady's voice was so quiet he almost didn't hear it over their lament. "We were in this Realm far too long. The way home was lost to us, lost to memory, lost . . ."

"Lost . . ." the others repeated, a thin whisper of sound.

But while they keened, their guard was lowered. In a sudden fierce rush of strength, Hauberin tore free—

Only to stop dead when he saw Matilde trapped in Fée arms, a bronze Fée dagger to her throat.

"And outside," the Lady said in her quiet voice, "the other, the spirit-in-flesh, is caught by us as well. Do our bidding, *chaikulai,* and they live. Deny us, and . . ."

"Damn you, what do you want of me?"

"Only one thing, only this: to follow where you are bid."

A Fée woman bent and scooped up the forgotten signet ring in one smooth motion. Hauberin took it from her, *feeling* the psychic thread once more. "But this is insane! There was no need for force—or for you to break honor! Following this trail is what I wanted to do from the first."

"Is it? Come."

She stepped with delicate grace from her throne, gesturing to him to follow, the stiff green folds of her gown

brushing softly against stone as she walked the length of
the cavern. There before them, almost beyond the reach
of the *lilialli'al*, was the mouth of yet another tunnel. But
this one was never a natural thing. About it flickered the
faintest hint of Power, as though there was something
very much not of mortal Realms at work.

"Look into this passageway," the Lady said softly.
"Mark it well."

Puzzled, Hauberin obeyed, the *feel* of the ring telling
him that yes, this was the way he must go, down this
corridor . . .

   . . . down this dark, featureless corridor. . . .

All at once he knew it. All at once the air seemed
turned to ice about him, crushing him, stealing his
breath, his thoughts, his life:

This was the corridor out of his nightmares.

I can't go down that, I won't!

"You must," the Lady murmured, and Hauberin realized he had shouted that aloud. "You must go, or your
friends must die. It is as simple, I fear, as that."

"No, wait!" Matilde screamed, and Hauberin turned
to see her struggling to pull free from her captors,
stretching out her arms to him with a lover's longing.
"You can't go without letting me say goodbye!"

Now, what . . . ? the prince wondered. But he'd play
along; before anyone could stop him, he rushed to
embrace her, a corner of his mind wryly amused at the
melodrama. But then Matilde's lips met his in a long,
fervent kiss, and for a moment Haubeirn forgot they
were only acting, for a moment forgot everything but the
passion suddenly blazing about them both. He straightened, seeing Matilde staring up at him with something
of the dazed wonder he felt.

Then Hauberin came back to himself with a shock as
the disgusted Fées around them muttered, "*Chaikulai*
and human . . . doesn't even honor what diluted Blood
he has."

"You're fine ones to worry about honor," he began
hotly, but Matilde hurriedly whispered in Hauberin's ear

what must have looked like an endearment but was actually, "I don't dare use this, not while they've got Alliar."

Impatient Fée arms pulled them apart—but not before Hauberin felt Matilde slip a cold, hard something into his sleeve, something with the cold fire of iron to it—

"Go with my blessing," she cried out as the Fées dragged her away. "Let it be as a blade to defend you, iron to cut through sorcery!"

Oh, clever woman: she'd given him her belt-knife, safely sheathed so the metal wouldn't harm him. "Thank you, my dearest," Hauberin said. "I gladly accept your blessing."

In one smooth movement, he'd drawn the little blade and the Fées shrank back in horror at the sight of iron. Hauberin laughed sharply, for once on the right side of the deadly metal, and lunged at the Lady. If he could take her hostage—

Ae, no. Too many of her people were swarming forward to protect her. Hauberin hesitated, threatening them all with a wave of the knife, seeing them cringe. But one little bit of iron wasn't going to hold them back for long, and he dared not risk the lives of Alliar and Matilde.

There was only one road open. As the Fées charged him, Hauberin gave a shout of defiance and plunged into the corridor of his nightmares.

Almost at once, he was seized by a swirling dizziness that could only mean the thing wasn't quite within the human Realm; he was being drawn across to the Powers only knew where, hearing the Lady's voice as from a great distance, saying yet again:

"Forgive us. Your foe has promised us the way home for this service."

As the psychic gateway closed, Hauberin shouted back in frantic revenge, "*I* know the way back to Faerie! If you'd dealt honorably with me, I would have shared it!"

Had they heard? Hauberin drew back from what was now a blank wall of stone, and turned with slow dread to see the empty expanse of corridor stretching out before him, the far end misty in shadow. The walls were completely blank, with not the slightest slits for air or light, yet the chill, dry air was breathable enough, and the way was lit dimly by what every sense registered as an alien, alien Power.

The only possible way to go was forward. But for a long time, the prince couldn't move, caught in the throes of sheer claustrophobic terror, the cumulative weight of all the nights of horror crushing him till he could do nothing but huddle against one cold wall and pray like a terrified child that this was only another dream, that he could awake. . . .

At last, disgusted by his own fear, Hauberin straightened, sheathing the iron blade with not-quite steady hands—he didn't trust himself not to accidentally jab himself with the thing in the state he was in—and forced himself to start down that blank-walled corridor.

But the dreams had conditioned him all too well. Terror would not be banished. It clung to him with every step, telling him that *now* he would surely hear the voice, *now* he would surely see his death, *now*—

Hauberin stopped short, gasping. Ah Powers, he couldn't go on! How Serein would have laughed to see this, to see his poor little half-blood cousin so terrified he could hardly walk, trembling with fright when nothing had harmed him. How Serein would have taunted him:

"Timid little boy. Weak little half-human."

But the familiar jeer had lost some of its bite. By now, Hauberin realized, he'd learned it wasn't so terrible a thing to be human. Oh yes, humans had such piteously short lives, and some of those lives were squalid and cruel indeed. But he'd met some bright, happy souls as well: friendly, honest Aimery; the fisherman who'd pulled Hauberin from drowning without thought of reward; that gentle-eyed monk in the cathedral of St. Denis, a man without much fire, perhaps, but with genuine kindness towards a total stranger in need of help.

And . . . there was Matilde. All too human Matilde, forbidden to him by bars of blood and honor. . . .

Hauberin started resolutely forward, refusing to think of what couldn't be, trying not to think of what might be waiting. But the dreams' miasma wrapped him close, tightening his nerves, hampering his breathing. For all his determination, the prince's steps faltered, then stopped once more. Ah Powers, Serein was right, he was weak, weak.

Was he? One firm little thread of logic slipped through the despair, making him question, *was* he weak? What of those years he had ruled? His proud and independent people would never have suffered a half-blooded prince to live, let alone to sit the throne for six years, if they'd thought him weak. They certainly would never have sworn him fealty!

As even Serein had sworn, submissive as a servant before his "weak" cousin.

The prince stiffened as though he'd been slapped. Why, then, had he been blaming Serein all these years for something that was his own fault? The man had been genuinely petty and cruel, yes, but no one, as the saying went, could truly be tortured without inner consent. Had he, Hauberin wondered, let his cousin torment him because, secretly, he'd believed Serein, believed himself inferior?

Not exactly inferior. The prince gave a long, shuddering sigh, remembering long, lonely childhood nights spent lying awake, too frightened to go back to sleep. "Human" had never been the true problem, not even back then, no matter how much Serein's taunts had hurt. In those empty hours, even though his night-keen sight had told the child-Hauberin nothing lurked in the shadows of his room, the stories of terrible cruel Others had seemed all too real.

Particularly when he knew that Other blood so terrible his parents never spoke of it ran through his own veins.

Particularly when he never knew when such blood just might turn him, too, to Other. When the very name or sight of his grandsire might be enough to spark the change—

Hauberin cried out in sudden fury. What in the name of all the Powers did such old fears matter now? Alliar and Matilde were risking their lives for him while he—he stood agonizing like a fool over What Might or Might Not be!

Ah, Powers, enough, the prince thought wearily. *What happens, happens.*

He was still very much afraid. But, sick with that inner cold though he was, Hauberin strode forward to meet whatever waited. One way or another, there would be an end to this.

XXVIII
THE UNRAVELING

Distance was deceptive in that long, narrow, closed world. For a time Hauberin fancied wearily that the corridor had no end, that his fate would be to simply walk and walk into death. He was too drained by the burden of fear by this point to really care.

But the perpetually straight corridor ended without warning in a sharp right angle, beyond which was a large alcove. And there, sprawled upon a pile of cushions, lay . . .

Ah, Powers, he couldn't look. Every childhood fear had rushed to the surface, screaming *here is the demon, here is the monster you truly are,* and he just couldn't turn his head to look.

"Grandson?"

It was so gentle a voice, so full of disbelieving wonder—so totally unlike the horror of his dreams—that all at once the tension sharpened beyond all bearing. With a gasp of surrender, Hauberin turned, and saw:

Himself!

No. The resemblance wasn't all *that* strong. This might be himself as he would someday look: the same slight, supple figure, the same olive-dark skin and sleek black hair, something of the same cast of features, but with quiet wisdom and experience in the dark eyes that could only come with age.

"Who . . . are you . . . ?" Hauberin breathed.

The slight figure, dressed in a rainbow of bright, silken robes, twisted about to study him, and the prince realized only now that the other was held to the floor by a network of narrow chains. A tender smile crossed the prisoner's dark, elegant face. "Of course. You couldn't possibly know me; your own mother never saw me." He spoke the Faerie tongue with easy fluency, but the faintest hint of an exotic accent colored his words. "Nevertheless, I am your grandfather."

"But . . . who . . . what . . ." Hauberin stopped with a shaky laugh, shivering. "You must forgive me. This is . . . you're not what I expected."

"Oh, I can imagine. Come, don't be frightened. I'm of Faerie, too, a distant branch: the humans call my people *peris*."

Hauberin started. "The desert folk! The folk who prefer human Realms."

"Exactly."

"But how in the name of all the Powers did you come *here*?"

The *peri* laughed wryly. "Not through my own choosing, certainly. As I slept, invisible and—I thought—undetectable, beneath the palms of my favorite oasis, a force, a Presence, snatched me away before I could defend myself. It left me here as you see me. To . . . ah . . . greet you." He raised a slim hand as far as the chains would permit, indicating the few cushions and bleak surroundings. "I'd offer you hospitality, but . . ."

The prince couldn't stop shaking. "Your name," he pleaded. "Tell me your name."

"In my language, Nasif-i-Khanalat. In yours, Moonflame."

And it was true, it was all true, because Hauberin *felt* the curse shiver and fall away from him, leaving him so suddenly free he staggered back against a wall, fighting to keep from laughing like a fool from the wonderful, unbelievable, incredible relief, from the sudden erasure of all the years of childhood terror.

Free, oh, Powers, I never thought I'd see this moment, free . . .

As Moonflame was not. Giddy with shock, Hauberin

bent over his *peri* grandfather, trying to find a beginning or ending to the chains. "Let me—"

"Wait." A flicker of alarm in Moonflame's eyes made the prince draw back in surprise. "First we should talk."

"Talk! When that—Presence could return at any moment?"

"The Presence has not returned once in all the while I've been held here. I doubt things will suddenly change."

"How . . . long has it been?"

Moonflame shrugged in a weary chiming of chains. "I've no way of knowing. *Peris* don't live off fragrances, silly human tales notwithstanding, but I haven't even felt hunger or thirst to help me keep track; this . . . place is quite outside time, as you've surely sensed. Waiting to see the son of my daughter—the grandson I never knew existed—was the only bright spot in it all." The *peri* shook his head. "Ey-ai, I can't keep calling you just 'Grandson'!"

"Uh, no. I am Hauberin, son of Prince Laherin and—and your daughter, his wife, Melusine."

"Ah . . ." The *peri*'s eyes were soft and achingly sad, seeing a time long past. "Melusine. Is that what you named her, my love, my dearest heart? Melusine. It has a sweet, magical sound to it." His gaze sharpened. "And is she happy, my Melusine?"

"She—she's dead," Hauberin stammered out, more bluntly than he would have liked. "As is my father. But she—oh, my parents loved each other dearly. She was very happy."

Moonflame sagged. "Both dead . . . mother and daughter. . . ."

"I'm sorry," Hauberin said helplessly. "Let me see about these chains, and—"

"No, not yet."

"Don't you *want* to be freed?"

"Need you ask?" But the dark gaze wouldn't meet his own. "But have you no curiosity as to how you came to be as you are?"

"Of course I do, but—"

Moonflame was already beginning, "I never thought to owe my life to a human, let alone a *ferengi* from the West. . . ."

With an impatient sigh, Hauberin settled down to listen. And soon, despite himself, he was engrossed in the intricate oriental tale of a *peri* trapped by an enemy he'd made among the *djinn*, "dark and cruel as the storms that sweep across the sands," of a fair-haired foreign knight, separated from his fellows "during one of the humans' incomprehensible wars," Moonflame said with a disparaging wave of a hand, "some crusade or other," who came to the *peri's* aid and slew the *djinn* with cold iron after a fight worthy of a true hero.

"Human or not," the *peri* mused, "he was a good man, this Gautier. I tended his wounds and did my best to comfort him while he raved in fever of his longings for home and wife. The fever broke; he seemed well along to recovery. But . . . the *djinn's* blood had touched him, burned him, poisoned him. As the days passed, I could do nothing but watch as Gautier weakened and . . . died."

Moonflame paused, eyes shadowed. "We had became something close to friends, human and *peri*, in that brief time. I buried him with as near to *ferengi* rites as I could manage. And then honor demanded I travel the winds to Western lands, to bring the sad tidings myself to Gautier's widow. The Lady Alianor." The *peri's* voice caught in his throat. "She was so beautiful . . . beautiful in her foreign human way, not delicate and dark like our *peri* women, but tall and strong, with hair the color of mortal sunlight. . . . Neither of us ever expected, human and *peri*, that love might touch us. But . . . as soon tell the lightning not to strike or the moon not to rise."

"I know the rest," Hauberin said softly. "Her brother found out. And banished you."

"With iron," Moonflame added bitterly, "and—secretly, so no one would doubt the purity of his oh-so clean mortal soul—with bought-and-paid-for sorcery. After long and long I managed to return, briefly, though it cost

me great pain, only to learn my love was—he had—
Aie, damn him to the humans' Hell, damn him forever!"
Moonflame broke off, choking. Haubeirn looked away,
giving the *peri* a chance to recover control. At last Moonflame continued quietly, "He died not long after, not,
alas, by my hand. In a hunting mishap. I blessed the
horse that had crushed him and, since I could no longer
endure the double charm of spell and iron still binding
me, I went my way. I . . . never saw my daughter."
Moonflame smiled faintly. "But at least I've lived long
enough to see you, my regal young grandson."

"And I'm honored to meet my grandsire, and all such
courtesies. Now, will you please be still and let me free
you?"

He bent over the intricate tangle of chains once more.
Moonflame said not a word, but Hauberin caught a quick
glimpse of the *peri*'s eyes. And in their depths burned
such sudden bitter despair that the prince drew back in
alarm.

"It's a trap, isn't it? And you've been bespelled so you
can't warn me. *That's* why you kept talking: You've been
stalling desperately, haven't you? Trying to protect me."
Though Moonflame never spoke, the love in the dark
eyes gave Hauberin the answer. "But protect me from
what? Not you, surely," the prince continued, watching
his grandsire closely. "The chains?" He saw pain flash
across Moonflame's face as the *peri* struggled against the
mind-binding spell, and cried out in dismay, "Ah, don't!"

"Can't . . ." Moonflame gasped out in anguish, "don't
. . . chains, don't touch . . . chains. . . . Sorcery . . . Touch
them, and die. . . ."

"Ah." But after a moment, Hauberin grinned sharply.
"I won't touch them. *This* will." He drew Matilde's belt-
knife, and saw Moonflame stare in horror at the deadly
metal in this grandsons' hand. Silently blessing Matilde,
the prince attacked the chains with cold iron, careful not
to scratch the *peri*. As he'd hoped, sorcery crumbled at
the contact. A stunned Moonflame staggered to his feet

from a nest of shattered chains and drew his grandson into his delighted embrace.

In the next moment, the not-world of the corridor shattered as well, tearing itself apart in a wild screaming of wind—

—that left them standing dazed on a windswept, barren slope nearly at a mountain peak jagged as a broken sword. On one side of the slope a tangle of huge boulders lay where they'd broken off from that peak in some long-ago upheaval of nature or magic. On the other sides . . .

Hauberin pulled away from Moonflame, staring out at a wilderness of savage gray mountains stabbing like knives at the sky—the clear, sunless sky. And the prince laughed aloud, a sudden rush of returning Power telling him what he already knew: this was one of the primal lands at Faerie's very edge.

"Hauberin!" exclaimed a startled voice. In the next moment, Alliar, sleekly golden, human guise dropped, came leaping spryly down the mass of boulders, calling back, "Matilde, he's safe!"

"Oh, thank the Lord."

As the woman started down more carefully, Alliar impatiently scrambled back up to practically carry her down, pulling her along to Hauberin's side. Fairly blazing with excitement, the being chattered, "One moment I was surrounded by Fées, then I was here, and Matilde was with me, and the Fées, for all I know, are still trapped back there, while you— How did you— What did you—"

"Alliar," Matilde said softly.

"Eh?" The being stopped short, staring, as Moonflame moved to the prince's side. Hauberin grinned.

"Grandfather," he said formally, "may I introduce the Baroness Matilde, and the wind spirit, Alliar. Matilde, Alliar, this is the *peri* lord Nasif-i-Khanalat."

"Moonflame," the *peri* added.

"Grandfather . . . ?" Alliar's eyes widened. Then, as the implications sank in, Li let out a high, shrill, wind-sharp shout of delight. "The curse is broken!"

"Quite." Moonflame smiled, and bowed with intricate oriental courtesy. "You are, I take it, my grandson's friend?"

"Oh, I am!" Alliar imitated the bow flawlessly. "And delighted to meet you, believe me."

Moonflame repeated his bow for Matilde, his dark eyes so appreciative that she reddened. "And this, I would think," the *peri* murmured warmly, "is my grandson's lady."

"Ah . . . no."

"No? A pity." With true Faerie suddenness, Moonflame had forgotten all about danger, his smile only for Matilde. "You are half of Faerie, too, oh flame of delight?"

"N-No. I'm human. Only."

"Oh, don't belittle yourself, lovely one. It's not 'only,' but—"

"Grandfather," Hauberin cut in impatiently (telling himself that no, he was *not* jealous), "this is hardly the time for flirtation."

Moonflame sighed. "Forgive me. I have been away from . . . gentle matters too long, and—" The *peri* tensed. "We're not alone."

Alliar had already disappeared, stalking. There was a startled shout, a curse, the sounds of a fierce struggle, and then Li was forcing a man, arm twisted behind his back, out from behind the wall of boulders, to the accompaniment of much fury.

"Damn you, you misbegotten wind-thing, let me go!"

"Not yet," Alliar snapped. "I don't like spies."

"I wasn't spying, curse it!"

"That's for the prince to decide."

Hauberin saw a powerful build (not quite as powerful just then as the strength of an angry wind spirit), disheveled red hair—

"My lord Ereledan! What are *you* doing here?"

The Lord of Llyrh finally managed to pull free, glaring at Alliar, too proud to rub what must have been a sore arm. "I think you know more about this than I, my Prince!"

"I don't."

The fuming Ereledan ignored that. "I was hunting in my woods, minding my own affairs, when—whoosh," he waved an angry hand, "I'm here. What game are you playing, my Prince?"

"I'm not—"

"It was bad enough when Charailis was trying to confuse my mind— It *was* Charailis, wasn't it? Or have you been experimenting on me?"

"Look you, I don't know what you're talking about!"

"Oh, don't you? I've sworn fealty to you, but if you have been practicing spells on me—"

"Enough!" Hauberin snapped. "I have *not* been bespelling you, I do *not* know what you're talking about, and I— Now, what?"

Ereledan wasn't even looking at him. Matilde had moved from behind Hauberin, and the Lord of Llyrh, face gone deathly pale, stared at her almost as though he saw his death. "Oh, Powers . . ." It was the barest whisper. "Blanche. . . ."

"I'm sorry," she said in the human language, "I—I don't understand. Blanche was my mother's name, but—"

"A daughter," Ereledan breathed. "I never knew, I never dreamed . . ."

To Hauberin's astonishment, he said it in the human tongue. The prince glanced swiftly from Ereledan to Matilde and back again, stunned to suddenly realize why Matilde bore Power, why she had a Faerie-strong love for music, why she had always seemed so vaguely familiar. *Idiot! How could you have missed it?* Those subtly Faerie features, that blazing hair—he'd even compared its redness once to that of Ereledan, yet never once stopped to think— It seemed so obvious now, like the trick of some small sleight of hand which, once revealed, can't *not* be noticed. *How could you never have guessed?*

"Grandfather," he murmured in the Faerie tongue, "you were very right: she's half of Faerie, indeed!"

Matilde whirled. "What are you saying? And why are you all staring at me?"

"Tell her, my lord Ereledan," the prince commanded. "You seem to speak the human language well enough. Tell her how you followed my father into mortal Realms. Tell her what you did there."

All the defiance had ebbed out of Ereledan. "I didn't know I'd gotten her with child," he pleaded to Matilde. "I never would have abandoned her, or you. Please believe me."

"Believe you about what? What are you trying to say?"

"That . . . that I'm your father."

"But—no, that's impossible! My father is *human*, only *human*, and my mother would never, ever have betrayed him!"

"Ah, my dear . . ." Ereledan's voice and eyes were gentler than Hauberin would ever have believed possible. "How could it be a betrayal? She had never given her heart to the man. The marriage was a forced thing, a lie arranged by others." He glanced at the prince. "Yes, I did follow your father. Or tried to follow; the transfer-spell worked for me, but I couldn't quite control the differences in time."

"And so you were years too late to interfere with him," Hauberin said without expression. "But not too late to interfere with human lives."

"I didn't mean . . . Blanche was so lonely, so unhappy. And she was so lovely. . . . When I first saw her, stolen out of her husband's grim keep to sit in the moonlight, I . . ."

He hesitated, and Hauberin could have sworn he saw tears glint in the haughty eyes. "What betrayal there was, was mine," Ereledan said dully. "She was human. And I—I . . . just . . . could not let myself love a human.

"It wasn't until after I had abandoned her that I realized my mistake. By that time, of course, I couldn't find my way back to her. Or to my . . . my daughter. Oh, please," he begged Matilde, "you must believe, I never meant to hurt her!"

"I don't know what to believe," she murmured, glancing at Hauberin in desperation. "To learn after all this time that my father isn't—that I'm a—bastard, and n-not even human. . . ."

"It's not such a terrible thing," the prince murmured, and she smiled wanly.

"Ah well, at least now I know why Faerie called to me so strongly. If Gilbert only knew—"

But Alliar had come suddenly alert, cutting in on her words with a sharp, "Look!"

A tall, lean figure stood above them on the sharp slope, a dark-cloaked figure with hood thrown back: a most familiar figure.

Matilde's cry could have been either of joy or pain. "Gilbert!"

But when she would have run to him, Hauberin, cold with sudden horror, caught her in his arms, holding her with all his strength.

"Hauberin! That's my husband up there!"

"No," the prince said as gently as he could.

"What nonsense are you—"

"Gilbert is dead, Matilde."

"No, I—"

"He's *dead*, Matilde. I *feel* it." Hauberin shivered, thinking of a similarly . . . empty human boy, dead even as he struck at the prince, and added softly, "What you see up there is nothing, only an empty shell."

As though his words had broken a spell, the baron's body crumpled. In the next moment, a fierce, cold force swept down on them, wild with hatred, whirling dizzyingly about them, staring briefly, terribly, from Ereledan's eyes, pulling at Hauberin's will, forcing a gasp from Matilde, Moonflame, Alliar, snatching at their minds, trying in vain to control them in that sudden rush, then whirling back up into Gilbert's body, which slowly staggered back to its feet.

"It was you," Ereledan gasped, face white. "You,

Thing, whatever you are. The times I couldn't think, couldn't act, thought myself mad . . . the time I duelled my Prince and nearly killed him: it was you in my mind!"

The voice was all about them, mocking, hating, shattering into a thousand rough, overlapping shards, all grating painfully at once on their ears so they could hardly make out the words:

Easy . . . so easy to control . . .

What manner of Thing could possibly dominate Faerie minds? Fighting to keep his voice level, the prince said, "Then . . . it must have been you behind Serein as well. Of course it was. Those sudden, inept plots against me: that was you feeding his ambitions. Controlling him. Letting him murder a child."

The weak, wanting creature . . . simple to push it into the proper paths.

Mockery echoed in the painfully alien voice, sharp as bits of ice stabbing at Hauberin. Grimly, the prince continued, "I never could believe Serein had found some mythical spell. You were the one who tore the spirit from his dying body, threw it across Realms into a human shell— Why? And why abandon him?"

A thing no longer useful is nothing. . . .

Alliar let out a sharp hiss. "No wonder we couldn't make sense of the curse! The Power fueling it had nothing to do with Faerie." The being stood tense as a predator ready to spring. "What are you, creature? A demon?"

"Nothing so trite, I think," Hauberin mused, and shards of alien laughter, empty and humorless, grated along his nerves in response.

Would you know? Then, come, feel

And Power, dark and chill and dazzling, engulfed him. In one endless, terrible moment he knew—as well as any finite mind could know—the emptiness beyond reality, the nonspace between the boundaries of the Realms. He *felt* the thing that whirled and eddied there, non-living yet alive, nonreal yet real, a force of living hatred left over from the dark side of Creation. He *felt* it swirling endlessly between those pathless boundaries, never able to enter any tangible world until—

Hauberin pulled free with a strangled gasp, realizing the truth: There hadn't been any pathway till Prince Laherin, in the process of creating his transfer-spell, had accidentally created one. Laherin could only have realized what he'd done; he'd been too skilled a magician not to have known. And he would have moved quickly to shut the pathway again.

But he'd been too proud, too determined to cross from Realm to Realm. Prince Laherin had never stopped to realize he had left the smallest psychic crack unsealed.

"And you seeped through it," Hauberin murmured, and *felt* the Other's painful nonlaughter stab at him. The Thing was all but mindless by any true-Realm standards, a segment of chaotic force: living hatred, indeed. It could never have felt anything as rational as gratitude for the one who'd let it into new Realms; hatred was all it could be. And so it had set out to destroy him for creating change.

Yes, yes, the Other taunted, *to destroy every trace of That One. This force was in the warrior that caught the male-form of That One as he crossed Realms and slew him. But first this force was the poison-illness that slew the female-part of him. . . .*

Hauberin heard Moonflame cry out in pain, "Not, 'female-part,' damn you! She was my daughter! They were separate beings."

That concept plainly meant little to the Other. *The useful/not useful one this force possessed is destroyed, too,* the thing continued blithely to Hauberin, referring, he guessed, to Serein, *and those others this force brushed are here. Only your fragment is left of That One. It was pleasant to play with you/fragment, pushing this way, that. You/fragment nearly was destroyed many times, yet this force always let you still exist. Not for much longer.*

Alien hatred enfolded Hauberin, so sharply he hadn't a chance to defend himself, hatred cold as the space

between the Realms, pulling the air from his lungs, choking him. Dimly, he heard the others shouting, but he
could concentrate only on the sudden battle to breathe.

As he staggered, Matilde snatched her dagger back
from him. Murmuring, "Gilbert, forgive me," she threw
it with desperate accuracy—but the blade crumpled to
dust in mid-flight. The crushing force vanished from
Hauberin in a rush as the Other gathered back its hatred,
doubled it with what it pulled from Matilde and hurled
the deadly force back at her—

"No!" Ereledan screamed. "I won't lose her, too!"

He hurled himself at his daughter to shield her. And
the full spear of hatred struck him. Dead on his feet,
Ereledan slowly sagged to the ground, leaving Matilde
standing in wild-eyed horror over his body.

But Hauberin didn't waste time on shock. *"Link!"* he
screamed to Alliar, and in the instant in which the Other
was distracted, still wearing its human shell, mind-joined
man and spirit shouted the strongest Spell of Binding
they knew. Even so Powerful a spell wouldn't hold the
too-alien Other for long, but for the moment their doubled strength was enough to trap it in Gilbert's body,
mortal as Gilbert had been mortal.

No-o-o! The savage shriek tore at their minds. Raging,
the Other hurled its fury at them, nonvoice splitting into
simultaneous messages of hate. But Hauberin could no
longer be hurt by ancient taunts of "half-blood, weakling,
unworthy half-human," not after that ordeal in the corridor,
not after the relief of learning his true lineage. But, still
partly linked with Alliar, he *felt* the being's anguish at enforced memories of lost, lost freedom. Aching for his
friend's pain, the prince drew Power into a death-spell—

No! Not against something so alien! The spell would
fatally recoil onto the flesh-and-blood.

But the damned thing is still trapped, still mortal, so . . .

Hauberin charged his foe, head down, colliding with
Gilbert's body with an impact that should have hurled it
right off the mountain. But even in its mortal trap, the
Other was far too strong for any one man. A backhanded

slap sent Hauberin staggering back against a boulder, breath slammed from him. Before he could defend himself, the Other grabbed him off his feet as though he was weightless. For one dizzy moment, Hauberin saw a blur of empty space, mountains, the long, long drop to the valley below and a river that looked like a thin silver ribbon, then the Other threw him down at its feet with bruising force, nonvoice shrieking in an ecstasy of triumph, *Fool, fool, this one cannot be hurt by you! This one cannot be slain by anyone of mortal birth!*

Inhumanly strong hands closed about his throat. Choking, dying, Hauberin heard a fierce, joyous, despairing voice cry, "Oh well, I suppose this is my job, then!"

"Alliar, no!" the prince gasped out.

Swifter than any of mortal birth, the wind spirit surged forward, crashing into the Other, sending them both plummetting off the mountain.

"*Alliar!*"

Hauberin shot out a frantic hand—

But it closed only on empty space.

XXIX
REVENANT

Hauberin had no memory of having buried the dead (Ereledan alone; the river far below had, mercifully, washed away the others) or returned the living to his palace. He accepted the commiserations of friends and courtiers without emotion; there was no room in his numb mind yet for grief.

Only one thing was clear: He must destroy his father's spell. Alone in his chambers, he took it apart, syllable by syllable (refusing to let himself remember the first time he had used it, with Alliar so nervously peering over his shoulder) and, syllable by syllable negated it, banishing each fragment from his memory as he erased it from parchment. With the erasure of the final spell-shard, there was the sudden sense of a distant door irrevocably, safely, shutting, and Hauberin sat for a time with head in hands, too drained to think.

But then the prince straightened. Oh, Powers, he'd forgotten about Moonflame and Matilde! He'd stranded them here without a thought. Matilde was off seeing to her father's estate; Hauberin had thought giving her something positive to do might help her over the shock of double bereavement. But Moonflame was still in the palace, and the prince asked to see him.

"Grandfather," Hauberin began uncertainly, "I . . ."

"Closed the Gate permanently. I know, I felt it."

"But—"

"No, dearheart, you haven't trapped me." Moonflame's smile was gentle. "We desert folk aren't quite like you of green Faerie. with us, *peri* calls always to *peri*. I don't need a formal Gate. All I need do to find a way home is . . . listen."

"You miss that home very much, don't you?"

Moonflame hesitated. "I didn't want to bother you with it, not with your friend's death so fresh in your mind, but . . . I'm sorry, yes. This land of yours is very beautiful but it could never be mine. Of course," he added thoughtfully, "that doesn't mean I didn't enjoy seeing my daughter's son in his rightful place on the throne. And it also doesn't mean I can't come calling on said grandson from time to time. If he'll allow it."

Hauberin had to smile. "Oh, of course. You'll always be welcome."

"Then," Moonflame said, smiling as well and bowing his most intricate and formal bow, "I shall not say good-bye, only farewell for now."

"Hauberin?"

The prince started, looking up from the scroll on which he'd been trying without success to concentrate. "Matilde."

She was dressed in a gown of Faerie design dyed black in human mourning style; her hair was at last free of those restrictive braids, streaming gloriously down her back, but its brightness was covered by a black silk scarf. Her face was drawn with grief, her eyes shadowed. And, Hauberin thought with a stab of pain, she had never looked so beautiful.

"They told me you were out here on your terrace," she said, "and that I was free to enter."

"Yes. Matilde . . . how are you managing?"

"I don't know yet. Too much has happened too swiftly. The moment I set foot on Erele—on my—my father's lands, I realized I'd found my own heartland, the place where I *belong*. And that was wonderful. But at the same time . . ." Matilde turned away, staring out over the fertile green fields to the mountains beyond. "I can't truly mourn my father; I never had a chance to know him. But Gilbert . . . I never really loved him, I won't lie about that now. But he—he was a good man, he didn't deserve to die like that, alone, unshriven . . ."

"The Powers won't mind."

She glanced at him. "Your people don't have any churches, do they?"

He waved a hand at the beauty before them. "When we have that? Why insult the Powers with something artificial?"

"But I . . . ah . . . never hear anyone call on Holy Names."

"By now you should know we never toy with Names of Power. That doesn't mean we don't have our own forms of worship. But you didn't come here to discuss religion."

"No. I . . . it's . . . oh, Hauberin, I'm so sorry about Alliar."

"Yes. I know."

"I—I wish there was something sensible I could say." She hesitated. "At least now—"

"If you're going to say, 'Now Alliar's free,' please don't."

"But—"

"If I knew for certain Li was free and happy, believe me, I would rejoice. But I *don't* know!" Hauberin turned savagely to her. "Because of that thrice-damned sorcerer's thrice-damned spell, a violent death such as Alliar faced might not have meant freedom, but total obliteration! And I . . . I'm sorry," he added, seeing her horror, "I didn't mean to put that weight on you." Hauberin breathed deeply, trying to regain control. "Matilde," he said softly, "I'm afraid I have something else to tell you. I'll be blunt: the Gate back to your Realm is closed. Forever." The prince hesitated, hunting in vain for comforting words. "Moonflame couldn't take you back with him; since you haven't a drop of *peri* blood, he assured me the transition would be fatal. I . . . forgive me. I can't return you to your native land."

But she didn't even flinch. "Weren't you listening to me?" Matilde asked gently. "I don't want to go back there; I don't belong there any more. Hauberin, my land is here."

The slow days passed. Hauberin, to all outward seeming, took up his life once more, sitting in court, settling what needed to be settled. Matilde, formally ceded the late Lord of Llyrh's lands and title after one of those sessions, was, he knew, settling into Faerie with wary joy, chattering with Aydris as though they were sisters of one birth and charming his people, learning the forms and strengths of her Power, even working her first careful healing spells under Lady Kerlein's haughty supervision. With all three possible rivals for the throne dead, the land and court were at peace.

But, alone in his chambers, Hauberin, unable to find relief in tears for all his bitter loneliness, mourned for his lost friend as for a brother.

A sudden voice asked, "Hauberin?"

The prince looked up, startled at this invasion of privacy. And then he was flattening himself against the far wall without realized he'd moved, staring out at this—this apparition, this seeming of— Oh, Powers, no, it was impossible. Panic-stricken, Hauberin rummaged through his memory for a spell of banishment, sure his mind had finally given way and—

"Oh Winds," the apparition said, and darted forward to catch him firmly by the arm. "Now, does *that* feel like a ghost?"

The hand was cool but undeniably solid. "Alliar . . . ?"

"No, you are not hallucinating, and yes, I really am here. Come, sit before you fall."

"But you—I saw you—"

"I . . . think I really did . . . die," the being said hesitantly. "I know the Other did."

"Of course it died; it was still mortal when it fell. Never mind that now. What happened to you?"

"I'm not sure. I remember falling, and then . . ." Alliar shrugged helplessly. "It's the first time I actually lost consciousness. Now *that*, you know, is a truly bizarre sensation. I don't see how you flesh-and-blood folk stand it every night."

Hauberin groaned. "Now I *know* it's you. Alliar, please, *what happened?*"

"Death or whatever it was apparently shattered the sorcerer's spell. The next thing I knew, I was free of solidity, whirling up into the sky. And oh, it was glorious for a time. . . ."

"But you returned."

"Ah. Well. You see, I've been tangible too long. I've learned too much of flesh-and-blood emotions, and . . . Ah, I never was able to put this into easy words. Hauberin, wind spirits, true wind spirits, have no sense of *I*, no real understanding of the concept. They're totally boundless, incorporeal in a way you'd find terrifying. But as *Alliar,* as *myself,* I've gained too true a personality. After a time I found myself longing for a body. And that was when I discovered Ysilar's spell wasn't quite broken after all. Just as he'd done to me, I used it to build myself a body out of motes of light and matter."

"Alliar . . ."

"Winds, don't feel sorry for me! You're missing my point: this time I wasn't forced to do anything. I freely *chose* to be Alliar again. And now that it's totally my choice, I realize that I *like* being Alliar. I suppose," the being added smugly, "that means you're stuck with me."

There had been too many shocks in too short a span. Overwhelmed, Hauberin let out a joyous whoop of a laugh and threw himself into his friend's embrace. There, to his mortification, he felt the long-postponed tears finally starting. Alliar said nothing, only held him patiently, pretending not to notice, till the prince had recovered.

"Sit," the being commanded. "The wine's still kept in this cabinet? Ah, yes. "

Alliar filled two goblets and handed Hauberin one. They hesitated, then clinked goblets in the human style, sipped, and burst into laughter.

"Now," said the being like a good gossip once they

had settled back into comfortable quiet, "what about you and Matilde? Is there anything between you two?"

Hauberin, about to deny it, stopped short, realizing with a shock that Matilde had completed her human rites of mourning some time back. She was quite honorably single by anyone's standards. And since he was now officially three-quarters of Faerie and she—that bright, brave, lovely lady—was at least as much Faerie as human . . .

"Why, there may be," the prince told his friend, "there just may be at that," and smiled.